Delicious

"Another winner from Black . . . will thrill erotica and mystery fans alike."

—*Romantic Times*

"A book to be savored over and over. I consider it one of the best books I have ever read."

—*Romance Junkies*

"Erotic, emotional . . . suspenseful."

—*Joyfully Reviewed*

"An absolute winner."

—*Fallen Angel Reviews*

Decadent

"Wickedly seductive from start to finish."

—Jaci Burton, national bestselling author

"A lusty page-turner from the get-go, *Decadent* lives up to its title, grabbing readers from the very first chapter and not letting go until the very end with a shuddering climax worthy of any keeper shelf."

—*TwoLips Reviews*

Wicked Ties

"I loved it!"

—Lora Leigh, #1 *New York Times* bestselling author

"Not a book to be missed."

—*A Romance Review*

"Absolutely took my breath away . . . *Wicked Ties* wound itself around me and refused to let go. Full of passion and erotic love scenes."

—*Romance Junkies*

continued . . .

Strip Search
(writing as Shelley Bradley)

"Packs a hell of a wallop . . . an exciting, steamy, and magnificent story . . . If I had to rate this book out of ten, it would certainly get a fifteen! Twists, turns, titillating and explosive sexual chemistry, and memorable characters—readers can't ask for more. *Strip Search* is highly recommended!"
—*The Road to Romance*

"An exciting contemporary romance with suspenseful undertones . . . the love scenes are particularly steamy. This book would be perfect for readers who enjoy their romance with a hint of suspense."
—*Curled up with a Good Book*

"Blew me away . . . a great read."
—*Fallen Angel Reviews*

"The twists and turns in *Strip Search* make for an intriguing climax . . . Bradley is a master of tying love and mystery together. I highly recommend this book."
—*MyShelf.com*

Bound and Determined
(writing as Shelley Bradley)

"This story explores one of my favorite fantasies . . . a desperate heroine takes a handsome alpha male hostage. Much sexy fun is had by all. Especially when the yummy captive turns the tables!"
—Angela Knight, *New York Times* bestselling author

"Steamier than a Florida night, with characters who will keep you laughing and have you panting for more!"
—Susan Johnson, *New York Times* bestselling author

"A searing, frolicking adventure of suspense, love, and passion!"
—Lora Leigh, #1 *New York Times* bestselling author

"A flawless story that grips readers from page one and doesn't let up."
—*The Road to Romance*

Titles by Shayla Black

Wicked Lovers series

WICKED TIES

DECADENT

DELICIOUS

SURRENDER TO ME

Anthologies

FOUR PLAY

(with Maya Banks)

Titles by Shayla Black writing as Shelley Bradley

BOUND AND DETERMINED

STRIP SEARCH

Surrender to Me

SHAYLA BLACK

HEAT BOOKS
NEW YORK

THE BERKLEY PUBLISHING GROUP
Published by the Penguin Group
Penguin Group (USA) Inc.
375 Hudson Street, New York, New York 10014, USA
Penguin Group (Canada), 90 Eglinton Avenue East, Suite 700, Toronto, Ontario M4P 2Y3, Canada
(a division of Pearson Penguin Canada Inc.)
Penguin Books Ltd., 80 Strand, London WC2R 0RL, England
Penguin Group Ireland, 25 St. Stephen's Green, Dublin 2, Ireland (a division of Penguin Books Ltd.)
Penguin Group (Australia), 250 Camberwell Road, Camberwell, Victoria 3124, Australia
(a division of Pearson Australia Group Pty. Ltd.)
Penguin Books India Pvt. Ltd., 11 Community Centre, Panchsheel Park, New Delhi—110 017, India
Penguin Group (NZ), 67 Apollo Drive, Rosedale, North Shore 0632, New Zealand
(a division of Pearson New Zealand Ltd.)
Penguin Books (South Africa) (Pty.) Ltd., 24 Sturdee Avenue, Rosebank, Johannesburg 2196,
South Africa

Penguin Books Ltd., Registered Offices: 80 Strand, London WC2R 0RL, England

This book is an original publication of The Berkley Publishing Group.

PRINTING HISTORY
Heat trade paperback edition / March 2011

Library of Congress Cataloging-in-Publication Data

Black, Shayla.
    Surrender to me / Shayla Black. — Heat trade paperback ed.
        p.   cm.
    ISBN 978-0-425-23655-0
    1. Triangles (Interpersonal relations)—Fiction.   I. Title.
    PS3602.L325245S87 2011
    813'.6—dc22   2010043027

PRINTED IN THE UNITED STATES OF AMERICA

10   9   8   7   6   5   4   3   2

For Cecil Robson, with love.
You will never know
the impact you had on my life.
You'll always be a vivid,
larger-than-life hero to me.

Acknowledgments

To the readers on my Shayla Black Facebook page, hugs on all your encouragement every time I posted a new excerpt of this book. You made me smile and kept me going through some tough days.

Thanks to Sylvia Day for cutting through the BS to give such sage advice. You're the best conference roomie ever!

Kris Cook, your friendship means the world to me. I don't know what I'd do without you.

Special appreciation (and much bowing and scraping) to Sophie Oak for saving my butt at the last minute—more than once—with this book. I am super grateful. I owe you margaritas on the patio!

Thanks to my wonderful editor, Kate Seaver, for all the extra time she gave me to pull this book together, and for loving it as much as I'd hoped she would.

As always, to my wonderful family for putting up with me during deadline dementia. I wonder sometimes how you manage it, but I'm always grateful that you do.

Prologue

Friday

RUBBING damp palms on his denim-clad thighs, Hunter stood in front of the door of the bathroom Kata had retreated to and let out a deep breath. It didn't help; every muscle remained clenched. If there was another fucking way . . . But there wasn't, and he knew it. This was it.

His heart pounded as he pushed into the room. The fragrant, humid air wrapped around him. Everything smelled like her: spicy amber, sweet lilies. Beyond arousing. Like always, he turned hard and aching in an instant.

God, he loved this woman.

Seeing him, she gasped and scrambled for her towel on the basin. He grabbed the damp terry cloth first, loving the hell out of her in nothing but a lacy, baby blue thong. Her smooth olive skin and lush breasts with those tight, rosy brown nipples tempted him like nothing ever had. The dark ropes of her wet hair dripped down her back, framing her freshly scrubbed face. He couldn't wait to get back inside her, to hold her again. Yesterday, she'd been dealing with too much, so he'd backed off, hadn't pressed his way into the snug, silken clasp of her pussy.

Tonight, all bets were off.

Realizing that he wasn't going to give her the towel and that he blocked the path to her clothes, Kata faced him squarely, chin raised. "What now? I've told you how I feel and what needs to happen. If you're here to stop me from leaving, you can't."

Ah, that stubborn streak of hers that intrigued him so much. Normally, he'd argue until he wore Kata down or seduce her until she gave in with a well-sated cry. This situation was far from normal. Until dawn, his most important role was to keep her safe. Nothing mattered more. Hunter had only one way left to do that . . . and give her what she wanted.

It was going to tear his fucking heart out.

He had no illusions; he'd never be the same. He'd be every inch the miserable bastard his father had been for the last fifteen lonely years, that Logan was now. Hunter had always sworn he'd do whatever it took to hang onto the one woman meant for him.

Goddamn it; in a handful of hours he'd have no choice but to let her go.

Hunter crossed his arms over his chest, restraining the urge to embrace Kata, stroke her tempting flesh—and never stop. "First, if you go home, you're not only putting yourself in danger, but your family, too. You might not know everything about this asshole threatening you, but he knows you. Why wouldn't he come after those you love?"

Kata's stubborn chin rose, but she nodded. Though she didn't want to, she saw his point. Now he had to put all his cards on the table, even though he had the losing hand.

"I have a proposition, honey: Today, I'll do whatever it takes to neutralize the threat against you. Tomorrow, you'll be free in every way." He clenched his fists. "I'll sign the fucking divorce papers."

As soon as he choked out the words, Hunter wished he could

take them back. For him, she was it—had been since the moment he laid eyes on her. He wished he could make her understand, but unless she came to love him in return, accept his needs and her own, they were doomed.

Surprise flashed across her face, along with something else—regret, maybe . . . or was that his own wishful thinking?

She smoothed out her expression. "Th-thank you for finally being reasonable."

Reasonable? In five seconds, she wouldn't think so. "I'll do that, *if* you spend tonight with me."

Chapter One

Saturday, six days earlier

THE first thing Hunter Edgington thought when he saw the laughing brunette across the crowded Vegas hotel suite, champagne in hand, was that he couldn't wait to fuck her.

His next thought was that it was a damn shame the curvaceous bombshell belonged to his former boot camp buddy, Ben.

"Does she know?"

Ben leaned against the wall and took the last swig of beer from his bottle, then yelled over the deafening party tunes. "Nope. Big surprise. She wanted to come to Vegas for her birthday and have her fantasy fulfilled. After the shit she's been through lately, when she requested . . ." He let loose a beer belch, tossing his brown hair from his unfocused eyes. "I delivered."

Maybe, but Hunter suspected Ben hadn't spilled the whole story. He'd spent the last half-dozen years as a Navy SEAL and was still alive because he always listened to his gut. "You're okay with this?"

"Yeah," Ben slurred. "Fuck, she's hot in bed. Passionate. All that

Latina blood." He leaned in and grinned. "She's a screamer and scratcher."

Ben's words created a visual that had Hunter stone hard: himself with her, naked, slick with sweat. Her fuck-me mouth gasping his name. Her red manicured nails digging into his shoulders as he nuzzled her lush breasts. While pounding her swollen pussy relentlessly deep with his cock.

He wanted that—and would do whatever necessary to make it happen.

The brunette was deep in conversation with a slightly older Hispanic woman and two twentysomething twigs in stilettos with fake blond hair and equally fake breasts. They made him yawn. But she . . .

As if sensing his stare, the gorgeous woman looked up. Their gazes locked. Oh, yeah. *She* exuded sex appeal with all the subtlety of a flashing red light.

Instinct jabbed his gut with a full-throttle attraction that raced through his veins. Damn, she was beautiful. Tangling his hands in her dark silk hair as he claimed her mouth and body—all while cuffing her helplessly to his bed—would be worth whatever it took to get her there. Even twenty feet apart, they generated combustible heat that singed him down to his balls. It was beyond chemistry. At thirty-two, Hunter knew the difference. He didn't merely want her; he wanted to unravel her, figure her out, possess her.

Why was that?

She looked at her companions briefly, then back to him. Hazel, mossy green laced with deep brown. Stunning against her hint-of-olive complexion. Another shock of awareness blasted through him. Her wide smile fell slowly. She held his stare, drew in a trembling breath. Her pulse fluttered at her neck. Her pink tongue peeked out, swiping across her plump lips.

Everything about her breathless expression told him that she felt the heat between them. *Good.* Because this goddamn searing lust made him wonder if he could ever sate his hunger for her, much less in a single night.

"What's her name?" He had to know, ached to.

"Kata." Ben slurred. "Short for Katalina, but she hates it. I call her that when she pisses me off, but then she calls me Benjamin and—"

"Got it." Hunter didn't need to know the ins and outs of Ben and Kata's relationship. He already envied the bastard like mad. "Boundaries?"

"Nah, man. Whatever she wants."

Idly, Hunter wondered if Ben realized that, without limits, he was going to be fucking lethal. Requesting leave from his team after being shot, Hunter had nothing more to do for a week than rehab his shoulder and devote himself to seducing Kata. But since he and Ben hadn't spoken much in the last few years, it was clear the guy had forgotten his ruthless side.

And why warn the competition? Hunter suspected he might lose a buddy over this girl. Poaching wasn't his style, but for her, he'd bend the rules.

He gazed across the room again at Kata, who sneaked another glance at him from beneath a thick fringe of lashes. Her nipples beaded as she held his stare. Satisfaction rippled through him.

Last warning . . . "You're a very generous boyfriend. Are you sure you want to share?"

Ben reared back in surprise, staggering drunkenly. "Kata's not my girlfriend, dude. She's just a friend with benefits. She knows I fuck other girls."

Evil glee wound through Hunter's system. *Just a friend?* Hunter vowed those benefits Ben received now would be very short-lived. He would be more than happy to start scratching Kata's itch.

"She fuck other guys?"

Lurching over to the six-pack on the nearby bar, Ben grabbed another brew and pried it open. "Not lately. Too busy."

This just got better and better. "Doing what?"

"She's a probation officer for Lafayette Parish. Works fuckin' terrible hours with the dregs of society. Been dealing with death threats lately, she thinks from a foot soldier in the Gangster Disciples. He got probation for a first-time drug trafficking charge, and she reported him for not checking in."

Hunter's gut clenched. Hearing about anyone being unduly threatened pissed him off, and it took a special kind of chickenshit to threaten a female. This particular asswipe made every combat-trained cell in Hunter's body want blood. "They arrest the motherfucker?"

Ben shook his head. "They got a warrant out. Kata's tough." Ben sent him a lopsided grin. "And she looks hot in a business suit with all that long hair in a prissy twist . . . Hmm."

Oh, Hunter could picture peeling away a hip-hugging skirt and a papery-thin blouse, working his fingers through her hair until it hung thick and wavy as it did now. Tearing away her exterior until all she wore were stockings, stilettos, and a welcoming smile.

But before he indulged, he had to ask the question that bothered him all the way to Vegas. "Why ask me to join you?"

Ben actually looked surprised. "You're like ice, man. Slick. You always fuck and leave. Perfect for a ménage."

Yeah, that had always been his MO in the past. Now? He suspected things had changed—in the last five minutes. His gut was telling him that he wanted more from Kata than a good fuck. Figuring out what, exactly, was Hunter's first goal. Making sure she wanted far more than a single night was his second.

"Ménage is her fantasy, huh?" He smiled. "Game on."

At least until he changed the rules.

* * *

"WHO is *that*?" Marisol asked, raising a dark brow as she stared at the tall, hard-bodied stranger Ben talked to.

The stranger who kept staring.

Katalina Muñoz had wanted the answer to her sister's question since he walked in the door as dinner ended a few minutes ago.

Nervously twisting her silver ring on her finger, she tore her gaze away, back to her older sister. "You don't know? You didn't invite him?"

Marisol shook her head. "The only person I invited myself was Mamá."

And they both knew that their stepfather, Gordon, would never allow their mother to leave the house merely to have fun. Why wouldn't she divorce the controlling son of a bitch?

"The way that blond guy looks at you, I can tell he'd like to know you much better," her friend Chloe murmured. "Damn, he's hot. He looks built, like he could kick even a pro wrestler's ass."

In total agreement, Kata stared at him some more.

Guys like him—gorgeous, well built, carrying an aura of danger that made her shiver—rarely went for girls like her, a little tall, a little on the plus side. But he'd hardly looked at anything or anyone else since stepping into the room.

"Will Ben be angry?" her sister asked in worried tones.

How did one tell her conservative, very married older sister that she and Ben were merely fuck buddies? Nope, not going there. "We aren't exclusive, Mari."

"I'd like to get to know that guy." Chloe sighed. "But clearly, you're the only woman he's interested in tonight. Happy birthday to you, chica!"

Amen. Almost twenty-five, single, and happy, why shouldn't she enjoy a few hours with a guy like him? Sure, Ben was here, but given all the girls he nailed, he would understand. And have no problem finding companionship for the night.

Unless Ben had invited this stranger to her party for . . . *Oh dear God.*

Even the possibility made her heart pound and everything below her waist want to tango.

"So no one knows who he is? This is *my* specialty. I'll get deets," her other friend, Hallie, promised with a sly grin. "Be right back."

Kata downed the last of her champagne and met the stranger's blue stare again, repressing a shiver. She knew just by looking at him that, whatever his reason for being here, he had sin on his mind.

As promised, minutes later, Hallie returned after working the room, and she looked ready to burst. "OMG! You will *not* believe this."

Kata's stomach danced with anticipation. Was he married? A male stripper? "What?"

"I don't know *why* he's here. Still working that angle. Apparently, he met Ben in boot camp eons ago. His name is Hunter. He's from Texas, and he's a Navy SEAL on leave after being recently injured. A real badass, by all accounts."

She had no trouble believing that. His don't-fuck-with-me air reached across the room. He had sharp eyes and an unforgiving chin, made more rugged by two days' worth of stubble. Dark blond hair cut military short, harsh jawline, corded neck, veined forearms and wrists. Everything about him conveyed stark power.

Damn, he filled out the shoulders of his gray T-shirt like nobody's business. The bulges of his pectorals and the ridges of his abdomen stood out, tempting her to tear the shirt off and run her fingers, her tongue, all over that amazing flesh. Jeans hugged his narrow hips and long, lean thighs. And in between . . . She swallowed. Even across the room she could tell he was hard. And still staring at her.

"Yeah? I'm feeling pretty badass myself." She tossed him a flirty gaze.

Chloe handed her the untouched glass in her hand. "Take this. And go get him."

Kata knocked it back in a few swallows. *Here goes nothing.* "Thanks. I will."

As she approached, Hunter's blue eyes heated, focused on her like a laser. Ben turned and looked at her with an unfocused stare. Her friend was shitfaced? Damn, he was always a sloppy drunk.

Hunter's hands were empty, and she picked up a beer from the cooler as she sauntered closer on her high heels, accentuating the sway of her hips—and never taking her eyes off him.

"This is the birthday girl," Ben slurred.

"Kata, is that right?" Hunter asked.

Even his voice made her quiver. Beyond deep, husky, with a bit of a snap, demanding an answer. He looked even bigger up close.

Kata forced herself to stop all the wicked thoughts in her head—at least long enough to reply. "Yes. And you're Hunter?"

His mouth curled into a grin. "Curious enough about me to learn my name?"

Of course. And if he wanted to flirt, she was all in. If he wanted more . . . she was definitely entertaining the notion. The thought of all that barely leashed power plunging into her made her hot and shivery.

Kata just smiled. "So what were you two talking about?"

Ben's crooked smile split his all-American boyish face. "That we're going to fuck you, Kata. And that you want it."

Heat detonated right between her legs. Ben was right; she'd had this ménage fantasy for years. The thought of a lover and a stranger of his choosing touching her with their hands, pleasuring her with their cocks, drove her out of her mind. Ben, a good friend since he'd moved into her apartment complex two years ago, had promised to help fulfill her fantasy. As he'd said, what were friends for?

She could have been embarrassed at Ben's drunken bluntness, but at least tonight's agenda was out in the open. Why cower behind false modesty? But Kata was desperately interested in Hunter's opinion on the matter. From beneath dark lashes, she saw that he looked supremely pleased. And a sweeping gaze down told her that his cock was still like granite. No reason she wouldn't finally get her wish tonight.

"Happy birthday to me." Kata winked and handed Hunter the beer. "You don't have a drink. Will this do?"

"Thanks, but I have a bottle of water somewhere." He looked at Ben's bottle. "Yours is empty. Here you go, buddy."

"Thanks." He ripped off the cap, guzzled half the bottle, then burped loudly. "I gotta pee."

"You do that," Hunter suggested with a repressed smile, then sent her a hot, lingering stare. "I'd like to dance with the birthday girl. Get to know you."

God, every time this man opened his mouth, her stomach fluttered. Stupid teenagerish reaction, given her very adult thoughts about him. But Hunter totally did it for her.

Before she could say a word, he curled an arm around her, his palm at the small of her back. That small touch was a jolt, and her entire body lit up like a supernova. She bit her lip to hold in a gasp as he led her to the corner where the amazing views of the Vegas Strip at sunset went on forever. A few nearby partygoers swayed in time with the sultry music. Then Hunter stepped closer, an olfactory aphrodisiac of musk, wood, summer rain, and pure male all mixed. He pressed his body flush to hers and left her no doubt how badly he wanted her.

Kata sensed he'd have no trouble delivering everything she'd ever yearned for . . . and more.

Chapter Two

Hunter pulled Kata closer. As the crevices and swells of their bodies slid perfectly together, his every muscle tightened with need. Pillowy breasts on his chest, her slightly curved belly warm against his own, and lush hips filling his hands. It didn't seem possible, but being this near her made him even harder.

Something about this woman flipped his every switch, and now that he had her close, desire detonated inside him with all the explosiveness of a megaton of TNT. He wanted to strip her bare, taste every inch of her skin, lay his scent on her. But he didn't just want to fuck her. He also wanted to know Kata, build her trust. Seduce her until she submitted completely.

For years, he'd known submissive females willing to succumb to his any and every dominant desire. He'd known intelligent, vibrant, multilayered women with whom he connected intellectually. Unfortunately, he'd never found both in the same person. He sensed that, in Kata, he finally had.

With her, his usual rules of engagement didn't apply, and his normal disinterest in something that lasted more than a few hours didn't exist.

The moment he'd touched her, something inside him had jarred, then settled in place. He'd known she would be his.

Hunter blew out a deep breath. Wow, he'd never felt this way, not even remotely, for any woman. He'd never imagined feeling this instant certainty. But just like his gut feeling about tangos on a mission, he wasn't questioning himself. It just was.

In case Kata didn't feel the same urge for something long-term just yet, he'd keep that under his hat, but already he was fascinated. He couldn't wait to figure out exactly why he was going to love her. No doubt, he would have to scramble fast to hook her as deeply as she'd already sunk her claws into him. No way was he letting her go.

Suddenly, Hunter couldn't wipe the smile off his face. Despite his recent hell, life was looking up.

Across the room, Ben emerged from one of the suite's bathrooms, grabbed another bottle of beer, and watched them with a glassy, puzzled stare. Yeah, he supposed Ben wasn't used to seeing him dance or chat with women he took to bed. Usually, Hunter made time with them because they understood the score, so there was nothing left to do but drop clothes and get busy. Vaguely, he wondered if Ben would be pissed that Kata was different for him . . . but the possibility didn't bother Hunter enough to change course.

Another group of friends clapped Ben on the back, distracting him. Hunter relaxed. Now, Kata's attention would be all his.

"I hear you're a SEAL," she murmured, her voice low, a little husky. "Recently injured?"

He grimaced at the memory of a bullet ripping through him three weeks ago, in nearly the same spot he'd suffered a similar gunshot wound only a few months prior. That night still bothered him . . . It almost seemed as though that fucking Venezuelan arms dealer, Víctor Sotillo, and his hit men had known of his prior injury and had aimed accordingly.

"Yes. He put a bullet in my shoulder, but I planted mine in his chest, so I think I got the better end of the deal."

Kata gaped. "Did he . . . ?"

"Die?" Hunter nodded. "As we were extracting, his pals were performing CPR, but intel was that he didn't make it. Good riddance."

"Bad guy?"

"*Really* bad guy. Sadistic and out for a buck, no matter how many died in the process." *Or how much it destroyed what little peace the world possessed.*

"Wow. And you were on a mission? Where?"

He shrugged, ignoring the twinge in his sore shoulder. "I can't say. Classified. But mission accomplished. The bastard played a mean game of hide-and-seek. Too bad for him I'm very persistent. And patient."

She swallowed, and Hunter wondered if she was getting the clue that those behaviors would apply to her as needed. If not, she'd figure it out soon.

"How long will you be Stateside?"

"Another week. You might be able to motivate me to stay longer."

Nothing coy about the sexy grin that broke out across Kata's face. She stared from beneath thick lashes, her teeth biting into her lush lower lip. He could imagine how she'd look cradling the width of his dick in that very spot.

"I don't know . . . If you decided to stay, what makes you think I'd be motivated to spend more time with you?"

"Honey, if you aren't, then I'm doing something wrong, and I expect you to kick me to the curb."

"Hmm . . ." She shivered and ran her hands up his arms, then clasped her hands together behind his neck. "A pleaser. I like that."

"I'd *love* to please you." He bent and nuzzled her neck, his mouth a whisper from her ear. "If you like that idea, we'll get along real well."

Against his chest, Hunter felt her nipples harden even more, and he'd bet every dime he had in the bank that she was wet. Ready. Still, he waited. Need tightened in his balls, and he forced back his impatience. What he wanted from her would take time and trust. This was too delicious to rush.

He fell back on small talk. "You're a probation officer, according to Ben."

"Yep, for the last two years. I love working with the people who have misstepped and genuinely want to change their lives. Some have just made a wrong choice and need the right tools or a little self-confidence. It's great to make a difference."

Hunter liked her all the more for wanting to. "I'm sure you're damn good at it, too. You've got a no-nonsense way about you, but I'll bet you make it go down smooth."

"Wow, a pleaser *and* a charmer. This might be my lucky night." Her kittenish laugh made him sizzle.

Hunter had to bite the inside of his lip to stop himself from kissing her here and now. Her lips, so red and glossy, were only inches away. Pouty. Sweet. He wanted that mouth under his, wrapped around his dick, open as she screamed through the orgasms he gave her.

"I hear you've had some work-related trouble lately."

Kata wrinkled her nose. "Cortez Villarreal is a piss-ass street thug who assumes that, because I'm female, I'll be easily cowed or bend to his threats. Not gonna happen. I've learned how to fend for myself, and there's no way he's going to scare me from doing my job just because he tosses out some nasty threats." She snorted. "The prick."

"He do anything more than threaten?" He had to suppress the growl from his voice.

"Not yet, but his warrant has only been out for a week. As the police and bounty hunters start closing in, he'll send some of his lowlifes to do his dirty work. Whatever. In both my purse and my apartment, I'm packing. So I'm ready."

Though Hunter didn't like the idea of Kata having to defend herself, the fact she was hell on wheels and didn't show fear turned him on even more. He hadn't expected this tough attitude from such a soft, curvy woman, but it made him even more eager to cement something with her. And confirmed his suspicion that there was more to this woman beneath her very pretty surface.

"Someone teach you to shoot?" He curled his hand around her hip, enjoying the hell out of touching her curves.

She rubbed against him, settling closer. "My older brother. He used to be a New Orleans cop before Katrina. He lives in Houston now, doing undercover work. We haven't heard from him in nearly a year, but last time he blew through town, he made me brush up."

"What about hand-to-hand?"

She grimaced. "I need to work on that. So far, I've relied on knees to the groin and a few pressure points that will take a man down."

"Remind me never to piss you off." He palmed his way down her ass and copped a quick feel.

Lush. Perfect. Taking her from behind was going to be a sweet visual treat. Getting deep inside her there would be even sweeter.

"Why would I do that to you?"

Kata circled her hips against him. A rush of tingles spiked down his cock and spread all through his body. Her stare singed him with sexual challenge. And damn if he wasn't going to take her up on that ASAP. Christ, he wanted to eat her up. Hunger clawed at him, relentless, so much deeper than anything he'd ever known. This mattered because, already, she mattered.

"Well, I suspect you're a vixen, and I'm not always the easiest guy to get along with."

"But if I kneed all that great equipment . . ." She trailed her fingernails right down the line of his spine, and goose bumps broke out over his skin. "Wouldn't I be cutting off my nose to spite my face?"

He grinned. "I like the way you think."

"Tell me more about you."

Hunter wasn't convinced her mind was on the small talk. He was certainly making a concerted effort to concentrate. Getting to know her was important. She was no meaningless fuck, and he wanted her to know it from the start. As hard as he was for her right now, he *liked* her. Respected her moxie.

"My father, whom we affectionately call the Colonel, retired from the army, so he was pissed when my younger brother and I both joined the navy and became SEALs. Logan will be on leave soon, too. I've also got a younger sister who lives with her husband in Lafayette and is expecting her first baby soon. You?"

"Lafayette? I live there. My mother and stepfather still live in the same house I grew up in. My older sister—the one glaring at us—that's Marisol. She lives a few blocks from my folks with her husband and boys. I already told you about my older brother. I'm the baby." Her head cocked to the side, and her sinful façade aside, intelligence gleamed in her hazel eyes. "What about your mom?"

The one subject he didn't discuss with anyone. Ever. Her question had merely been an attempt to be polite, so he didn't feel obligated to answer.

He swayed against her, palming her nape, brushing his lips over her cheek—all the way to her ear. "Is that what you really want to talk about?"

Kata sighed and slipped her hand under his T-shirt, and she scratched her nails lightly down his back, lighting him up like a Fourth of July fireworks show. Impatience to touch her, to spread her out and please her, flayed him.

He whispered his lips across her neck, a slow tease. Almost a kiss . . . but not quite. She gasped and tilted her head back, exposing the graceful arch of her throat to him. A sign of surrender that had his dick tightening, weeping for more.

With a growl, he rocked his erection directly against her pussy. She went utterly boneless against him. Her lips parted on a moan.

"Or do you want to talk about how I'm going to fuck you, Kata?"

"Y-you and Ben?"

He hesitated. "I can't speak for him. But I *know* what I'm going to do to you."

She met his stare again, now growing bolder. "Nice that you have plans. But you should be wondering what mine are."

Boldly, Kata pressed her mouth over his, kissing him. Her pouty lips molded to his, incredibly soft yet demanding, a hard brush. Then she eased back, a tease—there and gone—leaving behind a hint of her flavor, hot and intoxicating and impossible to pin down. Instantly, fire raged through his body, and he grabbed her tighter.

She ended the kiss with a husky laugh that scraped down his spine.

"Kata," he breathed in warning.

A brazen smile flitted across her mouth. She knew she was stringing him out, grabbing him by the dick and not letting go. He liked this playful side of her, so he let her lead—for now.

She rose on her tiptoes, closer, as she feathered her mouth over his again. Grabbing his arms, she deepened the kiss, her tongue like a butterfly, fleeting, flitting, elusive. She tasted like cherries, a hint of tequila, and pure sin. She made him so fucking hard.

When she broke away, Hunter looked up. Kata's sister frowned, but her girlfriends were smiling from ear to ear. Ben, still surrounded by buddies and nursing another beer, looked at them with an uncertain scowl. Hunter danced her farther away from them all, closer to the windows with the stunning views of the Strip just lighting up for the night.

Shoving all the bystanders out of his mind, Hunter thrust both hands into that dark, silky hair twisting down Kata's back and tugged gently until her neck arched for him.

"You're playing dangerous games with me."

A smug, sexy smile curled her fuckable lips. "I can handle you."

"You should find out what games I like before you get too confident."

"Tell me."

He stared right into her dilated eyes, took in the pulse beating at her neck. And he smiled. "I'd rather show you."

Hunter took control and unleashed the force of his kiss on her, past her lips, into that cherry-tequila mouth, to tangle his tongue with hers in a sensuous dance. He demanded. Took. Followed the clues she gave him, those little gasps and shivers that told him what she wanted. Then he delivered.

Still eating at her mouth, Hunter grabbed her wrists and clasped them together with one unyielding hand at the small of her back. He bracketed her thighs with his own and pressed against her—chest, belly, hips. He urged her back to the wall, holding her completely immobile.

She gasped, and he swallowed the sound with another kiss. *Fuck, yeah.*

His body shook with the need to strip her bare, fuck her mindless, master her utterly. As brutally sexy images flooded his mind and her flavor intoxicated him, she wiggled one hand free and slipped it between them, wrapping her fingers around his cock. And then she gripped. Need tore through Hunter. He gritted his teeth, swallowing back a hiss—and shoved her hand behind her back once more.

Kata was accustomed to taking charge. She wouldn't cede control to him easily, but he was determined and patient. He relished a good challenge. And he wasn't going to quit until she surrendered completely.

* * *

AFTER blowing out her candles, Kata set in to celebrate. Evening turned to night as she chatted, danced, and burned with the knowledge of the pleasure yet to come.

Two hours later, the cake was decimated, and most of the revelers had gone back to their rooms or out to gamble. Kata swallowed back her fourth margarita of the night, feeling more than a bit euphoric. But since a girl didn't turn twenty-five every day, tipsy was okay in her book.

Behind her, Hunter still stood very close, his hand slung on her hip. His body heat permeated her sweater and little black skirt—

while his stiff cock pressed into her ass. Everything about his stance screamed possession, and she kind of liked the thought that he wouldn't let her go until he was satisfied that he'd taken her as thoroughly as a man could. With Ben's help, of course.

Since their dance, Kata had found it difficult to focus on anything other than getting the clothes off Hunter's hard body and finding out just how capable he was of making her feel good. So why the hell had he cheered Ben on when her friend with benefits had suggested a drinking contest with another one of her neighbors?

For that matter, what was Ben thinking? This frat boy shit bored her. She'd never seen him down a six-pack like this. Why tonight?

"Go, go, go!" the small crowd surrounding them chanted, comprised of Ben's opponent's girlfriend and brother. Hunter remained silent.

Four minutes into the challenge, both opponents ripped open a new beer, Tim his fourth, Ben his fifth. They guzzled.

Two long minutes later, Ben belched and held up his sixth empty beer. "Did it!"

That, coupled with the copious amounts of beer and vodka he'd been drinking for the past few hours, made Ben a very drunk guy. His speech was slurred, and his limbs moved like wet noodles. Kata sighed and got up to make coffee. If he was going to be useful in helping fulfill her fantasy, she had to sober him up now.

His opponent, Tim, slammed his half-full bottle down. "Damn, I'm getting too old to drink anyone under the table." He sighed, then turned to his girlfriend with a scowl. "Let's go."

After Tim grabbed his girlfriend's arm and stomped out the door, his brother, Trey, hugged her. "Happy birthday, Kata. I hope it's a great night."

She smiled at the thirtysomething cop. "Thanks for coming to Vegas to celebrate with me."

"And miss a kick-ass weekend? Never!" He flicked a gaze over at Hunter. "You okay for the rest of the night, or you need me to stay with you?"

Translation: Are you okay with this stranger?

No one knew Hunter much except Ben, who had assured her that Hunter was a great guy with a boatload of medals. But even if the sexy soldier hadn't been a SEAL, Kata sensed that, while tough, he was good people. With his power play of a kiss earlier, he'd proven he had an uncompromising side. Then again, so did she.

Kata smiled. "I'm fine. Go enjoy the rest of your night."

Trey shrugged. "I got a hundred-dollar chip from Caesars burning a hole in my pocket."

She laughed and waved the trio out, then locked the door behind her and made her way to the suite's little kitchen. Hallie and Chloe had left a few minutes ago to seek out single, gorgeous males for the night. She'd catch up with them on their flight home tomorrow morning. Marisol had gone back to her room shortly after Kata had blown out her candles. The mommy of two rambunctious school-age boys wasn't used to late-night parties anymore.

So she, Ben, and Hunter were finally alone in the suite. Now the real fun could begin. After coffee.

She started the brew, then fished around the cabinets for mugs.

Suddenly, she turned, and Hunter stood *right* there. She yelped. "Oh . . . You scared me. Don't sneak up on me like that!"

A ghost of a smile played across his mouth. "Sorry. Can I help you with something?"

"No. Thanks. You want a cup?" She gestured to the coffee.

"I'm good for now. You need one?"

"I don't actually drink it." She looked out into the suite's living room at her slouching friend. His eyes were at half-mast. "But Ben looks like he could use it."

Ben sat up and barked, "I don' want no fuckin' coffee. I've just been waitin' for ev'rone to leave so we could fuck. You still game, Kata?"

God knew she'd wanted a ménage forever. People did it and enjoyed it, from what she'd heard. She knew she'd feel the same.

But Ben was flat drunk. She'd never known his equipment to

stop working, short of deep slumber, true. And she liked him, even if it was more as a friend than a lover. No denying that he was good in bed.

Hunter? Just being near the man made her tremble all over. Over the last few hours, she'd begun to sense that he was more than intense. That he crossed the line into forceful, maybe even controlling. That should send her running fast and hard. Given her family history, the idea of putting herself in the path of a domineering jackass terrified her. But Hunter just made her embarrassingly wet.

If she passed on this opportunity now because the situation wasn't perfect, would this chance—or a man like Hunter—ever come her way again?

In a few dozen steps, Kata could be face-to-face with her biggest fantasy, if she just walked down the hall to the bedroom.

"I'm game." She drew in a shaking breath and met Hunter's blue gaze. "You?"

Every time she looked at him, she went a bit more breathless. He was gorgeous, but she didn't feel this way with every gorgeous guy she met. It was *him*. He rolled up like a quiet storm, all cool and collected, but inside, barely leashed power filled him. Kata wanted to be the one to undo all that.

"I came here for you. I'm nothing but game, honey," Hunter drawled.

"Then . . . I guess we should go to the bedroom."

"Damn straight!" Ben rose to his feet, stumbled.

Hunter caught and steadied him, while gesturing down the hall. Ben lurched, walking unsteadily forward. Still, he managed to bounce from one wall to the other like a pinball on the boards. She watched, biting her lip.

Hunter approached her, his hot palm at the small of her back. "Second thoughts?"

"No. I'm worried about Ben."

He gripped her shoulder, squeezed. "It'll all work out. C'mon."

She nodded, figuring she was wasting time worrying about what *might* happen. Right now, she had two hotties willing to fulfill her fantasy. Why worry about anything?

Exhaling away her tension, Kata sauntered toward the bedroom, anticipation simmering inside her. And not just from the fantasy itself. She was familiar with Ben; they'd fallen into a twice weekly routine, so she knew exactly what to expect from him. But Hunter . . .

She cast a glance at him, and her breathing hitched. He sent her a slow smile that dripped sex. Kata looked forward to him. He'd likely drive her insane with the sort of pleasure she'd only ever imagined. She couldn't wait.

"If you move that pretty ass faster," Hunter drawled, "I'll get my mouth on your pussy faster."

Her stomach flipped over, and their gazes connected. Her breath caught. *Oh, holy shit. He meant that.*

She nearly ran the rest of the way to the bedroom.

Inside, against the backdrop of glittering Vegas night sky, Ben was already shedding his clothes, shirt half unbuttoned, one shoe on, the other off. The fly of his jeans and his eyes were both partially open.

After she drew shut the heavy hotel drapes along the south side of the room, Hunter took her cue and closed those along the east wall, shrouding the room in almost total darkness. Which brought her a measure of comfort. As a plus-sized girl, she liked her curves, but if her lover didn't, she didn't want to know. She preferred to leave the lights off. Ben had never minded.

Hunter flipped on the bedside lamp, and a white glow encircled the bedroom's huge king-sized bed. She hesitated, then crossed the room and switched it off, leaving them in shadow. "I'd feel better . . ."

Even in the semidarkness, she sensed his displeasure. Kata found herself regretting that. Why should she care what he thought? He'd be gone by morning. And she'd always been determined to please no one but herself. The minute a guy showed any sign of try-ing to pull controlling macho bullshit, she got out quick. Hunter hadn't said a word, but somehow, she knew that he wanted to see her exposed to his gaze. Vulnerable. The thought terrified and aroused her at once.

"Kata, I need help," Ben called.

Relieved to have something else to focus on, she dashed to his side, helping him off with his other shoe. "You really tied one on tonight."

"Aw, don' be pissed off. The guys challenged me, and—"

"And you weren't smart enough to turn them down, even when you knew you'd win? Seriously, Ben."

"So I'm a dipshit." Pulling off his shirt, he sent her a lopsided grin.

Kata couldn't help but smile. Even drunk, he was self-deprecating and funny. And true-blue. Impossible to hate, even if he wasn't showing his good side tonight.

"You are. You'd better not ruin my birthday."

"Hey, didn' I bring you someone?" He gestured vaguely in Hunter's direction as he pushed his jeans around his ankles. "He's done this before. And the girls who worked the bars near the RTC where we went to boot usta ooh and aah about him. I brought you the best. Happy birt'day."

Hunter had experienced a ménage before? Her gaze zipped across the room to him. What little she could see of Hunter's expression neither confirmed nor denied Ben's claim . . . but she didn't imagine for an instant that he'd been a choirboy.

So "yes" was a safe assumption.

His experience should have made her feel better. He'd know what to do, how to minimize any awkwardness and maximize the pleasure. But instead of feeling relief, the truth irritated her. Of course she wasn't special to him. He hardly knew her.

But logical or not, she wanted to be special. Or maybe she simply wanted the event to be special. Yeah, that made more sense.

"Do you want to talk about this?" Hunter asked, approaching her, his hand brushing over her hip—and sending tingles down her spine.

"No. I asked for a ménage because I wanted it. Nothing has changed." She shrugged. "So let's do this."

"My kinda girl!" Slivers of moonlight peeked through the drapes, enough to see Ben leer as he shoved the bedspread aside and kicked off his boxers. He bounced onto the bed, then lay flat across the mattress. In quick work, he started stroking his cock. "I'm waitin' . . . Why don't you strip for us?"

Strip for them? Even if it was mostly dark in the room, she was a little self-conscious. Ben knew that. Why the hell was he pulling this shit? Because Mr. Budweiser was doing his talking for him.

Kata opened her mouth to call him on it when Hunter leaned in and whispered, "Want help?"

Impossible to pass that up. Anticipation gripped her stomach in a vise. "Yes. Please."

God, she sounded every bit as breathless and eager as she felt.

"Very happy to," he murmured against her neck.

His voice vibrated inside her, and she quivered as every syllable crashed through her system. Damn, this man was potent. He knew just what to say, what to do, how to make her crave his next move. She wasn't sure she liked being so unbalanced around him. Sexually, yes, more than she wanted to admit. But being independent to the core, she refused to do anything but meet him on equal footing.

Smiling, Kata reached behind her and folded her palm over his hand. With her other, she pushed her red sweater up a bit, then guided his palm right over her breast. Even through the lace of her cups, his touch was electric. His fingers scorched her. With a catching little gasp, she melted against him.

Hunter cupped her breast, testing its weight, thumbing her nipple through the lace. Her head fell back on his shoulder, and she let out a full-fledged moan.

"From the bit I can see, that's hot. Get her clothes off, man," Ben barked.

"We're taking it easy here. Going slow . . ." Hunter soothed Ben's belligerent demand. Then he turned his attention back to her.

He kissed his way across her shoulder, one hand cradling her hip. She barely had time to process how good his touch felt before he smoothed his palm up her waist, swept across her back, then pushed her sweater over her head. He threw it at Ben.

A moment later, her friend let out a drunken holler. "*Whowee!* That's it. Get her bare. My dick is aching."

Hunter didn't say a word. Instead, he caressed her shoulders, then lower, before easing her bra from her body. Her large breasts hung heavy, aching, tips tight and sensitive. Then Hunter's palms were beneath them, lifting, thumbing, creating a new scatter of tingles everywhere. The ache between her legs had been a dull throb since their dance, but now? It had become a needy, demanding pang, made worse as Hunter pinched her nipples.

"I would love to see you bare for me. Panting. Wet. Eager. Even the thought of it turns me on more than I can tell you. You'll let me leave the light on and see you that way?"

It was a question . . . yet not. The command was subtle, but there. Normally, she balked when told what to do, but hearing the hunger in Hunter's voice made her yearn to arouse him more, whatever it took. "Maybe . . . if you admit that I'm making your dick ache, too."

"Oh, you have no idea." She felt him smile against her neck, just as he raked his thumbs across her nipples again. "But I'll do my best to show you."

He grabbed her wrist and led it behind her, right over his cock. What she'd suspected from her earlier stolen grope confirmed her suspicion. He was both very hard and sizeable—and surpassed her expectations. Taking every inch of him would be a tight fit, and Kata wanted him inside her so badly, she was nearly ready to beg.

Her stomach tightened, rolled. He was good. Really good. Had she ever wanted it so badly, even though he'd done nothing more than kiss and pet her? No.

Kata moaned. "Hunter . . ."

"Off with this skirt," he murmured against her skin.

She nearly protested when he nudged her hand from his cock,

but he set to work on her zipper. The light rasp of the little teeth filled the room, along with the sound of her own rapid breathing.

"Yeah!" Ben hollered. "She's got gorgeous thighs. I want them wrapped around my face."

"Patience," Hunter scolded. "She's not even undressed."

"You need help hurryin' that up?" Ben raised himself from the bed.

"No. Stay there."

The sharp command, though not directed at her, made Kata snap to attention . . . and caused her to ache in a way she didn't understand.

With a little tap on each leg, Hunter prompted her to step out of her skirt, then threw it at Ben, who caught the little leather garment—her silly birthday indulgence. "Oh, this feels good on my dick."

"Don't you mess up my skirt!"

"Then hurry, babe."

"Tell me what color panties you have on," Hunter whispered in her ear as he felt his way across her hip. "I can feel that they're lace, but innocent white? Black, to match your skirt? Red, because you're daring and naughty?"

His fingers crept slowly, ever closer, to the juncture of her thighs. Kata's knees went weak. *Dear God, please let him touch me there . . .*

He didn't.

"I'm waiting . . ." Hunter's fingers hovered a fraction above her mound, the heat from his flesh burning—but the absence of his caress was killing her.

"Me, too." She pressed her hips forward, but he evaded her, giving her the promise of a touch but never delivering.

"Answer me."

His demand pinged through her like a live wire. A jolt. A flash of desire. "Hot pink."

"Nice." In reward, Hunter slid his fingers under the elastic of her little panties and brushed his fingers over her clit.

Her breath stopped, literally, and her heart drummed madly as he rubbed a teasing circle at the top of her pussy, right where she needed him—but not hard enough to send her over the edge. Her clit swelled. She sucked in a hard breath as the ache gouged her belly.

"Please . . ."

"I can't wait to hear you beg when you really mean it." His fingers feathered over her clit again. "And you will."

Something about Hunter's tone told Kata that he wasn't just playing dominant games. He wanted to control her tonight. Kata bit her lip at the realization. Warning bells rang in her head . . . even as she melted against him. She gasped at the sensation that washed over her like hot rain. Looking for an anchor in a sea of drowning desire, she reached out for him, clung to his thighs, her back tight against his chest.

This was insane. She didn't give this much of herself or her control away—ever. Kata knew painfully well exactly where allowing a man to control her would end. She had to find the voice to tell him her limitations now. Equals all the way or she didn't play. But his touch on the hard, swollen nub, delving deep into her moist folds, was blinding, magical, as damn necessary as her next breath.

"You're wet. Perfect," he purred.

"Hunter," she panted. "I don't—*ooh!*—beg. I—I—" She gasped. "I don't submit."

"She doesn't," Ben slurred.

Her flesh tingled, burned. Orgasm was *right there*, and the only thing standing between her and it were his fingers. Still, she couldn't let this slide.

Gritting her teeth against the pleasure, she reached for her stern voice. "No man commands me. Period."

"Give me time," he murmured against her ear, making her shiver again. "I will."

What the hell?

Before she could protest, he lifted her, cradling her in his arms. Shock tumbled through Kata. Carrying a plus-sized girl to bed? Hell, no! Hunter could feel the effect of every tamale, every bite of chocolate, every day she'd overworked and been too late to hit the gym. . . .

"Put me down!"

Instead of complying, he raised her higher until his lips hovered over her own. "Trust me, Kata. I'm not going to hurt you."

"I might hurt *you*."

Hunter snorted. "Not likely, honey."

Before she could argue, he covered her lips with a hard kiss. Kata linked her hands around his neck and clung for dear life, expecting to have her ass meet the carpet at any moment. Instead, he sauntered across the room like he didn't have a care. Soon, she felt the mattress and slightly stiff hotel sheets against her back.

"All better?" he murmured.

"No. You didn't listen!"

"You didn't trust me."

Ben crawled across the bed to them. "Finally!"

Kata felt a hand slap down on her stomach and flinched. Was it terrible to admit that she almost didn't want Ben here? Not in his current state, anyway. Normally, they had fun and laughs, but tonight . . .

"Gimme those luscious tits," her friend demanded, his hand working up until he grabbed a breast and used it as a guide to pull himself closer. His mouth drifted across her shoulder, teeth slightly nipping. "You always taste good."

Ben licked his way to her nipple, and she settled into the bed, trying to relax. She was naked, he was there, and . . . where was Hunter?

No sooner had she wondered than she felt the bed dip at her feet. Two hot hands clutched her panties and dragged them down her legs. Then his fingers curled around her ankles and urged them wide apart.

As it had every time Hunter came near, Kata's stomach tightened and her heart galloped like a herd of wild horses. She offered no resistance as he crawled between her thighs and breathed right over her slick folds.

He brushed his thumb over her clit, and she sucked in a huge draft of air, fisting the sheets. Ben took that as a cue to suck the other nipple into his mouth, and before she could process the feeling and the rough slide of his teeth, Hunter dragged two fingers through her slick valley, then pressed them inside her deep. Almost instantly, he found a magically sensitive spot and rubbed. Arousal soared through her. She gushed, cried out, spread her legs wider, and lifted her hips in a silent plea for more.

"Ya likin' this, Kata?" Ben asked, dragging his tongue over her nipple.

Before she could answer, Hunter rubbed that one spot again, unmercifully, and settled his tongue over her clit, slow and sweet, like he had all day.

Kata couldn't find her voice except to whimper as pleasure bombarded her and the need grew from an ache to desperation.

"Guess that's a yes." Ben's laughter rumbled as he kissed a wet trail down her neck and flicked her wet nipple.

She barely noticed. She was too busy drowning in pleasure as Hunter's lips wrapped around her little bundle of nerves and pulled it into the heat of his mouth.

"Fuck, where're the condoms? Shit, left 'em in the john," Ben groused as he got off the bed, crashed against the wall, and stumbled to the adjoining bathroom.

Kata felt a guilty relief that she and Hunter would be alone for a few moments, and she sank back into the unending pleasure of his touch. He toyed and explored, wringing gasps and whimpers from her, driving her up higher . . . but always dangling her orgasm out of reach.

Seconds—minutes?—later, she heard a soft buzz and stiffened. What was that noise? Everything was still close to dark. Kata frowned. Had Ben never turned on the bathroom light?

Kata felt around on the bed beside her, but the mattress was empty. Was he still in the bathroom? Was that noise him . . . snoring? It sounded again, a light sawing, followed by a harsh exhalation. Ben had freaking passed out?

Hunter never missed a lick.

"Wait! Ben . . . Do you—? O*hh* . . . oh God, that's good." She fisted the blankets. "Yes!"

Instead of granting the orgasm shimmering just beyond her reach, he pulled back, teasing her.

Ben snored once more, and Kata tried to pull away. But Hunter held firm, his huge, hot palms holding her thighs open, wedging his shoulders between, his mouth hovering right over her pussy, silently promising ecstasy.

She tried to block it out. "Stop. I'm telling you that—"

"Ben is snoring?"

On cue, her friend's buzzing sounded again, this time deeper, longer.

"Yeah. We should wake him and—"

"He's not necessary tonight, Kata. Want me to prove it?"

Chapter Three

HUNTER didn't have to prove anything. He merely whispered in that sinful voice what she already knew: She wanted him far more than she'd ever wanted Ben. She'd had this fantasy of being touched by both her lover and a stranger forever and a day. But here, now, her panting breaths mingled with Hunter's, his unrelenting stare reached through the shadows, promising searing pleasure. Despite her misgivings about his bent for control, Kata wanted him. Badly.

"Don't stop," she whispered, raising her hips.

He hesitated, then levered himself up to shut the bathroom door—blocking out Ben's soft snores. He lowered himself to the mattress again, hovering over her, his stare drilling into her in the shadows. "I'm going to take you alone tonight."

"I know."

"Repeatedly," he vowed.

Her breath caught. Desire branded his masculine face as his hot palm caressed her breast, the curve of her waist, before settling inside her thigh—skating heart-stoppingly close to her pussy. And then he stopped. As she strained toward him, her ache ratcheted up.

He seemed to know exactly what drove her mad.

"Keep talking to me." His husky murmur whispered across her skin.

"Tell you what I want in bed?" Kata had no doubt he was capable of giving it to her.

"That, and more. I want you to be completely open to me."

"Sexually?"

"In every way." His eyes were solemn, startlingly direct.

Her heart skipped a beat. Kata pulled her lip through her teeth and peered up at the hard, shadowed angles of his face. "What is it you want, exactly?"

"All you're willing to give me." He smiled wryly. "And probably more."

Those murmured words raised all of her red flags. What did he want beyond passion? Surely not more than a night of pleasure with no regrets. They'd been ridiculously in sync so far.

Maybe hinting at possessiveness was his shtick. Maybe he thought women dug it. *Whatever* . . .

"I can't promise I'll agree to everything, but if you do something I don't like, we'll talk it out."

"Good." His fingers tightened on her thighs. He pried them apart a bit wider, then wriggled down her body. His mouth loomed closer to the ache she desperately needed him to sate. "Kata, I will push you."

"About the bedside light?" Kata frowned. Would he still want her if he actually saw *all* her curves?

"For starters."

She paused. "Hunter—"

"Trust me, honey."

The way he called her "honey" made Kata shiver. Usually, she hated that endearment, but the way he said it . . . *hmm*. Then the rest of his words registered in her lust-ridden brain. Trust him . . . with what? Was he trying to tell her that he was into some freaky shit? He'd done ménages before. What else did he have in his repertoire?

"Look, I don't know how your preferences run, but I have a few boundaries."

"Such as?" He breathed against her stomach, pressing mind-stealing kisses to her skin.

"I'm really afraid of knives."

His husky laugh warmed her. "No knives. I'm hard-core, not weird."

Kata relaxed. Maybe she was overthinking this. "I don't like pain."

Hunter shrugged and trailed his fingers through her very wet pussy. "You'll only get the good kind from me. The last thing I want to do is hurt you."

She frowned. "Look, in case you didn't get it earlier, I won't be dominated."

"You'll be fine."

His voice reassured her more than his words, but he hadn't done anything to give her pause, other than put out a dominant vibe. She'd run across that before and walked away unscathed. She could handle Hunter, too.

Kata shot him a cocky grin and let her knees relax to the sides, widening her thighs. "Okay, then. Do your worst."

"Oh, honey," he chided, his gaze fused on hers. "Don't doubt me. I will."

Before she could reply, Hunter bent to her again. He slid those long, still-slick fingers inside her, thumb grazing her clit just before his mouth took over. He sucked her slowly, a nuzzle, a gentle lick. A tease. She tensed, stared at him.

Hunter oozed confidence—and not just in bed. The man was clearly intelligent. Interesting. Dangerous. His touch gliding over her skin felt gentle . . . but his stare told her that he wasn't going to go easy on her tonight. Even the thought made her quiver.

He pressed firm fingers to her G-spot, and the question dissipated. Any cool perspective she'd gained in the past few moments . . .

gone. His bold licks made her dizzy, and he savored her swollen bundle of nerves—and sent her reeling.

God, he was good at this. *Really* good. If she tightened or gasped, he did more of whatever drove her mad, then found unpredictable ways to make it even better. A light scrape of fingernails into the nerve-laden tissue in her channel, teeth tenderly grazing her ultra-sensitive clit, sliding the pad of his thumb through her slick flesh, down, until he pressed in at her back entrance.

"No. Hunter, I—oh. *Ah . . .*"

"Don't think about whether you should like it," he whispered against her inner thigh. "Think only about whether you actually do."

Deeper, deeper, he eased his thumb into her backside, parting her flesh in a sting of pleasure that made her gasp. No one had ever touched her there. Ben had talked about wanting anal sex once or twice, and she'd always shied away. But now . . . A million tingles she'd never felt leapt to sizzling life, coupling with the quivering, begging sensations in her pussy.

"Do you like it?"

Kata gave him a shaky nod. "But I don't understand . . ."

"Just feel."

With that, he settled his mouth back over her clit, dragged his fingers relentlessly over the responsive spot inside her, and swiveled his thumb in her depths.

Hunter touched her as if he had already figured her out and now sought to use that knowledge to blow her mind. Maybe maintaining control wouldn't be as easy as it had always been . . . Her heart pounded, galloping so hard and loud, she couldn't hear anything but its roar. Her own moans rang in her ears. How could he both thrill and terrify her at once?

Her fingernails dug into her palms as the pleasure he gave rushed toward her like a towering tsunami. Kata had no doubt it would drown her. But she couldn't stop wanting it, crying out for it. Time stood still as she held her breath and waited.

Pressure tightened and burned under his fingers, multiplying, then rocketing until she felt as if her body would burst. Kata's back arched, her hips lifted, with the body-bending force of the orgasm. She screamed his name. Stars burst across her vision as ecstasy crashed over her. And Hunter's unrelenting focus on her with every touch of his fingers, every flick of his tongue, drove her deeper into the abyss of a pleasure so overwhelming, Kata wondered if she'd ever be the same.

Finally, her breathing evened, her heartbeat slowed. Only then did Hunter rise from the bed. Before she could stop herself, Kata whimpered at his loss. But when he took a step, she knew his destination.

"Please, don't turn on the light. I don't like . . ." God, even finishing that statement was too revealing.

"Being seen?" He flipped on the lamp as if she hadn't spoken.

Kata blinked against the harsh light. Apprehension seized her. He could see how thoroughly he'd devastated her by the flush that must surely be reddening her cheeks, by her swollen nipples and so-wet pussy. A look of dazed satisfaction, no doubt, filled her face. His blue, laser-focused stare peeled back her layers to see deeper still. She closed her eyes, but it was too late to hide.

In that suspended moment, Kata's stomach tightened. How had Hunter reached inside her, stripped the veneer of confidence from her, and dug down so quickly to the vulnerable woman beneath? The fact that he had, it terrified her. She didn't reveal that inner person to anyone, especially someone she barely knew.

With a curse, Kata rolled away, turning her back to him.

Hunter clamped a hand down on her thigh, another on her shoulder. "Don't hide."

Before she could argue, he braced himself over her thighs . . . and fixed his gaze on the heavy curves of her breasts.

"Don't stare." She crossed her arms over her chest and looked away.

Moving his weight onto his knees, he clasped her wrists and imprisoned them above her head gently—but firmly. "That's like telling me to stop breathing. Impossible."

"I told you I didn't want the light on. I don't want your eyes taking a walk all over me. Now get the hell off."

"Why don't you want me to see you?"

How pushy was this guy going to get? "Going down on me doesn't entitle you to an answer. Turn off the fucking light. I don't like being stared at."

"That's not true. If you didn't want men to look, you wouldn't have been wearing a black leather miniskirt or that attention-getting red sweater that was like a second skin. You wouldn't have that luscious gloss on your lips or the bright polish on your toes. You wanted to be seen at your party. But you're afraid for me to see you naked. Why?"

Kata blanched, her heart stuttering. He had noticed way too much.

She tried to calm herself with logic. So far, he'd made observations, asked a few questions, pressed a little—not behaved like a world-class asshole. He wasn't as loudmouthed as her stepfather, Gordon. That calmed her some. Taking back control would do the rest. Because whatever he was trying to pull, she wouldn't be playing. "Either turn the lights off or let me up."

He made no move to comply. "Did some prick criticize your body?"

Only her whole life. It wasn't any one prick in particular. Starting with Sean Lampke in the second grade and moving right up to football jock Mike McKindle in high school. Not that any of them had seen her naked, but all the teasing, especially after her breasts had developed in the fifth grade . . . Their opinions didn't matter. She was proud of herself. Fuck them if they didn't like her. But opening herself up to Hunter? She didn't do that for anyone.

"What are you after?" she challenged. "This is a one-night stand, and you don't need to know my innermost secrets for that. If you want me, then turn out the damn light and let's fuck."

"Kata, I need to see you. *All* of you. I want to watch your face as I slide in deep. I want to see your lashes flutter closed and your skin flush as your arousal surges, right before your pretty hazel eyes flash wide open and orgasm slams through your body." His eyes darkened with arousal. "I won't let you hide from me, honey."

There it was again: *honey*. The way he spoke to her made her sizzle. She shouldn't like that dominant tone of voice that went with it, shouldn't feel tingles down to her toes. Damn if he wasn't everything she shouldn't want.

"Won't *let* me?" she parried. "You came here to share me with Ben, then encouraged him to drink until he was too wasted to participate. Now you're trying to strip me of far more than my clothes. I barely know you. This control freak routine you're pulling? It's not happening."

His lips curled up, and it couldn't exactly be called a smile. "You're tough on the outside. But inside, there's a vulnerable woman. And there are times, like now, that you hate it. You don't want anyone to see anything but your independent façade. You're adventurous—when it suits you. You have a lot of friends but aren't really close to anyone. You don't like being told what to do, especially by a lover. Kata, I'm going to be the man who changes your mind. About everything."

Her jaw dropped, even as goose bumps broke out all over her skin. God, Hunter had read her perfectly. He was clearly used to sucking in the universe, examining it, then bending it to his will. She'd bet he did it as naturally as breathing.

Anyone like that wasn't for her, no matter how big a thrill he gave her.

"That's arrogant. I won't just . . . roll over and play dead. You're not dictating to me. You know what?" She pushed against his chest. "I'm done here."

He didn't budge, just held her still and sent her a considering look. "The last thing I want you to do is roll over and play dead, honey. Where would be the challenge in that?"

Her temper surged. He wanted to bring her to heel with his wit and his body for some sick thrill?

Kata bucked and wriggled, trying to displace him, to no avail. "Goddamn it, get off me. I'm not a fucking prize to win or some mountain to conquer so you can prove to yourself that you're the man. I told you I'm done." She shoved at his chest. "Get the hell off!"

Hunter's face softened. He trailed the back of his fingers down her cheek, his stare disturbingly intimate. "I don't want to win you like some cheap prize at a county fair to prove my masculinity. I want to be with you—all of you. Just like I want you to be with all of me. I'm stripping myself bare, too." As if to prove his point, he ripped that torso-hugging charcoal T-shirt over his head.

A hard ripple of mouthwatering abs gave way to pecs that made her fingers itch to touch him, followed by imposing shoulders that would eclipse a room the second he mounted her. That fact made a twisted part of her tremble with a secret thrill—and it bothered her more.

"Taking your shirt off is nothing compared to the way you're trying to bare my soul."

"It's a first step, honey. Believe me, I want you to know me inside out, too. Feel comfortable with me."

Kata frowned as she turned the words over in her head. "That . . . takes time. Don't you get the meaning of 'one-night stand'? It's just tonight, so none of this getting-to-know-you shit matters."

"I disagree. I want you to want me, trust me. And for you to give me every part of you that you've never given any other man."

She stared at him as if he'd lost his mind—because clearly, he had. "You don't want much, do you?"

"I know I'm asking for a lot. Give me a little tonight, Kata. I'll earn the rest."

His every word boggled her mind. Earn the rest, like he wanted not only to control her, but to *own* her? "I don't get you. I'm willing to fuck you. For most guys, that's enough. A little mutual pleasure and—"

"Before I met you, yeah. Now?" Hunter shook his head. "I'm

going to be totally straight up. I'm not willing to settle for less than everything."

His gaze told her that he was dead serious. She swallowed, her mind racing. They'd just met. This made no sense. Whatever. Just because he wanted something didn't mean it was going to happen. No way was she allowing him control of this situation or her.

"I told you, I don't roll that way. A simple romp between the sheets, great. But this . . . wanting me to give you permission to own me, or whatever . . ." She shook her head. "I'm no man's possession."

He considered her for a long while as the light from the bedside lamp burned over her shoulders, breasts, and nipples. Hunter stared fixedly, and Kata knew he could read her anger, uncertainty, and arousal simmering under her skin. The mix was a powerful cocktail of emotions.

She really wanted to look away, but damn if she'd give him the satisfaction of flinching first. But the longer their gazes clashed, the more her insecurities rose. Tears—honest to freaking goodness tears—burned her eyes, damn it. She had no idea where they'd come from, other than this horrible sense of exposure, of vulnerability, but no way she would reveal how much he rattled her.

Kata didn't know him well, but she suspected he was formulating some plan designed to have her eating out of his hand. Since he'd zeroed in on domination, one of her most potent fantasies—and her biggest fears—Hunter was off to a frighteningly good start.

"I know I've asked for a lot," he murmured roughly, making her hormones weep with need. "I'm willing to spend the time to earn your trust and show you what I'm made of. I'll be totally honest about who I am and what I want. Can you?"

Everything inside her clenched with desire. "I'm just here to scratch our mutual itch."

"And then what? We'll just go our separate ways? That's what you really want?"

Kata opened her mouth to say yes . . . then realized that, despite everything, the idea of their paths never crossing again disturbed her—far more than it should. Why? He was urging her to surrender more than her passion, cross a line she'd refused to ever go near, no matter how tempting. And part of her fantasized about things she could never endure. If she admitted half so much aloud, Hunter would engulf her—and right now, she was too raw, too needy to stop him.

But she'd offered to fuck him the simple way multiple times and he hadn't taken her up on it yet. If she wanted him—and she did, desperately—she must pretend to play his game.

As much as she hated to admit it, he intrigued her, sucked her into a drowning pool of desire. Walking away right now wasn't an option.

"How about this? For the next hour, I'll be honest." She gritted her teeth and forced the words out. "But if I say stop, you stop."

"An hour?" He didn't sound pleased.

Kata nodded. "That's all you're getting from me. Maybe, after that, we'll both be done, and it won't matter."

"I wouldn't hang your hat on that, honey."

For a long moment, he said nothing, and she stared up into his unwavering blue stare. Earlier his eyes had been shutters that allowed fleeting glimpses of the real man to peek through, veneered by challenge and hunger. Now he'd opened up. The desire was still there, but she read something almost profound on his face. This was important to him. Why? A guy like Hunter would—and probably did—have anyone he wanted. Why would she matter when they'd just met?

Whatever . . . He was a birthday fling she'd forget tomorrow. She hoped.

"All right," he agreed. "An hour, for starters. I want you to see me." Hunter stood and reached for the button of his jeans, slid his zipper down, toed off his boots, then shoved everything off to the thick carpet in a pile. And Kata got her first look at him naked.

"Oh, holy shit." The words slipped from her mouth before she could stop them.

Hunter was, in a word, gorgeous. Every inch of him solid, hard, imposing. Big . . . everywhere. She swallowed.

He chuckled. "Glad you approve. I'm going to make this so good for you."

She didn't doubt for an instant that he could.

Hunter slid back onto the bed, over her body, balancing most of his weight on his knees and elbows. Then he settled right between her thighs, chest to chest, belly to belly, lips inches apart. As she'd suspected, he eclipsed the rest of the room, leaving her nowhere to look but at him. His stare melted into hers. He wasn't yet inside her, but already Kata felt breathless, overwhelmed.

With a dip of his head, he covered her mouth with his own, a firm press, a gentle demand. She opened to him, and Hunter sank in with a groan that lit her up and sizzled all the way to her toes. His tongue curled around hers, holding her a willing captive to his seduction.

Just as she opened wider, he edged away, nipped at her lip, drizzled kisses down her neck so sweetly that she moaned and shuddered, clung to him and arched.

Suddenly, Kata realized Hunter was far more dangerous than she'd believed. He would use his knowledge of her body and her pleasure to lure her deeper under his spell. Control her. Apprehension burned a hole in her belly.

"Wait, Hunter, I—"

"An hour." The intensity in his gaze made her tremble. "I'm not wasting another minute of it arguing."

She couldn't do a damn thing without breaking her word. As much as he alarmed her, she refused to show fear.

Another part of her couldn't stand for him to stop touching her.

He rubbed the pad of his thumb over her lip. "You're so fucking gorgeous, honey. It's going to be my pleasure to prove to you that an hour isn't nearly enough."

A mix of thrill and foreboding zipped through her. God, he made her shiver.

Hunter eased down her body and latched onto her nipples. Kata gasped. They'd always been sensitive, but now? He nipped, sucked, licked, scraped, laved until she threaded her hands over his head, frustrated that his hair was too short to grab in her fists. She wailed, the sound high-pitched and desperate. Hunter didn't stop, just worked his palms farther down her body as his mouth worshipped one nipple, then the other, over and over.

The ache between her legs ramped up again. She arched toward him as more moisture seeped from her core. He must know how wet she was. Surely, he could feel it. But he merely continued his singleminded, voracious devouring of her nipples. They swelled, turned tingly-sore, felt so, so hard that it was a pleasure in itself. Still, he didn't let up, didn't veer.

With every lick and nuzzle she fell a bit more under his spell.

"Oh God. Damn! Hunter . . ." She clamped onto his bulging biceps, her nails digging into his skin.

He shuddered and sucked harder. "These are incredible." He lapped at the stiff points, taking turns making them even more rigid, more sensitive. "I'm never going to get enough."

"You're killing me."

"But you like it." It wasn't a question; he knew. "They will be sore tomorrow," he murmured like that pleased him. "But every time your shirt brushes these beautiful, swollen nipples, you'll think of me."

Shit, she would. And given how devoted he'd been to the two little buds, she would be thinking of him often. That gave him a whole new level of power over her. Still, she didn't want him to stop. Foolishly, she bowed her back in offering, settling her nipple deeper into his mouth . . . knowing she'd pay for her weakness tomorrow.

Hunter smiled against her skin and cradled the mound in his hand, thumbed its side in a slow stroke. Then he bit down tenderly on the rigid tip. And her arousal surged, so close to the edge . . .

Kata panted as lightning pulsed between her legs, leaving her on the edge of orgasm. "What are you doing to me?"

"Making a good first impression." He grinned.

She wanted to hate him for forcing this surrender on her, but she needed this climax more. He'd made sure of that, pressed and pushed and tempted her until she had nowhere to hide, nothing to do but beg with her body and incoherent words.

Lips parted, breath held, she waited for Hunter to suck her nipple into his mouth again. But he didn't. He stared instead, his eyes gleaming like a predator about to move in for the kill.

Apprehension jammed in her throat. No matter how much her body wanted this, she couldn't lie back helplessly and allow him to call all the shots. He'd overwhelm her. Consume her.

Kata swallowed down her need and reached out to him, wrapped her fingers around his thick cock. His whole body jolted as if he'd been shocked. But surprise charged through her as well. He was so big and alive in her hand, full of life, pulsing. Velvety hard. Addicting.

He gritted his teeth. His shoulders tensed, fists clenched. Oh, yeah. She'd put him on the edge, and a thrill shivered through her. But damn, driving him to the brink was driving her closer to her own.

"Kata . . ."

"You wanted to see me, feel me. I want to do the same to you." Slowly, she stroked her hand up and down the long shaft, thumb brushing the slightly slick tip, then cascading down the sensitive underside.

His strong jaw worked, as if trying to speak was beyond him. She smiled. This was more like it. Now *she* was in control. After all, why should she be the only one undone tonight?

"That feel good to you?" She sat up and purred against his chest. Then she slid her free hand under his testicles, cupping, rubbing, gently kneading. She definitely had his attention, especially when she spread kisses across his collarbones, down his pectorals. He tensed. Kata tongued his nipple, turning up the heat. "Yeah. It does, doesn't it?"

In her hand, his cock stiffened even more—along with his whole body. "Fuck."

Kata gave him a throaty laugh and pumped him faster in her

hand, licked furiously at his nipple, reveling in sweet victory rippling through her. But it was short-lived.

Hunter grabbed her wrist and thrust it away from his cock, then drew in a shuddering breath. Threading his fingers through her hair, he wrapped the thick strands in his fist, tugging just hard enough to snap her head back—and force her to take his heavy stare. His expression was nothing short of a silent, sensual warning.

Uh-oh.

Hunter reached to the floor and grabbed something that disappeared into his hand. A second later, he ripped open a small foil packet with his teeth. Single-handedly, he rolled a condom on, starting at the angry tip of his heavy cock prodding at his belly insistently, all the way down to the root surrounded by dark hair.

Anticipation and anxiety lanced through Kata, tightening her stomach. God knew how far Hunter was going to push her. Yet she was beyond aroused, ready to feel him stretching her, getting deep, stroking slow, giving them both mind-bending pleasure.

With a growl, he pushed her on her back. She bounced against the mattress once before he was on her, sliding against her wet folds, his lips at her ear. "I'm going to get so deep inside you, honey. You'll give me all of you, and I'll give you everything you need."

His words made Kata fear he'd settle for nothing less than her soul.

She looked him in the eyes and shook her head. "You'll fuck me. I'll let you. End of story."

"We'll see," he said cryptically.

Then her thoughts scattered as Hunter began to penetrate her, scraping along every one of her throbbing nerve endings with a molasses stroke in, designed to devastate. No way she could stop herself from lifting her hips greedily to him. She threw her arms around his neck, biting her lip to hold in her moan. She knew it would sound like surrender.

They'd barely started, and it already *felt* too much like surrender.

Hunter stopped his endless glide into her suddenly, and her entire body tensed in denial. Kata lifted her gaze to him, questioning, hoping like hell that he couldn't see her silent begging.

"You're holding back. Open that pretty mouth. Give me that moan, honey."

"Just fuck me."

He eased out of her weeping entrance. "Are we going to have this conversation again? You know what I'm going to say."

Yes, she did. And she already knew he was patient and controlled enough to withhold his own pleasure to prove a point. Damn it.

"You promised you'd give me everything for an hour," he reminded. "You've got forty-four minutes left."

Hell, she *had* promised, and she wasn't the kind of person to renege. She always let it all hang out with Ben, never had an issue if he wanted to take the lead. But Hunter? He was more potent. A frightening thrill. He got to her, and she wanted the pleasure he gave her so desperately. The decision to give in should be easy.

But in the back of her mind, she kept wondering . . . If she surrendered, could he take some part of her that she'd never get back? No way was she walking a mile in her mother's shoes.

Hunter stared, waiting for her response. Either she had to shut up and put out or walk away now.

She'd split as soon as it was over. No after play, no cuddling or conversation or round two. She'd get up, get dressed, and get out— before he could do more damage.

With a sigh, she trailed kisses along his hard shoulder, nipping at its bulging cap, dragging her nails down his back.

"Good." With a fist in her hair, he brought her face within inches of his and fused their gazes together. "I'm done talking now. I'm just going to show you what I want from you."

Hadn't he been doing that already with his lips, his fingers, his molten touch?

Kata drew in a shaky breath as Hunter lowered himself to her again and began sliding his cock inside her, one torturous, hard inch at a time, reigniting her need.

Her fingers tightened on him. A little gasp escaped her as he pushed his way in slowly, awakening more tingles. They shivered down her spine, boiled her blood.

When Hunter shoved the last few inches into her ruthlessly, reaching deeper into her than any man ever had, her gasp became a moan—in the sound of his name.

"That's it, honey. Feel me."

As if she could do anything else . . .

He swiveled, rotating and flexing his hips, catching a bevy of sensitive spots inside her, connected like a chain. Touching one ignited the others, and suddenly, she was on fire. Unable to stop herself, her fingers curled into his flesh, nails digging. He tossed his head back with a groan she felt all the way to her pussy.

"Perfect." He bit the sensitive spot where her neck and shoulder joined, nipped her lobe, kissed his way to her mouth, and devoured her.

Even as her mind railed against it, her body unfurled to him. Her lips parted further to taste him again, her back arched up to invite him closer, her legs spread wider to welcome him deeper. He took her up on every unspoken invitation, cementing the connection of their mouths until she knew his intrinsic taste, until he flexed his hips and her nails dug urgently into his back, until he gripped her hips so he forged even deeper.

Hunter was everywhere, every sight she could see, every scent filling her nose, every flavor on her tongue. And as he tunneled down again to the hilt and he filled all her empty space, he became every sensation she felt. He was every*thing* she'd ever thought of, ever fantasized about.

Like a force of nature, he overwhelmed.

With a hot palm, he caressed her face, his lips pressing with finessed demand. Mindlessly, she opened, and he captured her mouth. Hiding was no longer an option, so she threw herself completely into the kiss, into meeting each spine-melting stroke into her aching pussy.

"Hunter," she panted.

Sweat broke out along his forehead, at his temples, across his back. His body tensed, his cock hardened. And still he consumed her at that controlled pace that drove her mad.

"You feel perfect, Kata. So slick and tight. I'm never going to want to leave."

At that moment, she could never imagine being without him. That fact would scare the hell out of her at some point, she was sure. But now, she just drowned in pleasure . . . and wondered how she'd ever forget a man who'd so thoroughly jacked up her pleasure—and gotten inside her head. After her earlier killer orgasm, she'd expected to find reaching climax again somewhere between difficult and impossible. Losing control once was hard enough for her, but twice? With Hunter, that wasn't a problem. Already need clawed through her until all she knew was that little spot he prodded over and over with the tip of his cock and her own impulse to hold him closer.

God, everything inside her was awake and attuned to him. The salty-musky taste of his skin coated her tongue as she laved his shoulder. His husky murmurs filled her head as he encouraged her every response. But the most potent? The way he looked at her as if she was the only woman in the world while he filled her to burning capacity stroke after slow stroke.

"Faster," she demanded, almost not recognizing her own voice. "Soon."

His pace didn't change. He continued to slide his way in, angled against the spot guaranteed to send her reeling. Her mind fought it even as she craved it, until she didn't know what to want. Until her body took over.

She bucked under him, doing her best to take him deeper, faster, harder. "Now!"

"You're not controlling this, honey."

"But I need—"

"I'll give it to you, as soon as you're ready."

Ready? How could she be more ready? She was breathing fire, her heart pumping lava. Right behind her clit an inferno of an ache burst, threatening to singe her alive.

"I'm ready now!"

He shook his head, balancing his forehead on hers so that she had nowhere to look except into his eyes. "No, honey. Put yourself in my hands. I'm going to take care of you."

With her flat on her back and Hunter covering her completely, her anchor to the bed, it wasn't as if she had much choice. Kata bit her lip as both anger and arousal surged wildly.

The head of his cock scraped just the right spot again and again and again. The storm brewing in her body became a hurricane. Vicious need rushed through her. She clamped down on him. And the friction only grew more mind-boggling as he fought his way deep with every plunge.

As she gasped, her world spun out of control. Her stare clung to his. She knew he could read the panicked need in her eyes.

"Now you're ready."

Hunter turned on the jets, his thrusts into her a rapid rush of fire deep over her skin. Her body jolted, tightened, bucked. And the pleasure multiplied exponentially, zipping fire through her entire body. She clawed, screamed, begged.

And orgasm was still beyond her reach. Still in his hands.

Panting, Kata dug in her nails, desperately clutching what little she had left of her composure. She was giving Hunter too much, and he was eating it up—and with every stroke demanding still more. Yes, she'd promised him an hour of candor, never imagining he'd work *this* deeply into her body and her psyche and take over. Her mistake.

Now it was too late.

He hammered into her, shoulders flexed, concentration fierce. And still his gaze locked on hers, forcing her to connect with him, to show him exactly how he affected her stroke for stroke.

Inside her, pleasure pummeled her. A tingle built on a shiver, deepening the unrelenting ache between her legs. He capitalized on that ruthlessly, pounding, pounding her most sensitive spot.

The pleasure was like a chain reaction as it built, fed on itself, then took on a life of its own. Suddenly, the need for release swallowed her whole, and Kata feared how far under it would drag her. How far under Hunter's spell it would put her.

"C'mon, honey. Let it happen. I'll be here to catch you."

Wildly, she shook her head. "It's too—*oh* . . ." she whimpered, throbbing everywhere. "Too much!"

"Then it's perfect. Come for me, Kata."

As if her body had only needed that last stroke and his rough encouragement, the restraints around her pleasure sprang free. She screamed his name again as her entire body clenched with unrivaled pleasure.

"Yes! That's it," he chanted. "Watching you let go makes me so . . . Fuck!"

As the climax exploded, fracturing her, his entire body tensed, broad hands clutching her hips, keeping her suspended in the sort of ecstasy she'd never believed existed. Until Hunter. He shuttled deep and emptied into her, delving so far inside her, she'd never be able to look at him again and not think of how thoroughly he had controlled her body. The supernova he'd detonated inside flashed her even hotter—with no end in sight. The wrenching pleasure had her crying out until she lost her breath, her voice.

As soon as the climax slowed, leaving behind languid, liquid satisfaction and his addicting male scent, his gaze locked in on her, steady, open, letting her see forever into his psyche to glimpse his grit, his determination—and the fact that he only wanted her more.

A moment later, the aftermath of her orgasm split her wide apart, ripping her open from the inside out. Vulnerability crashed over her. A hot splash of moisture filled her eyes, burning like acid as her throat closed up. Tears were coming. There was no goddamn way she would expose her raw feelings to anyone, least of all the man who'd just stripped her down to her soul. Being with him when they'd talked and danced, fine. They'd simply been having fun. But now . . . he'd affected her emotionally, controlled her in a way that made it impossible for her to control herself. Shades of Mamá and Gordon. Game over.

For her sanity, there was no way she could ever lay eyes on him again.

Chapter Four

BENEATH Hunter, Kata shoved, trying frantically to dislodge him. She pushed with an intensity that hinted at panic. Her whole body shook. Was she sick? Had he, God forbid, hurt her somehow?

Frowning, he rolled aside, zeroing in on her. "Kata?"

But she was already off the bed, grabbing her clothes, refusing to turn his way.

Kata slipped on her sexy hot pink panties. The visual of her in naughty lace and nothing else made him instantly hard again. He tore off the condom and trashed it, restraining the urge to drag her back to bed and tie her to it.

Instead, he watched as she threw her sweater over her head, every movement rapid and stuttering. She was upset. Hunter scowled. Her mood wasn't about the lamp. She hadn't been thrilled, but whatever bothered her now went deeper. She reached back to the foot of the bed for her leather mini. The silent treatment had gone on long enough.

He clamped a hand around her wrist. "Kata, talk to me. Look at me."

In silence, she tossed her head back, and her dark tresses brushed that sexy back, making him want to get her flat on it again. But not until he knew what the hell was wrong.

"We're done here." Her voice cracked as she yanked her wrist from his grasp, then ran out of the bedroom, picking up her bra and shoes as she went.

The hell they were.

Getting deep inside her had been the most singularly amazing experience of his life. For him, sex had always been just that. Kata reached him on a chemical level he couldn't explain and didn't bother to try. Coming deep inside her while staring even deeper into her eyes, he'd known for the first time in his life what it was to feel something beyond desire. No way was he letting her walk out of his life without a fight. He wouldn't be the same brokenhearted fool as the Colonel, who had no one to blame but himself for his misery. Hunter knew Kata didn't feel the same devotion right now, but he damn sure hadn't thought she would dart out of his bed like her ass was on fire.

Stark naked, Hunter vaulted out of bed and raced down the hall after her. "What's wrong?"

She didn't answer, just kept running until she disappeared into the kitchenette. He followed her around the corner to find her slipping her shoes on, her purse perched on her shoulder. She splashed water on her face—and her hands trembled. She still refused to look at him, but he *knew* she'd felt the connection between them. Then he understood: He'd reached her on a level that disturbed her.

Shoving down his triumph, he approached her on silent footfalls. "It's okay, honey."

Finally, she turned to face him. Her eyes were red, slightly puffy. She'd been crying. *Shit.*

"Of course it is." She flipped her hair over her shoulder. "It was fun. Thanks. But now it's over, and I'm still in the mood to party. See you around." She shouldered past him, focused on the suite's front door.

Hunter hooked an unyielding arm around her waist and reeled

her close again. He didn't believe her for a second. "Tell me what I did to upset you."

Kata hesitated, then tossed him a stare full of mock confusion. "No idea what you're talking about. I had to get you off of me. You were heavy, I couldn't breathe, and time is wasting."

"And you're going to party with who? Ben is passed out, your girlfriends are out on the prowl, and your sister is asleep."

"What is this, an interrogation? You may be used to calling the shots when you go on your missions, but I told you, no one controls me. I'm ready to leave, so unless you want me to scream down the entire floor of this hotel, take your fucking hand off me."

Everything she'd said since crawling out of bed made his bullshit meter ring. What she didn't say was even more interesting. Her entire body was taut. She tried damn hard to repress a shiver as she licked her lips, looked at his. Definitely, he'd reached her on a level she hadn't expected. That connection between them had her panicking. Even if he couldn't get the why out of her now, he'd be goddamned if he was going to let her leave this suite alone wearing that curve-hugging sweater sans bra and those fuck-me shoes.

"Give me a minute, and I'll get dressed. We'll find a party and have all the fun you want."

She leveled a stare at him as if he'd lost his mind. "Look, thanks for the bedroom tango. But I'd rather spend my birthday with people I know. No offense."

He tightened his arm around her waist. "We've been as close as two people can get. Why don't you get to know me better? I want to know everything about you."

Kata shoved at his hold. "There you go again with your 'everything' talk, like this is some meaningful relationship. We fucked. It was nice. Now go away."

Nice? He snorted. "Walks on a sunny day are nice. Orgasms so powerful they incite tears aren't. We both know what's going on."

"I think you may have overestimated your prowess." She raised a dark brow.

"Yeah? So all the gasping, clawing, and screaming were you just stroking my ego? Okay . . ." He shrugged. "I think you're lying, but I'm more than willing to fuck you again if you'd like to prove me wrong."

Her mouth pursed with fury—then suddenly she went limp. Had she fainted? He nearly stumbled at the unexpected shift in weight but found his balance and brought her upright.

As he lifted her hair aside and whispered her name, she elbowed him in the belly. He released her to clutch his middle. The tricky woman darted out of the suite.

Vixen. Damn, he was used to fighting enemy combatants, not sexy females.

But by the time Hunter worked into his clothes and hit the door at a run, Kata was nowhere to be seen. He charged down the hall and made his way to the elevator, but all of the cars had moved to lower floors. He watched the indicators as one of the cars descended to the lobby. The ugly certainty that she was on that one sliced through him.

No way he could leave her upset. He'd come on strong, he knew. He was a soldier, and subtlety wasn't his forte. But once he found her, he could let her breathe a little. He just needed to know exactly what had spooked her so they could work through it. And he couldn't know that without getting her to open up.

Glancing at his watch, Hunter wondered where the hell she would go at this time of night, even in Vegas, alone and on her birthday. She'd said that she wanted to party. Pounding on the elevator's down button, he waited. Finally, a *ding* announced its arrival. Empty. He prowled inside, hit the button for the lobby, then scanned all the hotel's advertisements for its many bars and restaurants. In short order, he found one for a club that looked trendy and loud, with pretty people dancing and lots of alcohol. His money was on that place.

After picking up another person or two on the way to the bottom floor, the doors opened. Hunter surged outside, scanned the area, and cursed. Fucking people everywhere, milling around the lobby, checking in, flooding the casinos that flanked the bank of elevators.

As a bellman stepped past, Hunter waylaid him for directions. In less than thirty seconds, he was jogging through a casino, up a flight of stairs.

As he reached the top, the electronica music throbbed through his body. Ahead stood a set of frosted double doors. The club's name sparkled across them in glittery paint: SIN

Hunter stepped inside, letting his eyes adjust to the darkness, then scanned the area for Kata. Thirty seconds later, he spotted her at the bar, drink in hand, tossing clear liquid back with one swallow, then sucking a lime.

Shit, what exactly had he done to fuck with her head? He flipped through their encounter mentally, but nothing stood out except the explosive connection and earth-shattering orgasm that had obliterated any in his memory. She hadn't gotten her ménage, didn't like the lamp on. She hadn't seemed *this* disturbed about anything until the sex was over. But something about their connection had made her cry.

She'd panicked a little when he'd gotten possessive. That, Kata was going to have to learn to live with, because it wasn't going to go away.

Slowly, Hunter circled the room. He watched her push her glass forward, order another, then suck it down immediately, chasing with a lime. She repeated the process. Thank God for one small favor: She'd paused somewhere to put on her bra. Not that it kept guys from leering.

A tall punk in a baseball cap and baggy-ass jeans approached her, a come-on based on his body language. Hunter was close enough to read her lips and bit back a chuckle. His Kata knew creative ways to say no.

Then his smile fell. He couldn't let her use those creative ways on him. He wanted her again, bare skin sliding against his as he slid as deeply into her body as possible. In fact, "want" was a weak word. He itched, craved, needed.

When the would-be Romeo stalked off, and Kata was sucking down her next drink, Hunter approached. "If you're looking to get trashed, you're doing a great job."

She snapped around to meet his stare. "Why can't I get rid of you?"

Hunter considered his possible answers, then went for the one least likely to cause more conflict. "You can't party alone, honey. And you just pissed off the last guy who approached you. Looks like you're stuck with me."

"This isn't funny, Hunter. I told you we're done. Stop stalking me."

So she preferred straightforward? Fine by him. "I got to you enough to make you cry. What did I do to bother you so damn much?"

She ordered another drink from the bartender, refusing to look at him. "Just because we spent an hour between the sheets doesn't mean I owe you any answers."

"How about a little common courtesy, then? I won't leave until you tell me what the hell is wrong."

As soon as the bartender set down her drink, she tossed it back in one long swallow, following with another lime that made her wince. "That, right there. You demand and push. You try to control me. I told you I don't roll that way. Now fuck off."

An independent woman like Kata? No surprise she'd feel that way. But her body had said something totally different. When he'd taken control of her orgasm and granted it on his terms, she'd been afraid . . . right before she'd gone off like a killer fireworks display. She might not want to be controlled, but a big part of her got off on it.

"You can tell me to fuck off all you want, but I'm not leaving you. First, I'm pretty sure you're drunk. Second, you're alone, which makes you a target for any predator looking for an easy victim tonight. Third—"

"Third, I'm a grown woman and I won't put up with this shit." She shook her head. "I moved out of my childhood home the day I turned eighteen and lived in terrible rat traps to avoid more of the kind of shitty mind games you're playing with me. I don't need a carbon copy of my stepfather."

Her stepfather? *Damn*. She had family issues. Ugly ones, from the sound of it. That changed everything—including his tactics.

He softened, coming closer, encouraging her with a caress. "Tell me about him, honey."

At her signal, the bartender handed her another drink. With a toss of her head, she poured the shot down her throat. "Tell me where to find your off button."

Stubborn, independent, funny. She'd be pissed off if he told her how adorable she was right now. Not that she wasn't frustrating the fuck out of him. But no matter how grouchy she was . . . well, he'd been called a mean motherfucker more than once because he'd earned it.

"Did your stepfather hit you? Because I'd never lift a finger to you, ever. I'll beat the shit out of anyone who tries."

"My family is messed up, but we're not an episode of *Cops* in the making. You're loco."

"Not the first time I've heard that I'm crazy. I'm also persistent."

"No." Her mock surprise dripped sarcasm. "I would have never guessed!"

When it came to defense mechanisms, she had an arsenal. Good thing he had his own weapons.

As she signaled for yet another drink, he grabbed her hand. "You're going to make yourself damn sick if you keep that up."

"That's *my* choice."

Hunter couldn't dispute that. Stupid choice, but hers. "What are you drinking?"

She slanted him a suspicious stare. "Patrón."

He held in a wince. Very soon, she would be feeling no pain. Tomorrow, it would hit her like a ton of bricks.

"Hey, pal," the bartender called. "Want something?"

"Club soda with a twist of lime."

The beefy bartender, who could have been Mr. Clean's double, raised an amused brow.

"What, you can't handle Patrón?" Kata sneered, the effects of the alcohol beginning to show in her heavy-lidded eyes.

"I don't drink."

She frowned, lost her balance for a second, and grabbed him to stabilize. Whether she knew it or not, some part of her trusted him.

"Recovering alcoholic?"

"Nope. I just refuse to engage in something so obviously self-destructive."

With a roll of her eyes, Kata reached for the shot glass and lime the bartender set in front of her. "Are you determined to crawl on my every last nerve tonight?"

"No, but I am determined to make sure you stay safe."

The bartender with the shaved head slammed the glass on the bar. "Four dollars."

"I want to close out her tab, too."

In the middle of tossing back her latest shot, she choked. "What the *hell*?"

The other guy shrugged. "She handed me a hundred bucks when she walked in and told me to keep the tequila flowing until her money ran out. She's got a bit less than half her tab left."

And she'd have alcohol poisoning by then, too. *Fuck.* Hunter reached into his wallet and pulled out another hundred. "Close it out. Now."

Mr. Clean shrugged. "You got it."

"Hey!" Kata slurred at the bartender, who ignored her. Then she swayed on her feet and scowled at Hunter. "Goddamn it! There you go, trying to control me again. Why the hell did I ever let you fuck me?"

The bartender repressed a smile. Hunter cursed under his breath. Kata had definitely had too much to drink, and he had to get her out of here quickly. For a girl who wanted to retain control, she'd certainly drunk enough to ensure that she lost it. The tequila was to mask fear and pain; he got that. Now he had to figure out her issue before she erected permanent barriers between them.

The conflict with her stepfather, whatever the cause, was something bigger than he could deal with here with the music pulsing, artificial smoke pumping, and her blood alcohol way over the legal limit. Because while she might have been disturbed by the way he controlled her body, she'd loved it. So had he. If he pointed that out again, he'd only drive her farther away. Likely, Kata's stepfather had used his position in the family to somehow abuse her trust, so he must tread carefully.

She turned, staggering away. He grabbed her arm and pulled her against his body. "I'm sorry."

Kata looked at him with shocked, slightly unfocused eyes. "For what exactly?"

"Taking so much of the control without talking to you first. I tend to be dominant."

"*Tend* to be?" She rolled her eyes. "Thank you, Captain Obvious."

"If I had known how much it would bother you, we would have had more conversation."

"Before you fucked me into the mattress? Yeah, how would that conversation have gone?"

Hunter sighed. They weren't going to solve anything with the Black Eyed Peas making the walls shake.

He cupped her shoulder, caressed it. "Honey, if you don't get some food and coffee into you, you're going to be sick." Her face tightened, and fury cascaded over her features. He held up his hands in self-defense. "I'm not ordering you to sober up; I'm suggesting. You'll be in the same state as Ben, passed out on the bathroom floor and destined for a hangover, if you don't take care of yourself. Now, if you think drinking away great sex is worth the headache tomorrow, by all means, I'll stay while you get sloppy drunk and tuck you into bed safely. But if you want to be human when the sun comes up and you fly home . . ."

Kata didn't say anything for long moments. "Why is it when you

claim you're trying not to control me, you still sound like you're trying damn hard to do just that?" She shook her head. "Seriously, I
don't know why you're still here or why the hell what I do matters
to you."

He stepped closer, wrapped an arm around her waist, and pulled
her flush against him. Her eyes widened, and he knew she could feel
exactly how disinterested he wasn't.

"Oh, it matters, honey."

Actions spoke louder anyway, so he captured her lips under his
in a taking both ferocious and absolute. Against him, she stiffened
and gasped. But seconds after he found her fruity-tart tongue with
his own, she threw her arms around him and dove into the kiss
with her entire body. She lit him on fire . . . but it was more.

That something he'd felt the moment they'd met plowed through
him with a vengeance. It drove him to possess her. It wasn't enough
to say he'd fucked her. It wouldn't be enough to fuck her again. Not
nearly enough. He wanted the right to see her whenever he wanted,
touch her whenever—and however—he wanted. Protect her, care for
her. Call her his—always.

There it was, the truth that had been simmering in his consciousness, the reason he was pursuing her so hard. Suddenly, it was
crystal. He wanted her permanently.

Reeling back in shock, Hunter ended the kiss, stared down into
Kata's flushed face, her half-closed eyes, her swollen mouth, at the
sensual siren that lived under her skin.

No question, he wanted her forever. And right now, she wanted
almost nothing to do with him. He had eight days before he'd be
returned to active duty. With the flare-up of clandestine activity all
around Iran and their race to acquire nuclear weapons, along with
the Venezuelan government's perfect willingness to lend an illegal
hand, he had no doubt missions were piling up. If he left without
figuring out how to make Kata his . . . she might become Ben's—or
someone else's—before he could step foot on U.S. soil again.

Unacceptable.

"What is with you?" Kata pushed against him. "You annoy me, start to make up for it with that killer kiss, then pull away? And then you try to pretend that you're not a control freak? Whatever."

She turned and blended into a nearby crowd. After a moment of observation, Hunter realized it was a small party. Given one woman's short white dress and little bouquet of flowers, he'd guess they were preparing for a midnight wedding.

He watched them and smiled. He might be losing the battle right now . . . but the war wasn't over.

Lunging for her, Hunter grabbed Kata's arm and spun her around. "I have two questions. Will you answer that much?"

Frowning, she looked as if she was concentrating hard through the alcohol buzz. Hunter thanked her momentary infatuation with Patrón; she'd be more likely to tell him the truth now.

"Then you'll leave me alone?"

No. "If that's what you want."

"Oh." The slightly confused, crestfallen expression gave him hope. "Okay. What?"

"The sex between us . . . Help me understand why it made you cry." When she looked ready to object, he leaned forward and whispered softly, "I won't judge or give you a hard time. I need to know if I hurt you."

She sighed, her shoulders sagging in defeat as she slurred her reply. "Fine. You win. You were right. It was too powerful. I don't like feeling weak or needy. Happy?"

Very. Hunter kept his smile to himself. Good to know that his instincts weren't wrong. "Not weak, honey, human. Last question." And the more important one. "Are you against long-term relationships? Did you ever picture settling down?"

"What kind of question is that?"

He shrugged, pretending nonchalance. "Curiosity."

Kata sighed and shook her head. "I don't want to be alone for the rest of my life, and I love my nephews. I see them . . . and want kids of my own someday."

"Understandable. Most people want kids at some point, even me."

"It's just . . ." She scrubbed a hand across her face. "I keep looking for someone to share life with, someone patient. Not afraid of a mop or the stove. Even-tempered, understanding, not allergic to emotion." She closed her eyes momentarily. "Someone sweet."

Hunter stifled a grimace. She was describing a female with a penis. He'd make sure she figured out soon that wasn't what she needed.

"One who likes antiquing and long walks on the beach?" he said, tongue in cheek.

"*Yeah!* Instead, I keep running into the party animals. Or, *ugh*, the ones who think farting contests are good entertainment. I once dated a guy who loved his gaming console way more than he'd ever love a woman. And then there are all the heavy-handed, demanding bastards." She glared at him.

Hunter held in a laugh, feeling euphorically optimistic. Once she got to know him, she'd see they fit perfectly. He just needed more time with Kata and a way to keep them together. Letting her leave without a fight—taking his heart with her—just wasn't an option. His father hadn't had the balls to fight for his woman. After failing to man up, he'd curdled up into a surly, workaholic recluse. Hunter refused to follow in the Colonel's footsteps.

"You still want to party? There's a group who looks like they're having way too much fun to pass up." He pointed behind her.

Clutching his shoulder to steady herself, Kata glanced around and saw all the laughter, the embracing, the clinking glasses, the festivity. She flashed him a bright smile. "That looks fun!"

Chapter Five

SUNLIGHT slanted across Kata's face like an ax. She grimaced and flung a hand over her eyes, squinting against the bright pain exploding through her skull.

What the hell had she done last night to earn this monster hangover?

With a groan, she rolled over—and encountered a solid chest, a heavy thigh draped over her own. Her eyes flew open wide. Hard, male, dangerous.

Hunter.

Had she slept with him again? Given that she was completely naked and even small movement strained muscles she hadn't known she possessed, she guessed yes. Worse, merely sliding her bare skin against his hair-roughened flesh made her hot and wet. Again.

Despite the fact that Hunter was as subtle as a sledgehammer, and she usually refused to come within ten feet of such men, some part of her wanted to stay curled up next to him with his strong arms around her, and hear that deep voice rasp her name again.

Many men shied away from her big mouth and attitude. But Hunter? No matter how many times she'd told him to fuck off last night, he'd continued his pursuit. Their verbal sparring roused her, and he'd thoroughly proven he had as much upstairs as down. No matter what she'd said to him, he'd stayed with her and ensured that she remained safe. Kata remembered flashes of his brutal hunger and, oddly, his tenderness that, even now, made her shiver.

In every way, he made her feel more desirable than any man ever had. She'd be lying if she said she didn't crave more.

Not a good development. He was controlling, could clearly catch any female he wanted, and was shipping out soon—everything she didn't need.

Kata stretched, and her head started to pound in earnest. She winced again. What the hell had happened last night?

She scanned her memory but couldn't piece everything together past the black spots. She recalled her party and Ben passing out . . . and, oh, the incredible sex with Hunter before running out on him. There'd been a club with lots of tequila, and Hunter had tracked her down. She'd revealed more to him about her family and her fears than she should have. Kata cringed. What had possessed her to bring up a bottomless-pit-of-shit topic like Gordon?

Grimacing, she rolled carefully away from Hunter, sliding out from under his thigh. Kata ignored the fresh ache in her head—and the flesh between her legs that still throbbed—then stood on wobbly legs.

Clutching her rolling stomach, she kept sifting through her memories as she tiptoed around the room for her clothes. At the club, she and Hunter had eventually joined a happy group, who'd soon left the hotel. She had a vague recollection of passing all the bright Vegas lights situated on Hunter's lap, his lips whispering over her neck, his fingers swirling lazy circles on her clit under the cover of her skirt, as they squeezed into a cab with their new acquaintances. Everyone had been excited about going downtown, but she could only remember the orgasm she'd screamed into Hunter's kiss, not why their destination had been important. Was there a better casino down there? A show?

Everything after the car ride was a total blank.

Kata bent, still feeling around the hotel room in the semidarkness for her clothing. Her panties were toast, literally now in three pieces. She could only imagine Hunter had done that in his haste to fuck her again. The thought shouldn't make her wet, but . . . Kata cursed quietly. She had to focus.

Her skirt hung on the doorknob, her shoes just beneath. Her sweater strewn in the hall two paces into the room. Her bra? Missing altogether.

She had a vague recollection of Hunter stripping her down to her skin seconds after closing the door behind them, and she'd let him have his wicked way with her again. The wisps of memory made her hot all over.

Turning back to the bed, she watched the steady rise and fall of Hunter's powerful chest. Most people looked softer or more vulnerable in sleep. He looked every bit as formidable as he did awake. And given his occupation, if she didn't sneak out quietly, he'd wake before she could make a clean exit.

Running out on him seemed cowardly, but with attraction still tugging at her and her odd reluctance to leave him, she'd best find the door pronto. Besides, they'd shared a whole night, and her slightly achy throat told her that she'd screamed for him over and over. Hunter had to be satisfied with that. His oddly possessive behavior aside, what more could he want?

Kata glanced around for her purse, resisting the urge to take another peek at him. She didn't dare wake him, or he might be motivated to start round . . . what, fifteen? No. Her need to pee would have to wait.

Finally, she spotted her bag on the floor near the closet, grabbed it, and scampered for the door. It took forever to undo all the locks quietly. Hunter grunted, his breathing paused as she flipped the door's main lock. But she paused, letting silence slide over the room again. Within moments, his breathing became deep and even once more.

Kata opened the door and closed it behind her with a soft, final *snick*. Most likely, she'd never see him again.

As the thought hit her, she stopped dead in the hall. That was a good thing, right? Yes, their killer chemistry made her shudder even now, but he was a one-night stand. His job was pure danger. He dominated, pushing her, challenging her. Granted, when she'd been really furious, he'd listened. He wasn't a jerk. But when she considered spending more time with him, icy panic rolled through her. Foreboding churned. Being with Hunter could change her life. Change her.

It hit her then that she feared for her heart. What had passed between her and Hunter hadn't *felt* like a one-night stand. Despite her panic, something inside her screamed that she was making a terrible mistake sneaking out on him.

That feeling was so, so dangerous . . . but undeniable.

Kata spun around for his door again, then looked out the huge window near the bank of elevators. The sun was high in the sky. Crap, what time was it?

Pulling her cell from her purse, she nearly choked at the clock's display. Her plane left in less than two hours!

Okay, so she'd have to deal with her feelings for Hunter once she returned to Lafayette. Maybe some space was good. They could both cool down, decide what, if anything, should happen next. If she was still thinking about Hunter in a few days, she'd ask Ben for his number. If not . . . maybe leaving now would be for the best. Besides, now that they'd had lots of sex, maybe Hunter was done with her.

The possibility depressed her.

Kata dashed to the elevator and raced in, pounding the button to go up to her suite. At the door, she wrestled out her little plastic key and slid it in. Ben stood there in a towel, staring at her as if Medusa had just walked in.

"Where the hell have you been?"

"Drinking a lot and not remembering much."

He grunted, then held his head with a wince. "I hear that. I woke up on the fucking bathroom floor. What happened last night?"

"You mean after you got me half-naked with Hunter, then passed out?" She arched a playful brow at him.

"Fuck! I did?" He sighed. "I'm sorry, Kata. I ruined everything."

Surprisingly, he really hadn't. She smiled. "You had good intentions."

He sauntered closer, a lock of his wavy brown hair brushing across his forehead. "We might have time for a quickie now. What do you say, babe? I'll make it up to you."

No. Her reaction was immediate and confusing. Normally, she enjoyed quickies with Ben. He was at his best when he only had a few minutes and poured everything into making it good. But she pictured Hunter's face hovering over hers during the darkest part of the night, focused and intent, as he held her wrists above her head and drove hard inside her. She shivered.

Kata shook her head. "We're going to be late if we don't get out of here. I need a shower, and I still haven't packed up."

Ben sighed and backed away. "You're right. Damn it. I'll finish getting ready and arrange for a cab."

"I'll be ready in fifteen," she promised, as she grabbed a pair of denim capri pants, a T-shirt, and fresh undergarments from her suitcase, then darted for the bathroom and shut the door behind her.

"Chloe, Hallie, and Mari already left for the airport. Your sister called, looking for you. You were supposed to ride with them?" Ben called through the bathroom door.

Kata winced. "Sorry. I . . . overslept."

"With who? 'Cause looking at you, I have no doubt you didn't give yourself that whisker burn on your neck."

Turning, she peered in the mirror and pressed her lips together to stifle a shriek. Ben had looked at her as if Medusa had come through the door, because she had. Her hair was a rumpled mess, her mascara smudged, her lips incredibly swollen. Kata stripped off her clothes as if they were on fire and bit back a gasp at all the marks on her body. Whisker burns, love bites, faint bruises in the shape of Hunter's fingers on her thighs, hips, and ass. What the hell had they done last night? And God, she was still wet just thinking about him.

"Kata . . . Who? Were you with Hunter?"

No way in hell was she answering that now. She stuck her head in the shower and flipped it on, the sound of the water running drowning out Ben's inquiries.

Twelve minutes later, she stepped out of the bathroom with wet hair, a freshly scrubbed face, clean clothes, and sunglasses to find Ben, fully dressed, setting down the hotel room's phone.

"Hunter is looking for you. He's pissed that you left him."

Against her better judgment, excitement cramped in her belly, made her ridiculously giddy. Gathering the contents of her suitcase, Kata checked herself. Yeah, they had great sex, but no way in hell was she volunteering to be with a man like that. Too bad everything about Hunter flipped her switch. It was insane but . . . she missed him already.

Speculation flitted across Ben's face. "You fucked him. And you liked it. Gotta say, I didn't picture you going for his tie-'em-down-fuck-'em-hard sort of thing."

"Tie 'em down?" Her heart stuttered just asking the question.

"Yeah." Ben crossed his arms over his chest and stared like he was looking forward to imparting news that would totally shake her. "Hunter's a well-versed Dominant. That means he's into BDSM. From what I understand, when he takes a submissive, he insists on taking complete control."

Kata sucked in a breath. She'd been around enough to hear bits and pieces about people into bondage, mind games, and pain. She was no expert, but everything she'd heard scared the shit out of her.

Puzzle pieces snapped into place—Hunter's behavior. And, God, her reaction. Did he think that he could make her some submissive plaything, willing to bend backward and inside out just to earn his approval and a smile? Likely so, because she'd stupidly given him every indication that she ate that shit up. Kata shuddered.

Ben watched her carefully. She smoothed out her expression. He was the last person with whom Kata wanted to discuss her feelings for Hunter.

"We'd better get out of here." Before Hunter came pounding on the door, looking for her. And he would, Kata suddenly had no doubt.

With a practiced shrug, she closed up her suitcase, grabbed her purse, then reached out for Ben's hand. "C'mon. We have a plane to catch."

* * *

THE minute Kata hit her seat, she buckled up and closed her eyes. In the window seat on her left, Ben did the same and started snoring almost immediately. Hallie and Chloe were two rows behind her, looking every bit as hungover as she felt, but the smile on Hallie's face told her they'd gotten lucky last night. Kata didn't ask, though. She didn't want to answer in turn.

What happened in Vegas . . .

Yes, it should stay here, but Hunter had proven last night that he took intense to a whole new level. He'd find her if he wanted to.

Shoving the thought aside, Kata tried to sleep, but she couldn't nod off. She couldn't put Hunter out of her mind.

While Kata pored through her lost memories of the previous night, something tugged at her again and again, as if she'd forgotten an important fact. But that something proved as elusive as smoke. She could only latch on to bits of things that made no sense—an overbright government office with bored clerks, flashbulbs, strangers laughing, a moonlit garden. Vividly, she recalled Hunter pressing her into an elevator and kissing hungrily on the way up to his room. He'd called her *his*, the word emphatic, as solemn as a bond.

Kata opened her eyes to find the flight attendant standing beside her row with the drink cart. "Something to drink, ma'am?"

"Coffee, cream and sugar."

The fortysomething blonde nodded efficiently as she poured. "And your husband?"

Kata frowned. Why the hell would the woman think . . . Then she felt Ben's hand, warm and big, as he tangled his fingers with hers.

"Nothing for him," she whispered to the other woman so she didn't wake him.

With a polite smile, the flight attendant moved away.

A few minutes later, Ben stirred at her side. "Damn, did I miss the coffee?"

"You can have some of mine." She offered the cup to him with her free hand.

"That's okay, but thanks. I'll get some when we lay over in Dallas." He squeezed her hand affectionately.

Discomfort wound through Kata. She'd never had a problem with Ben's touch, so why now? She still considered him a friend—hell, he'd helped Mari throw her a great birthday party—but the idea of sex with him again didn't appeal. In fact, it turned her way off.

Ben was good in bed, but she didn't have romantic feelings for him. Kata had long viewed that as a blessing, hoping that after all she'd seen with Mamá and Gordon over the last decade that her heart had scabbed over—and permanently put her off anything too deep.

In a few short hours, Hunter had challenged all that. The thought of blazing up the sheets with him once more . . . even allowing him to tie her up. Instant arousal. God, how was it possible that, in a single night, he'd hardwired her body to respond so thoroughly to him? Her thoughts to revolve around him?

What the hell was she going to do about her comfortable arrangement with Ben? She searched his face, lax in sleep once more. Last night's doofus drunken behavior aside, he really was funny and kind. Attractive. Dependable. He'd make someone a great husband someday. But not her.

The pilot announced their initial descent into Dallas/Ft. Worth, where she and her friends would change planes before going on to Lafayette. She loved where she lived, but the lack of direct flights anywhere really sucked.

Carefully, she extracted her hand from Ben's—and the streak of sunlight shimmering through the little window's shade glinted off something unexpected. It wasn't the eclectic silver swirl ring she always wore. The weight was similar, but . . . this was an unfamiliar, endless band of gold.

Her stomach dropped to her toes. Suddenly, the obvious smacked her in the face. She gasped.

The sound jarred Ben awake. "What?

Kata stared at the ring in horror, puzzle pieces from the night before snapping into place.

They'd gone with the strangers in the bar to the county clerk's office because Christi and . . . what was his name? Nick, maybe. They'd wanted to get married, despite only knowing each other for two weeks. So they'd run off to Vegas. She and Hunter had tagged along, lured by the promise of a big post-wedding celebration.

At the county offices, Kata had remarked that her stepfather would freak if she married someone she'd only met two weeks ago. Hunter had sent her a sly look and asked, "Yeah, what about someone you met four hours ago?"

Since she always looked for ways to spit in Gordon's face and hadn't seen a reason to stop, especially with the alcohol giving her liquid courage, Hunter's words had given her a very bad idea . . . and Hunter hadn't objected.

"Kata?" Ben's voice shook as he stared warily at her left hand. "What is *that* on your finger?"

"I think it's . . ." She closed her eyes, withdrawing from Ben's grip. "A wedding ring."

Oh, holy shit. She was Hunter's wife.

* * *

THREE hours later, Hunter touched down at the Dallas/Ft. Worth airport, turned on his phone immediately, and called Kata. Voice mail—again.

His new wife had sneaked out of his room this morning. Granted, her plane had left before his, and she'd had to catch it. But he didn't have a good feeling about the fact that they hadn't talked since sacking out.

Would she regret last night's hasty decision today?

Kata ought to be in Lafayette now. He tried her number again. Nothing but her recorded voice telling him to leave a message. Anxiety balled in his gut as he made his way to the nearest airline representative to change his final destination. Once he caught up with her, no doubt, he would have to do a lot of fast talking to calm her down and keep her from running scared again.

How the hell had he slept through her leaving his room? Hunter mentally kicked himself for that. A three a.m. turn in, followed by another hour of the most hedonistic, extravagant sex ever, had wiped him out. Still, failing to hear her leave had been both sloppy and lazy, and he'd never allow it again. For his fuckup, he was paying the price, being separated from Kata during what he feared was a critical time in their new marriage.

He had to do everything in his power to keep that distance from becoming permanent.

After settling his plane ticket, Hunter searched for a decent cup of coffee. He reached Kata's voice mail once more with a curse, then he made another call he'd rather not . . . but one that might help his cause.

"Raptor," Hunter's pal and commanding officer, Andy Barnes, barked into the phone after the first ring. "Aren't you on leave, Lieutenant?"

Since being promoted a few months back, Andy had become like a label-conscious shopaholic, only his addiction of choice was rank. He was still in the phase where he liked to remind himself—

and everyone else—that he'd moved up to lieutenant commander, as if he was verbally pinching himself.

Hunter rolled his eyes. Andy had worked hard for the promotion, overcome his family's less-than-stellar reputation in the navy to earn it. The promotion had first come Hunter's way, and Andy had been completely mind-boggled when Hunter had turned it down. But desking it wasn't his speed. He'd rather take an M-1 Tactical blade to both wrists before subjecting himself to a shitload of paperwork. "Yes, sir."

"How's that shoulder? Healing up?"

"Pretty well. I'm following doctor's orders and continuing my strength training regimen."

"Never doubted that. So why are you calling? The world isn't falling apart without you. At least not yet."

"Glad to hear it. I called to request permission to extend my leave, sir."

"You don't report until oh five hundred next Sunday."

"I'm aware of that, but I have a situation that requires more time."

Andy paused. "What aren't you telling me? Shoot straight."

Fuck. Not that it was any of Andy's business, but if he was going to hook Kata up with all the benefits of being a SEAL's wife, the news would come out. "I got married yesterday."

"*You* got married?" He whistled. "Seriously? That's something I thought I'd never see. You've been married to your team for nearly half a dozen years. Is she pregnant?"

Hunter gritted his teeth against Andy's implication. "No."

"Is she navy?"

"Civilian." And Hunter itched to end this conversation so he could find her.

"I didn't know you were seeing anyone that seriously."

Hunter hesitated, and Andy drew out the silence. Damn, if Hunter wanted this leave, he was going to have to spill his guts. "I wasn't. I met Kata yesterday."

"And you met and married her on the same day?" Andy's question sounded calm, but Hunter knew it was a façade. Barnes didn't like outside interference in his SEALs' lives, and this likely had him broiling inside.

Ah, hell. "I'm crazy about her, Andy."

"I always knew you were decisive, but damn." His buddy blew out a long breath. "I'll need some info on her so she'll be eligible for your benefits. I can start the ball rolling while you're on leave, save you the time."

Nice of him, but Hunter supposed Barnes was softening the blow in case his leave couldn't be extended. "Katalina, maiden name Muñoz. She turned twenty-five yesterday." Thanking God he'd had the foresight to look at her driver's license and memorize her address, just in case, he rattled it off to Barnes.

"Got it."

"Look, I need extra leave to settle this situation so I can return rested and focused."

Andy scoffed. "You want extra leave to fuck her brains out. Damn it, Raptor. I don't suppose it would do any good to tell you this is irresponsible and stupid?"

"No. *Sir*," he added quickly.

Hunter sometimes forgot to treat Andy like his CO. But ol' Barnes liked hearing it, and this was one situation in which following protocol might help.

A gate agent in a nearby lounge made an announcement over the loudspeaker, and Andy pounced. "You're in the airport. Pretty sure of that leave, huh? Where you headed?"

"Lafayette, my wife's hometown. I need to meet her parents." Discern the problem with her stepfather so he could figure out exactly what not to do if he wanted to keep Kata and earn her trust.

"I'll see what I can do about your leave. But, to be honest, things aren't good here. Word is that Víctor Sotillo's former troops are rallying around his brother, Adan."

Hunter frowned. "The salsa dancer? That brother? He's all about parties and finding his next lover, by all accounts. Not the kind of guy to take over a bloodthirsty cartel."

"It's still a family business. Always has been. So after Víctor's death, Adan stepped in. Intel is that they're regrouping and planning."

Fuck. Even if Adan was ineffectual, this development didn't bode well for an extended leave. The situation would need monitoring . . . but he must cement things with Kata, too.

Hunter sighed. "Even a few extra days here would really help me. Then I'll be ready to roll."

"I'll be in touch."

Without another word, the line went dead. Hunter pressed the end button and shook his head. Well, that had been a clusterfuck. And the conversation with his father would, no doubt, be worse, though he'd bring Kata with him to see the Colonel.

As soon as he found her.

Originally, he'd planned to stay in Dallas with his brother, Logan. Now, he was focused on Kata, and the three-hour layover was chafing. He paced, picked at some lunch—and tried to call his bride a dozen times.

Finally, as he was boarding his flight, his phone rang. Kata's name and number appeared on his screen. *Bingo!* A bit of the tension in his gut eased . . . then ramped up again. What would she say about last night?

"Good afternoon, honey."

"Honey?" she screeched. "What the hell did you do last night, besides put your number in my phone?"

He froze. "It's what *we* did. You don't remember?"

"Not much."

Surprise and disappointment stabbed him. That changed a lot of things. Yes, she'd been drunk, but not incoherent. He'd assumed . . . Fuck. He'd assumed wrong and now had to deal.

"But I think it's coming back to me." Her voice shook. "Tell me I'm wrong. This is crazy. Impossible. We couldn't possibly have . . ."

"Gotten married? The keepsake certificate is in your purse. The officiant said we can write away to the county clerk's office for the real thing in a few weeks."

Kata gasped, choked in panic. "You sound pretty damn calm. Why aren't you freaked?"

Because he had no reason to be. If he showed the slightest bit of uncertainty, she would only panic more. Best for all concerned if he remained firmly in control.

"Listen, we're going to be fine. Our sudden marriage is unconventional, but—"

"Crazy!" Kata drew in a horrified gasp. "You sound . . . happy about this."

"Very. I want you, Kata, and my gut tells me we're right for each other. Give yourself some time to get used to the idea—"

"That my family is going to kill me? That I just did the most irresponsible thing of my life? Or that you went way beyond taking advantage of a drunk woman?"

Yeah, she'd see it like that—and maybe she was right. All he knew is that, unless Andy came through, he'd be going back on active duty too soon to resolve this. His time to make Kata fall in love with him was ticking away. It might be six months or more before his feet touched U.S. soil again. Last night, he'd known that if he didn't find some way to tie her to him quickly, she'd be gone. The decision had been simple strategy, like securing the bunker. Or in this case, marrying the woman.

If there'd been another way, Hunter would have chosen it, but time and her fears weren't on his side. Last night, he'd never expected to meet someone he connected with on every level, then marry her almost immediately, but things happened; he dealt. That was the nature of his job.

This wasn't his most noble moment, but if being a SEAL had taught him anything, it was that sometimes you had to fight dirty to complete the mission. And if his father had taught him anything, it was that a man must be ready to do whatever necessary to hold on to his woman or lose her forever. Unlike the Colonel, Hunter wasn't a quitter.

Resisting the urge to point out the fact their marriage had, in fact, been her idea, Hunter played along, using his calmest voice. "We need to talk this out. I know this is sudden, but I want this to work."

"We barely know each other!"

He sighed, pressing down his frustration. He wanted to howl that, while true, that wasn't the point. What they had now wasn't nearly as important as what they *could* have. But she was scared, and he didn't want to come off like a stalker. Nor did he want her unhappy. He wouldn't pursue this marriage and her so relentlessly if he didn't believe in his gut that they belonged together. But he had to ease up now, find the right strategy to help her to see the possibilities.

"Kata, we can fix that—and anything if we set our minds to it. Give me a chance."

"Hunter, I . . . Why? I know I have to take responsibility for my part, drunk or not, and I'm pretty sure I'm the one who suggested we get married like Christi and Nick—"

"Mick."

"Whatever. You were the sober one. Good sex wasn't a reason to get married."

"Just good?" he countered archly.

"Okay," she conceded. "Great sex. But still . . ."

"I think we've both been round the block enough to know that this is something more."

"But normal people spend more time getting to know each other. They talk. They date."

"We'll do those things, Kata. In fact, I want to."

"We should have started there."

Hunter tried to grab on to his patience. "If you weren't wearing that ring around your finger this morning and I'd called you to ask you out, what would you have said?"

Her silence told him everything. The emotional intensity between them still scared her. Most likely, she would have tucked tail and run. Only time would help her see that they could work.

"You weren't drunk. Why did you *marry* me?"

That question was easy to answer. "Because I wanted to."

Her sigh shivered down his back as he took his seat and buckled his belt. "Ugh, just when I think you're a pushy, dominating prick, you say something nice."

"I am a pushy, dominating prick." He smiled. "But honey, I'm always honest."

"How do you know I'm not a screechy head case with a bad credit score?"

"I don't. But what I do know is how I feel about you. Trusting my gut has kept me alive more than once. I believe it's steering me right now."

"This is so much, so fast. I need time to sort through it."

Hunter gritted his teeth. He could afford to give her latitude on a lot of things, but not about spending time with him before he went back on active duty. If he didn't, Kata would be gone.

"Where are you, honey? I think we should talk as soon as I hit Lafayette."

"Lafayette? Your plane ticket said Dallas/Ft. Worth."

So she'd looked. Interesting . . . "Easy change."

He regretted that he wouldn't get to spend time with Logan so he could straighten his brother out. That would have to wait for now.

"Y-you can't come here."

"That's where you are, honey. I'll come straight to your place."

"I—I'm not there right now. I had to leave. Ben . . ."

Probably wanted to pick up where he'd left off last night. Hunter would have to set him straight or kill him.

"I'll take care of it."

"Stop! I don't want you to take care of anything."

Hunter swallowed against sudden fury, his voice very low. "You're my wife. You're not going to fuck him again."

She gasped. "You thought . . . oh, that's just fucking perfect. Why the hell do you want to be married to me if you think I'm going to step out on you the minute you turn your back?"

It was a fair question, and Hunter grappled for a fair answer. "I don't know what your feelings for him are. And I know that a piece of paper between us probably wouldn't make a damn bit of difference to him. But let me be clear: It means something to me."

"He's a friend and he's been convenient, yeah. But he's not jealous, just pissed that I won't have sex with him anymore. I couldn't stay and listen to him rant. It was making my head hurt like a bitch."

Hunter repressed a smile. Poor baby was hungover. It pleased him even more that she didn't want to be intimate with Ben.

"Understood. Sorry if I upset you. No insult intended." He gripped the phone tighter. "Tell me where you are, honey. I'll come to you, and we'll have a thorough conversation. I don't want to change your life; I just want to be a part of it."

"You change everything just by being you, the same way Gordon does." Her voice wobbled with tears, and she sniffed. "Ugh, I need to shut up."

Who the hell was Gordon? "Give us a chance to work this out. Are you with your sister?"

She laughed through her tears. "You think I'd go near two rambunctious boys when my head is throbbing like a broken toe? Or sign up for the lecture from hell? No way. I came to my office. It's almost empty on Sunday."

"Street address?"

Kata paused a long time, and Hunter bet she was weighing the intelligence of giving him an inch versus the sheer futility of running. In the end, she sighed. "You win."

He memorized the address as she rattled it off.

"I'll be there in two hours."

"You know this marriage thing is a train wreck waiting to happen?"

He laughed. "Or the adventure of our lives."

"Well, I—"

Suddenly, he heard a blast on the other end of the line. It was unmistakably gunfire.

Kata screamed. Then the line went dead.

Chapter Six

HUNTER knew his fingers shook as he dialed Kata again. Four rings, then voice mail. The result didn't change when he tried once more.

Who the hell would be shooting inside her office building? He couldn't let himself think that she couldn't answer the phone because something terrible had happened.

Pushing down his fear, he fell back on his training. Stuck on a fucking plane, he could only reach out for help. And he had to do it before the plane pushed away from the gate and the flight attendants forced him to turn off his cell phone.

He didn't hesitate to hit one of the numbers on his speed dial. Thankfully, Deke had elected to move to Lafayette, closer to work and his cousin Luc, a few months back. His brother-in-law answered right away. "Hey, Hunter."

"I have a situation. There's a female probation officer, Kata Muñoz, who's been either shot or shot at." He rattled off the address. "She's had some run-ins with a local gangster who's been threatening her. Get to her, man. Now. I'll be there as soon as I get off this damn plane."

Deke could have asked a lot of questions and probably would later, but the soldier in him responded to the urgency of Hunter's tone. "Done. I'll text you."

"Sir, you have to turn off your phone." The flight attendant hovering in the aisle scowled.

"Thanks, Deke." He ended the call, moving restlessly in his seat, praying like hell that help wouldn't be too late for Kata.

He'd known her less than twenty-four hours, and already she was perilously close to being the most important person in his life. He'd never sought love, but now that it was breathing down his neck, anyone who wanted to steal his possible happily-ever-after would have to pry it out of his cold, dead hands.

Despite the fact that it chafed him raw, Hunter powered the phone down and tucked it into his jeans pocket. He had no idea how he was going to survive this flight without losing his mind. Scrubbing a harsh hand down his face, he tried not to picture Kata hurt, bleeding, alone. Dying. Goddamn it, he should be there to save her.

He swore that if she lived, he'd never leave her unprotected again—not for a single second.

* * *

THE sharp report of gunfire startled Kata, echoing through the office. She jumped and lost her grip on her phone. It skittered across the floor, under a colleague's chair about fifteen feet away as she hit the tile floor on her hands and knees, diving under her heavy metal desk.

Where had the gunfire come from? Given the deafening sound, inside the building, maybe even inside the room. She was the only person in the office, since it was Sunday. But God, who would shoot at her? Had Cortez Villarreal or his goons caught up to her?

Heart beating until she feared it would burst, Kata mentally raced through her options. Her phone had fallen in the intruder's direction. It was too far away to safely retrieve. Instead of retrieving it, she had to focus on escape. The main exit lay in the direction from which the shot had come. The emergency exit was to her right, on the far side of the room, a good twenty feet away. How the hell could she reach either door before this thug's bullet struck her? She had to try.

Her phone rang again, a jarring clatter in the thick, empty room. Hunter. God knew what he was thinking now. The ringing stopped, started again.

Then the phone fell eerily silent. Quiet, methodical footsteps echoed off the tile floors in the utilitarian room. There was no one here to rescue her—and they both knew it. If she was going to live, she had to save herself.

Clutching the leg of the desk, she peeked around the corner to see if she could get a bead on the shooter's exact location or any other possible escape routes. All she saw were rows of empty desks, piled high with outdated computers and paperwork. Then another blast ripped through the room, followed by a metallic ping an inch from her ear. She jerked back in time to see a dent shaped like a bullet in the side of the desk.

The shooter knew precisely where she was. Kata suspected the bastard was toying with her. Next time, he wouldn't miss.

She cursed the fact that her purse, with her gun inside, was in the top drawer of her desk. If she reached up to get it, she'd make an easy target of herself. But better to die trying than to sit and wait for the fatal bullet.

Slithering out from under the desk on her belly, she curled up in front of the drawers and reached for the handle of the top one, opening it slowly. It creaked, and the sound exploded through the still office. She'd already alerted him; better to finish and be quick.

After opening the drawer, Kata reached up and groped for her purse.

Another shot rang out, closer. With a sharp gasp, Kata jerked her hand down. She'd felt the bullet whiz just over her wrist and had to cover her mouth to hold in her scream.

Then she got mad. This unseen fucker was screwing with her head before he took her life. She'd be damned if she was going to let him do it without a fight.

Again, she reached up into the drawer. From her first foray, she knew exactly where to grope, and jerked the little Coach bag free.

It landed with a thump between her feet—just as she heard more whisper-light footsteps in aisles between the desks mere feet away.

He was coming closer.

Ripping into her bag, she pulled out the little semiautomatic, unlocked the safety, and popped off a round in the shooter's general direction as she ran, crouching behind the next desk over, one closer to the emergency exit.

She listened for his footsteps again, wondered where he was, how close. But she heard only her own panting, terrifyingly loud in the thin silence.

Biting her lip, Kata peeked above the desk. Her assailant was nowhere in sight.

A fresh wave of fear overtook her. He hadn't left; she could feel him plotting, creeping steadily closer. Her thoughts spun again. *Sit tight for a better opportunity, or run?*

A better opportunity might never come.

Sucking in a breath, she darted past a desk. No shots rang out. Holding her weapon in one hand and covering her mouth with the other, she listened. Waited. Though Kata couldn't hear this murderer, she knew he was coming for her.

Gasping a silent breath, she ran, crouching, to the next desk. Only one to go before she reached the emergency exit. Kata pressed her back against the cold metal, handles digging into her back. Oddly, the pain reminded her that she was alive. At least for now. She gripped her gun tightly, determined to stay that way.

Hunter crossed her mind.

Despite the fact that he hadn't called again, she had no doubt he was worried. If she didn't escape, somehow she knew he'd mourn her. For some reason, he cared, way more than she would have expected. Kata regretted like hell that she might never see him again.

God, she was in the most terrifying situation in her life, and yet she worried about a man she'd met less than twenty-four hours ago. Where was her head?

Kata paused, straining to hear the shooter's breath or footsteps, but she heard nothing. This asshole, whoever he was, was *good*. Where the hell was he? Kata knew all too well that he hadn't gone. He likely had her cornered. He knew it . . . and so did she.

She leaned around the far edge of the desk, until she could glimpse the right half of the room, including the path to the emergency exit. No visual, no movement, no sound.

Kata took a chance, scurrying over to the next desk on her knees. The emergency exit was about four feet away, but once she left the relative safety of the desk, she had no cover between her and the exit. She'd have to run in the open, pause to push the heavy door open, wait for it to part enough to let her through—plenty of time for a killer to do his job.

But she had no other escape.

Drawing in a shuddering breath, Kata began counting in her head. *One . . . two . . . th—*

Behind her, she heard a gun cock—not more than a handful of inches away. She froze, her entire body turning to ice.

"Stay on your knees," he demanded. "Bow your head."

No! She had read enough about crime scenes over the years, seen plenty of gut-turning photos. Her guess was that he planned to kill her execution style. Kata tamped down her panic.

"What is Villarreal giving you to kill me? I'll pay you cash to walk away."

He didn't respond, except to press the cold barrel of his gun at the base of her skull. Her heart pounded as terror and fight crept in. If he was one of Villarreal's gangster thugs, he wouldn't betray his colors. They were each other's family, often not having much of a real one. They sought power, were willing to kill for respect. Murdering a woman to help his "brother" was nothing, and no amount of money she could afford to offer him would make a damn bit of difference.

"Say good-bye," he growled, his Hispanic accent very pronounced.

Like hell.

Kata dove forward and flattened her belly to the floor at the same time she kicked out with all her might and struck her assailant's shin. A loud rattle of metal and a curse told Kata that she'd knocked him into the desk. Then she heard the clang of a weapon, whirled to find his gun skating across the tile.

Leaping to her feet, she lunged between him and his weapon, pointing her own gun in his face. She'd never seen him in her life. Hispanic male, average height and build, around thirty, shaved head, cold brown eyes. He possessed no visible tattoos but his black, long-sleeved shirt would cover most. His jeans were baggy, puddling over the tops of his high-end sneakers.

Suddenly, he smiled as if the joke was on her. "You won't pull the trigger."

Bullshit! Before Kata could mutter a word, he lunged at her, hand outstretched for her gun. She tried to get a shot off, but there was no time. She scrambled back to prevent him from tackling her, but he managed to grab her wrist. If he got his hands on her weapon, she was as good as dead. Yeah, she'd love to corner this bastard and call the police so he'd serve time. But she wanted to live more.

Hauling her free arm back, she let it loose and punched his face with every bit of her strength. After an audible crack, pain shot up her hand, but he stumbled. Kata ran for the emergency exit as if she were on fire, looking behind to see if her assailant followed.

She hadn't cleared the door before she felt a man's chest, hard as a brick wall, block her. Steely arms closed around her. She screamed at the unfamiliar man holding her. Tall. Sandy hair, green eyes. Gorgeous. Clearly, the guy was intimately familiar with the gym, and wore a look that said he meant business.

God, had Villarreal sent a damn hit squad to kill her?

Panicked, she struggled to reach the daylight beyond him, but she could not pass or move him. She yelled as loudly as she could, hoping someone nearby would hear, even though this business district was largely deserted on Sundays.

"Shh." The big guy pulled her away from the open door, into the alley, his voice oddly gentle for such a big man. "Hunter sent me."

Those words ricocheted inside her, and relief blanketed Kata, warming her cold panic. She was safe. No one in her life knew of her connection to Hunter except Ben, who'd come to her apartment and cursed a blue streak when she'd refused his advances and said she'd wanted to be alone. No one Villarreal had sent to kill her could possibly know that by uttering those three words, she'd instantly trust him. With a shaky sigh, she stared up into the stranger's calm green eyes.

"Thank God."

The blond guy cast her a reassuring stare and set her behind him, then turned back through the open door, looking into her department's office space.

At the sounds of a scuffle, Kata peered around her rescuer to see another beefy blond guy with a military haircut and a grim smile holding her attacker to the ground with a large, veined hand around his neck.

Who were these guys? How had they found her so quickly?

"Give me a reason to kill you," her second rescuer said. "Even a small one will do."

"Fuck you, *cabrón*!" The thug was all bravado. He was outgunned and outmanned—and from the panic in his eyes, her assailant knew it.

"I'm married, and you're not my type," said the buzz-cutted hulk. "Get on your feet, scumbag."

Her would-be killer resisted, and the big stranger manhandling him looked positively gleeful when he jerked the shooter up by the arm—in a way designed to dislocate his shoulder.

Suddenly, the thug screamed like a little girl.

"One more good tug will do it," the stranger warned. "You going to cooperate?"

The vicious bastard who had done his best to kill her gave a jerky nod.

His captor smiled. "Tyler, call nine-one-one."

"Already on it."

Kata glanced as Tyler, the man who had caught her coming out the door, looped a protective arm around her waist. He had a cell phone jammed to his ear and glared at her assailant as if he'd love to rip the guy in half.

Standing so close to the phone, she heard dispatch answer. He responded with all the pertinent information, his voice low and controlled.

"What's your name?" Mr. Buzz-cut asked her attacker.

"I have nothing to say to you," he spat out.

"Not going to cooperate? You get that's going to be bad for your health, right?"

His dead brown eyes narrowed. "You are not the police."

"Right. Which means I have no rules to follow. And if the cops get here before I can finish fucking you up as much as I'd like . . . well, I can make sure when you go to county lockup, you have a very horny cell mate, if you don't start talking. Now, why did you try to kill her?" He pointed to Kata.

Her attacker hesitated. "Just doing a job."

Kata's gut balled tightly at the answer. As she'd feared, someone, probably Villarreal, wanted her dead, enough to hire the job done. A quick glance at her rescuers' faces told her that both men were blazingly pissed.

"Who hired you?"

Her assailant pursed his lips and looked away from his captor, his refusal to talk evident.

Tyler pocketed his phone. "Police are on their way."

The big man holding her attacker grunted. "That means I've got about five minutes to make your face look like hamburger. No sweat."

The criminal flinched, then put on his tough-guy face. He had menace down to a fine art, but the other guys didn't seem to notice.

"Want help, Deke?" Tyler asked hopefully.

"Got it. This will be my pleasure. I hate pricks who threaten women. Cowardly motherfuckers." He grabbed her attacker by the hair and bunched up his fist, clearly ready to smash in his face.

"Wait!" she called.

Deke hesitated, glaring her way.

"If you hurt him too bad, they'll arrest you. A-and he won't be able to talk. Neither of those will help."

Grumbling, Deke reached into his back pocket for a set of cuffs. "You're ruining my fun, damn it, but if that's the way you want it . . ." Then he looked straight at her. "Kata, right?"

She nodded. "Hunter sent you, too?"

"Yep. He's my brother-in-law, so when he called, I came." He secured the criminal's wrists behind his back and lowered the guy on his belly like a snake.

Just hearing that confirmation made something in her flutter. Even hundreds of miles away, Hunter had protected her.

That sent shards of both delight and anxiety through her. She was beyond grateful that he'd sent reinforcements, but clearly he had no intention of letting her go anytime soon.

"I see." She heard the trembling in her own voice.

Deke planted his big combat-booted foot in the middle of her attacker's back, then grimaced. "Shit, you look wiped out. She's about to do a header, Tyler."

As soon as he said the words, her knees began to give way. The residual adrenaline that juiced her system bled out, turning her legs to Jell-O. She stumbled, but Tyler caught her and swept her up in his arms.

"Easy, baby," he murmured as he lifted her.

Kata didn't like this shaky, overwrought feeling, how vulnerable Hunter's pursuit and the assassin's attack made her feel.

"I'm fine," she choked. "Put me down."

Tyler rolled his eyes and kept walking. "Let's sit to be on the safe side. Hunter would tear me a new one if I let you faint and you hit your head."

She swallowed. Yeah, she could picture that. Even this poster child for bodybuilding didn't want to displease her—*gulp*—husband? Was this how everything had started for her mother, with a bit of flattering attentiveness and overprotection?

"And you know him . . . how?"

Deke and Tyler exchanged a glance. Then Tyler set her in a chair and knelt in front of her. He shrugged and hesitated. "I've . . . um, worked some with Deke's family."

At that, Deke barked out laughter. "My cousin Luc would take issue with that description. He would describe it as trying hard to get in his wife's panties."

"He could kiss my fucking ass, too."

Leveling a considering stare at her, Deke ventured, "How do you know Hunter?"

Kata froze. "He didn't tell you?"

"There wasn't exactly time. He barked at me to protect you. I figured there'd be opportunity for questions at some point. Spill."

Damn, she didn't want to be the one to tell Hunter's family they were married. And why should she? Hunter may not have any intention of ending this impulsive relationship, but Kata was having second thoughts about this marriage. And third and fourth. Not that she wasn't grateful to him for sending the cavalry, but . . .

Hunter's a total Dominant. Very into BDSM. Insists on taking complete control.

"We met in Vegas last night." A simple, safe response that didn't invite more questions.

Deke's sharp expression told her that he was mulling her answer. "It was *your* birthday party he flew out for. So, did he . . . make good on that favor for your mutual friend, Ben?"

Kata gasped. Deke knew that Hunter had flown out to participate in her birthday ménage? The sparkle in Deke's blue eyes said yes.

A flush crawled up her face. Why couldn't the concrete open up and swallow her whole? "Hunter told you about that?"

"Nah." Deke shook his head. "Tyler and I happened to be with him when he got the call from Ben. Otherwise, we'd still be wondering where the hell he went last night and why. So, did you get your birthday wish?"

"Not . . . exactly," she hedged.

Deke frowned. "Did Ben change his mind?"

Tyler looked her up and down and snorted. "If Kata was my girl, I would have changed my mind. Of course, I wouldn't have invited some other schmuck to help me fuck her in the first place."

Both men turned to her expectantly.

"Well . . ." Kata hesitated, mortification rolling through her. And more molten anger. Damn, who didn't know her business? And what the hell did she say now?

Deke's gaze zeroed in on her left hand, then he asked softly. "Shiny new ring. Did Ben marry you instead of share you last night?"

Kata swallowed, trying to figure out how to derail this train wreck of a conversation. "Not . . . exactly."

"Shit." Deke tensed, then pinned her with a hard stare that made Kata feel as if he could see straight through her. "Now I know what I heard in Hunter's voice, besides apprehension. I heard possession. Ben didn't marry you. Hunter did."

* * *

TO all outward appearances, Hunter looked as calm as a lake on a windless day. He exercised great mental control to not pace the aisle of the plane, not imagine that, even now, Kata could be dead. But inside, the waiting, the not knowing, was fucking killing him.

How she'd become everything to him in one night was a mystery to Hunter. Their eyes had connected. They'd danced and kissed, then poof. That quickly, he was completely taken. He didn't love Kata . . . yet. But that was coming, his gut told him. Soon.

If she survived.

Biting back a curse, Hunter palmed his phone, already turning it on as the plane landed. The flight attendant could kiss his ass.

As soon as the little device lit up, he saw a text from Deke. They'd found Kata at her office. She was fine. Attacker in custody. Detectives on scene. *Thank God!* Profound relief poured through him, and he sagged into his seat.

As soon as the gate opened, he strapped on his backpack and ran into the terminal to grab a taxi. Perched stiffly in the backseat of the musty-smelling vehicle, the need to hold her battling with an urge to kill the gunman, Hunter barely saw the Lafayette landscape whiz by.

Someone had tried to kill his Kata, probably for no other reason than she'd done her job and reported a criminal who'd failed to live up to the terms of his probation. Goddamn scum had fucked with the wrong man's woman. If the bastard tried to touch one hair on Kata's head again, Hunter swore he'd bypass the police and demonstrate to the asshole every way he'd ever learned to kill painfully.

The ten-minute ride to her office seemed to take two hours. Finally, the taxi pulled up in front of a nondescript office building crawling with myriad police cruisers, a pair of unmarkeds, and an ambulance. Hunter threw money at the taxi driver and bailed out at record speed.

"Sorry, sir." A uniformed officer stopped him at the perimeter. "This is a police investigation. You'll have to stay behind me."

"Someone tried to kill my *wife*. I'd like to see her."

The youngish cop frowned. "I know Kata. She's not married."

"She is as of last night, and I'm not playing this game with you anymore." Hunter dipped under the tape, dropped his backpack, and jogged off in search of Kata.

There. In a chair, she sat with her head between her legs, trying not to faint. The late afternoon sunlight glinted off the rich red and brown strands of her hair. Tyler knelt beside her, hand on her knee, pressing a bottle of water into her grip. A detective barked questions at her. Everything about the scene set Hunter's protective instincts off.

He jogged his way to Kata and cupped her shoulders, dragging her against him. She lifted her face, and he tried not to curse. She looked pale, shocked, exhausted, her mouth set in a grim line. Her eyes said she'd endured too much for one day.

"Hunter."

Even her voice shook.

"I'm here, honey. I'll take care of you."

"You'll have to back away, sir. I'm questioning the witness," the detective insisted.

Hunter got up in the idiot's impassive face. "My wife is in no position to be questioned right now. Have you goddamn looked at her? She's either going to faint or give out. She may be in shock. I don't want you saying another word to her until medical has checked her out."

"I'm right here, Hunter." She looked annoyed. "I can speak for myself."

The steel in her tone surprised him, though he guessed it shouldn't. That combination of strength and softness was one of the things that made him so hard for her. He would find other qualities that drew him to her, and once he knew her better, he'd add those to the list and fall deeper. *For better or for worse . . .*

"You don't have to," he offered softly.

"I *want* to. And I refused medical. I'm fine."

Was she fucking serious? One look at her, and he knew better. "Except that you're having trouble staying upright."

She glared at him, clearly not liking his sarcasm. "Look, it's been a really eventful twenty-four hours. I'm grateful that you sent Tyler and Deke. But I don't need you in my face, barking at me. I just want to finish up here, so I can go home and get some sleep. It's already stressful enough that this stranger won't admit why he tried to kill me or who hired him."

Hunter froze. "It wasn't Villarreal?"

"Not that he'll admit." Kata shrugged. "The police will figure it out. I'll be fine. I just need rest. I know work is going to be a bitch tomorrow, so—"

"Work?" *Oh, hell no.* "If you're on someone's hit list, then you're not coming here or going anywhere out of my sight until I figure out how to put a stop to this shit."

Kata bolted to her feet—and immediately had to brace herself on the chair.

Beside her, Tyler stood quietly, shaking his head. "Shit's gonna hit the fan now . . ."

Hunter and Kata both ignored him.

Drawing in a sharp, steadying breath, she looked her husband in the eye as she pulled herself to her full height—which meant the underside of his chin. But she didn't let that deter her.

"Ben told me what you're into, but I'm never going to be the meek little woman. That should have been clear in Vegas. I won't ask anyone's permission to do what I want, Hunter, especially not to go to work. One incident won't keep me from a job I love. As soon as I get some sleep, I'll be fine. I get that you're worried about me. That's sweet, but I've been trained to defend myself. This office will be full of people tomorrow, and I have folks I can call for backup, if necessary. But I fought this thug off today by myself. I got away with my brains, my gut, and my determination to fight back."

Hunter's gut tightened. She was a stubborn thing. Strong. That would only make her surrender all the sweeter. But for now, he needed to talk her off the ledge.

He gentled his voice. "I'm proud that you fought him off all on your own. I feel better knowing that you can. But I'm here to take care of you. I've defended people for Uncle Sam for the past decade. This prick won't even get in the same zip code until I catch him. I'll keep you safe; I promise." He held out his hand.

Kata backed away. "I appreciate your concern, but I'm a grown woman. I've lived alone and paid my own way for the last seven years. I make my own decisions. Don't pull this high-handed he-man crap on me." She raked fingers through her long hair, looking exhausted. "I've seen enough of it to last me a lifetime."

Damn, the stepfather again, he'd guess. Frustration pressed in on Hunter. Gritting his teeth, he pushed it down. Kata wasn't thinking with the right fear, hadn't realized that he wasn't the enemy. But he'd make sure she got some rest—and some peace. Then she'd realize he was right.

He snagged her hand, bracketed his thumb and forefinger around her new wedding band, wiggling it just enough to remind her that he'd put it there. "I spoke vows to love, honor, and cherish you. That includes protecting you." He leaned closer, spoke softly in her ear. "So if I have to tie you to my goddamn bed and keep you naked and busy until we catch this guy, don't think that will bother me one bit."

Chapter Seven

"Hunter, what the hell is going on?" a familiar feminine voice called from behind him.

Stifling a scowl, he turned to find Deke standing in the doorway with his arm curled around his wife, Kimber. Hunter's gaze swept over his sister. She looked happy, healthy—and very pregnant. He hadn't been Stateside in months. Seeing his baby sister preparing to have a baby of her own was a shock.

Wondering how much Kimber had heard of the speech he'd just given Kata made him wince.

"Hi, little sister. You look great! When did you say your due date is?"

"Hello to you. Next week. Don't change the subject." She glowered, pulling away from Deke to approach him—and cutting a sidelong glance at Kata. "Tell me what's up, or I'll beat it out of you. Pregnancy hormones can make a woman vicious."

"Shit's *really* going to hit the fan now," Tyler predicted with a laugh in his voice.

"Her temper is short these days," Deke confirmed.

"Can it, both of you," she tossed over her shoulder at the men.

"See?" Deke shot Hunter a look that warned him to cooperate.

If the situation had been less serious, he might have laughed. Instead, he glared at Deke. "Why is she here? No pregnant woman, especially my sister, should be anywhere near the scene of an attempted murder."

"As if either of you could stop me from coming." Kimber snorted. "Now, cut the macho crap, and start explaining why I'm hearing about your marriage from Deke, and not you." She stopped before Kata and held out a hand. "Hi, I'm Kimber Trenton, by the way. Can I get you something?"

Kata, looking both weary and rattled, shook her head and extended a shaky hand. "Kata Muñoz."

"Edgington," Hunter reminded, teeth gritted.

Kata looked away, and fresh dread sliced through his gut.

"So it *is* true that you got married? When?" Kimber demanded.

This wasn't the right time, but nothing was going to stop Kimber from digging for information except the truth. "Last night."

"God, you have steel balls. You got married without first telling your family? Did it ever occur to you that maybe we'd want to be there? In fact, not only was your family not invited, we've never heard the merest mention of Kata. How long have you two been dating?"

"We haven't dated at all," Kata piped up. "The marriage was a stupid impulse. A drunken mistake in Vegas. I'm sorry if I've caused your family any trouble."

Those words cut like a knife. Marrying Kata was dead-on right. Even seeing her now, shaken and skittish, he *knew* that. Since she still wore her wedding ring, he'd hoped that, somewhere deep down, she sensed that they belonged together, too. She just hadn't—or couldn't—admit it. Yet.

"It's not a mistake," he bit out, facing her with challenge in his eyes.

The women ignored him.

"Kata, I'm not yelling at you," Kimber assured, then she turned to Hunter. "But you . . . I don't even know where to start."

The wedding hadn't exactly been planned, damn it, and he wouldn't let Kimber rake him over the coals for not telling her in advance. But God knows, she'd try.

"Remember when you criticized me for my . . . unconventional relationship with Deke before my marriage? I could say, 'Pot, meet Kettle,' since you barely know Kata—pretty name, by the way. But I realize it's your life."

"It is," he growled.

"Yeah. But it's clear you know shit about being married. A year hasn't made me a huge expert, but one thing I can tell you is that if Deke ever threatened me the way you just did her, we'd be doing ten rounds of verbal smackdown in the parking lot."

Kimber had heard that? Damn . . .

Tyler coughed to smother a laugh. Deke pressed his lips together and turned away in a futile attempt not to burst out laughing. Hunter threw them both a killing glare.

Maybe Kimber was right, but Kata was independent, stubborn. She'd never admit to needing his help to stay safe. Begging her to accept his protection would likely fall on deaf ears, even though she could have been killed tonight. Besides, as Hunter glanced around at the crime scene, he got a bad feeling. Things weren't adding up.

"Kitten," Deke said to Kimber. "Kata's been shot at, and you know how we men are about protecting our wives."

"I'm totally familiar with testosterone overload. But if Kata's just been attacked, she needs comfort and kindness, not someone threatening to tie her to the bed."

"It's not the tactic I would have taken," Deke admitted. "But—"

"Bullshit," Tyler chimed in. "You'd tie Kimber to the bed for just about any reason."

"True enough." Deke repressed a smile as he met his wife's stare, then sobered again. "Kata thinks she's going back to work before we know why someone is trying to kill her and, in Hunter's shoes, I'd do whatever necessary to keep my wife safe, too."

"Because threatening her after she's just been threatened makes so much sense." Kimber rolled her eyes, looking like her patience was about to unravel. "Can I talk to you for a minute, Hunter? Alone?"

He sighed. Kimber's question was code for: *Can I chew your ass out in private?* But he figured he'd either pay now or pay in spades later. Whatever his and Kimber's differences had been in the past, he loved his sister. If she wanted to talk, hell, he'd listen.

"You going to be okay for a minute?" he asked Kata, smoothing a gentle palm down her back.

"I've been insisting for a while now that I'll be fine." Kata braced her hands on her hips and raised her chin.

Even her pose didn't mitigate how vulnerable and afraid she looked. Shaky. Rattled. Worry torqued his gut. Why was the woman being so stubborn? She said she'd seen enough of controlling men to last her a lifetime and likened him to her stepfather. But he couldn't afford to ease up now, not with such a short time line before he returned to active duty and with a killer on the loose.

He nodded. "Sit down, honey. I'll be right back."

"As soon as Detective Montrose is done with me, I'm going home and going to bed."

"Not alone. And not before you know whether someone dangerous might be at your place, too, waiting for you."

Kata hesitated, and Hunter knew that possibility hadn't crossed her mind. That fact alone told him that keeping her close, safe, protected, was the right move—even if she didn't like it. Without someone able to watch her back, she could be dead.

"This wasn't a random attack," he pointed out. "Why would some killer assume there'd be anyone to target in the probation office on a Sunday? Your car is the only one in the employee lot, honey. He knew you were here and alone."

"But how? *You* were the only person who knew I was here."

Hunter reared back. The implied accusation was far worse than a slap. "I was on a plane," he ground out, "talking to you from the moment you told me the address to your office until I heard gunfire over the line. How the hell would I have told anyone besides Deke and Tyler where to find you in those, what? Two minutes? Why would I call them to save you if I wanted you dead?"

God, he was pissed. Blazingly, furiously pissed. Not necessarily at Kata—though he couldn't claim to be thrilled, either—but at the situation. If she thought for a second that he'd be capable of sending a killer after her, they had bigger trust issues than he'd thought.

Regret tightened Kata's face. "You're right. That doesn't make sense. I'm sorry. I'm just . . ." She bit her lip, fighting tears. "I'm a little scared."

Hunter didn't want to scare her more, but he did want her to see reason. "I know. My theory is that this guy followed you from your apartment. Whoever wants you dead knows where you live. I want to make you safe again." He turned to the other men for backup. "Tyler, Deke, you know she can't go home alone."

"No chance in hell." Tyler crossed his arms over his chest and stood in front of Kata, effectively blocking her path to the parking lot. "Hunter's right, baby."

Hunter didn't like the other man's endearment directed at his wife. But before he could take Tyler's head off, Kimber grabbed Hunter by the arm and dragged him about twenty feet away.

"Are you hearing yourself?" she hissed.

"Yeah, I stated a fact. She can't go home alone until we know it's safe."

"Maybe, but it's the way you said it." Kimber smacked her forehead with her palm. "Damn, you're thickheaded, Hunter. But I know you would have never married anyone, much less a virtual stranger, unless you were sure she was the one."

Kimber's insight shouldn't have surprised him. His sister was a smart cookie. "Exactly. So I'm going to protect Kata."

"I know that's how you feel." She lowered her voice. "But you have to tread a bit more carefully. You heard her, right? She already thinks the marriage was a mistake and doesn't want to be bullied by you or anyone."

Yeah, it wasn't a surprise. Kata had been fighting him since just after they'd hit the sheets. She needed to know him better, be reassured, fall for him. Their first full day of marriage had begun inauspiciously, given that Kata hadn't remembered they'd married at all. Since then, everything had become a shit storm. Knowing she was in danger made him really edgy.

"If you want to keep her happy and keep her in this marriage, you can't run her over like a semi," Kimber argued. "Dad did that for years to Mom. Look where that landed them."

Hunter recoiled. "Amanda and the Colonel have *nothing* to do with Kata and me. I'm not giving up on this marriage without a fight."

"You're a goddamned idiot. Mom and Dad's breakup has everything to do with your behavior. Get a clue. All this pushiness is going to bite you in the ass. Unless you want to watch Kata walk out the door, back off."

* * *

"DO you know anyone who would want to kill you?"

Detective Montrose's voice jerked Kata's attention away from Hunter. What were he and his sister bickering about, while Deke and Tyler tried to edge close enough to hear? She was chewing Hunter a new one—and predictably, he wasn't backing down. Kimber hadn't given any indication that she disapproved of Hunter's choice of a wife, but . . .

Kata looked away. It didn't matter if his family didn't like her. She and Hunter weren't going to be married long enough for her to care about their opinion. But Kata had to admit that she already liked Kimber. And the sight of Hunter taking a verbal lashing from his very pregnant baby sister made her smile. That he'd stand still and listen said something good about him. Certainly, Gordon would have never tolerated this kind of dressing down from any female.

The fortyish detective pushed his sunglasses up his nose, looking both fried in the hot late May humidity and annoyed at her lack of attention. "Ms. Muñoz?"

"Sorry. You asked about people wanting to kill me? Yeah. Like I said, I'm a probation officer, so there's probably a list. I think you already wrote down Cortez Villarreal's name. He's my top suspect and one of the Gangster Disciples. There's a warrant out for him already."

He flipped back through his notes. "Right. I'll see if we've picked him up." The detective jerked his cell phone from his waist and punched a few buttons. "Boudreaux there? I'll wait." Then he looked at her again. "Anyone else who might want you dead?"

She mentally scanned through her caseload. No one else stood out. "I don't think so."

"A family member? A frenemy?"

No doubt, her stepfather disliked her, but Gordon had never been violent, just a manipulative jackass with a coal chip for a heart. She shook her head.

"Former lover?"

The only one who had any reason to be pissed at her was Ben, but he hadn't been jealous that she'd married Hunter, just annoyed that she'd refused him more sex. He'd apologize in a day or two, as he always did when they fought. Despite having been a soldier, Ben wasn't much of a fighter. "Definitely not."

Montrose jotted a note. "You said you'd never seen your attacker before. You're certain?"

"Positive."

"Any chance he could be associated with Villarreal?"

She shrugged. "I guess. When this guy arrives at lockup, they should check him for ink."

The detective nodded. "That's the easiest way to tell if he has any street affiliations. The suspect should be there now. I'll ask as soon as—" Suddenly, he turned his attention back to the phone. "Hey, Armand. You got a Cortez Villarreal in there? Would have come in on a warrant." A moment later, he cursed. "You don't. Talk to me about that perp who just came in for attempted murder, can you check—" The detective scowled. "What do you mean?" Then he flinched in shock. "Fuck! When?" The detective closed his eyes and sighed. "Keep me posted."

"What is it?" she asked impatiently, her stomach knotting painfully. "Did he get away?"

Montrose flipped his phone shut and hesitated. "Do you have anywhere to go? That's safe, I mean."

Home. A hot shower, then a nap in her own bed sounded heavenly . . . but Hunter's earlier warning and the detective's sudden jumpiness made Kata rethink that. "What happened?"

"The man who tried to kill you today was stabbed within ten minutes of hitting his cell. Inside job. Professional."

Kata started to shake. "He's dead?"

Nodding, Montrose ripped off his sunglasses and stared with grave, dark eyes. "Whoever is after you went to great pains to clean up his loose ends. He means business."

Hunter was right; this attack hadn't been random. In fact, her assailant had admitted that he was doing a job. Someone had hired him—then, once he'd been caught, snuffed him before he could talk to the police.

"They haven't ID'd your would-be killer yet. He had no ink linking him to the Gangster Disciples or anyone else. That doesn't mean anything, but maybe your murder would have been his initiation or . . ."

"He looked too old to just be hitting the streets."

He sighed. "Yeah, who knows? But you need to be careful. Stay someplace safe for a while."

No shit. But where? Kata started to shake again, reached out for the chair behind her to steady herself. Someone wanted her cold in a grave—quickly.

Home was too obvious. She couldn't go to Marisol's without putting her sister and nephews in danger. Nor could she risk her mamá. Gordon would only make her mother's life worse if she dropped by unannounced and asked to stay. After everything Mamá had been through, Kata couldn't make the woman's life harder. Besides, the less time Kata had to spend with Gordon, the better.

Where did that leave her? Driving to her brother, Joaquin? Was he still in Houston? She didn't know. For the past year, he'd been deep undercover—he'd never say who for. Joaquin was like a ghost to the family, there but not.

Kata sighed, raked her hand through her hair. Ben didn't deserve to be in danger, and their friendship had been strictly casual, convenient. Maybe she could grab her gun, withdraw some cash, then run for it, staying off the grid until things cooled down. But if there was a hit out on her, the matter wouldn't be resolved until whoever had hired the gun called it off or she was dead. Not palatable choices.

Through bits of conversation over the last few hours, Kata had gleaned that Deke was half owner of a personal protection business, along with some guy named Jack, who was out of town. Tyler, a former homicide detective, helped out from time to time. Could she persuade them to help her for the right price? Possibly . . . but they were Hunter's friends. They'd defer to him.

That left her with her new, unexpected husband. If she asked for his help, would he see that as some sort of implied consent to take over her life? Maybe that sounded paranoid, but she'd seen Gordon in action for too many years, and Ben had already warned her that Hunter liked to dominate. But both appeared to be control freaks with a deafness to the word "no" and a knack for manipulating matters—and women—to their liking.

Maybe it wasn't fair to lump Hunter and her stepfather together. Kata knew she hadn't been at her most magnanimous last night. And her husband appeared to lack Gordon's mean spirit.

You're so fucking gorgeous, honey. Hunter's voice echoed in her head, very different from the way Gordon talked to Mamá.

She sneaked a glance at Hunter. He stood tall, focused, his stance and body that of a warrior. He would be totally capable of keeping her out of harm's way. But haunting memories of his large hands heating her skin, shoving her thighs apart, his threat to tie her to his bed, plagued her. He'd gotten to her on every level, more than any man ever had.

Even so, avoiding the vulnerability and fear he pushed her to feel wasn't worth dying for.

"Do you have someplace to go?" Montrose barked again in low tones, breaking into her thoughts.

Where she wouldn't have to sleep with one eye open and a gun under her pillow? "No. But Hunter will."

* * *

GRIPPING the steering wheel of Tyler's truck, Hunter stared at the thin traffic meandering around Lafayette early on a Sunday evening. The sun shone, the birds sang. People on the corner ate ice cream. And the fury bubbling inside him tested his composure to its limits.

Some asshole wanted his wife dead. His brief but enlightening conversation with Detective Montrose made matters worse.

Hunter's only consolation was that she had come to him for protection. Somewhere inside that stubborn woman's head and heart, she trusted him. He would work with that—as soon as he figured out how to end this threat to her life.

"You did the right thing in letting me protect you," he assured. "I'll take care of it."

Kata shook her head, the inky, long hair brushing her arms, the tops of her breasts he remembered tasting. Her lips still looked swollen, her eyes a bit red and heavy from lack of sleep. The adrenaline crash had to be gnawing away at her energy, but other than one dicey moment earlier, she refused to show weakness.

Too bad his adrenaline hadn't come down yet. All he wanted to do was beat the hell out of whoever wanted to hurt Kata. Or fuck her. Preferably both. Didn't look like either would happen for a while.

"I appreciate your help, but let's get one thing straight." She turned to him in the cozy cab with a warning glare. "I turned to you because I'm not sure I can do this alone, but I don't want you to take over."

In his book? Same thing. She had no experience with this kind of shit, and he'd be damned if he'd let her put herself at risk for the sake of her stubborn pride. She could decorate the house however she wanted, name the pets, choose the vacations. He'd give her a lot of latitude during their married life, but he was in charge when it came to sex and her safety.

With Kimber's words ringing in his head and Kata's desertion this morning playing in an endless loop in his brain, Hunter wished he could afford to back off. He couldn't, but maybe he could find a gentle way to make her see his logic.

Hunter nodded in her direction. "All right. What did you have in mind?"

Her expression told him that she hadn't thought too much about the answer. "I—I guess a safe house somewhere, at least until the police catch Cortez Villarreal."

"I've got a safe house."

Logan probably wouldn't appreciate the added intrusion of another person on his leave, but tough shit. If Hunter knew one thing, it was that his brother was every bit as cautious as he was. Logan's bachelor pad was full of military-grade security. Hunter would handle the rest of his brother's special equipment on an as-needed basis.

"Good." She nodded, looking shaky and near her breaking point. "I appreciate that. As soon as I've had time to think, I'll start taking care of myself, but for now, I think you hiding me is the best move. Almost no one knows we're connected, especially someone on the street like Cortez Villarreal."

"About that . . ." Hunter wished he didn't have to give her bad news now, but there was too much at stake to withhold the truth. "Let's think this through. The assassin said he was *hired*, not that his street boss had told him to roll you over. From what the detective said, he couldn't see any tattoos that identified the shooter as a Gangster Disciple. For argument's sake, let's say that he isn't a street thug but a real hired killer."

Kata recoiled, looking even paler. Clearly, she hadn't let herself seriously entertain the notion before now. "B-but if that's true, why did he miss me when he shot? How did I get away?"

As much as he hated to burst her bubble, he had to press on. "I'd guess it's because you gave him more fight than he expected, and you threw him off guard. That he's a professional fits. When Deke tackled him, the guy was carrying a SIG 232. The barrel was threaded so he could use a silencer, if needed. It was in his pocket, in fact. We're talking about some of the best equipment. Not impossible to fall into a gangster's hands—"

"But unlikely." Her voice shook, then she closed her eyes, drew in a deep breath. "What else? I can hear it in your voice."

Smart girl . . . She'd been through a lot in the last twenty-four hours—marathon sex, an unexpected wedding, a hangover, and an attempt on her life. Kata was shaken but not defeated. His respect for her went up another notch.

Hunter tried to lay this out as gently as possible. "Usually assassins are like ghosts. They'll just 'clean up,' take out a target with a high-powered scope and sniper rifle at a distance. The closer an assassin is to the target, the greater his risk of being caught or ID'd and jeopardizing the mission. But if the person hiring the assassin wants others to know the target was intentionally iced, then when they hire the killer, they'll tell him to put on 'a show.'"

"Th-the guy who came after me was putting on a show." Kata didn't ask; she knew. Nervously, she swallowed.

"Yes." Why else had he come in such close range, onto the target's turf, eschewing his silencer, rather than waiting on the high-rise across the street until she walked into the parking lot? Whoever had masterminded this attack wanted to make a public statement. Question was, about what? And to whom?

This whole episode might be related to a gangster's revenge or

Kata's temporary disruption of his drug trade. But that didn't feel right. And if there was already a warrant out for Villarreal's arrest, why put on a show like this and piss the cops off more? There were a lot of ways to make an example out of someone without spending the time and money to hire an assassin.

Fuck. "We need to keep trying to figure out who would do this to you."

"I've wracked my brains, but—"

"I don't want you to worry about it now, honey. You're exhausted. Sleep for a bit. We'll talk in a few hours."

"Hours? My apartment is on the other side of town. I need a few things before we go anywhere."

Hunter steered the truck onto I-49. "No stops. We're going to Dallas."

"What about my suitcase? It was in the trunk of my car. Did you get it from Tyler before he drove off in it?"

"No. Getting you away from there quickly was more important."

Kata looked lost and frustrated. He understood that she was angry at the situation, not him—but he was the only available outlet for her irritation. He wished she wouldn't wear herself out unnecessarily . . . but Kata wasn't a soldier trained to contain her emotions, channel them to something useful.

"I—I need my vitamins, a toothbrush—"

He leveled a stare at her across the cozy truck's cab. "Is there anything at your place that's more important than your life?"

She sighed. "No."

"I'll buy you replacements once we reach my brother's place."

"I have to have clean underwear . . ."

Hunter did his best to distract her with a smoldering smile. "Honey, if I have my way, you'll never need those again."

Kata rolled her eyes and did her best to look annoyed, but he saw the blush crawl up her cheeks. "You think about sex all the time."

He smiled. "When you're near me, yeah."

She crossed her arms over her chest, but not before Hunter noticed that her nipples had tightened. "We have more important things going on, you know."

"Unfortunately, I do. Don't worry, honey."

As she closed her eyes for a moment, some of the starch left Kata. "Hard not to."

Hunter grimaced. Every mission he went on, he figured that he had an enemy who would kill him if he didn't finish them off first. Hell, he knew a few of those shadowy figures from his past had put hits out on him. In every case, they'd given up or Hunter had made sure they went down instead. Kata had no experience with this, and it had to be scaring the hell out of her.

Still, he tried not to step on her toes.

"Any plans beyond tonight? How are you going to rid yourself of the threat?" He didn't think she had the first idea. He'd love to be proven wrong, but if not . . . well, he needed her to admit that before he moved in and took over. Or she'd be blazingly pissed.

"I c-can call some of my cop friends, like Trey, see what they might have heard. If this wasn't Villarreal's work, I have to figure out who ordered the hit . . ." Kata paused, blinked, then looked up at him with a furrowed brow before wrenching away.

But not before he saw tears in her eyes.

Hunter hated seeing his wife, so assertive and sexy, looking ready to crumble. Once he figured out who the motherfucker responsible for this threat was, he'd be lucky to live long enough to take a last breath.

She exhaled on a shaky sigh. "But without all that, I can't hope to have anyone arrested or brought to trial so I can have my life back. Damn it, I've never been helpless, and I won't start now."

So fiercely independent. No doubt, she was going to keep his life interesting for the next fifty years.

He grabbed her hand, squeezed. "You're not. Far from it."

Kata scoffed. "Look at me. I'm shaking and confused. I don't know what to do next. I have to figure this out quickly."

"Have any interest in lying down and dying?"

She gaped at him as if he'd lost his mind. "Hell, no!"

"Good girl. Some people crack and, not knowing how to deal, they give up and wait for the inevitable."

"It's *not* inevitable."

Hunter smiled. It was good to see her moxie again.

"If you fight, it's not. You, honey, are a fighter. I needed you to realize that for yourself. I knew it because you fended off a professional today, got a jump on him. I'm proud as hell."

A smile crept across her mouth before it fell again. "But other than fighting constantly, I don't know any way of dealing with this . . . prick who wants to kill me."

"Deke and his business partner, Jack, will help us dig until we figure out who's behind this. Until we have more information, I don't want to trust any of the cops you know. I'll bet some of them were on duty when your attacker was processed today. And he was murdered. Until we know what's going on, let's not involve anyone else."

"But they're my friends. They would never—"

"Are you willing to bet your life on that?"

Kata hesitated, chewed on her bottom lip. "No, but why should I trust Deke and Jack?"

"Because they're the best." Hunter reached across the cab and grabbed her hand. "Honey, once we figure out who's behind all this, we'll have to act. As long as we wait for this guy to make all the moves, we're at his mercy. Once we figure out who's behind this, we'll take the fight to him, dictate the terms and the tempo, keep him guessing and off guard. He'll get sloppy, make mistakes. We'll be waiting."

"The best defense is a good offense?"

"Exactly. Are you up for it?"

"I don't have a choice."

She didn't, and Hunter was proud of her for facing it. A professional hit would send most women into a panicked frenzy. But Kata had done her best to remain calm. She'd acknowledged her shortcomings in tracking down a killer and listened to logic. Even at her most vulnerable, she'd refused to give up the fight.

Hunter damn sure wasn't giving up—on keeping her safe or preserving their marriage. He hadn't chased Kata this far to let her slip through his fingers. He tightened his grip on the wheel. Kata scooted across the bucket seat, closer, then leaned her head on his shoulder. As he wrapped his arm around her, she curled herself even tighter around his heart. This woman was meant for him. Damn. Less than a week—that's all the time he had to save her life and make her fall in love with him. Failure wasn't an option.

Chapter Eight

IT was damn near midnight when Hunter parked Tyler's truck in front of Logan's condo on the northeast side of Dallas. Long fucking day after such an eventful night, but he could go many hours without sleep. Days, if he had to.

Hunter looked over at Kata, snuggled against his side, sleeping peacefully with her head on his shoulder. He didn't like the smudges under her eyes or that she'd refused dinner when they'd stopped on the road. During the drive, she'd said almost nothing.

He'd refused to let her use her cell phone to contact her family, especially to say where she was going and who she was with. After he'd explained that her phone could be monitored, Kata had been frustrated but resigned. She'd used a pay phone to call Mari and assure her that, despite whatever the evening news said, she was just fine, and to let their mother know. Then Kata had called her boss to arrange a week off. Back in the truck, she'd curled her knees to her chest and stared out the windshield, looking shell-shocked. Damn, he'd do anything to wipe that expression off her face. When he caught the son of a bitch threatening her, he'd force-feed the bastard his own balls.

But first Hunter had to take care of his wife.

Gently, he shook her awake. "We're here, honey."

"Hmm." Her lashes fluttered. Her lips parted.

In an instant, she made him hard. Stifling his urge to kiss her until she was clinging and wet, then sink deep into her pussy so he could connect deep into her, he settled for a light touch, brushing the hair from her face. "I'll come around and get you. Gather up your stuff."

Finally, his words seemed to register, and she sat up and grabbed her purse.

Hunter hopped out of the truck, vaguely irritated with the muggy night, then circled around the vehicle to open her door. Before she could protest, he scooped her up in his arms.

Her eyes flew open. "You can put me down."

"You're not taking away my fun."

The amusement she tried to hide bled through her exhaustion. "Carrying me can't be fun."

"You're wrong. I like you right here." He raised his arms, lowered his head, and pressed a soft kiss to her mouth.

Her kiss was flavored with peppermint and a hint of the vanilla milkshake he'd finally plied her with a hundred miles ago. And sin. She always tasted like it, was made for it, and he wanted to share it with her again.

"I'm perfectly capable of walking," she insisted, even as she wound her arms around his neck and rested her head on his shoulder.

"Yes, and I love the way you walk, hips swaying, ass swinging. *Hmm . . .*"

She sighed. "Nice to know that you watch my ass so closely."

A moment of sweet harmony flowed between them, and satisfaction settled into Hunter's belly as he laughed. "I watch your everything closely, honey. Trust me, it's my pleasure."

Logan's front door loomed ahead. On the little porch, Hunter reluctantly lowered Kata to her feet. His younger brother wasn't due home for at least two days, and Hunter would be lying if he said he wasn't looking forward to the privacy with his bride. As honeymoons went, this sucked. But on his next leave, he'd make it up to her.

For now, spending time together here would have to do.

As he retrieved his key and inserted it in the lock, he hesitated, hoping that Logan's taste in décor had improved since last year. But Hunter wasn't betting on it.

The lock turned, then he entered the code on the keypad that controlled the dead bolt. The second trigger for that catch, a thumbprint scan, was located just under the doorbell. A green laser and a ding later, the door finally opened.

"Oh my God. Is your brother paranoid?"

He stifled his smile. "He's a SEAL, too. In our line of work, honey, you make enemies. It pays to be cautious."

"Guess he doesn't have anyone watering his houseplants while he's gone."

Hunter stifled a smile. "Logan doesn't allow strangers into his domain."

Kata shrank back from the door. "Then he won't appreciate me being here."

"You're family now. Inside."

Pressing a guiding hand to the small of her back, he ushered her over the threshold into the pitch-black room. One step in, a shrill beeping assaulted his ears. He grabbed her elbow, pressed her to the wall, then locked the door behind them. "Stay here. He's armed the motion sensors."

The warning chime of the interior alarm played hell with the headache developing at the base of Hunter's neck, but he zeroed in on the little backlit pad and punched the appropriate code. The high-pitched screech stopped immediately. Finally, blessed silence.

"Is there a light in this place?" Her voice trembled.

Hunter reset the exterior alarm and reached for Kata, wrapping his arm around her waist and leading her through the dark living room. He intentionally left the lights off. She'd see plenty of this place tomorrow. No need to add one more shock to her already-crazy day.

"Not necessary. Just stay near me. I'll get you settled."

She walked hesitantly, digging in her heels. "Wait! I'm going to trip and—"

"You've got to trust me, honey. Do you think I would let anything happen to you?"

Kata hesitated. Hunter knew the instant she realized that, if he was protecting her from killers, he'd keep her from hurting herself while crossing the dark room.

She relaxed. "No, but—"

"Never," he interrupted. It didn't matter what she planned to say. She needed to know one truth. "I would *never* let anything happen to you. I should spank your ass red for even thinking I would."

Her gasp shot straight to his cock. Sitting next to her for hours, her scent, soft and womanly, filling up in the cab of the truck, while she'd curled trustingly against his side with her hand on his thigh, had revved him up.

"You did not say just that. Don't you *dare* think you're going to spank me," she growled.

Hunter smiled in the dark. "Dare? Honey, I can't wait."

"Stop trying to keep me off balance and forcing me to rely on you. Just . . . stop."

He understood the trepidation in her voice. Last night, he hadn't expected to take the lead. By all rights, that had been Ben's honor, who was vanilla all the way. So Hunter hadn't come prepared for anything more than a good time. Then his buddy's drunkenness and Hunter's own possessiveness had changed the plan. He'd been unprepared to lead her in any sort of D/s scene. But here, alone . . . Yeah. He couldn't wait to show her exactly how much he'd dare.

A few steps more, and he ushered her into the master suite, setting the motion sensors in the living room, then shutting and locking the bedroom door behind them. He flipped on the overhead

light. A bright glow spilled out over the heavy two-toned gray comforter, its pattern thoroughly modern. The black upholstered and
brushed nickel headboard sat against the charcoal walls, between
two vertical windows with dark blinds drawn tight. A dresser, matching nightstand, and area rug—all black—added to the heavy air in
the room. The only shred of warmth was the Brazilian cherry floors
and the bridal portrait of Kimber. The rest? Off-putting and impersonal, just the way Logan liked things.

Idly, Hunter wondered how long it would take her to notice
the manacles dangling from chains down from either side of the
headboard.

"Wow." Her gaze skittered almost frenetically around the room.
"This is your brother's place?"

He nodded. "Warm, huh?"

"Not in the least."

Logan had been fucked up for years. But instead of his mental state improving over time, it was growing worse. By leaps and
bounds. Another reason that he and little brother were going to have
a heart-to-heart. Not that Hunter didn't understand Logan's dark
needs. They had a lot in common there. But lately . . . his brother
behaved as if he'd done a belly flop off the mental deep end.

Rather than giving Kata more time to rubberneck, Hunter pushed
her to the sleek adjoining bathroom. At least here, a patterned marble inlay and travertine relieved the black of the walls, cabinets, and
trim.

"He, um . . . has a real hard-on for contemporary décor."

Or black simply matched Logan's mood. But why debate the
subject? "Let me run you a hot bath, honey."

Without waiting for a reply, he turned the hot water on and placed
the stopper in the tub. Beneath the vanity, he found a towel and wash-
cloth and set them on the counter. He rummaged through a few
drawers and came up with a toothbrush still in the plastic and a new
comb.

Then he turned to Kata, watching her step away and look at

everything but him. Her evasiveness had to end, especially now
when he was dying to reconnect with her. Time would help her adjust to marriage and to him—but that was something he didn't have.
So, on to plan B.

He took a deep breath. Yes, he had to tread carefully, give her a
lot of latitude, considering all she'd been through, but . . . he couldn't
allow her to keep walls between them.

Begin how you mean to go on.

"Thanks," she murmured, stepping toward the door, presumably
to see him out.

Hunter stepped into her path. "You're welcome. Now strip."

Kata's hazel eyes went wide. "Excuse me?"

Her flippant reply didn't interest Hunter; he'd expected it, would
deal with it. But she couldn't hide when her pupils dilated and her
cheeks turned rosy. Kata's involuntary reactions sliced desire through
his belly, shuttling straight down to his cock. He leveled her with a
hard stare, raising his head a fraction, stepping far into her personal
space.

In response, her nipples beaded. She swallowed, dropped her
stare.

Definitely submissive. Last night, he'd suspected it, even as she'd
pushed back again and again. But she hadn't been his to test or claim.
All that had changed. Hunter planned to make sure she understood
exactly who and what he was—and uncover the submissive inside
her he felt sure she'd never trusted any man enough to let out.

Kata had some serious hang-ups about control. They'd get to the
bottom of those. Yes, the power to refuse always rested with the
submissive. But Hunter sensed that she needed reassurance that he'd
never want a doormat and didn't want her to change. He'd help her
understand what she secretly yearned for and teach her to ask for
what she feared to want.

"It's an order, honey, not a negotiation." He kept his voice low,
deceptively soft. "I'm waiting."

She hesitated, and Hunter sensed a million thoughts whirling in her head. Desire, anger, and exasperation crossed her gorgeous face. Finally, she raised her chin and crossed her arms over her chest.

Submissive . . . but not going down without a fight. He held in a smile.

"Don't do this now, when I'm exhausted and afraid," she murmured. "I know you want to exert your dominance or whatever, but why over something as inconsequential as a bath?"

Since Kata didn't understand him or his ways, that wasn't an unfair question. His cock was nagging him like a toothache, as was his impatience to reach the woman behind her defense mechanisms and bind her to him, but that was his problem. She deserved answers first.

"Everything about you concerns me. You're a smart woman, and I'm sure you've guessed by now that I don't merely like to dominate; I *am* a Dominant."

* * *

JUST like Ben had said. Kata wasn't exactly sure what that meant. That he was itching to restrain and spank her? That he liked to play Master/slave games?

A forbidden ache settled with horrific insistence right under her clit. She tried to ignore it. No damn way was she submitting an inch of her independence, even in the bedroom, just to get her freak on.

She mentally sorted through escape routes out of this mini Fort Knox. "Not with me. Hell no!"

Disappointment and anger tightened Hunter's face, settling in with the exhaustion. A pinprick of guilt pierced her before she checked it. He was bringing this argument on. They could be in bed even now, drifting off to a much-needed night's sleep. But no, he insisted on pushing her now. No way would she be his doormat, not after everything she'd seen in the last dozen years. She'd rather take a bullet to her brain than endure what Mamá had under Gordon's rule.

Hunter could tie her into a pretzel if he wanted to restrain her.

God knew he had the strength, the intelligence, and the balls. So she had to keep her wits about her. Kata retreated another step.

He grabbed her hand, his thumb brushing over the top of hers in a soft sweep unexpectedly soothing. "Kata, it's the way I'm wired. Everything I demand is aimed at providing you what you need, while giving me what I crave. Tonight, that's you relaxing in a hot tub while I massage the tenseness from your muscles so you reach a physical and mental state optimal for sleep." He shrugged. "And I'll have the peace of mind that comes with knowing you're safe and well."

That's it? She stared at him suspiciously. This was supposed to be for her benefit? What about the high he got from ordering her around? How much bigger did he feel by having power over another? "Why not just say that instead of bossing me around?"

"Part of what I need as a Dom is for you to trust me, so I won't explain myself unless you're genuinely concerned or frightened. I *need* you to put yourself in my hands, submit to me completely, and know that I have your best interest at heart. I understand you'll find that a challenge. Submission won't be easy for you."

Won't be easy? Kata would have laughed in his face if her racing thoughts hadn't been tangling with emotions she barely understood. The kicker was, he seemed so confident that she would eventually comply.

The fact that he thought she could ever submit proved he didn't understand her. Maybe he didn't want to. Maybe she hadn't made herself clear enough.

Kata stared, taking in every inch of his gorgeous face. She couldn't deny the attraction curling through her. Why couldn't he be more laid back like Ben? Why couldn't they just enjoy each other without the power trip? She wanted to be with Hunter. He definitely made her feel something no man ever had. Why couldn't they just have sex without her having to be submissive?

He sighed as he turned off the faucet. Water steamed from the tub. "Your face is an open book, honey. I get what you're thinking. We need to talk about what dominance is and isn't."

"It's a power play, pure and simple."

"It *is* about power—but it's mostly yours. I can only take what you're able to give. This isn't to inflate my ego. It's to form a bond. We'll test our trust every day. And each time I respect your boundaries, yet push you until you're satisfied mentally, emotionally, and sexually, our bond deepens."

Some part of her wanted to believe him. In fact, she ached for such a relationship. How goddamn dangerous was that? Bonds so deep that Hunter could see into her soul, and vice versa, sounded great—on the surface. But Kata had her doubts that's how it would actually work. In her experience, a man ordered, a woman complied and cowed, until it broke her self-esteem, and he got some sick kick out of the fact that he could bend her to his will. The next day, he'd bend her more, then still more, until she crumbled. The insides, her self-esteem and spirit he'd carved out, he tossed aside with unrepentant glee.

"That's crap." She snatched her hand back and crossed her arms over her chest.

"Have a lot of experience with Dominance and submission, do you?" Hunter arched a tawny brow at her.

"I don't have to in order to know I don't want any of this. So take your chains and ropes and floggers, and go f—"

"Don't finish that sentence." Hunter stepped closer. He didn't loom over her, but bent until they were eye to eye. "I want tonight to be about comfort and relaxation. But if you finish that sentence, I'm going to smack your ass so red, you won't sit for days."

She blinked. "So now you're going to abuse me?"

His smile wasn't pretty, and it made her belly clench with nothing she could remotely term fear. An answering chord tightened between her legs.

Slowly, he walked a half circle around her, settled his hands on her hips, and whispered in her ear. "It's nothing like abuse. You'll come, more than once. You're a hellcat, but deep down, I'll bet you have fantasies you won't admit to . . . but you want fulfilled. I'll be the man to do that for you."

Hunter caressed his way down her ass. As her skin burned, Kata tensed, sucked in a breath. Her heart careened against her chest in a painful thud. She couldn't string two words together to sling the tart reply trapped on her tongue.

He circled around her again, faced her. Then he sent her a long, hot stare. She could feel her thong going from damp to soaked.

God, was he reading her wayward thoughts? Based on the sex they'd shared the night before, she feared he could—and see all the way down to her soul. She didn't doubt that he'd be able to satisfy her body completely. But what about her heart? How could a relationship between them work if he demanded more than she could willingly give?

"I don't want this." Her voice shook. *Liar.*

"I won't tolerate dishonesty. That's your second punishable offense. I'll let you slide because you're tired and new to this dynamic. But one more . . ." He reached around and popped her ass once, then he soothed his palm over her warmed flesh.

Before she could stop herself, Kata gasped—and not in pain. Hunter sent her a satisfied grin.

A new fear wrapped around her. Why couldn't she understand—or control—her own traitorous reactions? Suddenly, the thing she'd long feared was the thing she wanted most.

"Let's try this again," he suggested. "Strip."

If she complied, he would turn her inside out. She knew it. After everything that had happened in the past twenty-four hours, she already felt raw. Kata couldn't take more now. "I'd rather bathe alone."

Hunter took his time responding. "Okay. But when you're hot and you need me to ease your ache, I'll make you wait for an orgasm until you beg. For hours." He shrugged. "It's your choice."

Kata had no doubt Hunter could—and would—do exactly that. Even the suggestion made her clit pulse.

He grabbed her shoulders. "I don't want to fight about this. Trust me, honey. I won't hurt you or let you down."

The blaze in his eyes sizzled her skin. The deep timbre of his seductive voice resonated through her, settling right between her legs. Hunter, along with his air of power and control, got to her like no man ever had. In his place, someone like Ben would have yelled, thrown a tantrum. Hunter had merely laid his cards on the table and now waited patiently, certain he'd come out victorious eventually.

Kata swallowed. Maybe she was being paranoid and looking at his demands all wrong. Denying herself a hot guy wasn't her style. Refusing to try something new wasn't like her, either. So Hunter played the game differently than Ben or any of her previous lovers. No big deal, right? She couldn't deny that she'd eaten up everything he'd done to her so far. Yes, he was a lot to handle. But she was strong. No reason to assume that she couldn't manage.

"If . . . we try this and I want out?"

"'No' isn't an acceptable safe word. Instead, say 'Ben.' If you do, I'll know you're not ready to move past your status quo yet, and I'll back away until you are."

It almost seemed too simple. Where was the loophole? Or did Hunter have so much self-control that stopping at any time wouldn't be a problem? "That's it?"

"Nothing more complicated than that. You know what I want. I'm waiting, honey."

Fine. If he wanted to see her naked because it turned him on, then she was all for it. Kata wasn't too cowardly to admit that the way he watched her like a predator getting ready to pounce aroused her.

She grabbed at the bottom of her T-shirt and pulled it over her head, tossed it to the floor. Hunter sucked in a breath, and Kata looked down. Ah, yes. The red bra with lace cups so sheer, he could see through them. His gaze caressed her wide, rosy areola, and she knew he saw her hard nipples almost poking above the delicate, low-slung fabric.

He didn't move, didn't say a word, but there was no missing

the sudden tension in his body or the erection straining the front of his jeans. He'd filled her utterly last night. But now . . . he looked even harder, bigger. He'd have to really work to bury all of that inside her.

Kata shivered, and her panties turned even wetter at the thought. She reached for the snap of her capris and slowly unfastened them. Her fingers drifted down over the denim . . . until she rubbed at the ache in her pussy. A muscle ticked in Hunter's jaw.

Holding in her smile, she slid her hand back up her stomach and found the tab of her zipper. She began tugging it down, torturously slow. A peek at Hunter only proved that he was even more rigid—everywhere.

When Kata had lowered the zipper, she hooked her thumbs in the waistband and began to shove them past her shimmying hips, over her ass, down her thighs. Finally, they pooled at her ankles, exposing her matching red thong.

"Fuck me, you look hot," he muttered, his stare harsh, electric. Possessive as hell.

Her pussy spasmed, clenched.

As much as it pained her to admit that Hunter was right, in her deepest, darkest fantasies Kata had imagined being overpowered and restrained. Imagining him dominating her, securing his ropes around her wrists and taking her at will, only turned her ache into an unrelenting throb.

"The bra, Kata. Now."

Strain showed in Hunter's voice, suddenly husky and gravel-filled. His deep tone, coupled with those electric blue eyes of his, seared her. She was hyperaware of every beat of her heart, every inch of her exposed skin, every long-held fantasy she'd ever repressed.

She reached behind her and grabbed the band, unhooked the fastenings one at a time. Before the bra slid down her arms, she pressed her palms to her breasts, precariously holding the cups in place.

"Let go." Hunter made a fist at his side. "Or I'll rip it off."

Kata had no doubt he meant that . . . but the devil in her prodded her to goad him. "But it's the only bra I have with me."

A nasty smile curled up the side of his mouth. "Oh well."

He tensed, reached for her. Kata let the bra fall, exposing her breasts.

They felt heavy, swollen. More blood rushed to the already-sensitive tips, and they hardened until the sensation became a pleasure/pain all its own. His stare lashed them like a live wire, a stunning jolt across each nipple.

God, she didn't think she'd ever been more aroused, and Hunter had barely touched her.

His gaze drifted down her stomach, hesitated on the winking ruby at her pierced navel, then lingered between her thighs. Kata squeezed them together, trying to ease the ache. That only made the desire sharper. She needed relief.

Kata shifted a hand to the lace shielding her pussy and pressed in, rotating her fingers over her sensitive flesh. She gasped. Euphoria rolled through her as tingles danced under her skin. The ache sweetened. God, she was so close . . .

Hunter grabbed her wrist, exerting just enough pressure to lift her fingers an inch. "Your orgasms are mine. I say when and how. You don't have permission to come."

That didn't fit in her fantasies. She jerked against his hold.

He didn't let go. "I more than warned you. You've got at least one punishment coming. Want more?"

"You have no right to—"

"Last night changed everything. Own up to the fact that you want this, and take off that wet thong if you want to keep it in one piece."

Anger and desire tumbled together, churning and roiling inside her. In that moment, Kata was royally pissed—but she also wanted him like hell.

With a curse, she grabbed the little thong clinging to her hips and jerked it down ungracefully until she was as bare as the day she was born. "Happy?"

"Nice." That cocky half-smile curled up the corner of his mouth. "Spread your legs shoulder-width apart."

"What? Are you going to inspect me?"

"If I wanted to, I would. In due time, I will. At some point, I'll have that pretty cunt waxed from top to bottom so you can feel every lick of my tongue. But right now, I told you to spread your legs. Hesitate again, and that will be punishment number two."

Kata gritted her teeth but complied. Not because she was afraid of him but because, despite the anger simmering just under her skin, heaven help her, she wanted to.

"Excellent." His stare lasered in on her pussy . . . then rose to meet her gaze. "You're very wet."

It was true, but she hated giving him too much power over her. "Maybe my wetness has nothing to do with you."

Hunter shook his head. "You're just racking the spankings up tonight, honey. That's two punishments. Unless you want a third, I suggest you get your fingers on that pussy and start rubbing. I'll tell you when to stop."

Her pulse jumped. Touching herself for show was one thing, but . . . "M-masturbate in front of you?"

"*For* me. Get busy."

The challenge in his tone both made her bristle and ache. She swallowed.

Kata had never done this for any lover, but she wanted to drive Hunter mad with lust, then hold out on him. Make him regret ever pushing her.

She smiled coyly. Their gazes met, fused for an electric moment. Then she caressed a line down her stomach slowly, finally reaching the apex of her thighs. She diverted from her clit, slipping lower to press two fingers inside her snug depths.

Sensation rolled over her in a hot wave, a delicious pleasure that had her gasping. Somewhere in the back of her head, she marveled at how hot and slick she felt, but the invasion stole her breath, her thoughts.

Kata tangled her free hand through her hair, pulling her fingers through the silky mass, until she reached her breast. She cupped it, pinched her nipple, and moaned.

Her head spun. The sugary ache stretched the moment as pleasure buzzed inside her. A wave of dizziness threatened to send her tumbling deep into a chasm of need. Kata groped for the wall beside her and hung on tight as she eased her fingers deeper inside her pussy.

Hunter tensed. The way he gripped his thighs told her he was exercising superhuman restraint not to throw her to the cold tile and fuck her into next week. "Rub your clit."

Gladly. The little knot of nerves had swollen to twice its normal size. As she withdrew her fingers and dragged them up and settled them over her clit, a new wave of tingles crashed through her. Knowing that Hunter's eyes were on her made Kata shudder, gasp. Normally with self-pleasure, it took at least ten minutes to orgasm. Now, after the barest of touches, she felt a heartbeat away from an explosion that would flatten her.

Kata's fingers shook as she dragged in a shuddering breath. So damn close. Oh God . . . One more good swipe would do it. Her knees were unstable beneath her, and her heartbeat roared in her ears. She anticipated this orgasm like crazy. *Needed* it.

"Stop." Hunter pulled her hand away from her pussy, then moved behind her, until he pinned her wrist at the small of her back.

"Damn it, no!" she groaned.

He said nothing, merely grabbed her other hand, then held both together behind her in an unyielding grip that aroused her even more.

Her breathing accelerated. Even without the stimulation to her clit, she still felt a split second from orgasm. And the heat of his body blanketing her back, his free hand moving her long hair off her neck, just before he kissed his way across her sensitive skin . . . Kata shuddered, her senses on overload.

"Please . . ." God, she hated herself for begging, but she couldn't stop it.

He edged to her side, caressed his way down her spine, rough fingertips sliding over her skin. She trembled, arched into his touch.

"You're so beautiful," he whispered.

Hunter made her feel that way, like a goddess. She loved the way he seemed crazy with desire for her.

Suddenly, his touch disappeared. Kata held her breath, expectation thrumming through her. Then *thwack*! He struck her ass with a solid palm.

She yelped. "What the hell are you doing?"

"I promised to punish you, so I am," he growled.

Fire began to crawl across the right cheek of her ass, stunning Kata mute. Only the rhythm of Hunter's hot breaths on her shoulder and his grip on her wrists told her that he remained behind her. Then he slapped her left cheek with equal force.

He repeated the process again. Then again.

Her rear began to throb, become a luscious starburst of sensation. That ache joined the one behind her clit. Need escalated. Her heart slammed into her ribs. Her knees buckled.

Hunter hooked an arm around her waist to hold her upright, his fingers hovering over her pussy. Kata sucked in a breath in anticipation, but he didn't touch her, leaving her to dangle at the edge of overwhelming need.

She whimpered. "Oh, God. Please . . ."

"Why should I reward your disobedience by giving you an orgasm?"

"I need it," Kata admitted with a moan.

"I needed you to strip, and you refused me."

"You *ordered* me."

Hunter's fingertips drifted down, rubbing light, lazy circles over the hood of her clit, the pressure too light and scattered to do any-thing but drive her up higher. Kata fisted her hands, trying to thrust her hips against his fingers, praying he'd rub her right into oblivion. But he clutched her hip tightly, controlling her every move.

"As I will again and again. Learn to take direction, and you'll find I can be very generous. If not . . ."

He let the implication sink in.

Damn him! He might have her in this moment. No way she was going to comply with him twenty-four/seven. She fully intended to repay Hunter for this. Then he could go to hell.

"Stay here," he barked. "Do *not* move."

Kata tensed at his order, spitting mad and scared. She itched to rebel, find some way to have him eating out of the palm of her hand. But if she tried, he'd only withhold orgasm again. And right now, she needed so badly what only he could give her. "I won't."

"Answer me properly with a 'Yes, Sir.'"

Sir? No way . . . That rubbed her independent streak raw. Seri-ously, payback was going to be a bitch.

Silent moments stretched on, and her body ached, screamed for the release she knew he wouldn't give her until she cooperated.

Squeezing her eyes shut, she finally choked out, "Yes, Sir."

"That was slow, and it lacked sincerity, but I'll let it pass tonight." He released her wrists. "Turn and face the shower. Brace your hands on the wall in front of you. Spread your legs wider."

Kata froze, her mind racing. Then slowly, she turned, glancing over her shoulder at Hunter.

He shook his head. "Eyes forward."

What the hell did he have planned? He'd reveal it in time, but if she questioned him now, no doubt he'd just keep withholding this orgasm. The thought made her chest tighten, a sob rise up.

Resolutely, she looked at the wall, pressed her lips together, and waited.

"Good. That's progress," he praised as he cupped her breast, thumb brushing her aching, beaded nipple.

She swallowed a gasp. God, every nerve ending was on fire. When his hand skated down her rib cage, her waist, her hip, her butt, she held her breath, so full of need. Then his other hand joined, and he spread her cheeks slightly. She tensed.

"You've never had anal sex?"

"N-no." She'd never wanted it. But with Hunter, it sounded so hot and forbidden. Sexy as hell.

He traced a finger from the small of her back, down through the hidden crevice, lingering over her back passage. "When the time comes, I'll be gentle. But you'll take me here."

His fingertip teased the little opening, and tingles skittered through her. She gasped. Oh damn . . . The thought of his cock in her ass scared the hell out of her—and yet she was desperate to know what it would be like, if Hunter taking her that way would make her feel utterly dominated. Suddenly, Kata craved that in a way that haunted her.

"Such beauty . . . and reluctant obedience." He caressed the curve of her waist again, his lips drifting across her shoulder—and his naked body pressed to her back, hard cock nestled against her ass. When had he undressed? "We'll work on that."

Her pulse jumped, and Kata was so ready for anything—everything—Hunter wanted to give her—as long as he let her come.

"Please . . ." She wiggled against him, pleading again.

She heard a tear, a crinkle. Thank God Hunter was donning a condom. Her entire body clenched in anticipation.

Hunter found her opening in the center of the slick folds of her pussy. He pressed the tip in—and paused.

"Don't come until I give you permission. Are we clear?"

In the past few moments, she'd regained a little control, not quite as high with need. But Kata had no illusions; he could push her to the edge again quickly and leave her hanging. It seemed she'd been achy and desperate for hours, though it had probably been ten minutes. He could likely make it seem like days if he wanted. Why take the risk that he'd deprive her?

Giving in both scared and thrilled her. "Yes, Sir."

"Your obedience goes straight to my cock, honey." He pressed his solid chest over her back and nuzzled her neck with soft kisses. "Hmm. I could get used to this."

She could, too. That's what scared her to death. But she was too high on need to think about it now.

His hands scooped up her breasts, fingers pinching her nipples until the edge of pain had her gasping and her pussy creaming anew. The need to orgasm rose once more, now screaming through her body.

Hunter grabbed her hips and slammed deep inside her in one savage thrust. "Fuck, yes!"

Kata cried out as pleasure-pain ripped through her. God, he was huge. She rose on her toes to put more space between them as she tried to adjust, but he still pressed inward, deeper and deeper. She hissed, trying to accommodate his girth, take the avalanche of sensation burying her. Climax loomed . . . but she needed just a bit more.

"Hunter, please . . . Fuck me," she cried out.

"I will, until you've screamed your throat raw," he vowed. "Once you've done what I asked, when I ask it."

Chapter Nine

UNDER him, Kata stiffened. No surprise, since he'd intentionally pushed her.

Hunter grabbed her hips and waited. His little spitfire wanted to give in—he could feel her need—but that independent mind of hers, riddled with whatever scars she carried, kept asserting itself, shutting off trust before she could truly grant it. He understood; she was having difficulty reconciling what she wanted with what she thought she *should* want. Hunter planned to get to the bottom of that contradiction ASAP.

"Damn it, don't keep doing this to me. Put up or shut up." She wriggled her ass, not in invitation but in challenge. "Sir."

So, she sought to lure him past his control and entice him to fuck her on her terms? Not happening, but damn if giving in and unleashing the full force of his lust on her wasn't tempting.

Immediately, he clamped down on the thought, ceased all movement, then whispered in her ear, "We can do this the easy way. You can be soft and submissive under me, and I'll make it worth your while. Or we can do this the hard way. I'll withdraw and tie you to the bed, and jack you up every hour on the hour, withholding your orgasm until I get my point across. But that's not what I want, honey."

He stroked down her abdomen . . . and lower, into the damp curls, grazing over her clit. She mewled. Her pussy tightened on his cock, and Hunter swore. His vicious need for her had sweat beading at his temples, all over his back. Hot blood scalded his veins. He fucking ached to pound Kata to their mutual satisfaction, but establishing control first was nonnegotiable. Once she submitted, they'd both be happier. Proving that to her was going to be a bitch.

"Damn it! Can't you just . . ." Whimpering, she thrust back on him, shoving him even deeper in her tight, silken clasp.

Only by literally biting his tongue did Hunter hold in a groan. Letting her know how good she felt, despite her disobedience, would only encourage her. "Don't push me."

"Or what?" Her voice was breathy, a heady combination of trepidation and demand, as she curled her hand around his neck, leaned back, and tugged his lips toward hers.

Hunter turned his head, refused her kiss. He'd answered her question, but she still tested him, trying in her way to top from the bottom. He wouldn't have it. "Spread your legs wider."

A long heartbeat passed before she complied. He breathed out, partially in relief, partially because the sight of her offering her body to him was flat-out one of the sexiest sights ever.

"Hold still. Don't move your hands. You may moan and scream my name, nothing else."

"I don't like your orders, damn it," she panted.

"I don't like your defiance. Final warning."

He held very still inside the hot grip of her cunt, dying to ease back, then slide deep, find that one spot that would send her reeling just for the sublime joy of hearing her shout his name. But he was prepared to punish her again if she disobeyed. She'd more than earned it. He was giving her a lot of latitude because she'd never submitted, and the last twenty-four hours would have exhausted even the hardiest of souls. He'd be lying, though, if he said the ec-stasy boiling in his balls and clawing up his cock wasn't strangling his good intentions.

She shuddered, hesitated. Then, finally, she nodded.

"Good. Bow your head."

If she refused, he'd already spelled out the *or else*.

"Bow my—" She sucked in a breath and tossed back her head, dark hair spilling all down her back. "No. I've given some, but that? I won't relinquish that much. I can't . . . be subservient."

Fuck. Slowly, he withdrew from her pussy.

"No!" She thrust back, fighting to keep him deep inside her. "Hunter."

Turning down that temptation almost killed him. He wanted to work deep inside her again, his balls pressed right to her wet pussy, tangle his fingers in the silky mass, inhale her scent as he listened to her whimpers become screams. But he didn't. Instead, Hunter fought for control as he brushed his knuckles over her clit in a soft, hyp-notic slide. He pressed his dick against her ass, grinding.

Kata glared at him over her shoulder, defiant.

Hunter lifted his fingers from her clit, stepped back, and crossed his arms over his chest. No matter how much his cock ached, he wasn't backing down. Her eyes simmered with fury, her lips pursed as if she was dying to spit acid at him. He braced for a long night.

"Apparently we're going to do this the hard way." Hunter shook his head and, in one quick stroke, tore off the condom. *Damn it to hell.*

She stood straight, her back stiffening. Eyes narrowed, she whirled to face him. He forced himself not to look at her heavy breasts, rosy brown nipples, and her traffic-stopping curves. Distraction now would only be detrimental.

"Bowing my head, are you serious? Why can't sex be equitable? Why can't we discuss what we both want, then do it together?"

Because she wanted his dominance as much as he wanted to give it to her. Her wet pussy proved that. She couldn't be satisfied until she submitted. Still, he never wanted her to think that he wasn't listening or didn't care for her needs.

"What did you have in mind?"

"First, sleep. I'm exhausted."

"If you could have simply complied with my commands—"

"Why should I? You don't own me."

He stiffened, then forced himself to relax. Kata would understand his possession soon enough. She knew the reasons he expected her compliance; he'd explained. Her protestations and questions were merely stall tactics. "All you had to say to stop me was 'Ben,' but you didn't. Care to tell me why?"

She sighed, her shoulders sagging. "I don't know. If you'll let me sleep first, maybe I'll be coherent enough to figure it out and I'll tell you."

Ah, the predictable dodging of the subject. So much easier for Kata than admitting that she was not only afraid to embrace what he ached to give her, but too aroused to turn it down.

As she bent and reached for her clothes, Hunter grabbed her by the shoulders and brought her body against his. "Listen, I will do whatever it takes to help you see who I am, what you are, and how great we'll be together. Get in the tub."

Kata glared at him, then turned to glance at the bathtub. Wisps of steam still rose from the water. He felt the tension leave her shoulders, signaling a modicum of surrender.

"Fine," she muttered. "But only because that bath looks heavenly."

Yes, and because she was finally learning that he wouldn't let her derail him. He also suspected that her arousal was beginning to overcome her reluctance. Her pussy was still throbbing; he'd bet money on that.

Hunter released her, and she made her way to the tub, sinking into the clear water with a sigh that went straight to his cock.

As she settled into the steaming bath, Hunter climbed in behind her, sitting on the wide ledge above. She stiffened and started to sputter something. Hunter silenced her by laying his palms on her shoulders and massaging away the tension. Seconds later, she turned to butter in his hands. He smiled.

"God, you're good at that," she moaned.

"If you're a good girl, you might find out what else I'm good at."

Kata shook her head. "You just don't let up, do you?"

"In case you hadn't guessed yet, I'm generally a relentless guy. You have to be, in my line of work."

Before she could say another word, he worked at a nasty knot just under her shoulder blade, then pressed his thumbs up either side of her spine until he reached her neck and began releasing the tightness there. Within minutes, she was totally limp under his hands.

"You always do something redeeming just when I'm ready to slap you," she mumbled.

He grinned as he reached for the soap. To his relief, Kata didn't protest when he lifted and washed each arm top and bottom, or when he gathered all the gloriously soft hair in his grip so he could soap up her back. After a quick rinse, he hopped out of the tub and leaned over her, urging her to lie back, then took hold of each leg and bent them at the knees until her feet rested flat on the bottom of the tub. In fact, she didn't have a hint of defiance left in her body as he gently smoothed the white bar and his hands across her abdomen, over her shoulders, and lingered on her breasts. Then he edged between her legs. As he'd suspected, she was soaking wet.

Suddenly, she gasped and pulled at his wrist. "I can do that."

Hunter didn't budge an inch. "Look at me." And he didn't say another word until she obeyed. "Get this through your head. I'm going to take care of you, Kata."

Biting her lip, she looked at him uncertainly. "It's not that I don't want you to touch me, but I'm capable of taking care of myself."

"I never doubted that. Tell me the real problem."

She looked down at his hand, still covering her pussy, claiming it. "That's so . . . intimate."

"Our relationship should be."

She looked away, seeming to search for a reply. "Hunter, getting comfortable with someone takes time. I can't just flip a switch inside me and be ready for whatever—"

"Time isn't the real stumbling block. Both people have to be open."

She hesitated a long time, then looked down. "And I'm not."

"Have I hurt you?"

"No."

"Would I?" he demanded.

"Physically, no. But you want more than that." Her gaze was earnest as it met his own. "Trusting someone with your body and trusting someone with your soul are two very different things."

"Agreed. But so far, you haven't truly trusted me with either. Or really tried."

Her eyes slammed shut. Pain pinched her brows. She struggled for a moment. Discomfort etched her face, and a part of him wanted to ease up on her. But he'd be sending the wrong message, and ultimately, not providing what she needed.

Finally, she let go of his wrist hovering over her parted thighs. Triumph slid through him.

Gently, he cleaned her slick female flesh. Kata closed her eyes. Her body remained tense, but she let him take over. When he'd finished, he moved back to massaging her neck, shoulders, mid-back until she wilted bonelessly.

At that moment, he pulled the plug from the tub and urged her to stand. She complied, her head lolling on his shoulder, granting him more trust than she'd ever given. His heart caught as he lifted her into his arms, out of the tub.

And right on cue, she asserted herself. "Hunter, this carrying me thing—"

"Is it really worth another argument?"

After a long moment, she sighed and sank back into his arms. A bit more progress. He smiled.

Hunter angled her through the doorway and back into Logan's room, dimly lit by one small bedside lamp. "Are you hungry? Thirsty?"

"No."

"Do you feel safe?"

Kata's black lashes fluttered over her pretty hazel eyes, and his heart stuttered again. What was it about this woman? Her independence? That she wouldn't give all of herself easily, but once she did, it would be *so* worth the battle? He didn't exactly know the answer, but he couldn't wait to find out. But she was, without a doubt, his.

"Yeah," she murmured huskily. "No one is getting in here, past you. I hate to admit it, but I probably wouldn't have been able to sleep alone at my own place. Thanks for watching over me. Though I don't appreciate the whole 'withholding orgasm' thing."

"We'll rectify that." He smiled. "Eventually. Rest for now."

Without another word, she grabbed the sheet and snuggled next to him, then drifted off to sleep. When she closed her eyes, when her brain shut off, she trusted him. Her back nestled against his chest as though she found his touch comforting. They fit together as though they were made for each other, missing puzzle pieces that had finally snapped into place.

Hunter released a shuddering, exhausted breath. No matter how tired he was, when he felt Kata warm and naked beside him, his cock stood at full staff. *Shit*. He glanced at the clock. Thirty-eight minutes until the hour. He set a vibrating alarm on his cell phone and closed his eyes.

No matter how soft and accepting Kata seemed now, this was going to be a damn long night.

* * *

KATA lay across the sheets like a sacrificial virgin, arms and legs spread, in the near dark. She could make out a shadow between her thighs. Male. Stark, intriguing face not quite visible. Tremendously wide shoulders blocked the rest of the room. Powerful hands glided over her thighs, up to her hips. She tingled everywhere he touched. Then he settled his palm *there*, and sensations converged into an unrelenting ache. He fueled it by rubbing his thumb, hot and relentless, over her clit.

She shifted restlessly, trying to capture more of the sensation. Desire multiplied, tightened, gathered like a tropical storm, swirling, growing. With a gasp, she reached out for something to anchor her, but found nothing. Certainly, there was no escape. He made sure she felt every skillful, slow touch of his hands . . . but never gave her enough to hurtle her into release.

More. Please! She moaned, her entire body thrashing in need.

He stopped, not moving a muscle, not persisting with that perfect attention to her clit. The sweet ache between her legs turned vicious.

Kata wanted to beg but couldn't speak. She wailed in frustration. As if he understood, he lavished attention on her clit again, harder, faster—the pressure precisely perfect to launch her into a supernova of an orgasm. Then he added to her sensory overload, slipping something inside her, prodding a spot that sent her careening faster and farther into a drowning pool of need.

Somewhere in the back of her hazy mind, she knew she was dreaming this unabashedly sexual fantasy, but it was too delicious to force herself to consciousness. Knowing it was all in her head, she opened her mind to the mounting pleasure. God, this dream man knew his way around her body, and wasn't that heavenly?

Her back arched, her body lifting and clenching as she thrashed madly, seeking that little bit extra she needed, exactly where she needed it. She was nearly there, so ready to explode. But he eased back, gave her a gentler touch, avoiding her most sensitive spots. A mewled protest rose up in her throat.

Damn, she wanted this—bad. For a dream, it was so vivid. She wanted to see her lover, ask him why he tormented her, beg for relief.

"Kata."

The whisper was as real as the breath hot against her breast.

She flung her eyes open. Hunter knelt between her legs, his big body casting a shadow over her, his stare hot, predatory. The buzz cut of his hair made what might have been a pretty face look harshly male, throwing every dip, plane, and jut into stark relief. His washboard abs tightened above his faded jeans. They were zipped but not snapped, giving her a tease of what was behind that bulge in his fly. She nearly swallowed her tongue. Desire bloomed fiercely inside her.

With an unrelenting stare, Hunter gripped her thighs, his hands pushing their way up her flesh, back to her very wet sex. His thumb toyed with her clit.

And Kata knew then that none of what she'd been feeling had been a dream. He'd brought her to the very verge of climax and left her there to ache and twist. Just as he'd vowed that he would.

She wanted to bite his damn head off, tell him to stop messing with her. But if she said anything of the sort, he'd take her defiance as a personal challenge. There'd be no orgasm in her future—immediate or otherwise. And Hunter had done his job, as she imagined he did all things, capably and well. Thanks to his expert touch, she *needed* what he could give her . . . if he chose to.

"Hunter?" She raised her hips to him, begging in the only way her pride and apprehension allowed.

Verbalizing how badly she ached for him left her exposed in a way mere nudity didn't. Admitting that she yearned to be covered, taken, powerless under his touch, seemed as smart as swimming with chum in shark-infested waters. Hunter was definitely capable of chewing through her resistance and eating her alive.

The wicked gleam in his eye, the half smile on his mouth, told her that he knew everything she felt and feared. "Want something, honey?"

Kata pressed her lips together. She was a big girl who could see to her own orgasm. She'd had plenty of practice.

But when she tried to lift her arm from above her head and slide it into her wet flesh, she found it cuffed to the bed. Attempting to move the other netted the same result. Fury and panic raced through her.

"You *tied* me to the bed?"

"Manacled, actually. They're fur-lined but made of steel, attached to chains, soldered into steel supports behind the headboard, and anchored into the studs in the wall."

In other words, she wasn't going anywhere until he was good and ready to let her go. Panic surged ahead of fury. But a fresh curl of arousal wasn't far behind. From the moment they'd met, Hunter had been trying to control her verbally, sexually. But now he was getting really serious. Manacles and chains and steel. *Oh my.*

"I'm not ready for this," she choked.

"Your body is. It's your mind that's fighting. We're going to get past that. And you've earned these punishments."

"So you've chained me to the bed and you're going to, what? Refuse to give me an orgasm?" The thought only made her crave it more.

"Every hour on the hour, until you cooperate. Just like I promised."

Oh, God. She already wanted him so badly, she was about to crawl out of her skin. How desperately would she need him by then? She didn't like being controlled this way. She didn't like being controlled, period. "Piss off."

"If that's what you want." Hunter leaned over her, supporting his weight on his elbows. "Or you can learn some compliance. Then you'll find I can be as accommodating as hell."

Kata felt the lethal spread of his chest over hers, his steely six-pack pressing into her belly. He nudged an erection of killer proportions between her spread thighs. Her clit burned with arousal. When she tried to close her legs and squeeze her thighs together, she found them tethered, too.

A gasp slipped from her lips. Her helplessness excited her even more. God, why did she find that so damn sexy?

Above her he smiled, a flash of disconcerting white in the near darkness. "Yes, your ankles are manacled, too, attached to chains, set in titanium supports under the floorboards. I helped Logan install them, so I know."

"You plan to keep me tied up until I give in?" Her pussy clenched at the thought.

"Nope. I want to make defiance unpleasant, but I don't get off on forcing a woman to do anything. Once the punishment is over, I'll release you. But since this all started with your refusal to cooperate, you can end it now by—"

"You mean my refusal to roll over and play dead?" she snapped.

Granted, she wasn't making a strong case for that orgasm she craved, but his I'm-all-big-and-bad routine, along with his mastery of her body, scared the crap out of her. This power-trip, steamroller shit was beginning to remind her too much of Gordon. If she gave an inch now, Hunter would take a hundred miles later.

"I want a submissive woman, not a well-trained dog. And my attempt to go slow and put you at ease is getting us nowhere."

"Get the hell o—oh!"

He drowned out her protest by laving her nipple with his tongue in a teasing glide, prodding the hard bud with his thumb. His nip was an electric jolt of pain, teeth to burning flesh, followed by a soothing lick. He paid similar homage to her other breast until both nipples felt swollen, alive with need. Kata wanted to hold out, throw his seduction back in his face . . . but she ended up arching to his mouth with another silent plea.

Hunter slid down her body, his lips gliding across the sensitive undersides of her breasts, caressing over her rib cage. His tongue dipped into her navel, swirling around as his humongous hands gripped her hips in a way she could only describe as possessive.

Kata swallowed. This "punishment" she'd supposedly earned felt more like Hunter wanting to overwhelm her senses to prove that he could command her at will.

Fear jolted her. "Why are you doing this to me?"

He froze, raised his laser-precise gaze to her. "What is it you think I'm doing?"

"Trying to show me that you're the man and can bend the little lady to your will, no matter how much you have to trample my independence or self-esteem. You may make me beg for an orgasm because, God knows, you've figured out exactly how to put my body in the palm of your hand. But in doing so, you're trying to steal my soul. And you can kiss my ass. I'm not giving it to you."

His brows shot up. He looked affronted, then considering. Finally, concern settled into the sharp angles of his face. "Honey, you're still not getting it. I'm not doing this *to* you. I'm doing it *for* us. We can't really be together until you're honest with me and with yourself. Your body craves domination, takes to it like surrender is the most natural thing in the world. It's your head getting in the way. God knows, I've made myself clear enough that I want to be the man who grants all your fantasies for the rest of your life. But you persist in thinking that I'm trying to belittle you and break you down, rather than build *us* up. You couldn't be more wrong. Explain."

He punctuated his demand by nuzzling his lips across her low belly, then followed with another nip of teeth . . . at the same moment he brushed his fingertips across her clit. The combination of pleasure and pain was nothing short of hypnotic, cajoling.

Panic, anger, and fear collided, compounded by this dangerous arousal. Regardless of his little speech, Kata felt overtaken. Hunter had nearly crushed her free will by hurtling her to the very edge of desire again and again. She bucked, trying to dislodge him. He wasn't moving an inch.

Really, she should refuse to bend, keep him in the dark. Except that he was relentless enough to keep her manacled to this bed until she told him everything. If he wanted the shitload of 411, that was his stupid mistake.

"I'll tell you why. Did I ever mention that my mother isn't allowed to choose her own clothing every day? Gordon insists on doing it for her."

Hunter's brows shot up, and he shrugged. "If they're a Dominant/submissive couple, that's not uncommon. I don't want a twenty-four/seven slave like that, but some Doms—"

"I don't know if he's a Dom. Even if he is, the real problem is that he's an asshole. Every day for the past dozen years he's been telling my mother that she could look better. He started by picking her jewelry, because, according to him, he has an innate talent for such things, which she lacked. Then he started choosing her shoes, then shirts, skirts, pants. Now she doesn't wear a stitch without consulting him because he's convinced her that she's a train wreck without him."

Even in shadow, she saw the concern deepen on Hunter's face. "Kata, I—"

"No!" How *dare* he suffer remorse now for pushing her to talk. He wanted this Pandora's box opened, so he'd better deal. "That was just the beginning. He cut her off from all her friends, scheduling conflicting events, inventing 'crises' whenever she had plans to go out. Soon, even the friends who'd stood by her after my dad died, fell by the wayside. So Gordon convinced her that he was a better friend than all of them put together. She'd had a great career as an OR nurse, but five years ago, she and the surgeon lost a little boy on the operating table. My mom was crushed. You know what Gordon said? Maybe she wasn't as talented as she'd thought, and that everyone would be better served if she stayed home. She fucking loved that job. Poof, it was gone. He's made her too afraid to pursue getting another. Her driver's license expired, and he's been dragging his feet for two years to take her to have it renewed."

"You're right; he is an asshole," he said softly.

Kata paused, stared at him in the dark. It wasn't a line. He sincerely meant that. Somehow, all the jumble of anger, panic, and desire that had been biting her morphed into grief. Tears stung her eyes.

"Gordon calls *all* the shots. Since about the time I began driving, Mom hasn't been the same woman I grew up with. She's afraid to *breathe* without precious Gordon's permission. She's a . . . shell. Then three years a-ago . . ."

Hot tears rolled down Kata's face. She tried to wipe them away, then realized the manacles made that impossible. Helplessness and impotent anger infuriated her all over again. God, what her mother must go through . . .

Kata paused, unable to relive the horror of the night everything had spiraled down the proverbial toilet of life. Hunter had only wanted her to vomit up the painful past so that he could unravel her. But she was already there, feeling a hairsbreadth away from giving in to something that could destroy her.

Granted, Hunter hadn't belittled her. She prayed he would see why the amount of control he wanted to exert over her life scared the hell out of her and stop trying to make her surrender her soul.

"Three years ago . . . ?" he prompted, wiping her tears away.

Kata slammed her eyes shut. As she pictured how that sentence ended, a sob buckled her chest with the horror her family lived with each and every day. The pity, the pain. No way she was sharing that so Hunter could rip her wide-open and make her even more vulnerable to him.

"Stop! God knows that, all trussed up like this, you can do whatever the hell you want with me, and I can't stop you. You'll probably even make me like it, but I—I'm done talking."

"Okay. Shh." Hunter kissed her forehead, caressed her cheek. "Thank you for sharing your mother's situation with me. I appreciate the courage and trust that required." His voice, surprisingly tender, soothed her. "I understand better, I think. You're afraid that my wanting to control you in bed will spill to the rest of your life. Before me, you'd never spent ten minutes with a Dom. Clearly, you've been through a lot with Gordon. Your fear is fair."

Of all the things he might have said, that surprised her most. And incited more tears. "You're not bullshitting me?"

"No. We married quickly, and you don't know me well yet. From your perspective, I took advantage of a drunk woman by hustling you to the altar, spent the night with you, and chased you to your hometown when you wanted space. When danger came your way, I ordered you not to return to work, which I'm guessing felt a lot like something Gordon would demand." He cocked his head in thought. "Then I suppose you think I dragged you to Dallas, away from your family and friends, so I could isolate you. I got in your panties and your head until you gave me the information I needed so I could somehow use it against you. Do I have it right?"

Her eyes watered over again. She wanted to believe it was nothing more than exhaustion and a decided lack of the orgasm she'd so desperately craved. Or that her damn eyes leaked because she'd dredged up so much stuff about her mom that she usually shoved way down. But mostly, it was Hunter. He was so insightful, actually able to see the situation from a point of view other than his own.

Wow. She wasn't used to that.

"Right now, you don't seem like the kind of dickhead who makes himself feel better by making others feel worse." She sniffed, paused, still thinking through her reply. He was trying hard to be fair; she needed to do the same. "I know that, though stupid and drunken, getting married was my idea. I have no doubt after having a bullet whiz a quarter inch from my face that the danger I'm in is real. I'd escaped him, yeah." It pained her to admit this. "He would probably have found me again pretty quickly. I know you alpha males can't fathom not protecting your woman or whatever. I admit that I don't know the first thing about hiding from an assassin."

"But?"

Damn if the concern in his prompt didn't start the tears again. "I don't think I can deal with you always trying to get in my head. Fun, casual, *normal* sex—yes. But what you want . . ."

"The intense bond of people who fuck not just with their bodies for the sake of orgasm, but with their minds and hearts to share the ultimate pleasure? Who give themselves to each other so completely that you and I become an *us* that's so solid, nothing can ever shake it? You don't want that?"

Kata couldn't look away from his solemn, unwavering stare, half-hidden in the gray shadows. She trembled from head to toe.

When he described the relationship he saw, it sounded so beautiful. But so not real. Wasn't that, like, a Hallmark card or a Lifetime movie? "Not when it starts with you ordering me around. I—I can't . . ."

"You're not the kind of woman who runs from herself. I refuse to believe that, rather than face me and your fears, you'd prefer tepid orgasms with someone like Ben, who will never fulfill you or truly earn your love."

She wasn't a coward. She already knew she couldn't go back to Ben. He'd propositioned her three times since she'd breezed into his hotel room—had that been just this morning?—and she hadn't hesitated to turn him down.

"You can't tell me you've had that sort of relationship with every woman who's ever submitted to you."

"You're right." He sighed. "You are the first one. The only one."

Those words touched her, despite the danger they represented. And the goddamn tears just wouldn't stop. Hunter had broken something open inside her. Even last night she'd wanted what he seemed to be offering, but now that he'd laid it out on the table so totally? She wanted it more. Desperately. Even though it terrified her.

And cue more tears. *Damn it.*

"Honey, trust me. I'm not Gordon. When something is bothering you, we'll talk about it. I want to know how you feel and what's on your mind." He sighed and swept the hair back from her face with gentle palms. "Too many Doms want some sweet little sub who won't give them any challenge. I could pick up the phone now and call any one of the dozens of such subs I know. But your submission is only as good as my dominance. It's your vitality and your passion I want, and your full life contributes to those. Under normal circumstances, I would never interfere with your job or your friends. If I ever behave like Gordon, you have my permission to string me up by the balls. I want to master your body, not put a lockdown on your life."

Really?

Kata bit her lip as she stared up into his hard male face, his eyes so blue in the semidarkness. He met her, moment for moment, not blinking. Not rushing her. His words bounced around in her head.

Hunter had spelled out the situation perfectly. Now she had to decide: return to her casual lovers and sex with them that meant nothing, or submit?

Chapter Ten

"ALL right." Releasing a harsh breath, Kata sent him a jerky nod. "If you don't overwhelm me too much, I'll try to submit to you."

He smiled. "Not to sound too much like Yoda, but 'do or do not; there is no try.'"

Yeah, Hunter was an all or nothing guy. And so far, she'd done everything halfway. If she wanted this, wanted to find out if he was really going to fill that empty, aching need in her that had never been quite satisfied, she was going to have to cooperate. Hunter couldn't give her that elusive, ultimate satisfaction if she didn't let him.

"Okay." She swallowed. "I'll do it."

Satisfaction settled into his stark features. "Thank you."

That look suffused her with pleasure. Normally, she wouldn't give a shit what any guy thought. Gordon had rearranged her wiring so that she didn't go out of her way to please any male. For some reason, Hunter was different. Yes, he was often pushy and unyielding, which sometimes translated to teeth-gritting annoyance. But he didn't appear to command her simply for the sake of pumping up whatever chest-thumping, knuckle-dragging caveman lived inside him. He had a purpose. And if she wanted more of his smiles, affection, and sugary-perfect touch—and that orgasm he'd been withholding—she was going to have to rein in her temper.

He brushed her cheek with a tender caress, settled his mouth over hers. Her thoughts scattered. His kiss drifted over her lips, softer than a whisper but with more impact than a sledgehammer. She drew in a shaky breath. An ache bled through her chest, until her nipples peaked again. This feeling went beyond a mere craving for his touch to an insane desire to be meaningful to him. It speared her heart, the terrifying yearning for all of him to merge with all of her.

Because she wanted it so badly, Kata realized that Hunter was holding himself back.

She raised her head, as much as the manacles allowed, and fused their mouths together in another silent plea. She opened to him, arched to him, told him in a thousand subtle ways that he was welcome.

Instead of taking what she offered, he eased back and stared at her as if she were a puzzle to solve. Lying naked under the muted, grayish light, prisoner to his perceptive gaze, made her so aware of her own skin, of the ceiling fan's cool breeze brushing her exposed nipples, the swollen, wet flesh between her legs. Manacled, open, she could hide nothing. Instead of squirming with the usual discomfort, more blood swelled her nipples and her clit pulsed under her skin.

His gaze was intimate. Ravenous. A thick ridge of cock stood behind the fly of his low-slung jeans. The fact that seeing her all spread out revved him up gave Kata a ridiculous thrill. She arched, thrusting her breasts out, silently offering what she so badly needed him to take.

As if he read her mind, Hunter ran a finger over the hard point of her nipple, down her belly, into her wet pussy. Light, toying, teasing, every touch was designed to take her up higher. A new ripple of pleasure crashed over her.

"What do you want, honey? Tell me."

His body on hers, every inch of that erection tenting his jeans deep inside her while they strained together for a mutually amazing climax.

She lifted her hips to him in silent invitation, hoping he'd get the hint.

His gaze dipped lower, right between her legs, but he didn't move toward her.

"Kata," his tone warned. "Any good Dom/sub relationship starts with clear communication." His phone dinged with a reminder alarm in the charged room. He leveled a heavy stare her way. "Top of the hour, honey. Time for another punishment. Tell me what you want or brace yourself."

That calm, unblinking stare of his unnerved her. How did you tell a man so full of control and command that you wanted him to do his worst, even if it scared you senseless? He *knew* all this. Why did she have to make herself more vulnerable?

"I—I . . ." *Am so afraid.*

"All right, then. Pity." As he opened the drawers of the nightstand, his jaw clenched. No mistaking his disappointment, edged in anger.

That didn't bode well for a quick orgasm. And some part of her really hated to disappoint him.

"Wait!" she gasped. "If you want me to admit that I'm hot for you, I am. Totally."

He shook his head, no longer even looking at her. Instead, he prowled through the drawers of the nightstand. "I can see that by looking at your hard nipples and your wet pussy. I didn't ask what you felt. I asked what you *wanted*."

Crap. He'd given her another chance, and she'd blown it with her reticence and her big mouth. Why was it so hard to admit her feelings and desires to him? Why did it feel too revealing? Gordon . . . and her mother. Their twisted relationship terrified her. But would Hunter really throw her feelings back in her face, use them against her? Or was she just too afraid to find out because baring her feelings gave him so much power?

Wincing at the ugly truth, Kata watched his quick, precise movements. The displeasure on his face was like a stab to the heart. And she had an inkling that whatever he was doing in that drawer would light up the ache in her unsatisfied body, quickly eclipsing any mental discomfort she would suffer by being honest.

"Hunter, you're right. I'm sorry. *Please.*" Kata willed him to look at her. He didn't. "This is hard for me."

He sighed, looked her way. "I know. What's happening is unfamiliar and uncomfortable. I've taken that into account. My problem is, you're still trying to submit on your terms. I won't let that happen, honey."

He trailed his fingers through her drenched folds. She gasped at the immediate resurgence of pleasure. He could make her want him so easily, so completely. That unnerved her to the core.

"Your body wants this." He drilled a serious blue stare into her, as if willing her to understand. "Now your mind must accept it. I see a submissive's need to be taken and to please on your face, but your fear is in our way."

Kata wanted so badly to tell him that he was wrong. But she'd be lying. As his thumb grazed her clit again, need jolted her entire body. She arched to him, trying to increase the pressure on her little bundle of nerves.

He withdrew his hand from her needy flesh, then began taking items from the nightstand and placing them above her head, just out of her line of sight. "Let's see if we can get you past that."

She broke out in a cold sweat. Handing the key to unlock her body—and her heart—to someone as alpha and ruthless as Hunter scared her. But if she didn't truly submit, what did she have to look forward to when Hunter was gone except more meaningless flings?

"I want you," she blurted. "I want you to do anything. Everything . . . even though it terrifies me."

A smile eased the harshness from his face. "Good girl."

He understood. Thank God. She released the breath she'd been holding. "So what are you going to do?"

Instantly, his stare turned thunderous—and made her shiver. "That's for me to decide. And for you to take without comment or complaint. Because you *trust* me."

Kata bit her lip. Her first urge was to tell him to go to hell. She swallowed it. As much as being bound and helpless disturbed her independent nature, she couldn't deny that her body loved it . . . and craved him.

What would it be like to give herself completely—no worries, no responsibilities or fears—over to him for a night? If the only thing in the world that mattered was the connection between them? That seductive thought whispered her name, a terrifying pleasure drug waiting to become addictive.

Hunter stood at the side of the bed and did nothing more than watch and wait as thoughts pinged through her head.

"I'm sorry," she finally whispered into the silence. "Please, don't stop."

He sent her a curt nod, then grabbed one of the items he'd placed on the mattress above her head. The crinkle of plastic filled her ears. He drew in a deep breath of anticipation, his chest lifting, looking lethally strong. Kata was dying to know what he planned to do but didn't ask. It would only prolong an argument her body knew she was going to lose.

He bent and sucked a nipple into his mouth. Immediately, heat assailed her, and the little bud tightened almost painfully. Moisture gushed from her, slicking her folds even more. Straightening, he lowered his gaze squarely to her pussy and rubbed a pair of fingers right over the slick hood of her clit. Sensation struck her like lightning. She bucked, arched. Moaned.

"Hunter . . ."

"Who am I in bed?"

No way she could hold back her reply. "Sir. Please."

"Good. Ever been clamped, honey?" He set his mouth on her other nipple, still looking her way.

And she watched his mouth move over her, working her, his cheeks concave, his teeth gently nipping until she moaned.

Then he nipped harder. "I asked you a question."

Since she wasn't exactly sure what he meant, she figured she had the answer. "No." At his raised brow, she added a hasty, "Sir."

A ghost of a grin broke across that gorgeous male mouth. "I'm looking forward to this. Remember, if this is too painful, just say 'Ben.' Otherwise, no complaining. No coming."

No coming, still? Kata whimpered.

Hunter ignored her and lifted his hand to her breasts, hovering above her nipple. He pinched something between his fingers then lowered it.

Oh shit. Nipple clamps.

Tight and vicious, they sank their teeth into her tender flesh, and she cried out. Dizzying pain—at first. It blurred quickly into searing, fiery pleasure.

Her nipples soon felt swollen to twice their normal size. Her skin tingled, electric and alive, unlike anything she'd ever felt. More moisture seeped from her pussy. She fisted her hands. "Hunter!" She gulped. "Sir."

"Better," he praised as his fingers surrounded the clamps and gave them a light twist. "You like it?"

Yes, yes, yes. Kata couldn't withhold the truth. "I do."

"Excellent. Do you want me to fuck you?" He gave the clamps another pinch and twist.

She hadn't imagined that her nipples could throb as badly as her clit, but now they felt connected by an invisible wire, each jumping anytime the others were touched. His every move brought her to the edge of pleasure and pain, and knowing that she couldn't do a damn thing about it was one of the biggest turn-ons of her life. That had to make her twenty kinds of sick in the head. She'd never thought that she'd get off on being bent to any guy's will. But somehow, Hunter made that work for her.

"What do you think?" she cried out. "Of course I want you to fuck me!"

All softness left his face. The arctic was downright balmy compared to this stare. "I would have preferred a polite 'Yes, Sir.'"

No doubt. And as lousy a job as she was doing curbing her tongue, it could be another decade before he allowed her to get off.

"Yes, Sir." She swallowed down her impatience . . . at least as much as she could.

Hunter laughed. "Even when you say the right words, the tone is still so much closer to 'fuck off.' Curbing your sass is going to be a long-term project."

And likely one doomed to failure. "Damn it, I'm trying."

"Silence." A moment later, he raised his hand and slapped his fingers down on the pad of her pussy.

Oh. My. God. Her head told her that she should feel degraded. Infuriated, at least. But no. Fire spread through her. Tingles danced behind her clit. She gasped. Desire grew to a seething, throbbing ache, magnified until every beat of her heart was echoed between her legs.

"W-what are you doing to me?" she wailed.

He swiped a finger through her sopping flesh, then lifted a glistening finger. "Are you going to try to tell me that you didn't like it?"

Now he was taunting her. She bit her lip, holding her response inside.

Hunter sat at the edge of the bed. "We're not going to make any progress until you start being honest with me—and yourself. Right now, I have all the patience in the world. How about you?"

Kata had reached the end of her rope—and he knew it. Hunter wasn't like Ben or any other guy she'd dated. She couldn't manipulate him with a pout or a sexy look. Damn it, he'd dug into her psyche and learned all her fears, her darkest secrets and wants. He was arousing her more than any man ever had. Still, she had no doubt he'd hold out on her until she lost the attitude and submitted with honesty.

Her need only grew worse when he dropped his jeans.

Oh dear God. Tall, broad, those shoulders nearly as wide as the doorframe behind him. And his cock stood thick, tall, ready. She couldn't tear her eyes away, wanted him so badly she didn't know how she'd stand even another ten seconds without him working his way inside her. When he took her, he did it with a single-minded determination that made her feel so desirable and special—something she'd never had before. Something she needed now.

"Please, Sir. I can't take much more."

"Hmm," he mused aloud. "We're getting closer. But there's still a lot of starch in your spine."

Already, he'd trashed through so much of the electrified barbed wire and GET THE FUCK OUT signs around her defenses. But Hunter had made it perfectly clear that he wasn't resting until she gave every part of her submission, her soul. She must put her tongue on lockdown in order to relieve this seething, burning desire eating her alive.

She swallowed her anger. "No . . . Sir. No starch."

"I've been reading submissives for a dozen years. I know your signals. In your head, you're trying to figure out how you can placate me to get what you want, not how to please me so I give you what you need."

Kata felt more exposed than she'd ever been . . . but he was right. One look at his implacable face told her that he wasn't going to let this go.

His challenging stare scraped her raw. She closed her eyes. "I'm doing my best to open up. Sir."

Hunter sat at the edge of the bed and rubbed the back of his knuckles over her breasts. "I realize that I've breached your comfort zone, and that, given your family dynamic, this isn't easy for you. You haven't come close to giving me everything, but you've given a lot. Wars aren't fought in a day." He smiled. "At least you're being honest and polite now. I'll reward that."

Hunter slid his body over hers, everything about him heart-stoppingly male. He kissed her with a desperate edge, under control . . . but just barely. Somehow, that made her feel better. Slightly mollified, she blanked her mind and allowed herself to drown in his kiss.

It went on forever. He angled his head to deepen the penetration of his mouth, his tongue stealing inside and raiding every bit of her breath and resistance. His hands gripped the sides of her face, keeping her exactly where he wanted her as he took—and gave. His kiss tasted of sweet comfort, even as it overwhelmed her with the spice of desire. His devotion flooded her next, a tangy aphrodisiac that lured her deeper.

From the first, Hunter had affected her like no other man. Now, he proved over and over that, for her, he was different. Special.

If they ended this crazy, spontaneous marriage, would any other man ever do again? They'd shared a bed only a few times, and already she felt wrapped up in him, desperate to soak in his determination and the ecstasy he gave her. Aching to give herself utterly to him. She shut out the voice inside her that was still trying to scream in protest and sank into his embrace.

Hunter lifted his head, looked down at her through the shadows. "Better." Firm with demand, his lips took hers again with a dark, lingering insistence. When she responded in kind, without closing anything off from him, he moaned. "Incredible."

His praise suffused a glow all through her. Just by being totally in the moment with him, she'd pleased him. After spending so long not giving a shit what anyone but her mother thought, that felt good. Scary still, but sublime.

He made his way down her body, pausing to lap at her nipples around the clamps. The dizzying pleasure/pain scattered the gentle glow of the last few moments, slamming her with a craving so strong, it seized her breath. Intense. Gripping. Impossible to ignore.

"Hunter . . ."

"I know, honey. These will come off soon. And you'll scream like you never have. So fucking sexy. I can't wait."

His words were an erotic riptide, sucking her under even deeper. Drowning was inevitable, and the anticipation made her shudder.

Then he eased down her body, his mouth drifting so, so softly over her stomach. A lap here, a nip there, awakening her even more. Kata's entire body clenched. Her yearning to put her fingers in the short strands of his hair, feel him alive and warm under her hands, assailed her like an addict craving his drug of choice.

"Free my hands. Please."

Hunter shook his head, his thumbs brushing her erect nipples so softly, a breathless madness closed in on her. "The control is mine. This is you trusting me to give you what you need, to push you farther than you think you can stand and still make you love it."

Kata arched, head tossed back, as she tried to endure his torment. But her body had become one giant ache that knew only the need for his possession.

His hand drifted down her stomach, into the wet curls between her legs. "Hmm, so wet and swollen. You might struggle to understand what's happening between us, but when I touch you, I *know* your body is on board."

He dragged his thumb over her clit again. A second later, he followed with a wicked slide of his tongue over the little bundle. She moaned, and he repeated the motion until her hips thrashed, until she cried out with a constant mewl of need.

"No coming until I say so," he reminded.

She snapped her head from side to side in a silent scream of denial. After all the kissing, the touching, the repeated ramp-ups and cooldowns, her body was beyond primed. "I . . . can't stop it."

"You're strong. You can. I'll release you at the right time. Just trust me."

He pressed two fingers inside her, then dragged fresh moisture over her sensitive little nub, rubbing in an unceasing, endless circle that completely unraveled her. His tongue followed once more, a hot lash that damn near destroyed her. Kata stopped breathing, stopped thinking. Every muscle in her body tensed with effort to stave off the inevitable. But oh . . . holding this orgasm at bay felt like trying to stop an avalanche with a paper plate.

"What will you give me tonight, honey?"

"Everything." The ache for release screeched under her skin, and she whimpered with need.

"How badly do you want to come for me?"

God, he wanted her to beg. "I've never felt so . . . on fire. It's like"—she panted—"an exquisite pain. Please, Hunter. Sir. Please."

"You're fucking gorgeous, honey. Are you on birth control?"

"Yes." Please let that mean he intended to fuck her now.

He paused, his fingers unmoving, and her entire body seized up. *No!*

"Because of Ben?"

The question slammed across her brain. Was he jealous? Would he punish her again by leaving her to ache and burn even more?

"The truth," he demanded as he shimmied up her body, his hot body pressed against her side, flaying her with heat. "Now."

"No. Irregular cycle. Since I was fourteen."

"You're clean?"

She gave him a jerky nod. In truth, she'd never had sex without a condom, but with the broiling heat of his cock hovering like a promise and a threat above her throbbing clit, she found it too hard to speak.

"Answer me."

"Yes . . . Sir," she choked out.

"Excellent. You're doing really well, your gorgeous skin all warm and damp and flushed." His hot breath caressed her ear. A shiver scratched down her spine. "Do you trust me?"

A dozen smart-ass replies died a fiery death before she whimpered, "Yes, Sir."

He smiled as he removed both clamps on her nipples at once. Blood rushed back in, the flood painful and yet . . . She screamed with the cacophony of sensation assailing her.

"That's it." He eased aside and settled his fingers back on her clit and circled the responsive flesh mercilessly.

The sting in her nipples converged with the fireball between her legs. Oh God, she couldn't stop it. The orgasm was headed her way like a freight train with no brakes, a steamroller with no off button, a supernova about to burst across space.

"Come!" he demanded.

With that one word, ecstasy climbed even more, a pleasure beyond her every fantasy, exploding across her senses, absorbing her in the earthy musk of cotton and sex, the deep timbre of his command ricocheting inside her, the salty tang of his sweat rolling down his neck, the sight of his demanding gaze electric with approval.

As the Mount Everest–sized peak broke over her and she struggled for breath, the blistering heat of Hunter's skin seared the insides of her thighs. Shaking, keening, trying desperately to grab the headboard in her hands, Kata could only watch in helpless thrall as Hunter fit the head of his bare cock to her opening and shoved into her spasming sex.

She screamed, her back bowing at his entrance—a conquest without mercy, he compelled her surrender. It should have hurt, she thought vaguely. Instead, she welcomed his invasion as his hard flesh scraped along every brilliantly alive nerve ending inside her.

The climax grew, swelled. Hunter gritted his teeth and planted his elbows on either side of her head, gripping the headboard for leverage as he slammed into her. Then he did it again and again in a rapid rhythm. Every stroke sent her up higher, and she shouted in pleasure—for him.

"Yes, honey. Fuck yes!" He grunted out between gritted teeth. "That's it."

Every time Kata thought she'd catch her breath, Hunter was there to steal it, his body keeping her rolling between one incredible peak and the next, his mouth slamming down on hers as his tongue took possession and demanded all she had to give.

She lifted to him, everything inside her reaching for him, meeting him, feeling like . . . one with him. Whatever this was, it in no way resembled mere sex. This transcended pleasure, became pure energy and connection and . . . God, she could barely put words to the dazzling, overwhelming sensations.

Kata knew in that moment that this man had changed her forever.

Hunter tore his mouth away, the breakneck speed of his thrusts steady as he fused his stare to hers, his eyes so blue in his flushed male face. Sweat dripped from his temples. Every muscle in his shoulders bunched with the effort of each thrust. The cords in his neck strained with every slide deep against her cervix.

"Again," he demanded. "Come with me now."

God, once she'd started climaxing, she'd never stopped. But when he swelled inside her, Kata's breath caught. He bit her shoulder, groaning against her skin, and shuddered above her. A flood of heat scorched deep inside her, sending her over another cliff with a scream.

"Hunter!"

Fire poured through her all over again. As he drove deep, his pace slowed until every measured glide against her wet flesh was a pleasure all its own. Her body convulsed again. She gave a last wail and went limp against him.

Moments later, he shifted. She heard a snap, then a click. Her wrists were free. He spent a long minute massaging each with strong hands, trailing kisses across her shoulder, her cheeks. Wearily, she closed her eyes and snuggled against him in contentment as he petted her softly.

"Put your arms around me," Hunter requested. His voice sounded deeper, gravelly, almost desperate. "Will you?"

Their gazes met in the shadows. A zing of awareness burst over her. He'd been as affected by their lovemaking as she'd been. Inside, she sang chorus and verse of *Hallelujah*.

Hunter lifted a shaking hand to her face, caressing a stray curl from her cheek. "Please."

Wow, after that, no way she could deny him a simple embrace—or anything, she feared.

Lifting her heavy arms, Kata wound them around his neck, pressing her fingers into his shoulders, her body so close to his. And God, more tears welled up. He'd shaken everything inside her, forever ruined her for anything simple or casual, for anyone other than him.

"Kata," he murmured, his voice more like a growl. "You have to know . . . I love you."

Those words sent a shock wave through her. She gasped, her eyes going wide. Love? In less than thirty-six hours? Insane. Unheard of.

Her heart stuttered, lurched. Unfortunately, she feared she wasn't too far behind.

"You don't have to say anything right now," he whispered, his mouth lifting in an exhausted smile. "That look tells me everything I need to know."

Kata knew what he saw—a woman on the precipice of losing her heart. It scared the hell out of her. She'd rather give a public speech to millions just before she jumped off a skyscraper with no safety net. But she didn't think even fear was going to stop this plunge.

She swallowed, hid her face in his neck, but even then she was surrounded by his musk, his sweat, his strength. And as he caressed her hair, lips whispering over her temple, she felt his love most of all.

A shrill ring sliced through the breathless silence. Hunter cursed and leaned toward the nightstand, refusing to withdraw from her body. That meaning wasn't lost on her.

He glared at the display. A scowl tightened his face, and he cursed again, longer, uglier. "Barnes. What?"

This close to Hunter, Kata couldn't help but overhear the conversation. "I know you're on leave, buddy, but we just received critical intel. You know that development we discussed about your last mission? We have a problem."

Chapter Eleven

"KATA?" Hunter reached across the cab of the truck to caress her shoulder.

She pulled away and looked out the passenger-side window.

Son. Of. A bitch.

Jerking his hand back, Hunter wrapped it around the steering wheel of Tyler's truck as he drove east into the rising sun. The last thing he wanted to do while on leave and this spontaneous "honeymoon" was to report for duty, especially after coaxing Kata's stunning surrender. She'd also revealed sensitive information about her family. Now, with his pending departure, she probably felt abandoned. But he and Barnes and other members of SEAL Team 4 had spent years trying to take down Venezuelan prick Víctor Sotillo and his arms-dealing gang. If there was even a chance that the prick's brother, Adan, had reorganized the group after Víctor's demise and was trying to do a big deal with his Iranian contacts in the next twenty-four hours, then Hunter had to do whatever necessary to stop them, hopefully for good.

So he'd promised Barnes that, after returning his wife to Lafayette, he'd be on a plane to the base in Virginia Beach by noon. No
doubt, he'd be out of the country before nightfall.

Beside him, Kata looked shell-shocked and hurt. All his plans
to make her safe, well sated, and head over heels in love had swirled
down the toilet with that one call. *Fuck.*

His timetable to persuade Kata to fall for him would run even
shorter now that he had to take an unexpected detour to a jungle
shithole. He heard the damn ticking clock in his head. Worse, he'd
blurted out his feelings before she was ready to hear them. And this
morning, all her defenses seemed to be back in place. Hunter began
to wonder . . . He might be able to compel her body, but her heart?
The sinking dread in his gut warned him that this might be one mission he couldn't complete in time. Her stepfather had fucked up her
psyche good. The question was, how could he fly a continent away
to fight tangos, then heal her during the precious little time of his
remaining leave so she could be free to love? It sounded fucking
impossible, but Hunter refused to give up.

"You okay, honey?" He reached across the cab of the truck to
grab her hand.

"Where are you taking me?" She tensed and tried to tug away.

Hunter held firm. "Back to Lafayette. I'm hoping to be gone
two days, three at most. While you're there, you'll be guarded by
friends, men I have no doubt will do everything possible to protect you."

Kata scowled at him. "You're dumping me on your buddies'
doorsteps and asking them to *babysit*? Hell no. I'll get some of my
cop friends—"

"We've already discussed this. With your assassin killed so quickly
in jail, we don't know if we can trust the police. I usually only dominate in the bedroom, but when it comes to your safety, all bets are off.
While you showered, I made some phone calls." This part pissed him
off most, and there wasn't a damn thing he could do about it. "You'll
stay with Tyler for the first day or two."

"Tyler? The flirty beefcake who called me 'baby'?"

Hunter strangled the steering wheel, wishing it were Tyler's neck. "Yes. He's a former detective who's done some bodyguard work. He'll keep you safe. I'd rather leave you with Deke, but my sister went into labor about two this morning."

Which was a fucking shame. Not only would he miss the birth of his niece or nephew, but the worry that Tyler was hitting on Kata would be niggling in the back of his mind. His brother-in-law would never touch her. Hunter had no such warm fuzzy about Tyler.

"I'm happy for Kimber, but—"

"Jack Cole is due home tomorrow night, so he'll relieve Tyler of duty. Jack is the best." And the guy was so deliriously in love with his gorgeous submissive wife that he'd barely notice Kata was female.

"I know you're trying to keep me safe, but I don't know any of these people. I wouldn't be comfortable camping out at their place and having them hover. There must be another way."

He leveled a stern stare her way. "I'm going to be halfway around the world, up to my eyeballs in terrorists and their illegal shit. I'll be more focused if I know you're with professionals who can and will do whatever necessary to protect you. I get that it's awkward, but I need to know that you're safe while I'm gone."

She leveled a *get-real* glare at him. "In other words, do what I say or I might be so unfocused that I'll die? That's blackmail."

Hunter flashed her a grin. "Is it working?"

"Ugh! You annoying son of a . . ." She shook her head, glossy black curls skimming her back. "Fine. I'll stay with your pals for a few days."

He squeezed her hand, smoothing his thumb over her knuckles. "When I come back, I'll have a bit of leave left. We'll work on us. I want to meet your parents, help you with your concerns. I want you to feel free to give yourself to me without fears or worries."

Kata yanked her hand from his grasp. When Hunter slanted a glance at her tight face and downcast gaze, his guts seized up. *Uh-oh.*

"What's on your mind, honey?"

"I saw your brother's living room, if that's what you want to call it. That hardly put me at ease. What the hell? Is regular dating just too bland for you guys?"

Hunter had dreaded this discussion. As he'd led her through the predawn shadows of Logan's living room, she'd finally gotten a first-hand peek. No sofas or big screens for his younger brother. Instead, a St. Andrew's cross, a spanking bench, a restraint table, spreader bars, and chains dangling from the ceiling beams filled the space.

To a woman terrified of giving up control, Logan's living room would be a nightmare. Hunter's thoughts whirled as he tried to figure out how the hell he could do damage control.

"So Logan and I are both dominant. His décor has nothing to do with you and me."

"Are you going to try to tell me that you've never used any of that equipment?"

No, he was well versed, and she was too astute not to know it. "I prefer restraint tables and spanking benches. Not as fond of the crosses." He shrugged. "But it doesn't matter what I use. I'd never hurt you."

"You'd just restrain me and do whatever the hell you wanted so you could turn me inside out. Both you and your brother are intent on locking down the women in your lives. What the hell is that about?"

He'd already explained his need to protect and sate her . . . yet push her to take all of him in any way he felt necessary to truly connect them. He'd been over this—and over and over it. He definitely wasn't going to explain that he'd discovered BDSM the summer after his mother's desertion. Okay, so the two were probably linked, but at this point, why explain it? It was what it was.

"That *was* you screaming in my ear a few hours ago while I restrained and satisfied you, right?" Hunter challenged her. "Did you think, for even one minute, that I was going to force any act on you that your body didn't fully respond to?"

"No, but my body and my brain are having one hell of a disagreement about what I need in a man for the long term, and you're trying to push past my boundaries faster than I'm ready." She looked out the passenger window.

That, he believed. If not for this mission, he'd spend more time reassuring her . . . before putting some of the items in Logan's living room to good use and giving her a darker taste of his dominance. She needed to experience more of the deep, incredible power exchange between them so she could see that she had nothing to fear. His mission put all that on hold. No wonder she felt a little lost.

"Kata, listen to me—"

"No, Hunter, you listen to me. We have awesome chemistry. I won't deny that, but . . ." She sighed. "I liked last night. I won't try to say I didn't. You make me feel adored and aroused in a way I never believed possible. But I don't think I can handle this. Getting married was a stupid impulse. You want something I can't give you. We should be smart now and end it, before we both get hurt."

Fear sent dread resounding all through him. She wanted a divorce? "I'm not letting you go."

"Be reasonable. We've known each other for less than two days."

He shook his head. "Not happening. I love you."

She shook her head, gaze falling away. "You don't mean it. You don't know me."

He gritted his teeth together, wanting to strangle her "logic" with his bare hands. The only thing running her brain was fear. "Honey, I meant every word." Hunter had no idea how to explain what he knew in his gut was true. He shook his head, sorting through his thoughts. "Why did you invite your sister to your party?"

Kata frowned like he'd lost his mind. "She's my sister."

"But she's married and has kids, and this wasn't her sort of party."

"Yeah . . . but the celebration wouldn't have felt complete without her." Her mouth turned down a moment later.

"You wanted your mother there, too."

Now Kata looked downright unhappy. "Fucking Gordon wouldn't let her come."

Another strike against the asshole in Hunter's book. Little wonder Kata hated him. "I'll bet you called your brother as well."

"Joaquin didn't answer," she shrugged glumly. "Guess he's undercover."

Hunter put his arm around her. "You knew he might not, but you still tried. You'll always try because you care. You're the glue holding your family together, aren't you? That's one reason I love you. Honey, you're smart and sexy as hell, and even when you're pissed at me, your razor-sharp humor makes me smile. I know underneath that is a scared girl, and I want to show her that she's loved and doesn't always have to be in control."

She bit her lip. "But I don't like not being in control."

"Some part of you does, at least in the bedroom. You found that out last night, and the depth of your submission scared you."

For the first time since he'd met Kata, she didn't have a cheeky comeback on the tip of her tongue. "Yeah."

He cradled her cheek in his palm. "Our marriage was no mistake. And when I come back from this mission, we're going to spend a lot of quality time together, until you're comfortable with me. I'll keep doing whatever it takes to earn your submission and your love. Don't doubt that."

Sadness furrowed Kata's brow. She pursed her lips together, as if she were holding tears inside. "I don't think it will work. I'm independent. I can't *stand* people telling me what to do. I'm stubborn and decisive . . . everything you don't want. You're a logical guy—"

"But one who knows when to go with his gut. So our courtship was in fast-forward. So I don't know your favorite color or TV show. So you don't know which of my scars are from a childhood bike accident and which are from military service. So fucking what? Those are details." He shook his head. "Don't confuse a Dom with an asshole. The truth is, you've been in 'easy' relationships so your heart would never be threatened. If you were to ask yourself—and be really honest—you know that you can't ever be truly happy with guys like Ben, who let you call all the shots."

Pressing her lush lips together, Kata stared out the window. Only the hum of the truck's engine and the faint twang of an old-time country western station broke the silence. Hunter wasn't deterred. Even if she didn't admit it, she was thinking.

"What do you know about me?" he prompted, his tone brooking no refusal. "And watch the sarcasm. You should know I have no problem turning your ass bright red."

Kata paused, shrugged. "You're gorgeous, but you don't act like you know it. You have loyal friends and family, which suggests that you must be loyal yourself. You seem confident in almost every situation, but not cocky. You're smart and quick . . . and probably good with kittens and babies, too." Kata quipped with a twist of her lips that gave Hunter hope. "But you're also relentless and too damn perceptive. Every minute you find some new way to twist me inside out. I hate the word 'submissive.' It implies that I'm some simpering, brainless—"

"Never you. I told you, that's one reason I want *you*. Some subs lose themselves and their identities to their Masters. If they're uncollared, in other words if the relationship ends, they're so used to being dependent, they don't know who they are anymore. I'll never worry about that with you. I have no doubt you'll always challenge me. Honey, the big difference between me and Gordon—and listen closely—is that, with that selfish prick it's all about his desires. With me, I can't be happy if I'm not giving you what you need. I'll concede that our marriage was quick. But give us a fucking chance before you bow to your fear and quit on us."

* * *

RUSH hour, or Lafayette's equivalent, was nearly at an end when Kata and Hunter approached the city. She stretched, then applied some lip gloss from her purse as her—she still could barely say the word—husband drove with a pair of aviators covering those perceptive blue eyes. With one hand, he held the wheel. With the other, he gripped her hand.

Before last night, the wound he'd made in her defenses in Vegas had just begun to scab over. She could have resumed her life without him, granted, with some regrets. But after last night . . .

Kata trembled. Hunter had introduced her to a whole new pleasure. Electric. Breath-stealing. Once-in-a-lifetime wow. No way was she going to delude herself and say that she hadn't enjoyed his manacles and firm hand. Hunter had forced her to see deep inside herself and admit her fears to him. In his domination, she'd felt utterly adored, almost pampered, which was contrary to everything she believed. He'd ripped off that scab and permanently scarred her defenses.

Today, she hated the raw, vulnerable feeling left behind. His every move had been designed to shove his way into her life, her head, her heart. He'd made her feel something for him that was way bigger than she could handle. Sure, other women craved being controlled. Kata wasn't cut out for letting anyone that deeply into her soul.

And whether Hunter fessed up to it or not, he wanted to control bunches beyond their bedroom play. That's where she had a problem. No, he wasn't Gordon. Hunter was her stepfather on steroids, smarter, more determined. Under all his pushiness he was probably a decent guy, but he could also act like Asshole version 2.0 when it suited him. He claimed that his behavior was about giving her what she needed. Smooth line. Bet Gordon wished he'd thought of that. Granted, Hunter hadn't torn her down to build up his own ego, but did that matter if she had no power in the relationship? She'd eventually lose all self-respect and feel like shit anyway.

On the other hand, he'd accused her of not really giving him and the marriage a chance.

She glanced his way. He met her stare, and the electric zing between them charged through her.

Had her mother felt this pull to Gordon, even as her friends, her job, and her individuality slowly slipped away? Hunter even admitted that some subs lost themselves to their Dom. Besides the fact that she couldn't imagine wearing anyone's collar, like some pet, Kata worried that if she allowed him complete mastery over her body, she would soon lose herself in the extreme pleasure he gave her, and surrender her heart and soul.

"Are you okay, honey?" Hunter murmured.

Kata chose her words carefully. He terrified her emotionally, but his point about being distracted on a mission was well taken. She didn't want to do anything that would place him in greater peril. They'd sort out everything when he returned.

"Just tired. Overwhelmed."

He sent her a searching stare as he pulled into the parking lot of an upscale apartment building, then eased the truck into a spot under a shade tree. Twenty feet away, Tyler stood in the doorway, waiting. *Whoa!* She'd forgotten how big he was built. With a guy like him, she'd normally assume he was a gym rat whose fantasies revolved around increasing the circumference of his biceps, but she'd already seen him in action enough to know he possessed a sharp watchfulness that promised he could totally kick someone's ass.

Yeah, he'd keep her safe, but Kata wasn't at all happy about this arrangement. How contrary did it make her that she'd been dying to put space between her and Hunter, but already she felt the pangs from his withdrawal?

They stepped from the truck, and Tyler jogged down the exterior stairs to greet them. "Hi, baby. I got your suitcase from the back of your car."

"Thank—" She frowned at the green-eyed beefcake in the killer tight black tee. "How did you get into my trunk without my keys?"

Tyler smiled smugly, then turned to Hunter. "I talked to Jack. He'll be by to get her tomorrow night." Then his grin turned sly. "That is, if she still wants to go."

Hunter lunged into Tyler's personal space, then growled, "Let's get one thing straight: Kata is not your 'baby'; she's my *wife*. You don't touch her. You don't even *think* about touching her. Or I swear to God, I'll rip your face off."

Really, Hunter had nothing to worry about. Tyler was attractive . . . but her life was complicated enough.

Tyler looked amused. "Possessive much?"

"Focus on the fact that someone wants to kill Kata. I get that other men's wives turn you on, but—"

"I'll make sure he's all bluster, Hunter." A familiar guy emerged from Tyler's apartment, with dark, shoulder-length waves that would seem feminine on another man. On him, it looked drop-dead sexy as he sauntered down the steps into the morning light.

"Luc Traverson?" Kata stared, stunned. "Wow, I love your cooking show!"

And he was even more gorgeous in person.

"Thank you." He extended a hand to her. "Great to meet you. You're Hunter's wife, Kata?" At her stilted shrug, he drawled, "My deepest sympathies."

"Funny." Hunter didn't sound amused as he glared at Luc. "You're here because . . . ?"

Kata frowned. "How do you two know each other?"

The two men exchanged a glance, and she knew something was up here. Finally, Luc nodded. "Kimber's husband, Deke, is my cousin."

He was cousin Luc? Wow. . .

Tyler snorted. "He and Deke used to share *everything*."

Did he mean . . . ? From the looks on everyone's faces, yes. Kimber and Deke and Luc? Kata's jaw dropped.

Luc cast a sidelong glare at Tyler. "Shut up." Then he turned back to Hunter. "I'm here because I know the hell of wondering if you're wife is screwing this asswipe." He jerked a thumb at Tyler. "I wouldn't put anyone through it. I'm happy to babysit until I have to start prep for tonight's dinner service at Bonheur. Besides, Alyssa is wrapped up in Sexy Sirens' rebuild, despite being thirty weeks pregnant. So my very curious wife sent me to collect the juicy details about your marriage."

"Thanks for staying with Kata for as long as you can." Muttering a curse under his breath, Hunter glanced at his watch, then winced.

He turned all his formidable attention on her, his face tight with regret. Damn if just being near him didn't make her tingle from head to toe. Damn if he didn't make her feel everything for him, even when she didn't want to.

"I'll miss you, honey." He layered his lips over hers.

So often, Hunter had kissed her with possession and overwhelming passion. He was always like a cat-five tornado barreling at breakneck speed for the protective walls around her heart, frightfully eager to mow them down. Now he was like a wisp of smoke, so light she almost wondered if she was imagining the kiss. All too quickly, her lips began to tingle, like they did after eating her *abuelita*'s homemade salsa. But this sensation couldn't be cured with cold milk. Hunter just impacted her. And this kiss, so tender, hit her right in the chest.

For her, there really was something about him—both incredible and terrifying.

Needing more, she leaned into the kiss, opening to him, fingers digging into his shoulders. She trapped a whimper at the back of her throat.

With a caress of his knuckles down her cheek, he eased back, then gripped her face in his hands with a desperation that further crumbled her defenses.

"I'll be back soon," he murmured. "I promise."

"Be safe," she choked on a whisper.

After another lingering kiss, he strutted down the steps to the blacktop parking lot already giving off shimmering heat waves, despite the fact that it was just after nine a.m.

Watching him go hurt. Kata realized that he'd been reassuring her that no third world asshole would prevent him from coming back to her. It hit her then . . . Hunter had an incredibly dangerous job. Worse than a cop or a firefighter. He was knowingly walking into a fight with people who wanted to kill him each and every time he stepped into his role. Fear quivered in her belly, and she had to fight herself not to call him back. She doubted that she and Hunter were meant for the long haul, but if anything happened to him? God, she'd crumble and die.

Why?

A taxi arrived to take Hunter away. He waved, and she watched until the ugly yellow and black vehicle rolled out of sight.

As soon as it disappeared around the corner, Tyler put a hand under her elbow and smiled. "Why don't you come inside and make yourself comfortable, baby? We'll find some way to have fun." He winked at her, then glared at Luc. "Even with the third wheel."

* * *

AFTER a quick trip through a nearby drive-thru for a burger and a stop at the video store, Kata settled beside Tyler on the sofa as he cued up their movie.

"When I said cuddle up on the couch after Luc left, this isn't what I had in mind." His pained expression said he'd rather be boiling in oil. "Are you really going to make me watch this?"

Hot, funny, attentive without being overwhelming, Tyler was everything she normally went for in a guy. Sure, they'd flirted. It was like breathing for him, both constant and automatic. But she wasn't feeling a serious vibe between them—which was a relief. Usually, she loved flirting, too, but Hunter had invaded every last brain cell and filled it with thoughts of him.

"I'll take your silence as a no." Tyler reached for the remote.

She yanked it out of his hand, then had to laugh at his mock pout.

"I love Edward and Bella. Have you even seen any of the movies?" she challenged.

"Hell no. She looks constipated, and I swear he plays for the other team."

Kata stifled a laugh. She really shouldn't encourage him. "It's called angst. Guess you've never felt any."

Tyler leveled a hard stare on her that told her she was dead wrong. Then he saved her from muttering an awkward reply by starting the movie. She stifled what she'd planned to say, since his life was none of her business and she was in no shape to be giving advice. Instead, Kata focused on the familiar Bella Swan voice-over that began the film.

About halfway through, he shuffled into the kitchen for popcorn, and Kata noticed that while it popped, his stare barely left the screen. Pulling one of the sofa's throw pillows to her chest, she smiled.

"Oh, come on," he groused. "Helen Keller and Stevie Wonder could both see this love triangle coming. And this movie made how much money?"

Kata threw the pillow at him. "Shh!"

"Don't shush me, woman, or I'll take you over my knee."

She froze. "You roll that way, too? What am I saying? Of course, you do. You're friends with Hunter."

And didn't she feel stupid for failing to figure it out sooner?

A frown creased Tyler's face. "Roll what way?" He frowned, then shook his head. "Oh, Hunter is into the BDSM thing. Control freak. No, that's not my thing. I leave that to him and Jack Cole."

"The Jack who's coming to get me tomorrow night?"

"One and the same. He's one cool customer, man. And his wife is a doll. You'll like Morgan."

"Because she's . . ." Kata searched for the most flattering words so she didn't insult a woman Tyler obviously admired. "Easy to get along with?"

Had Jack erased Morgan's personality and replaced it with that of a "yes, Sir" kind of woman?

Tyler howled with laughter. "Morgan, easy to get along with? I made that assumption once. She nearly strung me up by the balls. That's one scary woman when she's pissed. Even Jack is smart enough to steer clear of her then."

Kata wasn't sure how to interpret Tyler's words. If her mother tried to assert herself, Gordon found a thousand not-so-subtle ways to tell Mamá that she was wrong and her "tantrum" ridiculous. But when *he* got mad . . . watch out. But Tyler made it sound like Jack heeded his wife's moods, rather than belittled them. Was that the norm in a BDSM marriage, or just Jack and Morgan's?

It didn't matter. As much as she had feelings for Hunter, as much as they were explosive between the sheets, she didn't belong married to someone she'd met less than two days ago, who could wring both her body and her heart inside out.

She needed to talk to someone. To Mamá, who always understood her.

"Hey, um . . ." she called to Tyler. "I'm going to take a pee break."

Thoughts whirling, she headed down the apartment's lone hallway to the bedroom, which was pure masculine—heavy woods, comforter striped with three shades of brown and a touch of black. Guns everywhere, along with a dizzying array of electronic devices.

Kata found her suitcase in the corner and dug into it. *There* was her cell phone charger. The damn phone had died early this afternoon, and she'd been unable to fish it out under both Luc and Tyler's watchful gazes.

"Want me to pause the movie?" he called back.

"No, I've seen it, so I won't be lost if I miss a bit. You go ahead."

With Tyler occupied, maybe she could sneak in a quick, whispered call. Yeah, Hunter had told her that her phone was traceable, but it seemed far-fetched for most anyone outside of a government agency to have access to that kind of technology.

As soon as she plugged the phone in, she silenced the device. Text messages and voice mails started pouring in. Mari, Chloe, Hallie, Ben. She knew what they had to say before reviewing the messages. Sure enough, Mari wanted to know if she was all right after the shooting and if she'd gone insane, marrying a man she'd only just met. She'd insisted that Kata call immediately and bring

Hunter around for dinner on Sunday. Clearly, Chloe and Hallie hadn't yet heard about the shooting because they only wanted the deets on how hot he was in bed. Ben . . . was hurt and confused and angry. And she didn't blame him. He'd tried to give her the birthday present of her fantasies, and from his point of view, she'd stabbed him in the back. Definitely, she owed him a return call . . . and some sort of explanation.

Another voice mail popped up from an unfamiliar local number. Kata listened to this latest message. When she first heard the woman's wheezy, scratchy voice, Kata frowned in confusion—until the caller identified herself as Mamá.

"*Mija*, I heard that someone shot at you." Concern laced her voice. "Please let me know that you are all right. Gordon is on a trip and took our phone, so I am calling from my neighbor's." She coughed, a long string of hacks resounding from deep in her chest that made Kata wince. "Sorry. Gordon says I suffer from allergies, and he is probably right."

"If that's allergies, I'm Bigfoot," Kata whispered, worry toxic in her veins. Her mother's chest rattled with every breath.

"He left me some ibuprofen and decongestant, so I will be fine soon." Mamá paused to cough for another long spell. When she resumed speaking, her voice sounded even weaker. "Come by as soon as you can, *Mija*. I love you."

As her mother hung up, she began coughing again. Panic raced through Kata. Her mother had bronchitis—or worse. Damn Gordon for being too blind or self-centered to care that Mamá might truly be ill. He'd left her with no car, no phone, and probably no money. In his mind, if she went nowhere, spoke with no one, and did nothing, why would she need it? The bastard knew well that Mamá's dependence on him made her weak, and nothing gave him a hard-on faster than bending someone to his mercy.

She clutched her phone and tried to decide what to do. Mamá had no way to call a doctor, and she wouldn't have lingered at the neighbor's. It would only piss off Gordon if she made a "scene." Mamá should call Mari, but since her older sister was now a mother herself, Mamá didn't want to make Mari's life any busier.

For now, the only way to truly assess how sick her mother might be was for Kata to see her herself.

Kata dropped the phone and reached for the bedroom door. She didn't know much about Tyler, but he'd been reasonable so far, friendly. Surely, if she explained the situation, he would help her. That seemed logical . . .

Except that Tyler had already refused to take her anyplace she usually visited, like her apartment. His point that the bad guys could have all her usual haunts staked out was well taken. And Tyler's first allegiance wasn't to her but to Hunter.

Gripping the knob, Kata froze. What if Tyler didn't agree to help her? He wouldn't simply let her go. And all his banter aside, he was very capable of keeping her both safe and sequestered. She had no doubt that if he refused to take her to Mamá, she'd never be able to escape his watchful eye.

Mamá had no one else to help her. Mari was reluctant to help Mamá, since she didn't want to "help herself" by leaving Gordon. Besides, on Mondays, her sister would be doing some pro bono work in Baton Rouge with several of her colleagues. Her sister's husband was home with the boys, up to his eyeballs in homework and soccer practice. If she sent Tyler alone, her mother would refuse to answer the door for fear of Gordon's reprisals. Mamá needed her.

Kata bit her lip. Yes, she knew running off was dangerous; she wasn't too stupid to understand that. But Mamá had a history of respiratory problems, and Kata had successfully nursed her back to health every time.

"You okay in there?" Tyler called through the door.

She started. How had he made it all the way up the hall without her hearing the footsteps? Tyler might seem like a nice guy, and he definitely flirted, but under all that charm, Kata suspected that he'd be lethal.

"Fine," she called before he got suspicious. "I'm . . . looking for something more comfortable to wear. Mind if I take a quick shower?"

He hesitated. "No problem, but, um . . . don't be long. I paused the movie so we could watch the end together."

Think, think. How was she going to get out of here?

"You mean you do care about Bella and Edward?" she teased to throw off suspicion—and because he deserved it.

"Fine. It's not total trash. That's the most you're getting out of me. Ten minutes, Kata."

"Perfect. No problem."

How the hell was she going to escape him in ten minutes?

An idea hit her. She dashed into the bathroom and turned on the shower to mask the sounds to come. Then, hoping this didn't put her on the grid and in danger, she sent out a quick text to the one person she trusted implicitly and hoped would never refuse her.

Chapter Twelve

SINCE sneaking out of Tyler's apartment, Kata had experienced the worst twenty-four hours of her life. She paced her mother's hospital room as dusk turned to dark, raking a hand through her heavy hair. She needed a shower and a meal—and some way to stop herself from strangling Gordon.

"Control yourself, Katalina," her stepfather snapped. "You look like an elephant stomping from one side of the room to the other. You have your mother's grace, which is absolutely none, and I—"

"Shut up!" she whirled on him, fists clenched, menace boiling inside her. "How could you fucking leave her alone with no way to help herself when you knew she was sick? She could have died!"

From her chair in the corner, Marisol gave an imperceptible shake of her head. Kata knew what her sister was saying. This would only make Gordon more angry and defensive, something he'd take out on Mamá. Mari was definitely of the don't-get-mad-get-even school of thought. But Kata couldn't keep pressing her anger down. She wanted this asshole to pay.

Gordon rolled his pale eyes in his pale face. "You're being dramatic. Of course the doctor will say she's at death's door. He makes more money that way. But this cold isn't as serious as you imagine."

"*Cold*? It's full-blown pneumonia. If we'd waited much longer, Mamá's situation could have been life-threatening. Doctors don't make this shit up."

"Katalina, no man wants a woman who yells and curses at him, questions his sanity, or corrects him. Coupled with your weight, it's no wonder you're still single."

She was mad enough to chew nails—and spit them in his face. Then tell him that she was no longer single. But now wasn't the time to start more family drama. She needed to focus on Mamá.

"Well." Mari rose between them on long legs to her lean, elegant height. "It's nearly eight. The cafeteria will stop serving dinner soon. Did you eat, Gordon?"

He shook his head and glanced at her mother. "I'm going home. I'll eat there."

"After visiting for ten minutes?" Kata's jaw dropped.

"*CSI* is on. Carlotta knows I never miss it."

Even when his wife lay sick in the hospital? She supposed if he could work late tonight to prep for a meeting that wasn't until next week, he could leave early to watch some stupid-ass TV show. That was so like Gordon. Self-centered to the core.

Kata swallowed back her fury. "Fine. There's the door."

"I don't like your attitude, Katalina." He gathered up his suit coat and jangled his car keys in his pocket.

Yeah? She didn't like him, period. But what good would telling him again do? He already knew exactly how she felt.

"Get the hell out of here."

He harrumphed, then marched for the door like he was the freaking king of England. *Loser.* The only thing exalted about Gordon was his opinion of himself.

"Good night, Mari." He speared Kata with a narrow-eyed glare, then left.

If he thought for one minute that she cared about his snub, he couldn't be more mistaken.

"God, I hate him," Kata said to her sister once he was down the hall and out of sight.

"No more than I."

"But you never say anything to him!"

Mari's raised brows and somber gaze showed thin patience. "No point in making things worse for Mamá."

Kata knew that her temper often got the best of her where Gordon was concerned. "Sorry."

Her older sister shrugged. "You do it to defend Mamá. She knows you love her. I do, too, but I won't get involved again until she decides to leave him."

Yeah, Mari had made that crystal clear. "Why won't she divorce him? I know she's unhappy and thinks she has no other options, but damn, she's still young and bright and kind."

"And thoroughly stripped of her self-esteem. He's left her dependent on him financially and emotionally. Until she figures out her options, we're just making a bad situation worse."

Kata gnawed on her lip. "You're always so logical, and I know you're right, but . . . it just breaks my heart. I wish I could *do* something."

Mari hummed noncommittally, then reached into her briefcase to extract some papers. "I'm worried about you, as well."

"Me?"

Spearing her with that older sister look, Mari nodded. "When you disappeared after the shooting, I called Ben. To say I was shocked that you'd *married* Hunter was an understatement. I didn't tell Mamá, but . . ." She sighed in exasperation. "What were you thinking? You know almost nothing about him, and what Ben has told me—that Hunter is dominant and controlling—doesn't give me a good feeling."

"He's dominant sexually." Kata winced at the blush crawling up her face but forged on. "He's not an asshole like Gordon," she defended.

"Are you sure?" Mari, ever the level-headed attorney, got right to the heart of all of Kata's concerns.

How could she convince her sister that it might walk and quack like a duck—but this time, it really wasn't a duck? She wasn't completely convinced herself. Hunter wasn't mean-spirited like Gordon—but he possessed a ruthless streak. She had no idea what sort of husband that would make him.

Mari went on with her cross-examination. "Why couldn't I find you after that shooting? I had no idea where you'd gone until you stopped to call."

"Well, it's partially my fault. There wasn't a lot of time, but I also didn't want you to fuss over me."

"Hmm." She didn't sound convinced. "Would Hunter have let you tell us where he'd taken you?"

Kata winced. "Probably not."

"Yet you're assigning yourself the blame?" her sister asked incredulously. "Who does that sound like?"

Mamá, but . . . "After the shooting, Hunter didn't want anyone knowing where I was, for safety's sake. Since I was fine and you knew it, I didn't think it would be a big deal."

Mari raised a dark brow, looking decidedly skeptical.

"Look, I admit Hunter can be overbearing, but he's not all bad. He makes me feel really special. Sometimes . . . he says just the right thing." She sighed. "And I melt all over."

One thing Kata knew for sure, if she'd suffered her mother's illness, Hunter would never leave her hospital room to watch *CSI*. He'd probably never leave her side, period.

Mari slanted a hard glance at Kata. "If you'll remember, we liked Gordon once, too."

That knocked Kata back in her chair. Mari was right. Years and years ago when her mother and Gordon had been dating, he'd been a peach. Once, he'd taken her, Mari, and Joaquin to an amusement park, then for ice cream later that night. He'd always brought candies and toys when picking up Mamá. He'd done magic tricks and sang karaoke, played Super Mario Brothers . . . And after Gordon and her mother had married, he'd slowly morphed into the asshole they all knew and hated.

"Kata, think about it. You don't know anything about this guy except that he's a Navy SEAL and good in bed."

Great in bed, but Kata understood her sister's point. She *so* wanted to believe that Mari was wrong that it was like a physical ache. But the warning dredged up all her own uncertainties and magnified them. Mari could be dead-on. Kata really didn't know.

"He's just . . . really protective," she said, oddly determined to make her sister understand that Hunter had good qualities.

"He *claims* that he's protecting you, but don't you think that cutting off communication from all your loved ones and making you take a leave from your job is awfully extreme?"

"A professional assassin was after me." Kata defended Hunter—even as Mari's words sank in. Hadn't Kata told him just yesterday that the marriage had been a rash mistake? So why was she trying to sway her sister?

"How do you know that isn't what he told you so he could lock you away for himself?"

"Hunter wouldn't lie about that. Besides, the shooter pushed his gun to the base of my skull." Kata shivered just thinking about it.

"I'm not saying that you weren't in danger. But how do you know it wasn't one of Villarreal's street punks or someone else you pissed off along the way, rather than an assassin? How does Hunter know?"

"The gunman told me that he'd been hired to kill me."

Mari pressed her lips together. "Would a professional assassin bother to announce that? I'm concerned about your safety; don't get me wrong. I panicked when I heard you'd nearly been shot. But Hunter's behavior concerns me, too. I could be way off base here . . ." Her voice said she didn't think so for a minute. "But you should think seriously of getting out of this marriage before he smothers you."

Her sister's words made Kata go numb from the gravity of the situation. Her own confusion weighed her down even more.

Mari finally held the sheaf of papers out to her. "I took the liberty of drawing these up earlier today."

Kata took the papers with cold fingers and opened them. *Petition for Divorce.* Even though she'd talked to Hunter about ending it, seeing this document . . . Her knees buckled.

"All you have to do is sign them and get Hunter to do the same; then it'll be over. If he really cares about you, he can always call you, date you like a normal guy, make the effort to get to know you. If he doesn't, if he fights this like I know Gordon would fight Mamá, then . . ."

Then she'd know. Thing was, she couldn't picture Hunter just dating her. The way he'd immersed himself in her, tied them together almost immediately . . . he wouldn't have bothered if he'd merely wanted to date. Besides, Kata had mentioned ending the marriage earlier, and Hunter had flatly refused. But Mari had a point, though Kata wished her sister didn't. In fact, everything inside her resisted it. Then she looked at Mamá, pale and drained, lying frail in the hospital bed. A woman so unlike the vivacious mother she'd grown up with.

If she stayed with Hunter . . . could this be her in twenty years?

Kata clutched her middle, anger and confusion ripping her apart. She'd known Hunter for three days, and they'd been apart half that time. The thought of leaving him shouldn't hurt so badly. But she already missed him now.

As she bit her lip, tears welled. She fought them, but the last few days and her mother's ill health stacked on top of her until she struggled under the weight.

Mari crossed the distance between them and hugged her. "You like him?"

How did she answer that? What she felt went way beyond like. "I hate the way he argues, especially when he's right. Then . . . two minutes later he's everything I could have ever wanted and more, and . . ." She sobbed. "I don't know if I want to go back to life without him."

"Are you in *love* with him?" Mari sounded incredulous at the possibility.

For her sake, Kata wanted to say no. But she couldn't. "I—I . . ." She blew out a deep breath. Part of her had been relieved when Hunter had been called away. Part of her had been terrified and bereft. "I don't know."

Mari looked shaken. "It's possible?"

Given that Kata had never responded with such abandon to any other man? That everything inside her had begun dancing the samba when Hunter had said he loved her? "Maybe. But he scares the hell out of me."

Her sister didn't look at all pleased but somehow managed to smooth out her expression to something neutral. "I haven't met him, so I should reserve judgment. But those papers give you power. Sign them, *hermana*. If there's really something between you two, do this the right way, not by skulking off to a ratty chapel in Vegas for a drunken wedding. Get to know each other, meet your respective friends and family, *then*, when you're ready, stand up in front of us all and profess your love."

What Mari said made a hell of a lot of sense . . . in her sister's ultra-logical world. Kata wasn't wired like that; she didn't make decisions with her head. And every emotion she had now was one huge jumble.

Kata gnawed on her lip again. She either needed to throw herself into this hypersonic relationship or end it now, before a decade passed and she was older or too dependent or—God forbid—had to drag kids through a divorce.

Kata put the papers in her purse. "I'll think about it."

Mari pursed her full, red mouth like she wanted to argue but merely nodded.

A moment later, Ben returned, juggling two cups of steaming coffee, and rubbernecked the room. "Gordon's gone? That was a quick visit."

"Mercifully, yes," Kata murmured.

"Call me later." Mari gathered her purse. "If I leave Carlos alone too long with the boys, Javi and Robby are likely to tie him up and burn the house down."

Mari's husband loved the boys, and sometimes discipline was shoved aside in favor of fun.

"Go," she urged. "I'll let you know if there's any change with Mamá."

"You need to rest, too." Mari put on her older sister face. "Think about what I said."

Kata nodded as Mari exited, her charcoal gray skirt swishing with each efficient step. Exhaustion set in. A million thoughts skimmed the top of Kata's head, but she was too tired to actually grasp one. She needed a meal and sleep—and to decide what to do about Hunter.

"You all right?" Ben handed her a cup of coffee, then caressed her shoulder with a warm hand. "You want to talk about anything?"

The last person Kata wanted to discuss Hunter with was Ben. Her former friend-with-benefits wasn't furious that her husband had stolen her—but he wasn't thrilled, either.

"No, thanks."

"But something is on your mind. I can see it on your face. Did Gordon say something that upset you? He's such a prick."

"I don't care what Gordon says to me, but the way he treats Mamá is unforgiveable. If it's the last damn thing I do, I will convince her to leave his sorry ass."

Ben guided her over to the chair beside her mother's bed, where tubes stuck out from everywhere and monitors beeped. As soon as her butt hit the ugly mint green vinyl, she focused on her mom.

She drank some of the coffee he'd given her with a sigh. "Thanks—for everything. Smuggling me away from Tyler's place and watching my back, helping my mother get to the hospital, for not leaving my side since we got here."

Setting aside his coffee, Ben shook his head and knelt in front of her. "That's what friends are for. That"—he worked his hand up her thigh—"and other things. Kata, come home with me. You need a shower and sleep and someone to comfort you. I miss you. I don't know what's up with you and Hunter. And I don't care."

Once upon a time, she would have whispered an easy "yes." Ben was so familiar and easy to be with. Strong arms; a laugh or two; pleasurable, if predictable, sex. A guaranteed orgasm.

But she wanted nothing to do with his offer now. Kata knew her indefinable feelings for Hunter were to blame. It made no sense. How could she feel this aching attachment to Hunter when he terrified her emotionally?

"Ben—"

Suddenly, a man with dark sunglasses swaggered into the room, exuding menace like an expensive cologne. Inky hair, head-to-toe black, and a mean SOB scowl all screamed, "Don't fuck with me."

Was he one of Villarreal's men? Kata snatched up her phone to dial 911.

"Put it down," he growled, his hard stare moving to Ben, who cupped her thigh. "Hunter will care very much that you're propositioning his wife. Get your hand off her. Now."

Ben scowled but didn't move. "Who are you?"

"Someone more than happy to fuck up your face. Leave, or one of my buddies will set your truck on fire in the next two minutes if you're not driving it off the lot."

Sputtering, Ben jumped to his feet and glared at the stranger, a terrier taking on a pit bull. "Y-you can't . . . Don't touch my truck!"

The ominous stranger looked at his watch. "A minute forty-five. You're wasting time."

"How do I know you're not going to hurt Kata?" Ben challenged, shoving her behind him.

Kata loved that Ben was willing to defend her, especially at the risk of losing his beloved truck. But he was going to get his ass kicked . . . or worse. She started dialing the phone.

"Put it down," the stranger demanded of her, then said softly. "I'm one of Hunter's friends."

"Yeah? Me, too." Ben crossed his arms over his chest.

The stranger took a menacing step closer. "I'm pretty sure he wouldn't feel too friendly toward you, since you're trying to get in his wife's panties."

Kata stood and faced the guy. "I don't know who the hell you are or why you've come, but you don't get to strut in here and threaten my friends."

A dirty smile lifted his lips. "Actually, I do. Your husband sent me. I'm Jack Cole."

* * *

TWENTY minutes later, Kata still stared at Jack as he lounged against the sterile hospital room's wall and sent her an unnerving glance. Ben had left for the moment, ostensibly to call in sick to his bartending job, but she didn't doubt for a second that he'd also gone to move his truck.

"You don't have to hover," she told Jack.

He shrugged. "Occupational hazard."

Everything about Jack Cole unsettled her. His every loose-hipped move was calculated and full of controlled power. Danger rolled off him. Jack was one bad son of a bitch she wouldn't want to meet in a dark alley. And she had no trouble believing that he could totally, utterly dominate a woman. He and Hunter had too much in common.

Instead of pointing out that she hadn't asked Jack to do this job—a waste of breath—she grumbled, "Where is Tyler?"

She'd rather have him as a babysitter than the menacing Cajun.

As if Jack had read her mind, he smiled smugly. "Checking with the security detail in the hall. He hasn't had a chance to confer with them much since he put them in place nearly twenty-four hours ago."

Kata nearly choked. "Tyler's been *here* all that time? But I sneaked out of his apartment. How did he . . ."

"Know? *Cher*, when you left his place, he wasn't three minutes behind you," Jack drawled, looking amused. "He didn't drag you back to his apartment because he realized why you'd gone and that your mom needed help."

Relief and gratitude poured like a warm shower through Kata as she looked at her mother, still heavily medicated and asleep. Mama's color appeared rosier today, but her lingering, hacking cough hadn't improved. The doctor hoped her mother would be well enough to go home tomorrow. But even if she was, who would care for her? Certainly not Gordon.

"So . . . Tyler watched me from afar?"

"No. He blended into your surroundings. He knew that if he showed his face and played the heavy, you were likely to run again, which wasn't optimal for you or your mother. The hospital environment is chaotic, but along with some of the local off-duty officers who are buddies of ours, he put together a detail to keep you safe until I could take over."

Wow. Tyler had done all that seamlessly, invisibly. Kata had been on edge since arriving at the hospital, worrying not only about her mother, but fearful that somehow the threat would find her. But Tyler had managed to keep her safe with quiet efficiency. Behind all the charm and bluster, he was a badass.

"I'm not leaving my mother," she vowed, raising her chin.

Jack smiled, and it wasn't pretty. "Hunter loves a challenge. I can see why you fascinate him." He shrugged. "But it's not my job to give you the spanking I think he'll be itching to give you when he returns."

"A spanking? For taking care of my mother?" She advanced on him with narrowed eyes. It was probably stupid to provoke someone so much bigger than her, but she was exhausted—and he'd just crawled on her last nerve. "I'm being a responsible adult, not a bratty child. I don't need some *man* to put me back in line."

"So responsible adults sneak out a second-story window and away from their security detail, putting themselves in danger?"

Kata winced at his question. Okay, so she'd done that. Still . . . "I wasn't sure if Tyler would let me go."

"But you didn't ask. You didn't advise him of the situation." Jack edged closer, his tone dropping to dark steel. "You're not a bratty child, Kata. Hunter will want to spank you because you didn't give his protection a chance. A Dom's job is to know what you need and to provide it. To protect you. He's trying to do all that from halfway around the globe and went to a hell of a lot of trouble to see you safe. Instead of trusting him, you cut his protection loose and acted rashly. What good would you have been to your mother if the assassin had been waiting for you at her house and put a bullet between your eyes on her front lawn?"

Horror assailed Kata. She'd imagined that she'd be safe enough if she moved quickly, then spent all her time in a public place like the hospital. Yeah, she got Jack's point that she'd been reckless, but something in her rebelled at the idea of punishment. "Can't he just talk to me? Tell me his concerns? Spanking is so—"

"Simple and effective. People respond to the unpleasant and generally avoid behaviors that lead to it. Not that he'll hurt you in the traditional sense, but he'll make sure you feel remorse. I'm pretty sure the orgasm he'll withhold will be its own kind of pain."

Kata wanted to deny that she'd find any such spanking arousing enough to be on the edge of climax, but she knew better. Just like she knew that he could hold back her orgasm for hours and hours, if he chose.

She braced her hands on her hips. "You don't think spanking is condescending?"

"Am I offending your feminist sensibilities with the truth?" Jack raised a dark brow. "Look, we know you're women, not children. But the spanking isn't all for you, *cher*. When a Dom feels his woman has endangered herself, sometimes he needs to reassure himself with your skin under his hand and your cries in his ears. We're only a few thousand years from cavemen. In evolutionary terms, the blink of an eye. Now, from my perspective, you can remain at the hospital as long as we can keep you safe. Just don't imagine that Hunter will be as calm when he comes back."

It was on the tip of her tongue to ask who the hell he thought he was to give her "permission" to stay with her mother. But he was Hunter's stand-in, the assigned watchdog who had no compunction about doing whatever necessary to keep her safe. That he wasn't shuttling her back to a secure facility was probably cause for celebration. When Hunter returned, she'd have to pay the piper—and damn if the idea of an erotic spanking didn't make her wetter than it should.

Or should she just give him the divorce papers and end this before she got in deeper?

Kata chewed on her lip and retreated to the corner to sort through her tangled thoughts.

"Oh my gosh, the baby is gorgeous, Jack!" a petite redhead gushed as she hustled into the hospital room, her blue eyes lit with excitement as she placed a soft kiss on his intimidating face. "Wait until you see him!"

This must be Morgan Cole.

With every step, a sparkling gold and ruby choker bobbed at the hollow of the woman's throat and her slim hips swayed with a well-sated sensuality. A huge diamond winked on her left hand. Jack had both married and collared her?

The woman's lips looked swollen, as if she'd been thoroughly kissed recently. And she looked sublimely happy. As he put his arms around her, Jack's expression was nothing short of smitten.

An inexplicable bolt of envy pierced her. Not that Kata wanted Jack, but she yearned for the affection Morgan had, wanted to be steeped in that sort of tenderness and sexuality with someone who meant everything to her. Kata had never been aware of such a need. Hell, until recently, she would have denied it with her dying breath, especially after having Mamá and Gordon as her role models. But now the craving for a relationship like Jack and Morgan's blindsided her. The kind Hunter had described. His face swam in her mind.

"Tell me all about Deke and Kimber's baby, *mon coeur*." Jack smiled at his wife.

He worshipped Morgan with just a gaze and a few words, bowling Kata over again. Did being a man's submissive make the relationship deeper—or just more dangerous? Morgan looked like a vibrant woman, full to the brim with happiness. But Kata didn't know how to reconcile that vision with the reality she'd seen her stepfather dish out for all these years. How could the woman be anything but miserable under her domineering husband's thumb?

"Ten little fingers and ten little toes. He's so pink and chubby and perfect." Morgan sighed. "The maternity ward isn't very busy, so they brought the baby in, and I got to hold him."

"And now you want one?" Jack's smile was nothing short of indulgent. "I've been telling you since our wedding night that I would love babies with you."

Morgan glowed. "And I've appreciated your patience."

The big man returned her grin but didn't say another word. No pushing. No pressure. Just sparkling dark eyes that matched her excitement. Looking at Jack and Morgan, Kata wasn't sure exactly what to make of their exchange. Who had the power here?

"Can we . . . ?" Morgan asked with hope in her blue eyes.

Jack's smile only deepened. A warmth she would have never imagined him capable of suffused his face. "Whatever you want. You know that. Of course, I'd be thrilled."

"It's definitely worth . . . discussion." Morgan kissed her husband, then shivered at his touch. "But first things first. Where is . . ." Morgan whirled until their stares locked. The little redhead started, a hand to her chest. "Oh, I didn't see you in the corner. Kata, right? And, oh God, I just talked about having a baby." She blushed, then punched her husband. "Why didn't you tell me we weren't alone?"

Jack laughed, wrapping an arm around his wife's shoulder with a wink. "If Kata has been married to Hunter for more than ten minutes, I'm sure she knows where babies come from."

Morgan did a poor job of repressing a smile. "Yes, and no doubt, Hunter will want, um . . . lots and lots of practice when he returns."

That's what Kata feared—and yearned for so desperately. Memories of their night in Logan's condo kept swirling in her head. Hunter had controlled her body so completely that it still stunned her. The thought of giving that much of herself again both thrilled and terrified her. He would return in the next twenty-four hours, and those papers were burning a hole in her purse.

She'd come to a fork in the road. Take a chance that her relationship would be more like Jack and Morgan's? Or was that a fairy tale? Were she and Hunter destined to be more like Gordon and Mamá?

* * *

SIX a.m. Hunter shoved his phone in his pocket with a curse and headed inside the hospital. He didn't like any of this one bit.

The past forty-two hours had been a total waste. Hunter had encountered no arms-for-drugs deal going down by Víctor Sotillo's old gang. From everything he could tell, the thug's organization was barely limping along. They'd slowed their pace on funneling money to the corrupt local and national governments who, in turn, did business with Iran to fund terrorists and nuclear weapons. Hunter had no idea who was leading the Sotillo gang now. His local informant had assured him that Adan Sotillo, Víctor's salsa-dancing brother, was dead, though he had no details or proof. Provided Hunter's local snitch wasn't wrong or lying, if neither Sotillo brother was alive to turn an illegal profit, then who was running the show?

Even more perplexing was why he'd been sent to Venezuela in the first place. The pending deal that had created this blazing fucking emergency? He'd been unable to find even a hint of it. Usually, when he and the other members of SEAL Team 4 went anywhere near Sotillo's haunts, the meeting was fast, ugly, and brutal. This time, unnerving silence.

Was it possible that Adan's sudden death, so soon after Víctor's, had forced the criminals to slow their plans? Or had someone tipped them off? Either way, the "emergency" that had called Hunter to Venezuela and interrupted his honeymoon hadn't materialized. And he was beyond pissed off.

As soon as he got ahold of Barnes, Hunter vowed to chew his commanding officer a new asshole. Respectfully, of course. He'd probably be reprimanded anyway, since Andy liked exercising his newfound power. But he had a bigger problem now that he was back Stateside.

Hunter understood the need to drop everything and assist a sick loved one. He respected Kata for putting her mother's welfare above her own, since he did it every day as a soldier. But goddamn it, she wasn't trained for these situations. She'd disobeyed every direct order he'd given her and shed every safeguard he'd put in place. She hadn't asked for help when she needed it.

He had no doubt she was going to balk at her punishment, though she damn well deserved it. And he needed to feel her around him, under him, taking him. He needed to connect with her in a way he'd never needed anything or anyone.

Hunter wasn't one of those pussies afraid of commitment or his emotions, but he wasn't the only part of this equation. He'd pushed Kata to her mental and physical limit before leaving on this mission. He was coming off three days of adrenaline rush and sleeplessness. His mood was bad, his temper worse. Normally, he wouldn't go near Kata until he was rested and calm. But since he had to leave again Sunday morning for what would likely be months, he couldn't waste time. He had to see—and deal with—her now.

Inside the hospital's too-white lobby, Hunter bypassed the sleepy receptionist and headed for the bank of elevators. He counted to ten . . . twenty. Fuck, counting to a thousand wouldn't calm him down. If Tyler hadn't been on top of the situation, Kata could have fallen prey to an assassin's bullet; the heart Hunter still sought to earn could have stopped beating. The very thought turned his blood to ice.

With a muted *ding,* the elevator stopped on the third floor. Hunter jogged down the hall, spotting Tyler tucked in the shadows at the nurses' station, just as he'd promised. Jack and Morgan had gone home for a bit of sleep. Deke had stepped in while visiting his wife, then left around midnight. None of them could convince Kata to leave the hospital and rest someplace safe.

Hunter's palm itched. He was going to spank her but good. After they settled her mother, they were going to spend hours and hours sleeping and making love and resolving their problems. He'd do whatever necessary to make her damn well promise not to put herself at risk again. And he'd earn her love by Sunday.

Finally, room 304. Though less than a few dozen steps, the jog had seemed interminable. He rounded the corner and stepped into the hospital room.

And stopped cold.

In one of the room's two chairs, Kata sat, all curled up on Ben's lap, with her face in the crook of his neck and her arms around him, fast asleep. Ben had curled his arm over her thighs, his broad hand anchored near her hip. The other clung to her nape as he dozed. They looked cozy. Intimate.

The sight felt like a battering ram decimating his solar plexus.

Behind him, he heard familiar footsteps, and without looking knew they belonged to Tyler.

"How long has he been here?" Hunter swallowed, but nothing could keep the jagged fury from bubbling up inside him.

"He brought Kata and her mother here Monday night and has barely left since. Kata hasn't gone anywhere with him, but . . ."

Tyler's unfinished sentence suggested that, given their snug, sleep-warm embrace, it was only a matter of time before Kata fell back into Ben's bed. And from where Hunter was standing, that looked like an accurate assessment.

Fuck.

The bottom line was, Ben had been there for her when she needed him; Hunter hadn't.

What did you expect? An absent husband can't give me what I need. He *can.* His mother had screamed those words at his father fifteen years ago. No one in his family had seen or heard from Amanda again, divorce papers excepting, before she'd died.

Fisting his hands, Hunter stared at his wife curled up on another man's lap, a million thoughts racing through his head. He could turn around, leave, and never come back. But the Colonel had done exactly that when his wife had fallen for someone else, despite the fact that it cost him his heart. No fucking way was Hunter waving his white flag.

His dad had never quite healed after the bitter divorce, and Hunter knew if he let Kata go now, he'd likely crawl down that same emotional path. Unlike the Colonel, Hunter wasn't going down without a fight.

"Do you want to kill him, or should I?" Tyler whispered.

Personally, Hunter had assumed the man would understand Ben's position, mired in an unrequited love for Luc's wife, Alyssa, for about a year. But Tyler wasn't his focus now.

"Neither. I took Kata from Ben. Maybe he thinks this is tit for tat. I'll deal with him later. Since the doctor isn't releasing Kata's mom until later today, I'm going to have a long . . . chat with my wife."

When he finished, she'd understand exactly the lengths he'd go in order to keep what was his.

Chapter Thirteen

A HEAVY presence woke Kata from a deep, tangled sleep. Had the doctor returned? She opened her eyes to find herself on Ben's lap and frowned. How had she gotten there? Shaking her head, she stood on shaky legs, then turned—and gasped.

A forbidding shadow stood directly above her, face inscrutable in the predawn dark. Heart pounding, she gasped, adrenaline jolting her. Then recognition hit.

"Hunter!" Her first urge was to throw her arms around him, but she suddenly saw his taut shoulders and cold, cold gaze shift down to Ben before lifting back to her with the sharpness of a lethal blade. Trepidation tightened her belly.

Kata glanced back at Ben, who shifted restlessly in the chair, then faced Hunter once more. "It's not what you . . . I—I was just exhausted. I guess we fell asleep. I don't remember. But nothing—"

"Not here." His voice sounded like the snap of a whip. "The doctor says your mother will be discharged this afternoon. Once she is, we'll get her home and settled. When was the last time you showered or ate a whole meal?"

Kata swallowed a lump of dismay. She knew better than to think that he hadn't asked why she'd been sitting on Ben's lap because he didn't care. Rage vibrated off of him. No, he was saving this ass chewing for later. Ben had originally agreed to share her with Hunter, but she didn't think for one second that Hunter would be at all willing to share with Ben.

Jack's warning about the spanking Hunter would undoubtedly give her dive-bombed her thoughts. Had she, in his mind, added to her list of infractions by falling asleep on Ben? Would Hunter strip her bare, force her to lie across his knees, and take every hot, commanding swat of his hand on her ass? What self-respecting, independent female would want that? Yeah, his few swats back at Logan's condo had been . . . nice, but to actually want him to truly spank her? No way. Not her.

Still, the thought made her heart stutter . . . and made her pussy dismayingly wet.

God, her whole relationship with Hunter was confusing, destructive. Kata had fallen asleep trying to decide if she should give him the divorce papers. She still didn't know what to do. All the ways he'd touched her as if staking his claim, everything he'd said about loving her . . . She wanted so badly for that to be true, even though it terrified her.

"Kata, your last meal and shower?"

The way he barked questions rattled her. All his warmth, passion, and fire had been replaced with barely checked thunder. An odd shame crawled through her. She'd displeased him, and for some reason that bothered her. A lot.

She didn't like it one bit.

"Hello to you, too." She thrust her hands on her hips. "Glad to see you're still in one piece. Thanks for telling me all about your trip. Things have been rough here, since you didn't ask. But I'm handling it."

He clenched his jaw and softened his voice. "I'm sorry your mother's been ill. Tyler updated me on the situation earlier this morning. I'm glad she's recovering. Now I'm concerned about you. Answer the question, Kata. When?"

"The way you're glowering at me doesn't exactly make me want to answer, but it's been two days."

If she'd seen thunder on his face before, it now held a storm of fury. "Goddamn it—"

In the chair behind her, Ben groaned, stretched, and opened his eyes. He froze when he saw Hunter. "Oh. You're back."

Ben didn't even try to sound happy about that fact.

Hunter gave him a single nod, then grabbed her hand. "I'll take care of my *wife* from here. I'll make sure she gets a damn meal."

Ben stood and edged right behind her and added fuel to the fire by wrapping his arm around her waist. "Fuck you! I begged her to eat. I've been by her side for the last day and a half while you were off playing soldier. In fact, I've been with her for the last two years. I'll stand by her, no matter what, and she knows it. It's up to Kata to choose who she wants to . . . help her."

"Help" clearly being a euphemism for something much more meaningful. Kata gaped at Ben over her shoulder. They'd been casual lovers. Was he seriously trying to stake some claim *now*?

"Ben?" She sent him a questioning stare, tension gripping her insides.

His arm around her tightened. "I guess I didn't realize how important you were to me until you weren't there anymore. But you are, and I'm here for you."

Kata was there for him, too, but as nothing more than a friend. She didn't know if she'd just naturally outgrown him or if Hunter had played a role, but she knew that whatever had once been between them was over.

"Back off." Hunter pulled Kata out of Ben's grip, then held up her left hand. Her wedding ring glinted in the white hospital light filtering in through the hall. "I take care of what's mine."

"You're such a bastard," Ben snarled.

The testosterone in the room was so thick, Kata thought she might choke. She stepped away from them both.

"You knew that when you invited me to Vegas." Hunter smiled coldly.

Ben clenched his fists and looked to her, his expression a plea for reassurance. Kata's stomach cramped with guilt. If she'd led him on, it had been unintentional. No doubt, they should talk this through at some point.

She turned and gave him a friendly hug. "Thank you for everything. I wouldn't have made it through this difficult time without your help. I'm fine now. Rest. I'll call you."

Ben closed his eyes. Despite her gentle rejection, the sting of it tightened his face. Abruptly, he stepped away. "You're living in Fantasyland if you think this controlling prick will ever let you call me again."

He brushed her shoulder with his own as he exited the room.

Was Ben right? Would Hunter try to forbid her from even saying hi to someone she'd considered a friend for two years? Kata wouldn't put up with that.

"Your mother isn't set to be released until at least thirteen hundred, in seven hours. She's out of danger, and you haven't left her side in days. You need to rest and refuel. You and I need to talk. Tyler will watch her and call if anything arises." He tugged on her hand. "Let's go."

Kata dug in her heels. "I can't go anywhere until Mamá does. She needs me to take care of her."

Hunter's cold eyes narrowed. "She's in a hospital filled with health-care professionals. You can't take care of anyone when you're falling down on your feet. If you're not going to take care of yourself, I'll do it for you. Don't think I won't carry you out."

She absolutely knew that he would. A part of her reveled. Another part railed. How could he expect her to leave when Mamá needed her most?

"If this is your way of taking care of me, it feels more like bullying."

He crowded into her personal space, then glanced down at her breasts, his gaze a hot caress. "But you respond to it."

Shit. Kata became aware of her nipples, tight and hard, poking against her shirt. A few minutes in his presence did that to her. Her body felt heavy, her breathing shallow. Her panties? Best not to think about how wet those had become.

"You haven't even begun to discover all the ways I'm going to take care of you. Come with me now." Each word he spoke in low tones, his voice like smoke and steel, infused with that controlled demand she knew so well.

Kata knew she should just shut up . . . but she couldn't bring herself to simply give in. "If I don't?"

His grip on her hand tightened, and he stepped even closer, his chest brushing hers. "Itching to add to all the punishment you've got coming?"

Kata's pulse leapt. Lightning flared through her nipples. Fresh moisture slicked her sex. She pressed her thighs together, but that only made the ache worse. Damn Hunter. His touch could too easily become an addiction. Already, she felt the slide into craving.

She looked up, and their gazes locked. The fury in his blue eyes was so cold, they were nearly gray. A glance farther down revealed an erection that made her body tighten with need all over again. But when Kata looked up again, she saw the exhaustion in the deep hollows of his eyes and compressed lips. Concern bled through defiance.

Kata curled her hand around his shoulder. "When was the last time *you* slept and ate a whole meal?"

He paused, seemingly disarmed by the question. Some of his starch softened, and he sighed tiredly. "Days ago."

Which explained why he was particularly short now. Ben's presence at the hospital hadn't helped the cause.

"All right. Then let's go. We'll be back in time to get Mamá?"

"Of course. Kata, if you'd let me, I'll always take care of you. That includes helping the family you love."

That right there. When he said things like that, how could she not melt in a puddle at his feet? How could she not care about him? God knows, Gordon had never given a rat's ass about anyone but himself. After this declaration, all the times she'd compared the two seemed unfair.

"Thank you. Once we bring her home, I'll need to stay with her while she recovers—"

Hunter started shaking his head before she even finished her sentence. "Until we know who's after you and I figure out how to make you safe again, you can't stay there. It's too obvious. Whoever is after you will pick you off like a target in a shooting gallery. Do you want your family near that?"

Kata didn't have misplaced bravado, nor did she want Mamá in danger. Put that like, she shouldn't have come to the hospital with her mother at all.

"No. You're right, but what about Mamá's recovery? Gordon won't take care of her. She's this sick because he didn't care enough about her to see to her welfare to start with, and my sister—"

"Shh." He pressed a finger to her lips, making her tingle from head to toe. "I admire the fact that you want to take care of your mother, but there are other ways to accomplish it without putting yourself in danger. Trust me to make that happen."

Jack's words came back to Kata. She hadn't trusted Hunter's watchdog, Tyler. Which Hunter would, in turn, interpret as a lack of trust in him. She'd never looked at it that way, but Jack's explanation made that logic seem so obvious. Hunter might be dominating and stubborn, but he was also very capable and resourceful. She was exhausted after the past few days, and knowing that she could count on his help was both hard to swallow and pure relief.

"Did you have anything in mind? Gordon won't allow another man in the house." So Hunter sending one of his buddies was out of the question.

"Duly noted. Let me make a few phone calls. I won't do anything to make your mother's situation more difficult."

She squeezed his biceps, absently noting that she couldn't even come close to wrapping her hand around it. He was solid through and through. "Thank you."

Kata hoped that Hunter would kiss her. He didn't.

Instead, he stepped back, agitation still pouring off him. With a sigh, she walked into the shadows of the room hanging over the bed and pressed her lips to her mother's pale cheek, then followed Hunter outside just as the first fingers of dawn were spreading across the sky in hues of orange and gold.

Without a word, he helped her into a black Jeep she'd never seen. He slid into the driver's seat, pulled out of the parking lot, then immediately reached for his phone. With two phone calls, he had a place for them to crash, courtesy of Jack, and a capable female to nurse her mother back to health, thanks to one of Kimber's fellow nursing friends who was in between jobs.

Gratitude burned through her, and she felt ashamed that she'd leaned on Ben so much in Hunter's absence. "Thank you."

"You're welcome."

"Nurses aren't cheap. How much do I need to pay—"

"I'll take care of it." His tone warned her not to say another word on the subject.

She'd offended his masculine dignity. Did he think she'd suggested that he was incapable of doing it himself? Kata winced. Stubborn man . . . even if the sentiment was sweet.

Silence prevailed for the rest of the ride. Traffic began to pick up, and he dodged it smoothly, gripping the steering wheel, his shoulders bunched with tension. He flexed his fingers, then wrapped them even tighter on the wheel. Kata peeked at his profile. Sharp, clenched.

That wasn't a good sign.

Suddenly, Hunter pulled into a parking lot and stopped the Jeep. An office building. What were they doing here? Before she could ask, he threw open the vehicle's door and jumped out, slamming it behind him.

He marched around the Jeep, glaring at her through the windshield, then opened the passenger door, putting his body between hers and the street. "Let's go."

Kata had no illusions. Given Hunter's agitation, once they got behind closed doors, there would likely be a hard spanking and a thorough fucking in her immediate future. Ignoring her shiver of anticipation, she eased out of the vehicle. She had to talk to him now, before they got too busy.

"I'm sorry about running out on Tyler. And about being on Ben's lap."

With a fierce scowl, he stalked across the parking lot, dragging her and her suitcase behind him, heading for the building's gleaming black door. "We'll discuss it later."

"I need to say this now." She followed him across the blacktop and lifted a hand to the steely solid width of his chest. "Because if I don't, you'll have time to stew and get more pissed off and mentally convict me of shit that never happened."

Hunter grabbed her wrist. His blue eyes, usually filled with laughter or passion, looked like an arctic deep freeze. She'd never seen him close to the edge of his temper, but she imagined this was it. Discreetly, she tried to tug her wrist from his grasp. He held firm.

"Later. After we're inside and this asshole trying to kill you can't do an easy drive-by."

He released her, dismissed her, and focused on the silver pad to the right of the door. After he punched in a code, she heard an audible *click*. Hunter wrenched the door open. "Get in."

Kata hesitated. The independent woman in her wanted to fight his command. The logical part of her knew that loitering outside the building wasn't smart. Somehow, the female in her hated disappointing him even more.

"Yes, Sir," The words slipped out as she entered the building.

He rewarded her with a caress to her back, and she ached to burrow closer to his touch.

The door shut behind them with a deafening thud before he turned the lock and engaged the security system.

Tinted glass, sleek chrome, and ambient lighting filled the lobby. A couple of leather chairs, an empty desk.

"This is Jack's official office. He only uses it for client meetings. It's secure and out of the way. Come with me." He grabbed her arm.

He led her to another door, swiped a key card in front of a plastic panel, then thrust her through the next open door—and into an apartment of sorts. A small living room decked out with a leather love seat and a long, padded ottoman, a kitchenette with everything modern, a dining room less than half filled by a little bistro table and some giant cross affixed to the wall. Hunter flipped on a soft, golden overhead light, then shoved her straight into a bedroom both stark and lavish.

Cream-colored walls except the one that anchored the wide bed. That was painted a deep, passionate red. Gleaming marble floors, two pedestal nightstands, and a massive headboard that looked positively medieval decorated the space. There wasn't a single window in the shadowed room.

Hunter shut the door behind him, then turned sharply to face her. "Did you know that Ben has feelings for you?"

Well. Now that they were alone, he wasn't wasting any time.

"N—not until this morning. He's never indicated that I meant anything beyond—"

As Hunter tensed, Kata closed her mouth. Best not to remind him just now that she and Ben had shared a bed. Just a guess, but he probably wouldn't appreciate the recap.

"A casual fuck?" he finished for her, his jealousy roared through the room like an inferno.

Kata tried to play it cool with a shrug. "He never seemed to care that much."

"C'mon, Kata. He threw you a Vegas birthday party and went to a hell of a lot of trouble and expense to try to make your ménage fantasy come true. You *must* have guessed. And when you got your mom's message, he was the *first* person you turned to, the one you trusted. What am I supposed to make of that? What are your feelings for him?"

"I'm not in love with him, if that's what you're asking. And I didn't want to have sex with him, either. I just knew he'd come if I needed help."

"Yeah, because he fucking cares. You care for him, too."

"As a *friend*. And friends help friends, so yes, I knew he'd come."

Hunter raised a brow. "Do friends also cuddle up against their friends' hard-ons?"

She'd already said that she didn't want Ben. "Damn it, stop twisting my words. You're pissing me off!"

"*You're* pissed? I've been prowling jungle shitholes nonstop for the last thirty-six hours, hunting terrorists more elusive than ghosts. We accomplished nothing but exhaustion and dehydration. One of the things that kept me going was knowing that I'd see you again. I've been harder than steel, dying to fuck you, since I got on the plane in Venezuela. I came back to find you on your lover's lap."

The way he growled, his eyes seething fury, all screamed that he was at the end of his rope. How pissed would she be if she came home from exhausting days away to find a woman on Hunter's lap? Enraged . . . and beyond hurt. Maybe they both needed to count to ten.

She sighed. "I tried to tell you earlier, I don't even remember falling asleep. And you knew from the start that Ben and I are hardly strangers. But, I swear, we're not lovers anymore. I've been dodging his advances since Vegas. I don't want him anymore."

"Then why did he try to get territorial about you with me?"

"I really have no idea."

Hunter pressed his lips into a grim line. "That doesn't solve my real problem: You trusted Ben before you trusted me."

Kata recoiled at the hurt in his voice. "You weren't here for me to trust. I know you had to leave, and I don't blame you, but my mother needed me. I barely knew Tyler. If he refused to let me help Mamá, I had no recourse, and I knew it. Why would I ask the guy locking me up on your behalf to let me go?"

"Tyler was there to protect you. If you needed help, you should have told him, not sneaked behind my back."

"I've had, what? All of four days to reconcile myself to our marriage—while being shot at, grappling with your dominant expectations, and as my mother has been at death's door. Excuse me if I don't adjust my thinking fast enough for you."

"That pretty little mouth is going to get you in deeper trouble, honey. You should have trusted that I would see to your needs."

"Just like you should be trusting that falling asleep on Ben's lap means absolutely nothing to me?"

Hunter swiped a hard hand at the back of his neck and stared at the ceiling, clearly willing patience. Then he exhaled and stared at her with blue ice chip eyes. "Strip."

Her heart stuttered. Here? Now?

"Are you going to spank me?" Kata remembered the way he'd heated up her backside, then commanded her body to the ultimate pleasure at his brother's condo. The thought that he might do it again stirred up a confounding, alluring mixture of fear and anticipation.

He didn't answer. His glare silently repeated his demand, promising more punishment if she didn't comply.

She and Hunter had already played this game once, and she'd wound up naked and at his mercy. Better to admit that she enjoyed being naked for him and save her strength for the battles yet to come.

With a bravado she didn't feel, she kicked off her shoes, dropped her purse, doffed her shirt, shucked out of her capri pants, unhooked her bra, then shimmied out of her panties. The instant she was bare, a terrible sense of vulnerability, of being naked down to her soul, crashed through Kata.

At the sight of her, Hunter's eyes flashed with heat. He fisted his hands at his sides but made no move to take her over his knee.

Maybe there was no erotic spanking in her future. The possibility filled her with a disappointment that made absolutely no sense . . . but sat like a boulder in her belly.

"Now what?"

Hunter stared, remained silent, almost dissecting her with his gaze.

She sucked up her fear and thrust her hands on her hips. "If you're going to blame me for shit I didn't do and sulk, screw this. I'm going back to my mom." She bent to pick up her clothes.

Hunter stepped on the garments and blocked the exit, his lean, tightly muscled body squarely in her path. "You aren't leaving." His face seethed with fury . . . and unmistakable lust. In that low, authoritative voice that made her shivery and hot, he ordered, "On your knees. Bow your head."

Kata's womb cramped at his command. She froze. Her instinct screamed at her to leave. Her logic told her that trying would only be stupid and futile. Might as well get this over with.

Hunter pressed his lips together in an angry line as he waited wordlessly in the lengthening silence. Slowly, she dropped to one knee, then the other, wincing when she fell too hard on the tile. But she wasn't going to show him any weakness. And damn it, she wasn't going to bow her head in repentance when she'd done nothing wrong.

She looked past the tempting erection about to burst Hunter's zipper and sent him a challenging stare. "I said I was sorry. I admit I should have asked Tyler for help, but this is all the obedience you're getting from me. Deal with it."

Hunter moved so fast, Kata barely saw him. But she felt him, massive hands around her waist, lifting her. Suspended in his grasp, she flailed, only feeling solid surface under her belly when he drew her over his lap.

Something hot in Kata flared at the helplessness of her position. Clearly, he liked it, too. His erection, which had grown even larger, prodded her, taunted her, as she wriggled for freedom.

Above her, Hunter nestled a forearm against her nape and another across the back of her thighs, immobilizing her instantly. He leaned over to whisper hotly in her ear, "How far do you think that sass is going to get you?"

Though her pussy ached, her mouth still had a mind of its own. "You mean the truth? Nowhere, clearly. Because you're being churlish and overbearing."

"You're being disrespectful and obstinate. And you know what I think? You're pushing me on purpose so that I'll either give up or get so angry that I'll force my dominance on you, and you won't have to submit. Neither will happen. Either use your safe word or take your punishment."

If she was smart, she'd blurt out Ben's name and demand that Hunter let her go. But that would also leave the rapidly climbing ache inside her unfulfilled. "And give you an easy way to blame this on me? Fuck you."

"Oh, we'll get there—after all the punishment you've got coming."

Kata's body pulsed at his words. She bucked under his touch, though she knew he'd never let her loose. That added to her twisted excitement. Was she some closet deviant?

"I want to be clear," he said. "Are you refusing to use your safe word?"

She tensed. "Don't touch me."

He relaxed his hold enough for her to look over her shoulder at his dark, dirty smile. "You know I will. Just like I know you'll soon beg me to fuck you, and you'll come like never before. Since you're refusing to use your safe word, we'll start with ten swats, Kata. Count them."

Before she could prolong the argument, he raised one hand and brought it down across her ass, smacking her hard. She shrieked as a hot sting exploded across the center of her left cheek, searing her skin. A conflagration quickly spread across her ass. *Oh dear God!* Within seconds, her sex liquefied. Tendrils of desire began curling through her, even as she struggled to process the pain.

"Count," he insisted. "Or I'll start over."

Kata's entire body trembled. "One."

"Good. Why are you being punished?"

"Because you're a—a brute!"

"Wrong answer." Then he struck the fleshy part of her ass again, this time low on her right cheek, in the crease of her thigh, where she'd feel it every time she took a step.

Agonized pleasure whipped across her senses. A burning flush followed. Her blood turned thick like honey. Gasping for air, she braced herself with flat palms on the mattress, trying—and failing— to push away from him. Her breasts dangled, their nipples desperately tight. If Hunter saw them, he would *know* this spanking aroused her.

Hunter grabbed her wrists and forced them together at the small of her back, rendering her utterly helpless again. That made her even wetter, damn it.

"Kata?" he held her wrists with one hand and spread his palm across her ass with the other, grinding the burn into her skin.

She gasped, pressing her thighs together for relief.

"Stop that. Or I'll keep adding," His low growl warned as he forced her legs apart. "You've got five seconds. Count."

More blood rushed to her pussy. She swelled, throbbed. Drawing in a shuddering breath, Kata wondered how the hell she was going to make it to ten without falling apart. "Two."

"Good girl. Why are you being punished?"

Hunter's hand hovered above her ass. Kata could feel its heat, craved the intimacy of his skin on hers. She'd always appreciated a man with large hands, she thought because he'd likely have sizeable equipment. Now she knew why the size of a man's hands could turn her on. As the ache between her legs coiled ruthlessly, she prayed Hunter would give her more.

"Because I ran from Tyler."

"Yes." He smoothed his hot hand across her burning ass once more, priming her, before he spanked her again three more times in rapid succession, strategically striking her flesh in new places: low on her left cheek, high on the right, dead in the middle.

Desire ratcheted up. Now her entire backside felt tender, on fire. Moisture slid from her sex, coating her so that she felt every little quiver of her hips across Hunter's lap acutely. Her clit pulsed in time with her heartbeat. Her breath caught. "Three, four, f-five."

Arousal made her voice breathy. Kata squirmed again, then realized she was dampening the fabric of his pants under her pussy. Frantically, she tried to wriggle away before he figured out how much this excited her.

Hunter pressed a palm between her shoulder blades, holding her in place, then slid that hand between her legs. God, no way he'd fail to notice how wet the insides of her thighs were, how swollen her labia had become. Once he spanked her again, he'd likely feel her moisture seeping back between her cheeks.

"Hmm. You going to try to tell me that you're not enjoying this spanking?"

Enjoying it? Just knowing that she had five more swats coming forced her to bite back a moan. Kata closed her eyes as a shiver of both shame and excitement ran through her, but that didn't mean she was about to surrender. "You're entitled to your opinion . . ."

"Stubborn wench." Hunter's laugh wasn't pleasant as he slid a hand between her legs again, gliding one finger over her clit. Pleasure lit her up, a fireball sizzling right *there*. Kata clenched her fists, fingers desperate, nails digging into her palms. Her heart pounded, her blood blazed, her entire body felt electric.

Instinctively, she ground her hips down into his hand. He pulled back. "Stop. Why else am I punishing you?"

"Because I turned to Ben," she sobbed out.

He landed another two swats to her burning ass, both in the fleshy parts of each cheek. "That's right."

Amazingly, the pleasure expanded, and she felt herself sinking into it, embracing both it and the white-hot bite of pain that hurtled her ever closer to climax. "Six, seven. Please . . ."

"Very good. I love the way you're sticking your ass in the air, waiting for me to give you more."

Kata froze. She was? As Hunter ran a warm finger down her hot rear, she arched her back and strained up, anticipating his next blow. Need and confusion poured through her.

He struck her ass with his palm twice more, again with more force than before. "You will never put yourself in danger again. Ever. Are we clear?"

No, she was consumed by the ecstasy just beyond her grasp. The pain flowed through her backside, her thighs, her skin tingling and alive. Her sex throbbed in demand. The sensations licked her with flames of need, torqued her up, driving her close to the edge. She whimpered.

"Kata?"

"Eight." She exhaled raggedly. "N-nine."

"Are we clear?"

Hunter wasn't going to give her that orgasm beckoning with its overwhelming power yet. God, she wanted it. The strength of her desire splintered her. She squirmed on his lap, trying to rub herself on his thigh.

"You can't stop pushing, can you? I am your husband and your Dom. I say when you come. I say how you stay safe. You will not sneak out behind my back again. If you do, I won't be responsible for how far I push you or how hard I fuck you. Your role is to surrender."

The independent woman in her wanted to tell him to go blow himself. The trembling submissive in her lay braced for his last smack, praying it would send her over the edge.

"Ask me nicely for what you want, Kata. And do it right the first time." Or else there would be no orgasm. She heard the implied threat in his voice.

Nipples and mound both rubbing over the denim covering his strong, spread thighs, Kata held her breath, needing the intoxicating thrill of his hand on her ass again. She'd never imagined that she'd like it. But this stunning pleasure-pain . . . She could almost hate him for giving this to her, making her vulnerable, but she needed him too much.

"Please, Sir, may I have another? Please make me come."

"Will you consider your safety more carefully in the future?"

"Yes." She would have said anything for his next touch.

"Will you trust me to take care of you?" He rubbed his hot palm across her ass.

She gasped. "Yes, Sir."

"Good girl."

His body jerked, and Kata heard the whistle of his hand as it whipped through the air. She braced herself, but nothing could prepare her for the final blow, again in the center of her right cheek. An inferno blasted across her skin. Tingles sparked from her reddened flesh down, brutally invading her pussy. Need coiled tighter. She hovered on the edge of an orgasm that was both terrifying and essential. Without it, she'd die.

"Please, Hunter, Sir. Please . . ." Her entire body jolted, shuddered, pinging with a towering, unrelieved desire she'd never felt in her life.

Without warning, he released her wrists, lifted her, then rolled her over. Her sore rear rested on his chafing denim. She hissed at the sharp sensation, wishing it was enough to send her over. It only sent her higher.

"Look at me."

Kata lifted her frantic gaze to him. The unmistakable lust in his eyes added more fuel to her fire. But that wasn't all. Every moment, every breath, teemed with his possessive fury.

Hunter settled a palm on her knee, then slowly slid it up her thigh, his thumb achingly close to her pussy. "Who do you belong to?"

She whimpered and thrust her hips to him. "You."

"Will you ever forget that?" His thumb grazed her slick flesh, whispering just over her hard, demanding clit.

"No," she mewled.

"Will you ever disobey me like this again?"

To feel these million racing sensations again . . . this sublime journey into another realm where Hunter put this mind-blowing stamp of possession on her? For that, she'd do nearly anything to please—or provoke—him.

She closed her eyes, sinking into the drowning pool of need. "No. Please."

"Look at me, Kata." The second her eyes fluttered open, he murmured, "Now come." Then he slapped her mound, right above her clit.

It was everything she'd ached for and needed.

Kata let loose a guttural scream as pleasure drew up, in, blood swelling her flesh until she exploded in ecstasy. Her body jerked as she unraveled. And Hunter forced his hand between her legs again, circling her clit, prolonging the staggering clenching of her womb, until she could no longer think or breathe or do anything but feel rapture pour over her.

Though he had yet to be inside her, she felt utterly possessed. He grounded her, became her reality. In the haze of pleasure, his body, his arms, were the only things that seemed real to her. She met his gaze helplessly, losing herself in the commanding blue fire of his eyes. Needing something to hang on to, she grabbed his shirt and silently pleaded with him. For mercy? For more? She wasn't sure. In response, he shoved two fingers into the tight clasp of her sex, his thumb working her sensitive nub, and shoved her over another towering cliff of pleasure.

After Kata eked out the last whimper of need, she opened her eyes. Hunter leaned over her, knuckles brushing her cheeks and wiping her tears away. She'd been crying? Yes, and she still sobbed as the power of their shared moment hit her all over again. Hunter had taken her apart and turned her inside out, opened her up in a way that left her both terrified and exhilarated. Though limp and weeping in his lap, she felt inexorably tied to him, body and heart, in a way she'd never been connected to anyone in her life.

Gently, he dried her tears again, then lifted her, setting her on her knees between his thighs. "I need you, honey."

Kata glanced up into his tight, flushed face. His need was apparent and compelling, just like the hard bulge beneath his zipper. As she basked in afterglow, the urge to please him totally sank into her bones. For some reason, she knew she would not breathe easily again until he was every bit as satisfied as she. The feeling was foreign and illogical but undeniable.

With trembling fingers, she worked his zipper, looking to him for approval. Desire flared in his eyes. Hunter's heavy breaths punctuated the rasp of his zipper as she lowered it. Her heart raced. As she worked his jeans and briefs down, Hunter stood. Kata shifted at his feet, squarely onto her knees, and stripped his garments down his lean legs. He kicked them across the room as he tore off his shirt, leaving his muscled chest, washboard abs, and every amazing inch of his cock bare.

He filtered his fingers through her hair, then planted a tender but firm grip on her crown, slowly pulling her toward his open thighs. She reached for him and grabbed his thick cock, licking her lips as she went down.

When she ran her tongue across the damp purple head of his erection, his fingers tightened in her hair. Hunter tensed, hissed. "Yeah, honey. That's it. Open your mouth just like . . . *ahhh*. Yeah."

At the intense pleasure in his voice, a shiver rolled through her. Kata curled closer, opened her mouth wider, took him deeper. Slowly, eyes closed, she filled her mouth with his thick shaft. She cataloged everything about him: his silky-hard texture, the faint smell of sweat and musk, the tang of salt concentrated at his weeping slit, the dusting of brown hair on his thighs that thickened at the root of his cock, the way he groaned and jerked as she took him all the way to the back of her throat.

His fingers tightened on her as he arched his hips, stroking into her mouth. "Fuck, you feel so good."

Kata heated under his praise, yearned for more of it. Sucking hard, she drew her lips up all the steely inches of his shaft, rubbing and cradling him with her tongue, dragging her teeth delicately over the swollen head.

Hunter hissed again. "Damn. I've been dying to feel that heavenly mouth. Swallow me, honey."

"Yes, Sir," she whispered.

Then he was palming the back of her head with one hand and guiding his cock to her with the other.

In the past, oral sex had been merely a means to excite a lover before sex. But this was a pleasure all its own. He filled her senses with his musky scent, unique tang, and growling moans, as the hard bands of his hair-roughened thighs tensed beneath her fingers. He threw his head back, eyes closed, and lost himself. The woman inside ached to please him completely, deepen the undeniable bond forging between them.

The swollen velvety head of his cock brushed her lips again, and she took him deeper, faster, unable to resist giving him all he sought. She teased him with a sly flick of her tongue. His fingers tightened in her hair, guiding her, establishing a fast, hot rhythm. Kata complied, drawing him to the back of her throat. A long groan spilled from his chest. Kata relished the sound.

She cupped his heavy testicles in her palm. They drew up as she dragged her tongue up his shaft and curled over the sensitive head again, giving him another gentle nip of her teeth.

"You feel so fucking good. Suck me dry."

His command sent a thrill through her. The thought of giving him enough pleasure to completely empty him aroused her to a fever pitch. Her breasts hung heavy, ached. Her sex cramped with a hungry clench. She slipped a hand between her legs and fumbled for her clit.

Hunter dragged her hand away from her slick folds. "No, honey. Save that for me. That orgasm is mine to give you."

She whimpered, but he merely took her wrists in his grasp and lifted them high above her head, restraining them against his chest in one powerful hand. He directed her mouth back to his waiting cock with the other.

Even as he denied her self-pleasure, blood rushed through her body, heart pumping. Hunter was becoming an addiction. Kata knew it, felt herself rushing headlong into the danger. Despite knowing she'd crash hard eventually, in that moment, she was willing to do anything to experience the ecstasy he could give her.

He filled her mouth, leaking more fluid. His urgent need ripped through her. She sucked harder, faster. His words slowly gave way to tortured groans. He hardened again and pulsed on her tongue. Desire clawed at her. She wanted this, needed to know that she could hurtle him into pleasure, as he did for her.

"Kata." He barely got her name out between harsh breaths. "Now, honey."

She moaned, nodded, sucking him deeper than ever before.

Seconds later, his every muscle tensed. He shouted and flooded her mouth with the salty taste of him, filling her ears with his long, guttural moan. She swallowed him, sucking him through his climax, electric pleasure jolting her simply because she'd pleased him. And she knew it when he looked at her moments later with soft blue eyes, gave her that tender stroke of fingers across her cheek.

"Thank you."

Kata hadn't just wanted to give him pleasure; she'd *needed* to earn his praise and tenderness, and still ached for his approval. In the past, she'd assumed that lovers would find their pleasure in her, just as she did with them. Hunter was different. Why?

"God, you're incredible." His raspy voice went straight to her heart. "I'm so glad you're mine."

His. Yes, and she felt it down to her very core. Hearing his appreciation settled her anxiety, brought about a sense of peace that she didn't quite understand. In one way, she felt cleansed, almost happy.

With a groan, Hunter sat back on the bed. Kata rested her head on his thigh, sighing when he filtered his hands through her hair in tender thanks.

Kata had never felt anything like this sweet bond. Tears sprang to her eyes again. God, she wanted to experience it again and again, would do anything to have it. Clean his house, bake him cakes, worship at his feet. Whatever he wanted.

How did that make her different than her mother?

The question zinged through her brain like a bullet. Her blood chilled. Kata jerked away, avoiding Hunter's sudden quizzical stare.

Given her mother's weakness for Gordon, the fact that she was willing to prostrate herself to earn Hunter's pleasure and approval terrified her. After the way he'd handled Ben's challenge and her defiance, she knew Hunter wasn't like Gordon in the ways that mattered. But what if she was more like her mother than she imagined? What if she lost herself to her unbearably sexy, powerful husband and ceased being Kata, the snarky, independent probation officer, and merely became Kata the eager submissive?

For a decade, she'd despised that weakness inside her mother that allowed her to subjugate herself to the asshole she'd married. It devastated Kata to realize she carried the same weakness.

Suddenly, she could see herself as Hunter's plaything, waiting, hoping—begging—him to bestow pleasure and admiration on her because she couldn't do without them. After all, he'd dismantled her with a mere ten swats and a single touch to her pussy. How easily Hunter had taken her under, to a place where she didn't recognize herself, to a world where she'd do anything to make him happy. Kata could too easily lose herself in this, in him.

"What's running through your head, honey?" He reached out for her. When she scrambled away, he frowned. "Let's talk."

Kata tried to take a deep breath. Maybe she was overthinking this. Morgan didn't seem lost to Jack. Then again, they were like some fairy-tale couple, totally happy in a way most spouses could only pray for. That wasn't reality. The way she'd given herself over to Hunter so completely was. As was her terrible yearning to do it again.

She saw now that Hunter wouldn't *take* her independence. He'd be hard, demanding. But to feel this staggering pleasure again, to please him, she would willingly give her soul away until there was nothing left.

Kata closed her eyes and sobbed.

* * *

HUNTER frowned at his overwrought wife. They'd been perfectly in sync, her submission so natural and freely given. He'd been so proud. Now he saw panic ripping across her face. She'd fallen hard into a post-scene plunge, where she felt stripped to the bone and emotion ruled.

Hunter gritted his teeth. She needed aftercare and reassurance—fast.

He approached, ignoring her when she scrambled away, and lifted her to the bed. "Lie back." He settled her head on the pillow, rubbed a soothing hand over her shoulder. "Tell me what's upsetting you."

Kata refused to look at him. *Fuck.*

Digging for patience, he curled his body around her own. She turned her back to him, sobbing harder. Shit, was this something more than a common emotional swell?

Hunter realized that he'd argued without listening much, mistake number one. He understood the urgency of her mother's situation and should have told her so. God knew, she'd been under pressure and confused. But damn it, she hadn't even tried to hear his perspective, hadn't trusted his protection. The words necessary to describe his betrayal at seeing her on Ben's lap, knowing she'd run to her fuck buddy for help before her husband, weren't in his vocabulary.

With that spanking, Hunter had punished her. She'd submitted so beautifully. Now, after experiencing their stunning connection and tasting heaven, she was trying her best to put distance between them again.

"Honey. Don't do this. You've got to tell me what's wrong so we can work on it."

Kata scrambled off the bed. "Where's my purse?"

She scanned the room with haunted eyes. Worry slithered through him.

Damn, he should have known that if he was going to ask her to open up to him, the revelations couldn't be one-sided. He had to open up as well and explain why her refusal to trust him with her feelings was unacceptable . . . and painful. Kata had to understand. He felt so fucking vulnerable, revealing his anguish to someone with the power to devastate him. But she deserved the truth, especially if he wanted the same. They'd have nothing without honesty.

"Honey, take a deep breath. I'll find your purse. Then we'll talk."

She wouldn't meet his stare.

Reining back his anxiety, Hunter prowled around the room until he found her little clutch. Reluctantly, he handed it to her. Kata tore it open. From inside, she withdrew a sheaf of papers and a pen, scrawled something across the last page, then thrust the crisp document at him with shaking hands. "Sign it."

Trepidation tightened his gut. With one hand, he shook the papers open and found the only three words in creation that could have fear exploding in his belly—and him seeing red.

Chapter Fourteen

"Petition for divorce?" The blast of his voice echoed off the walls like thunder. Hunter crushed the paper in his hand. He swallowed, nostrils flaring.

Kata flinched.

"I—I don't think I can do this for even another five minutes. We're not going to be right together for a lifetime."

"But you're not willing to stick around and find out?" Hunter crowded in on her, his gaze locked on hers. "This. Will. Never. Happen." He spoke slowly, clearly, every word a vow. "We're going to work this out, Kata. I won't make my dad's mistake and watch my wife walk out the door."

She froze. His statement explained so much. He tried to hold emotion back, but sadness and rage bled from his expression. Kata's heart caught as their gazes connected, hers silently asking what had happened.

"At the start of my senior year, my mother served my father with divorce papers so she could be with her lover. My dad did *nothing* to stop her."

His father's inaction had disturbed Hunter deeply, she could tell. "Maybe your dad didn't love her anymore."

Hunter's laugh was grim and ugly. "He would have cut his heart out of his chest to have her back. I'm not making that mistake, Kata. I will fight to keep you until I stop breathing."

That's why he'd refused to talk about his mother in Vegas. Now every line on his face was stamped with determination and pain. She had to fight the urge to wrap her arms around him and comfort him.

No wonder seeing her with Ben had been such a nasty shock for him. Hunter was possessive and protective to start with, but coupled with his mother leaving for a lover . . . Of course, when she'd told him that she wanted a divorce, she'd dredged up the pain of his past. She, of all people, understood how emotional issues from parents could bite one in the ass. Clearly, they had that in common. Her heart ached for him.

But that didn't mean she could stay.

Hunter dropped his head, shoulders tight. "None of us ever saw her again. She was dead less than a year later."

Kata gasped. Not only had the woman left, but she'd *died*? Another terrible blow to a young man still reeling from his parents' divorce. "How?"

"The murderer snuck into her apartment, then raped and strangled her. She'd been living alone, had no one to protect her. To this day, the crime is unsolved."

No wonder Hunter took the threat against his own wife so seriously. He knew firsthand what could happen.

"I'm sorry that you lost your mother to senseless violence. My father died of a heart attack when I was ten, so I empathize about losing a parent. I'm truly sorry for all you and your family have been through." She took his hand, squeezed gently. "Hunter, I'm not her. I can't replace her. And you're not your father. You'll be fine when I'm gone. Our marriage was a whim, so you'll barely notice I'm gone."

While Kata feared that Hunter had imprinted himself on her forever. Even so, she couldn't stay and put either of them through the pain she knew would come.

"Bullsh—"

"Don't try to make me stay. We'll both just end up hurt."

"Do these"—he gripped the papers—"have anything to do with Ben?"

Why didn't he see that this whirlwind marriage just wasn't meant to be permanent? She couldn't be with someone who could not only make her give herself to him so completely, he demanded it. He was only clinging to her so hard because he didn't want to have his father's regrets. They didn't make sense for the long haul . . . but he deserved her honesty.

"No, I really don't love him. I am not leaving you for someone else. I'm just leaving so I can go back to my life."

Hunter swallowed again, fists clenching at his sides. And for all that he looked furious and proud, his vulnerability was unmistakable. The fact that she wanted a divorce was killing him. Even though parting was the sane choice, guilt and anguish sliced her stomach like a machete.

"This is all crap. You want to leave because you submitted so totally that it scared you. I won't let you run from us." He crossed his arms over his chest. "I'm not signing those unless I'm convinced that you have no feelings for me."

Frustration roiled inside her, and angry tears filled her eyes. "You can't refuse to let me go. That wouldn't make you any better than Gordon."

Flinty eyes raked over her. "Do you honestly think I would ever degrade you until you lost your self-esteem?"

They'd already crossed this bridge. "No."

"That I would fail to seek medical care for you when you needed it?"

"I know you wouldn't," she admitted softly. "You've spent a lot of time and effort trying to keep me alive."

"So you think that I would take away your job and your friends to make you completely dependent on me?"

Kata glared up through the thick fringe of her lashes with furious eyes. "No. But to make you happy, I worry that I would let you do anything you wanted to me in bed . . . and eventually in life. I can't respect myself like that. Please, just sign."

* * *

NEVER.

In disciplining her for not trusting him and trying to bring them closer together, he'd taken her too deep and too fast into submission. It had frightened her. His mistake.

As much as Kata's family dynamic messed with her head, Hunter realized that he should have at least guessed this could happen. But he'd been running on too much emotion and not enough sleep. Now, he'd have to swallow all the destructive feelings that thinking of his mother dredged up and tread carefully with Kata—or she'd walk.

Hunter gulped deep breaths, willing self-control. She was right; four days wasn't a long time to get to know someone or adjust to a marriage. He'd already admitted his feelings to her. Reestablishing the trust they'd been building during her punishment was important. Proving that she wouldn't lose herself, no matter how submissive she became, was critical. Kata had to know that she had a deep well of strength, and he didn't want to change that. Nothing between them would mean a damn thing if she was running from the dominance he needed to give her—and she craved.

The papers, still balled up in his hands, had been her attempt to control the situation. A part of him wanted to be angry all over again that she didn't trust him not to take her over the edge. That was counterproductive.

With hands less steady than he liked, Hunter set the divorce papers on the dresser, then clasped her other shoulder. "Honey, I want you submissive, but I never want you to feel weak. I never want to take over your life. You have so much power over me that it scares me fucking spitless. In just a few days, my feelings for you have taken root. They run deep, lifetime deep." He fused her gaze to his. "I don't believe for one minute that you'd ever surrender every bit of your free will to me. You're an amazing, strong woman. You have to know that."

"I don't, not anymore." Her hazel eyes looked so green swimming in unshed tears. "You're so intense. So dominant. Over time, you'll break me down, and I'll give and give to you until I wake up one day and find that there's nothing left of me, just like Mamá. You may not mean that to happen, but I wonder if, deep down, it's your way of ensuring that I never leave. If that happens, I will hate myself."

Hunter understood her fear, but Kata was dead wrong. He just wanted to love her.

The instinct he'd had to meet her parents after they'd married was kicking him in the balls now. They should have done it sooner, but with someone trying to kill Kata, they'd been unable to check the meet and greet off his to-do list. He needed to fix that.

"How can you think that you'll lose yourself to me when, from the moment I met you, you've done so much to fight for what you wanted and believed in? That straightforward attitude and conviction are some of the biggest reasons I love you. You've fought for your mother, for yourself—even your pleasure. Kata, you're not a woman who could ever lose herself."

Emphatically, she shook her head. "After the spanking I should have been furious with you. Fucking spitting mad. But all I could think about was pleasing you."

"A submissive's nature is to want to please her Dom."

"Great, so you'll be thrilled while I'm slowly losing my self-respect."

He cupped her cheek. "It's not one-sided. I want to please you, too. Always. Sometimes, I have to balance that with what you need. Don't you think that, instead of spanking you, I would have ten times rather made love to you?"

"So you spanked me for my benefit?" She sounded incredulous. "You didn't enjoy it at all."

"Maybe a little," he confessed. "But yeah, mostly for you. Afterward, didn't you feel a sense of happiness and calm? A desire to give that back? Didn't you feel closer to me?"

Her stunned expression told Hunter that Kata was, even now, wondering if he could read her mind.

Hunter drew her closer, both soothed and fired up by the feel of her naked body and lush breasts against him. "I want to protect and love you, not crush you. Not cage you. I push you hard in bed because you're a woman with backbone and you have the strength to submit with grace. For me, earning your submission is a pleasure unto itself. If you ever feel like you're giving too much of yourself away, use your safe word. We will pause whatever's happening and talk. Once I return from active duty, we'll go more slowly. But you don't need those papers, honey. You need to trust that I know what's best for both of us."

In his arms, Kata stiffened, backed away, shaking her head. "Tonight, how badly I wanted to please you? It scared me. I know you say it's natural, but it's a slippery slope to hell." She choked. "You deserve to find some sweet girl who will be content to obey and never leave your side. But it can't be me. Sign the papers."

As more tears flooded her eyes, she pressed her mouth into a grim line. Hunter realized that, even though she thought divorce was the right option, actually leaving him was hurting her. It warmed his heart—and hardened his resolve.

"That someone *is* you. I won't undo this marriage without a genuine reason. Fear alone doesn't qualify." He thrust his fingers into her hair and gripped, pulling her mouth just under his. "I'm going to earn your trust, show you how good it is between us. You'll give a lot to me, but honey, I'll give back everything and more. I'm back on active duty Sunday. Just give me until then to prove it."

She blinked as she considered his words. It took everything inside him not to lay his mouth over hers and ravage it. Her mind rebelled against how incredible their dynamic was, but when he commanded her surrender, she stopped thinking and started feeling. He had to get her back to that place, where her sensations and emotions ruled, not her fear. He'd given her his discipline, and she'd need more, but she also needed his tenderness.

Dipping his head, he nipped at her bottom lip with his teeth, then soothed the little sting away with his tongue. She gasped. He covered her sweetly parted lips with his own, barely restraining the urge to throw her on her back, spread her thighs, get deep inside her, and love her thoroughly so she'd know he cherished her.

She tasted sweet, and Hunter's knees all but melted out from under him as he thrust slowly into her mouth. For a thin moment, she stiffened. But he soothed her with a gentle caress up her back, held her nape with a firm grip. She softened against him and clung to his biceps.

Like diving into warm waters in search of treasure, he patiently eased down, ever deeper, until she rose up on her toes, welcoming him unconsciously. His tongue danced around hers, a long caress, a silent promise of more to come. Her soft whimper went straight to his cock.

As soon as he heard it, he eased back, softly brushing her lips with his own, laving at them for the span of a heartbeat before pulling away. Rising on tiptoes, Kata pressed closer, throwing her arms around his neck, grabbing at the short strands of his hair. At the moment she merely wanted him. But he intended to stay at her until she begged. Until she couldn't walk away.

Dusting kisses across her jaw, Hunter smoothed his free hand down the small of her back, over her hip, caressing one fingertip along the outside of her thigh, edging toward her ass . . . but never quite touching her there. He repeated each movement in a random pattern, adding a press of thumb along her upper thigh, a sweep of knuckles over the curve of her hip, a feathery touch to the sensitive bit of flesh just above her butt. He breathed against the soft skin behind her ear.

Kata mewled and shivered.

"Those sounds you make, honey? They undo me," he whispered into her ear.

She shifted her body restlessly against him, her pebbled nipples brushing over his chest. Closer, she moved, her hips sliding against his own. Hunter grabbed her, stilled her. So the little vixen sought to rob his control by rubbing that sweet pussy against his cock? He'd allow that . . . eventually. But not until she was ready to hand complete control of her body to him and able to see that she would be just fine.

"On my flight back here," he murmured, "I spent hours fantasizing about you. I'm going to find every way possible to make you come."

Her breath caught. She arched against him now, silently pleading with her body. That was good . . . but not good enough. He wanted her mind, her heart, her soul.

Hunter trailed his mouth over the soft, musky scent concentrated in the groove of her neck and shoulder. He nipped at the tender skin, then sucked it as all the nerves awakened. He licked her in that same spot, teasing her with sensation. When she shuddered, he smiled.

"You can't."

The hell he couldn't. He drifted a hand up to her waist, trailing lightly over her ribs, to rest just under one of her heavy, swollen breasts.

"Why not, honey?" He nestled his thumb just beneath it in a barely there touch and forced himself not to move, knowing it would leave her wanting more. "You think we shouldn't or that I'm incapable?"

No hiding her shiver from him. "I'm sure you can. It's not a good idea."

"I would love nothing more than to spread you across my bed and find out exactly how much I can arouse you with my hands," he murmured into her ear, the hand at her nape tracing light little circles on her skin. "Discover the exact pressure to apply to your gorgeous, rosy nipples to make them stand up and beg for more. I want to make your pussy not just wet, but juicy. My goal is to run my hand across every inch of your silky skin until I've touched you every way possible."

Kata drew in a shuddering breath and pressed tighter against him. Her nipples engorged again. Repressing a smile, he eased back just enough to see the flush crawl up her chest. *Perfect.*

He kissed the corner of her mouth. When she tried to press her lips flush to his, Hunter veered away to dust kisses along her jaw. Slowly, he worked his way to her other ear.

"Then I want to put my fingers inside you."

"Hunter, stop." The tone was forceful, but her breathing sounded harsh and shallow.

He smiled, then nipped at her lobe. "Honey, I'm just getting started. I can't wait to feel my way into the hot clasp of your cunt. It's a silky vise, and I'm dying to find that so-sensitive spot inside you again, brush my thumb over your clit, and watch you go crazy for me."

Kata grabbed his face and forced him to meet her stare. Her eyes looked wild and startlingly green. A dusky rose flushed her normally olive cheeks. And her lips were red, swollen. Everything about her grabbed him by the cock, the heart, and refused to let go.

"Don't do this." Her pleading voice was a low mewl.

"Don't tell you how good I'm dying to make you feel? I don't want to stop, honey."

She shook her head, tried to back away. "We have great sex, God knows, but you're not hearing me. I can't be what you want, and sex is only going to muddy the waters."

They needed sex to reconnect, so he could show her that she had no reason to panic. That she didn't have to fear what she, deep down, wanted. Hopefully, he could break through her wall enough so they could talk out the rest of their issues afterward.

"I want that pretty ass of yours." He went on as if she hadn't spoken, refusing to lend credence to her fear. "I'm going to run my palms up and down that fine backside. Those sweet cheeks took a spanking so well." He feathered the tips of his fingers down her back, then drifted over the tender line between her cheeks. "I'm sure it will take a fucking the same way."

She gasped, tried to step back. His hold was too tight.

"No one's ever penetrated you here, and I want to be the first one." *The only one.* "I could give myself wet dreams just thinking about prying those sweet cheeks apart and sliding my dick, dripping with your juice, back here, then plunging deep. I want that, honey. Just like I want to see if anal sex will make you come."

Kata dropped her gaze, her brows drawing together tightly, like she was fighting hard to resist the lure of his seduction.

Hunter grasped her chin and raised her stare back to his. "No running, no hiding. Eyes on me. Until Sunday, Kata."

A mulish expression tore across her face—along with need. Hunter waited with a patience that chafed.

She sighed, opened her mouth, closed it.

Hunter seized the opportunity. "Until I figure out who is trying to kill you and why so I can stop them, I *know* you're safe with me. Stay. I'll protect you."

"No one else has threatened me since Sunday. Maybe they've given up."

He'd wondered at the pause, too, but in his gut, he knew the threat wasn't over. "Or whoever is behind the hit is just waiting for us to get sloppy."

Kata hesitated. "All right. Until Sunday, but you have to consider what I'm saying and give me some space."

That was the last thing Kata needed. Still, her concession to give him more time was big. If she'd trust him, he'd give her something wonderful in return.

"I'll do my best." He cupped her jaw and stared directly into her eyes. "But you have to try to trust me."

She sent him a solemn glance, and he hoped like hell that she was considering his words. Finally, she nodded.

Sighing in relief, he wrapped a hand around Kata's hip and pulled her in close, whispering against her lips, "Now, where were we? Oh, yeah . . . After I found all the ways to make you come with just my hands, I'll start in on you with my mouth. Did you know I have a *huge* oral fixation? I'm always going to be tasting some part of you. Your lips . . ." He pressed a slow kiss across her mouth, then bent to whisper in her ear. "Your neck." Another achingly soft brush of lips along the silky skin there made his mouth water. "Your nipples."

Hunter dragged his thumbs across those hard points, thrilled when she gasped and arched to him. With one hand at the small of her back, the other cradled her breast, and he brought the little bud to his mouth.

Hell, yes. He loved the hard candy tip just sitting on his tongue, the way he could pucker his lips around the engorged flesh, just before he bit softly. Kata moaned, shifting her hips not just against him, but into him, wriggling, flaunting, silently pleading for more.

Not quite success . . . but getting there.

Passion flowing like lava in his veins, he sucked one nipple deep while he worked the other with his thumb and forefinger. They'd be tender tomorrow, but she wasn't feeling anything now except growing arousal. She clutched his head, fingers digging into his scalp. The little bite aroused the hell out of him.

Easing away, he studied his handiwork. Gorgeous nipple. Red, hard, swollen. He leaned into the other and gave it the same treatment, massaging the first with a firm pinch. Soon, she had a matched pair, each looking engorged and dark and eager.

Then Hunter clasped his hands around her waist and sank to his knees, his tongue tracing circles across her belly, dipping into her navel.

He clasped her hips and eased down a fraction, gratified when she canted toward him. She might not understand why, and her head might not agree, but she wanted him.

With one hand drifting down her stomach, he inched closer to her pussy. Easing back, he studied her. Goose pimples stood out on her thighs. She sought him with little jerks of her hips. And she was beyond wet. He smiled.

Clasping his fingers around her thigh, he settled his thumb low on her belly, then began a torturous descent. Down, down, in an unhurried stroke. Kata caught her breath, held it. He could feel her silently willing him to touch her and send her over. Another whimper escaped her throat, hardening his cock again, testing his will. He held firm.

It seemed like an eternity later when he finally felt her clit beneath his thumb, swollen, hard, peeking out from beneath its hood.

She gasped, thrusting her hands into his hair and holding him against her. "Hunter . . ."

Leaning in, Hunter hovered his mouth over her clit, his hot breath hitting the sensitive bud. "And here. I'm going to want to put my mouth right here all the time."

"Do it now," she demanded in a high, thin voice.

"You'd like that?"

Above him, Hunter felt more than saw her vigorous nod. "I ache all over. Why the hell can you make me want you too much?"

He brushed his thumb over her slick clit again, a ghost, there then gone. "Never any such thing, honey. Do you want to come?"

"Yeesss," she hissed. "Please."

Ah, a polite little plea. Definite progress.

"Soon. I need something from you first." And just to ensure her assent, he swiped his thumb across her needy little bud once, then again, ever so slowly.

"Anything," she gasped.

There it was, that beautiful, dangerous word. "Good girl. It works both ways. I'd do anything—and everything—for you."

Hunter rose and smiled, covering her mouth with his own again and sinking into the honey-sweet kiss, as slow as molasses. Kata wriggled, moaned, clutched his shoulders, the edgings of desperation apparent in her every move.

"Come with me." He took her by the hand and led her to the padded table in the living room for two reasons: First, he wanted to be as far away from those fucking divorce papers as he could manage. Second, what he needed to do to her would be much easier to achieve here.

Once they reached the low black table, he eased her down to the surface, stomach first. When the cold leather hit her skin, she tensed. Casting a gaze over her shoulder at him, panic tinged her hazel gaze. He could not let her brain kick in again.

Flattening his palm over her back, Hunter caressed his way down her ass until he curled his palm between her legs, right over her pussy, and toyed with her clit enough to keep her on edge.

"I love the feel of you, so wet." He circled an idle fingertip around that hardened bundle of nerves. "I wonder how long I can draw this orgasm out. Two minutes? Ten? An hour?"

"Damn it, no. Don't try to wring me inside out!"

Hunter flipped the switch under the table, turning it from a stylish, black studded ottoman to a fully functional play table. The compartments that concealed a set of O-rings retracted. He reached into the drawer beneath the table and pulled out two pairs of cuffs. In less than ten seconds, he had one attached to each of her wrists and the other end secured to the table.

"Let me please you," he said firmly.

She pulled at her wrists, her body beyond taut with anxiety. "What are you doing?"

"You want this orgasm."

Shaking her hair out of the way, Kata glared at him over her shoulder. "So?"

"But you don't *need* it. Yet."

"Don't torment me." She wriggled in vain. "Damn it, uncuff me!"

Not until he'd given her more of what she needed. Unless she used her safe word, he'd keep pushing her boundaries. Anything else she cried out was just for show.

Reaching into the drawer beneath the table again, he pulled out a tube of lube. And God bless Jack, there was a new multipronged vibrator sitting there, still in the wrapper, perfect for what he needed.

He grabbed it and rose. "I'll be right back."

Striding across to the kitchen, he unwrapped the toy, washed it, then inserted batteries, which he thankfully found in a drawer. Back on the ottoman, he slid Kata over his lap, then lubed up his fingers and the toy.

"What the hell are you doing?" The edge of fear was back in her voice.

"You're doing well, so I'm adding something to your . . . experience." He traced a finger down the line of her ass and pressed in, finding the tight little hole he knew no one else had ever touched.

"Stop!"

"Does it hurt?" He knew it didn't; he'd barely put a finger on her.

"N-no, but . . ."

"Then don't speak unless I ask you to or you wish to use your safe word. Do you understand? If you don't, I'll stop touching you altogether. Your choice."

Kata paused for a long moment, so long Hunter thought he would have to make good on that threat. Finally, she whispered. "Yes, Sir."

Relief poured through him.

Slowly, he pressed his finger inside her tight entrance. She clamped down hard on him, but with a gentle nudge, he pushed past the ring of resistance, all the way inside. She gasped. When she tried to peer at him over her shoulders, he pressed down on her shoulder blades with his free hand. She needed not to rely on her senses, but on their bond. Kata struggled for a moment, then fell still.

Easing out, he ringed the entrance again, spreading more lube, then pressed in with two fingers. She clenched her cheeks, and he rubbed her hip softly. "Ease up."

Slowly, she relaxed. "This isn't comfortable."

Yeah, for him, either. She was like an inferno, burning his fingers. The hot, tight pressure . . . God, when he got his cock back there, not only would it feel incredible, but many women said that taking a man anally felt like one of the most submissive acts possible. It sure as hell felt both dominant and intimate to him—exactly what he craved with Kata.

He spread his fingers apart. "This is for you, honey, to make taking me easier when the time comes."

Hunter worked his fingers inside her tight recesses, back and forth, in and nearly out, massaging her and coaxing her each time she clenched up. It didn't take long for Kata to draw in a long, shuddering breath and grip the edges of the table until every muscle in her arms and shoulders stood out. Her breathing hitched, her skin flushed red. More moisture gushed from her pussy. She was damn close.

"Need to come, honey? You don't have permission."

And wouldn't that reminder drive her insane?

Withdrawing his fingers, he took the vibrator in hand and set the tapering anal stimulator against her entrance. "Push down for me."

"What are you—oh!"

Hunter pressed in with the flexible toy, pushing past the tight clench of muscles there. She hissed as the wider end of the plug began to stretch her. He slowed. No way did he want to hurt her, but he did want her to feel every inch.

"Oh . . . God!" She gasped. "I—it burns and I . . ." She panted, and he waited patiently while the sensations sank in and she worked it out.

"I didn't give you permission to speak." He continued pressing in ever so slowly.

"But Hunter—"

With a slap to her thigh, he cut her off. "How do you address me?"

"Sir. I know, but—"

"Safe word or shut up." Eventually, she'd learn.

In the silence, he eased the toy completely inside her ass, the base flush with her cheeks. God, now there was a pretty sight, her ass still rosy from his spanking, her untried entrance slowly stretching, her stubborn submission nearly ripe for his taking.

He palmed the crown of her head in a soft stroke. "Kata, turn your head. Meet my gaze. Good girl. Honesty now. Are you all right?"

"It burns."

"I know." But he could tell from the way she spoke that there was more. "And?"

She wriggled her ass, jostling the wand inside. Her white teeth clamped down on her bottom lip. "I ache."

So she liked anal penetration. Some women hated the sensation. Personally, he loved the power and intimacy of taking a woman that way, the forbidden sharing. He was relieved that translated for Kata.

"We'll take care of that soon. He grabbed her thighs so she couldn't slink away. "First, we're going to talk."

A fine sheen of perspiration covered her body. Her skin flushed even rosier as she sent him a pleading expression. "But . . ."

"You hurt me, Kata. You can't hurl something like a divorce at me without talking to me or trying to work it out."

"I didn't know about your mother." She gritted her teeth against the rise of pleasure. "My sister, who's an attorney, gave me the papers."

Knowing she hadn't sought the divorce was a consolation. That fact gave him hope. "And?"

"I wasn't sure if I should use them. Then you overwhelmed me."

"And you thought that was a good reason to end us?" God, was his voice cracking? He frowned. "I'll never punish you for your feelings. They're real and honest. I will, however, punish you for not talking to me. What we do in the bedroom aside, marriage is a partnership. This 'decision' was all you."

Kata said nothing for a long moment. Then tears pooled in her eyes. "You're a caveman, and you're still not listening. You might be the perfect man for some little submissive—"

"I'm the perfect man for *you*. If you need to talk a scene or your feelings through, fine. Communicate with me, don't divorce me. I love you. You have feelings for me, too. That scares you, so you lashed out at me. That's not how this works. We're partners, and we work things out." He hesitated. "You've got more punishment coming."

Her jaw dropped. "See, *you're* deciding to punish me. That's not a partnership."

"This is where our Dom/sub relationship comes into play. For us to succeed, you need to communicate. Since that hasn't sunk in yet, it's my job to help you along."

"That's bullshit."

"You using your safe word?"

"That, right there. You're being a pushy asshole."

He cocked a brow at her. "I guess not. Hold still."

"But the plug . . ."

"Stays where it is."

Slowly, Hunter twisted the toy, aligning the bulbous G-spot stimulator up with her wet pussy. When she gasped, he merely smiled while he inserted it. There, now it would be perfect. Then he flipped it on the lowest setting, while sliding his other hand between her legs, right over her clit.

"Oh dear God!" she cried out as fresh moisture gushed onto his hand. She groaned once, then again when his finger circled her needy bud. Kata ground against his hand, looking for relief. Instead, he eased back—and turned up the vibration.

Kata's entire body jolted. As he reached her clit again, he slid his other palm over her ass, transfixed by the gorgeous rosy color from her previous spanking. Her hips gyrated wildly as she sought a relief that wasn't coming anytime soon.

He turned up the vibration again. Kata clenched, whimpered, trembled. Her clit swelled again, hard like a stone. She was so close that he damn near held his breath with her. "It's too much! Damn it. Please . . ."

"Please what? You want to come?"

Her body bucked again on his lap as she searched futilely for relief. It would come when he chose to grant it, and certainly not because she'd wiggled for it. In no way would he reward her behavior over the last few days.

"You know I do," she sobbed. "Touch me. Fuck me. Make me come."

Willing patience, he caressed her ass once more. "Are you demanding or begging, honey?"

"Begging . . ." She dug her fingernails into the padded leather, still wriggling. "I promise that I won't get on Ben's lap again. I won't run away from your protection. *Please.*"

"In the future, you'll talk to me about how you're feeling instead of springing nasty surprises like divorce papers on me?"

"I swear . . ."

Kata was many things: impetuous, headstrong, sharp-tongued, vulnerable, and sexy as hell. But she wasn't a liar. Hunter smiled.

"Good girl." He stroked his way down the dark tangles of her silky hair, then the smooth line of her spine. When he feathered a light touch across her ass again, she shivered. Then he eased out from under her and stood.

"Hunter?"

He didn't answer. Instead, he stood behind her and gingerly withdrew the toy, ignoring her protest, then set it aside. "Knees under you, ass in the air, honey."

Panting, Kata hesitated, her aroused body struggling to process his request. But she finally complied, drawing her knees up under her and sticking the luscious globes of her rosy backside high in the air for him.

"In addition to finding all the ways I can make you come with my hands and my mouth . . ." He stepped to the edge of the table and grabbed her hips in his hands. "I'll definitely find every way possible to make you come on my cock, over and over. Starting now."

Chapter Fifteen

HUNTER aligned his cock with the slick heaven of her entrance and inched inside. Every blood cell in his body urged him to take her fast, hard. He held back, determined to build her climax up higher than ever. But the slow press inside the tight clasp of her swollen pussy had him gritting his teeth. Desire turned to hot lava in his veins.

God, getting inside Kata was always the most stunning experience. She gripped him like nothing he'd ever felt. He lost himself to her silken clasp, the little catches of breath. The closeness they shared. He'd fucked plenty of women but never given himself this completely to any. Now, he'd never want sex any other way.

"Hunter . . ." She moaned his name, a question, a plea.

Nothing could get to him faster than hearing her cry his name. He wanted to hear it every day for the rest of his life. Wanted to connect with her, form something so never ending that she'd never think of leaving him again.

"Yeah," he croaked. "Kata, ah . . ." He slid back inside, all the way, and tossed his head back on a groan. "Fuck. You're amazing."

She sucked in a thin breath. "*Ahh.* I shouldn't like the way you force all this sensation on me."

Bullshit. "It feels good when I'm deep inside you, doesn't it?"

"Yes," she whimpered.

Determined to keep her on edge, he withdrew almost completely, then fell into her again. It was like diving into honey, so slow and sweet, her clinging passage all around him. He thought he'd go insane.

Finally, he nudged her cervix. She clawed the padded table again and bowed her head, unconsciously submissive. The sight nearly undid him. She might not want to acknowledge her nature, but he felt it, tasted and smelled it. That very nature colored so many of her responses. She would never be truly happy with anyone who couldn't give her the dominance she craved. And Hunter intended to make her very, very happy.

Jesus, she was wet and so close. The warning pulses of her pussy gripped him, trying to shove him over the edge. He gritted his teeth, his lungs about to burst, his skin on fire—but he managed to slow down, hold back.

"I shouldn't give in to you the way I do," she gasped.

More bullshit. "I love to please you, honey."

He punctuated the statement by leaning over the damp flesh of her back, settling his palm over her clit, then grinding into her.

Kata tossed back her head and cried out. "Hunter!"

"You want to come now?"

"Yes. Yes!"

"You'll talk to me before making any decisions about us?"

"I will," she sobbed. "Please . . ."

Satisfaction burned through him like an inferno at her words. All the leashed power he'd been holding back, Hunter let loose. He surged into her, throwing his body into each thrust. Kata mewled, gripped the edge of the ottoman with her nails. Her pussy clenched tight on him.

She wailed with pleasure, the skeins of her dark hair covering her shoulders in a silky brush of sable. God, everything about her was sexy. He thrust again, giving her even more, settling into a rhythm that was both blistering and merciless. Around him, she tensed, drawing in one shuddering breath after another, exhaling with a cry.

Sweat spread across his back, over his scalp, rolled down his temples. And still he kept at her, determined to give her both total devotion and absolute pleasure. He wanted this night to be like nothing she'd ever experienced—or would ever forget. Because in another three days, he'd be shipping out. He had to be certain she had no interest pursuing that divorce in his absence. Losing her would kill him.

He molded his body more tightly to hers, luxuriating in the feel of her under his hands as he thrust deep, hard, fast. He spread kisses along her shoulder, shoving her hair out of the way so he could slide his lips up her neck, breathe in her skin. Musky, tinged with female perspiration and arousal, and ripe with something that would forever remind him of Kata. The smell and feel of her drove him toward the edge.

"Hunter!" She clamped down on his cock now, dangerously close. In response, pleasure rolled down his spine, flash-heated his blood. His balls drew up tight. Damn it, he was going to be a heartbeat behind her.

He pressed his palm into her clit again. "Now! Come, honey."

She did, screaming out her release. She squeezed him so tightly, he couldn't move for a long moment. *Damn!* Her walls closed in on him, pressing, stroking. Had he ever felt anything more mind-blowing? Pleasure was like a fresh razor blade up his spine—sharp and cutting through him with so little effort. He bit gently into her shoulder and let loose, spilling all he had—seed, need, and soul—inside her.

Kata was everything to him. The submissive he'd always sought, the gutsy, smart wife who'd always challenge him. Somehow, with

the few days they had left, he had to stop her would-be killer, ensure Ben stayed away, and convince Kata that she felt the same way
for him.

* * *

KATA struggled to find her breath. Hunter's legs were tangled in
hers, his arms banded around her middle. His mouth hovered over
her neck as he breathed heavily against her skin. God, he was everywhere, made her feel everything.

She trembled. The floodgates of her fear and exhaustion poured
over the reality of her submission, threatening to drown her. She
bucked under Hunter, doing her best to dislodge him. But strapped
to his table and held captive by his heavily muscled body, Kata
couldn't move.

The rising tide rolled up and over her head. She swallowed hard,
trying to force the feeling down, but the giant sob tore at her chest,
even bigger than the release following her spanking. She choked as
it came up. Tears burst out, and her arms and legs gave way.

In the back of her head, she knew that he wanted her to feel free
to show him all her emotions. He'd shown her his. She'd never forget
the haunted, angry look on his face when he talked about his mother,
about the fact that his father had simply let the divorce happen.
Their split was a scar on his heart, festering.

The way he'd commanded her entire body just now proved that
he didn't intend to allow his own wife to leave. His ruthless domination of her body was his way of fighting back. He'd do anything necessary to make her stay. He'd consume her in the process. And she
feared that she'd eventually just let him.

A shudder rolled over Kata. Damn it, she'd already given him far
more than she'd ever given any man, more than she'd ever thought
she had to give. But he would never rest until he owned her through
and through, all the way down to her soul.

She must put some distance between them. Every time Hunter
touched her, he stripped her a bit more. After every encounter, she

didn't think he could leave her any more exposed or feeling any more raw. And she was always wrong.

What would another three days with Hunter do to her psyche? Or a lifetime with him? How long before she became his doormat? He pushed, and shoved, and demanded. Then, when she was defenseless, he brought in the steely tenderness, digging his way into her soul. Where Hunter was concerned, she was so weak, some part of her ridiculously eager to submit. Already he was so firmly entrenched, it scared her to death. Kata feared that she'd never be able to get him out of her heart.

She tried to crawl into a ball—but couldn't while strapped to the table. More sobs wracked her chest, overpowering, unstoppable, painful. Hunter watched her with all-seeing eyes, petting her with a soothing touch. She couldn't give all of herself like this to him day after day, year after year, for a lifetime. He didn't understand what it meant to feel as if he'd been broken down again and again. He'd never know how this submission made her question her sense of self . . . and whether she'd have anything left if she kept giving to him like this.

But after giving her the most stunning sex of her life, she had no way to hide.

"Kata, honey," he whispered in her ear.

She curled up tighter and shook her head.

"Was it too powerful?"

For her, yes. Always.

"Don't," she managed to gasp out through another sob. "Just stop."

"Shh." He trailed a soothing hand down her back, then back up, up, until he reached the cuff at the corner of the padded table. With a quick click, one unfastened. He repeated the same movement with the other. Then her wrists were free. With Hunter still buried deep inside her, he drew her back onto his lap, rubbing her forearms and wrists, caring for her gently. Kata refused to look over her shoulder at him, but she could feel his gaze delving past the curtain of her hair. No escaping the feel of his cock stiffening inside her so-sensitive pussy once more.

She couldn't share herself again now and not bare her soul to him. God, there'd be nothing left.

Gathering her strength, she pushed away from him and rose to her feet. Her legs had all the strength of rubber and gave way beneath her. She crumpled back to the ottoman.

Hunter sighed and lifted her onto his lap. "Stop, Kata. Let me take care of you."

He carried her to the bedroom again. She tensed against the sublime pleasure of feeling his skin against hers. Part of her wanted him to go . . . but the thought of not being with him again shot panic through her.

That was a bitter pill to swallow. She sobbed harder.

Kissing the top of her head, he curled up on the bed and brought her onto his lap.

"J-just give me a minute alone," she begged. And she hated the pleading note in her voice, but he'd stripped to the core. The only thing left was the scared girl inside so terrified of becoming her mother.

Hunter hesitated, then eased out from under her. "I'll be right back. I'm not going far."

A precious few moments passed, but Kata couldn't center her thoughts or calm herself in the silence. Moments later, he returned, only to sit her on his lap again, then reach for the tray he'd placed on the bedside table.

"Open," he demanded, placing a pastry with cinnamon and brown sugar right in front of her mouth.

She shook her head. Sugar wasn't going to solve her problem.

He frowned. "You haven't had a meal in hours. Eat. No arguments."

Could the man never listen? "I don't need this many calories."

"By the time I'm done with you, you will. Open up."

Exasperated, Kata opened, accepted the bite—and nearly groaned at the flaky, sweet texture of the pastry as it crossed her tongue. She reached out to grab it and feed herself. He pulled back.

"No, honey. Take from me what you need."

Eat from his hand? She finally looked up, met his so-blue eyes, questioning. Yes, that's exactly what he meant. He intended to feed her himself. The notion both thrilled and disturbed her. How intimate. How frightening that he was encouraging her dependence on him.

Even with those thoughts running through her head, Kata felt oddly contented to be so close to him, so connected. She couldn't find the will to say no. He coaxed her into eating the whole thing, then followed with some grapes and a banana, taking a few bites for himself.

With his free hand, he stroked her back slowly, tenderly, dusting sweet kisses on her shoulder and neck. Finally, she relaxed, her disquiet waning under exhaustion.

Then he propped a finger beneath her chin and drew his mouth to hers. "You're incredible. When I'm with you, I feel like the luckiest man in the world."

And she felt like the people of Troy must have with the Trojan horse, succumbing to a handsome, seemingly harmless beast, only to realize that she was under a siege that would only end in total surrender.

He fitted his mouth over hers. At first, she stiffened, but he kissed her long and deep and slow until her body went liquid. Until she sagged against him. Then he took her by the hand and led her to the shower.

After setting her under the steaming spray and easing into the small stall, he refused to let her wash herself. He did it in reverent silence. With a pounding heart and hollow, aching eyes, Kata watched as he kissed her shoulders, washed her breasts, soaped her backside.

"I know today has been a lot to take in. I pushed you hard. But I'm so proud of the way you took everything I gave you. And you're still here with me, the same you."

She didn't feel the same. Her body hummed, her mind was blank. Emotions swirled in a giant morass that terrified her, but telling Hunter that would only start an argument that she was too over-wrought to win. Instead, she stood still as he shampooed her hair, then knelt to wash her feet, calves, thighs, pussy.

He lingered on the last, toying, teasing with his fingers until Kata had to brace herself against the wall to avoid falling. She bit her lip hard against the rise of pleasure, but nothing could stop it—or him—despite the knowledge that, if she came again, there would be virtually no part of her soul he hadn't claimed.

As if he sensed that, he knelt at her feet and lifted her foot to the shower bench, leaving her pussy open to him.

"Hunter," she whimpered. "Please . . ."

"No holding yourself back from me. You're so wet and sweet. I need all of you."

She didn't have an opportunity to say another word. He set his mouth on her so-sensitive flesh, coaxing her arousal until he surged past her fear, until she knew only the feel of his tongue flirting with her clawing need for ecstasy, until she craved only the orgasm he dangled just beyond her reach.

He slid through her wet folds, tearing through her defenses. She couldn't help it; her hands slid across his scalp, trying to hold him in place. But he didn't need to be forced. That wicked tongue of his kept driving her up, hotter, higher, until she'd have given her soul for release.

"Yes!" she sobbed. "Yes . . ."

"I want to hear you scream, honey. Come."

As if the words were some mysterious catalyst, the climax pounded over her, flattening her. She grabbed him, her nails mak-ing half-moons on his shoulders as her deafening cry resounded through the shower. And still, he lapped at her, wringing every pos-sible tingle and twinge out of the orgasm.

Then he sat her on the corner bench as he washed and rinsed

himself quickly, then helped her out, drying her off like a child, running the comb through her wet hair carefully.

Kata watched him, watched herself, in the steamy mirror. He looked so big, capable, and content caring for her. So utterly reassured, almost at peace. She looked like a refugee from a war zone, one of those women who had survived but had seen too much.

Once finished, he led her back to the bed, checking his phone. "We have another five hours before your mother's release. You look exhausted."

She nodded. Sleep. She could escape this overwrought feeling when she slept. Eagerly, she curled up on the bed, rolled to the far side, tucked the sheet beneath her chin.

With a soft grip on her arm, Hunter rolled her to her back again. Without any warning, he slid his thigh between hers, his body over her own. Then he plunged the iron length of his cock inside her, all the way to the hilt in a single stroke.

That quickly, her body flashed electric with need.

"Again?" she panted.

Even as she asked, she parted her thighs wider, threw her arms around him, and clasped him close. Plunging deep, he gave her more of the powerful dominance that her mind could no longer fight. Pleasure soared inside her.

"Yes, again. And again. I will always give you more than you think you can handle. And I have no doubt that you will always thrill me with your surrender and your strength."

Shock pinged through her. Before she could think of anything to say or any way to stop him from dismantling her even more, Hunter proceeded to undo her with one deep, destructive stroke after another.

From his very first thrust, moans fell from her lips, and Kata couldn't stop them. They weren't the pretty kind, not from any normal sexual soundtrack. These were animal pleas, punctuated by her nails digging their way into his back and thrusting up at him wildly.

Hunter held her hips down, controlling her movement, forcing her to take the torture of his slow thrusts. Every inch of him glided over swollen, sensitive flesh as he entered her repeatedly, each stroke ending with a nudge against a spot high and deep inside her. She jolted, gasped, clamped down on him.

"Ah, there. Perfect, honey. That feel good?"

It did, and he damn well knew it.

He withdrew, then slid back in to rub over that same nerve-laden spot. "I asked you a question."

As he pulled back, her body clung, trying to keep him deeper, the intimacy of the act more stark and stunning than ever. Robbing her of the last of her feeble defenses.

Kata pressed her lips together and closed her eyes to shut him out. If she didn't, she would say or do anything Hunter wanted.

"I want to make love to you, Kata, sweet and slow. But if you keep pushing me, I won't hesitate to punish you again."

Punish. Spank. Sensually torture. He'd drive her to the brink of sanity, then throw her into a black chasm of pleasure so overwhelming that the shelter of his arms were her only chance of survival. But his touch came with a price: her soul. He was fast becoming an addiction, and she didn't know how to break free of something she wanted so desperately. Or what she'd do when she could no longer cope.

"It feels *so* good," she admitted.

He caressed her face. "Open your eyes."

Reluctantly, knowing he would strip her raw once more, Kata did. As their gazes connected, he surged deep inside the clasp of her body again, prodding that hungry spot.

No way could she hold back her needy moan.

"That's so sweet, the way your pussy tightens on me while your eyes are all but begging. I look forward to taking every opportunity to push your limits, strengthen our bond."

With his methodical thrusts, Hunter continued to nudge the nerve-laden spot inside her again and again, at a slow pace that set her on fire. She mewled and clasped him tight, panting. God, she was close.

"Come, honey. Don't hold anything back."

His whisper filtered down her ear, vibrating inside her. Pleasure gripped her, settling with a dark throb between her legs. The pulses started, shaking her body, bursting her wide open. A guttural roar sounded around her, ringing in her ears, and Kata realized she'd made the sound. Hunter fucked into her again, and the need bubbled over, jolting her entire body. Again, she screamed. A moment later, he spilled inside her with a possessive roar.

His stare locked on hers, and their breathing synced up, foreheads touching. Hunter was buried deep, as if he'd always be a part of her. Kata had never felt closer to another human being in her life—and it scared the hell out of her.

"I love you," he murmured and kissed the tip of her nose before quietly withdrawing.

Kata closed her eyes. Minutes later, she felt a warm washcloth between her legs, soothing, cleaning. Exhaustion beat at her as she watched him caring for her so intimately. It, like him, was simply too overwhelming.

When he curled up beside her, spooning his body against hers, Kata knew that she should fight, not give him every part of herself.

A voice in her head whispered that it may already be too late.

* * *

AFTER a few hours of sleep, Kata and Hunter returned to the hospital. The doctor was in emergency surgery and hadn't yet signed her mother's discharge papers. Kata waited impatiently, wincing every time she looked at Mamá lying amongst her sheets. Despite the fact that her color looked a bit better today, she still appeared frail.

Finally, Hunter tracked down the nurse and pushed a few buttons until he'd arranged the release. Now, Kata looked down as he entwined his hand with her own. Even now, she didn't know if she should grab on tight or push him away.

* * *

THEY pulled up in front of Mamá and Gordon's house near dusk. The lights inside weren't on, except the alternating flare and darkness of the TV visible through the front window. So, her stepfather was home. *Yippee.*

Kata wanted to curl into a ball and sleep for a month. For her mother, she had to deal.

"You all right, Mamá?" Kata asked, turning in her seat.

Lying down in the back of the Jeep, her mother smiled. She looked pale, her cheer forced. "You worry too much, *Mija.* The doctor said I will be fine. All the medicine, it has helped."

But the doctors also prescribed a great deal of rest, and Kata knew she wouldn't get any here with Gordon. "Please stay with Mari for a few days. Let her wait on you. I'm sure she'd love to have you."

"We discussed this. She is busy with Carlos and the boys. I will not trouble her. Besides, I belong at home. Gordon will be waiting."

Damn it, what did she see in that manipulative bastard? "You need someone to take care of *you* now, Mamá."

"Truly, I will be fine."

Out of the corner of her eye, she caught Hunter frowning in question. He didn't understand why she was fighting so hard to keep her mother from returning home. She'd explained Gordon, but . . . maybe it would compute once he saw the asshole in action. After the way Hunter had fed her from his own hand and bathed her himself, she didn't think Gordon's neglect would go over well.

She should be happy that Hunter would finally see the sort of woman she feared becoming and why. Maybe he'd pull back, give her space. But her immediate concern was that he and Gordon would come to blows.

"Ready?" she asked her mother as Hunter stopped the Jeep and jumped out.

When her mother nodded, Kata opened her door, then gathered her mom's luggage. Mamá tried to get to her feet. Hunter was having none of that. Instead, he bent and picked her mother up as if she weighed nothing.

"Mr. Edgington, I am older and not quite so healthy as you, but I can make my way up the walk. You need not trouble yourself."

"My name is Hunter. It's no trouble, ma'am."

He glanced her way. Despite the tension between them, Kata couldn't help but smile. "You won't win this argument, Mamá. Trust me."

The three of them made their way to the front door. Kata fished out her key, knowing that Gordon would only be more annoyed with them—and take it out on her mother—if they made him get off the sofa to let them in. He was a selfish prick who'd do anything to assure his own comfort. Her mother was a convenience for him, like an electric razor or a cell phone. And he behaved this way because Mamá was too lost to stand up to him.

Kata wondered if, after months or years of Hunter's intensity, she'd be like her mother, resigned to taking the path of least resistance.

She pushed the front door open. Hunter followed her inside, her mother tight against his broad chest. She looked slightly gray, and it scared the hell out of Kata to think of leaving her here. What if Mamá didn't recover because she didn't get any rest? Hunter had hired a nurse, which was a relief, but Kata wished she could be here herself to oversee her mother's recovery.

Not for the first time, Kata damned whoever was trying to kill her. The asshole had shoved her into Hunter's arms and now away from the one place that duty and love dictated she be. It fucking pissed her off.

"Where is your bedroom, ma'am?" Hunter asked her mother.

"Through the living room and at the end of the hall."

"Thank you, ma'am." Hunter nodded and made his way through the foyer, into the living room. "Your nurse's name is Becka. She'll be here in an hour. She's picking up your prescriptions along the way. We'll stay with you until she arrives."

"That's very sweet of you. You never said, how do you and Kata know each other?"

Kata's heart stuttered. She'd asked Hunter to keep their marriage quiet. Now wasn't the time to rattle her mother. And really, why bother, when Kata wasn't sure she'd remain his wife past Sunday?

"Is that you, Carlotta?" Gordon called over the blare of the TV, his feet hanging over the arm of the sofa.

Kata caught an unfortunate glimpse of the weasel lounging flat on the couch in a T-shirt and his boxers. His salt-and-pepper hair was askew, his pale blue eyes as washed out as the rest of his face.

"Yes, dear." Her mother sounded breathy. Was she merely tired and winded, or actually anxious to see this bastard?

Gordon grunted. "You're late."

The man could crawl on Kata's last nerve faster than anyone. "It's not her fault. We had to wait for her discharge papers. Which you would know, if you'd bothered to pick up your wife."

"Kata . . . *Mija*, don't." Her mother pleaded, meeting her stare around Hunter's bulging biceps.

"Shut up, girl. I work hard to keep this roof over your mother's head and food in her belly. All I ask for when I come home is a little peace and relaxation. I already called someone to do the yard work while she was laid up. Back off."

As Hunter passed Gordon's line of sight, her stepfather jack-knifed into a sitting position and scowled. "Who the hell are you?"

Kata knew she should leave it alone. Knew it . . . but couldn't. "Someone willing to help Mamá, since you're too fucking lazy and self-absorbed to even put her to bed."

"Bed? You're treating her like an invalid." Gordon stood, his brows drawn together in incredulity. "It's nearly seven o'clock. I've been waiting for dinner."

"Mr. Buckley, your wife is in no position to be out of bed for any reason. Kata, hand him the hospital's instructions."

With an angry shrug, she reached into her purse, then tossed them at her stepfather. "Here you go. It says in black and white that she should get as much rest as possible for the next week. Hunter found a nurse who will come in and take care of Mamá—"

"No strangers in my house. Carlotta doesn't need coddling." He turned to Hunter. "Put my wife down. She can limp to the kitchen from here."

"She's going to bed." Hunter's voice rang with steel. "You're a capable man who has two arms and two legs. You should be the one cooking."

Kata zinged a glance at Hunter. He sounded seriously pissed off. She had to repress a smile.

"You don't tell me what to do in *my* house," Gordon snarled at Hunter, then sneered in her direction. "Katalina, no nurse. You'll stay and take care of your mother and me."

"I can't." And she absolutely would not tell Gordon why. If he could write Mamá's pneumonia off as a mere cold, Kata knew he'd never believe that someone was trying to kill her.

"Can't?" He poked a thumb in Hunter's direction. "Because you can't stop spreading those fat thighs long enough to take care of your own mother?"

"Gordon!" her mother protested.

Beside Kata, Hunter's entire body tensed. He sent Gordon a murderous glare. "You don't *ever* talk to my wife that way again. I don't usually bother threatening. But you're part of Kata's family, so I'll give you one warning: Show her respect, or I will pound you into the ground until you whimper for mercy. Don't expect me to have any."

Suddenly, her stepfather apparently found his self-preservation instinct and stepped back.

Her mother gasped. "Wife? You got married, *Mija?*"

Kata closed her eyes. So much for laying low and seeing how the relationship panned out.

"Mamá, let's get you settled. We'll talk later. This is too taxing for you right now."

Hunter marched out of the room, into the long hall, her mother wrapped in his arms, then pushed open the first door on the left, entering the room that used to be hers.

"My room is at the end of the hall," her mother reminded politely.

"Yes, ma'am. But perhaps you'd be more comfortable in a room of your own. And you wouldn't disturb your husband in here."

"Yes, I do cough loudly." She patted his shoulder. "You married my Kata?"

"I did, ma'am. And I love her."

Mamá turned her head to smile at Kata. "I do not know when this happened. I want all the details later, but he seems to care for you very much, *Mija*."

Yeah, her mother would say that.

"Mamá, you need to rest. I'll tell you everything soon." *Fat chance.*

Inside what was now the guest room, Kata ran around Hunter and pulled down the bed. Once the sheets were smoothed and the pillows fluffed, he set Mamá down and tucked her in like a child. Her mother fell back with a sigh, head lolling back into an exhausted sleep.

Kata sent him a grateful look. Hunter might strip away every one of her emotional defenses mercilessly, but he'd been true to his word in helping her mother. He'd even put Gordon in his place. As soon as they left, her stepfather would berate her mother and refuse the nurse entrance; that had to be dealt with. But the moment Hunter had handed Gordon his ass had been so sweet.

"We should let her rest," Hunter commented. "I have something to ask you."

He grabbed Kata's hand and led her out of the guest room, then down the hall to the master. The second he closed the door behind him, he clenched his jaw, obviously holding on to his temper by a thread. "Why is your mother still with this asshole?"

She closed her eyes. He saw the bastard her mother had married, but his question implied that he didn't understand why Mamá hadn't removed herself from the situation. Did he not see how dependent her mother had become, see everything Kata feared?

"I've tried to get her to leave. So has my sister. Trust me." She sighed. "Now that Gordon has stripped her of any semblance of a real life, taking care of him is her only purpose. He's robbed her of her job, her friends, and her independence. He's taken her self-worth. I've tried to talk her into moving in with me. She won't."

"She's a beautiful woman. Plenty young enough to have a full life."

"I agree, but she doesn't see it that way. And whenever I talk to her about it, she always says that she's happy. I know it's a lie. She's afraid of being a burden to me. Besides, Gordon would only find her and drag her home. He's not about to do without his personal maid, cook, and sex slave."

"Then she needs to go elsewhere."

Kata bit her lip. He was right. "I'll call Joaquin again. Mari can't keep Gordon away from my mom, but Joaquin can. Hell, Gordon would never find him. But I'm not sure I can, either."

Hunter shook his head. "If he's undercover, he may not be able to break free. If you want this asshole out of her life, I know a place where she'll be waited on hand and foot. Gordon will never find her, so he won't be able to coerce her back. Anything more permanent will be up to her, but I can at least give her the chance for a clean start."

"Where will you take her?"

"You leave that to me."

That would require a lot of trust, but Hunter spent his life protecting people. He wouldn't let anything happen to her mother. "I don't know if she'll accept a stranger's help."

"Let me worry about that. Pack her bag. If your prick of a step-father is going to work her to death and fail to care for her, then I don't want your mother here another three minutes."

"Right now?" Kata gasped. "Gordon will give you twenty kinds of hell."

Hunter snorted. "The little pissant can try."

Kata hesitated. "She may not want to go. The one time I convinced her to leave him three years ago, I helped her save up enough money to buy her own car and a prepaid cell phone. We packed her bags . . . and about three hours out of town, she was crying too hard to see the road and got in a car accident. It shattered most of the bones in her left shin and foot." Kata swore she wouldn't cry. Swore it, but hot tears stabbed her aching eyes anyway. God, how did she have any more tears to shed? "Her surgery and recovery lasted for months. I took care of her. Gordon all but refused. After all, she would never have been hurt if she hadn't been trying to leave him. Mamá walks with a limp now. He constantly tells her that she's lucky he's benevolent enough to take care of damaged goods."

Hunter clenched his fists. "Shit-sucking pond scum. Don't worry about your mother. I'll convince her that leaving temporarily for her recovery is in everyone's best interest, even Gordon's. By the time she's better, she'll have no interest in returning. Trust me."

As tenacious as Hunter was, Kata knew exactly who would win that battle. Hope for her mother's well-being filled her. With Hunter on her side, Gordon would have a fight on his hands. "You'd do that for my mamá?"

"And for you. Anything for you, honey." He placed a soft kiss on her lips.

Looking into Hunter's blue, blue eyes, she knew he meant every word he said. He might demand so much that she feared she'd give away her soul. But she knew with every cell in her body that he would help her mother begin a better life. If Kata hadn't already suspected that some part of her was perilously close to being in love with Hunter, this sealed the deal.

Chapter Sixteen

HUNTER drove down the highway, the Jeep sliding through the night as Kata's mother slept in the backseat. After Kata packed a quick bag for Carlotta, and he threatened Gordon within an inch of his life, Hunter had called the nurse to cancel her services, assured Kata's mother this was the best course of action until she recovered, then picked up her prescriptions and began down the road.

Kata stared out the window into the nothingness of the night, looking bleak and exhausted and lost.

He held in a curse. She'd had a tough day, and he hadn't made it easy on her. In fact, he realized that he'd fucked up. After watching Carlotta allow Gordon to treat her as if her wants and wishes were of no consequence, Hunter understood Kata's fears a whole lot more. Before today, he'd comprehended on a theoretical level that her stepfather was a controlling dirtbag, but it hadn't really clicked that Carlotta simply let it happen—and that's what Kata feared becoming.

Kata's tart, sexy vivacity had intrigued him. Coupled with her natural submissiveness, she'd drawn him in like no other. Though she'd tried repeatedly to explain, he'd stopped thinking with the head above his shoulders. Wasn't that biting him in the ass now? The confidence he'd felt in their relationship after making love to her this morning was gone now that he'd seen her mother and Gordon in action.

"Are you sure your father won't mind the company?" his wife asked into the inky silence.

Hunter glanced at Carlotta sleeping in the rearview mirror. "Now that he's home from his latest mission, he'll welcome the company, honey."

In fact, they might be good for one another. At the very least, they would make steadfast friends, and no one could ever have too many of those.

"I hate to spring this on him. I'm sure he has better things to do than babysit."

"The Colonel needs to slow down, and this will give him a reason. He has plenty of operatives willing to do his work for him, and he continues to globetrot to the shitholes of the world, chasing an adrenaline rush." He had nothing else to come home to—and hadn't since he'd let his wife walk out the door.

"Thank you." Kata finally turned to him, grabbed his hand, and squeezed. "For . . . back there. For putting Gordon in his place. I really appreciate it."

Hunter wished he could do more. "He deserved it. I wanted to pound his face into the ground, but he's the kind of weasel who would only call the police. And the entire incident would upset your mother, I suspect."

"Very much. I can tell the restraint cost you." A faint smile lifted her grim face. "Thanks."

Sliding his thumb across her soft hand, Hunter gathered his thoughts, then sent her a solemn stare. "I hope you know I'd never treat you like Gordon."

Kata swallowed, looked away. "I know you'd never purposely

demean me or want me to feel weak. But, like Gordon, you want me all to yourself. Eventually, I fear that I'd . . . let you have your way."

Just as he'd suspected. "I'm possessive, honey. I don't deny it. But I'd never want you isolated and unhappy. And if I ever had so little respect for you, I'd end the marriage. But I suspect you'd do that long before matters became that bad."

She blinked and pressed her lips together, fighting tears. "You're not understanding. I'm not afraid of you; I'm afraid of *me*. A part of me would love giving myself over to you totally, the way my mother seems to enjoy at times. I won't lie, I love having your attention. You make me feel special. But your intensity terrifies me. And after sex . . . I'm always afraid of how much I've given you. I couldn't live with myself if I lost my spine for good."

Kata knew that he wasn't like Gordon, but Hunter had no fucking idea how to assure her that she wasn't like her mother.

He didn't have a lot of time left with her; what they had was ticking down quickly. As much as he wanted to give her the full-court press and totally make her his in every way, she wasn't ready. As afraid as she was—clearly with cause—he wondered if she ever would be.

But he couldn't give up.

"What happens between us sexually has no reflection on the rest of our life. I have at least another six months on this contract. Another eight years in the navy if I want to retire with benefits. The reality is, I'd be leaving you in charge of our lives when I'm overseas. I couldn't do that unless I know you're strong and capable, which you are. You'd never, ever let me take away your job, your friends, your car, your phone, your free will . . . And I would never ask you to give those up. Would I like you to have a safer job? Yes. Would I like you to avoid Ben? Yes. Would I force you to do without either for the rest of your life? Never."

"But I have this insane urge to please you that I've never felt. I don't want to give up either right now, but eventually . . ." She shrugged.

The shame in her voice made him ache. He didn't see her ever giving up what she needed in life. But she had to learn that. He had to help her. Hunter gripped the wheel, his mind racing. He'd have to think on that. Maybe more information would help him know which way to turn.

"Why did you ask Ben for a ménage for your birthday?'"

Kata blinked, the question clearly surprising her. "I didn't, per se. I told him that it was one of my fantasies. This was months before my birthday. He told me that he'd try to make it happen. Then you showed up and . . ."

Hunter winced. He'd stomped in the middle and busted up the situation.

"Why did you want it?"

"It's . . ." She shrugged, looked out the window again. "Not important."

But something told him it was. "We have a couple of hours to kill until we reach my dad's, and your mom is going to sleep for a while, since we gave her that codeine cough medicine. If it's important to you, it's important to me. Please."

"Wow, a 'please' from you?" she teased, then sighed. "I guess I should have known Ben wouldn't really understand, and it's probably a dumb fantasy . . ."

"How did Ben not understand? He arranged the ménage. I'm the one who derailed it." And he'd taken great pleasure doing it.

She squirmed in her seat. "It wasn't really a ménage I wanted. I had this fantasy of a man I was with . . . giving me to someone else. Like, demanding that I be with someone of his choosing because he thought I was so sexy and amazing that he wanted to show me off, and I wanted to please him so badly that I let him. It's dumb."

Shock pinged through his system. The depth of her submissive nature stunned him. "Not if that's what you wanted."

She might fight his commands because she wasn't accustomed to being under anyone's control and didn't know where and how to draw the line, but to learn that she wanted to be so utterly owned by a man that she could be shared . . . That was into slave territory.

Hunter had no interest in sharing, but her words confirmed every-thing he believed about her true desires. She saw submission as a weakness, but she needed this on a core level. Somehow, she must see that succumbing to her needs didn't make her a doormat. But understanding that could only happen when she accepted herself and learned to trust him.

"It's never going to happen, so it doesn't matter. Let's just drop it." She withdrew her hand and looked away as if she suddenly found the dark, empty road fascinating.

"How long have you had this fantasy?"

She shrugged.

Hunter turned a stern glower her way. "I expect an answer now, or I will stop this car and take you over my knee. I don't care if pass-ersby see."

She gasped. Her breath came more rapidly. Jesus, she was al-ready aroused. So was he.

"Fine. I've had the thought for about seven years. I read a book once where a man shared his girlfriend with his best friend, and . . ." She shrugged. "It just stuck with me."

"Were you excited about the scene Ben had set for you?"

"Being touched by two guys at once was something I'd al-ways been curious about. But in my head, since he'd arranged it, he was supposed to take control. But he didn't. He was too drunk, and that's not his style. Then you totally overwhelmed me, and I forgot about the silly fantasy. I got lost in you and your demands. So that's that. Can we drop the subject?"

"All right." *For now.*

"Tell me why you agreed to Ben's proposition."

"He told me you were very hot." Hunter shrugged. "But you were more than I expected. For years, I've wanted a submissive woman I hadn't met in a club. So many of them are jaded or head cases or so damaged that they want to be abused. I wanted to meet a strong woman . . . with kink. I never imagined that I'd meet Mrs. Perfect-for-Me."

She smiled wanly. "Who would have thought we'd wind up here? Amazing that a week ago I didn't know you even existed."

Ditto that. She'd changed his life completely. Hunter didn't want it any other way. He wouldn't ask if she regretted marrying him; it was too soon for that. But he could tell her how he felt and hope that she understood.

"I am glad we're here. You're everything I've wanted."

She turned to him with a furrowed brow and an expression he could only call puzzled amazement. "You're not afraid of anything— marriage, my stepfather, my emotional baggage. If I were a braver woman . . ." She smiled sadly, then sighed.

"You *are* a brave woman. Submission takes courage, and you've given me more raw honesty in mere days than some subs manage to ever give. Don't give up on us."

"I'm not sure I'll ever be ready to handle this. It would be better if you signed the papers."

Hell no. Never in a fucking million years. "Better for who?"

"Both of us, but you're not listening to me." Kata looked away.

Because she was wrong.

A ballad turned low filled some of the silence. Hunter had never paid that much attention to music. Now, he felt the singer's maudlin ache down to his bones. He had hungered for Kata's touch for a long, lonely time without knowing it. He did need her love. What the hell was he going to do if he couldn't convince her to believe in them before he left?

"What was our wedding like?" she asked softly.

Despite the turn of his thoughts, Hunter smiled. "Loud. Crazy. Christi and Mick married right before us."

"Who?"

He laughed. "The couple we met in the bar. During the cere- mony, the officiant kept rubbing his eyes, complaining that he'd pulled a double shift with a hangover. His assistant turned the music up loud, either to keep him awake or annoy the hell out of him." He chuckled again. "Elvis tunes at a Vegas wedding. How cliché is that? But I don't regret it."

Kata didn't say a word, just stared out the windshield, as if she were imagining the scene.

He frowned. "Did you have a dream wedding in mind?"

Her expression turned wistful. "I think most women do. I wanted to wear white and look beautiful. I wanted my brother to walk me down the aisle, with my mom and sister beaming in the first row. I wanted to hold a big bouquet of white roses, have a long train, and meet a man at the altar who's crazy in love with me."

If he could keep them together, Hunter vowed that, someday, he'd make that dream come true. "At least you got the last part right, honey." He reached out, grabbed her hand. "I love you. I know you have feelings for me, too, that scare you, but I think we can work everything out."

"How? We're running from a killer, my mother is sick, we don't see eye to eye, and what we have scares me half to death. You're leaving town and—"

Hunter leaned over and planted his lips on hers, silencing her. "Window dressing, all of it. We're going to find the killer. Your mother will recover. We'll get along just fine once you realize we're perfect for each other. There's no reason for you to be scared. As for me leaving, yeah. But I'll be back. It's that simple."

She gnawed on her lip. "Hey, is that the golden arches up there? I'm starving."

A not-so-subtle change of subject. But pushing her now would be counterproductive. Four days wasn't a long time for anyone to fall in love, be comfortable with a new sexual lifestyle, and overcome years of relationship fear. She needed time. Hunter glanced at the clock, then stifled his urge to curse. He shipped out in seventy-two hours. They'd come a long damn way in a short period of time. And he prayed they'd make it . . .

But his hope was beginning to dim.

* * *

KATA swallowed nervously as Hunter ushered her mother into the darkened house on the outskirts of Tyler, Texas. As they entered the classic southern brick house with large windows, a tall shadow fell over the threshold, same height and build as Hunter. Same haircut, same mien. This man also looked handsome as hell, but drawn, almost haunted. Would Hunter look like that in twenty years if she left and he never found love again?

"Son." The man relaxed, as if he'd just identified the person entering his house as a non-threat. "Glad you're here."

"Colonel, this is Mrs. Buckley." He nodded to Mamá, who looked so tiny in his arms.

"Carlotta," her mother smothered a cough. "I don't mean to intrude. If this is inconvenient—"

"It's not. Call me Caleb." He addressed Hunter. "Set her on the sofa. I'll take her up to her room when she's ready."

The Colonel even sounded like Hunter, a bit gruff, very to the point. Kata lingered in the doorway. Was leaving her mother here really a good idea? It *was* doubtful that Gordon would find her or fuck with someone as intimidating as the Colonel, but could Mamá recover with a terse stranger hovering?

"Will do, sir," Hunter said.

As soon as he moved to do his father's bidding, she sensed more than saw the Colonel's gaze zero in on her. Kata's heart stuttered. Though she couldn't see his face clearly through the shadows, something about his stance said he wasn't pleased.

The Colonel stepped forward finally, the foyer lights spilling across his face. God . . . it really was like looking at Hunter in twenty years. Tawny hair, though his had sprinkles of gray. Blue, blue eyes. Attractive, hard, demanding.

"Hello, sir. I'm Kata." She held out her hand, praying it didn't tremble.

Silently, she berated herself. If she and Hunter weren't going to remain married for long, it hardly mattered whether his father liked her or not. But that logic didn't smother her anxiety.

"Hunter's bride?"

"Yes." At least for the moment.

He took her hand and stared hard. Damn it, there was no way she would allow herself to feel inferior under that assessing glare. She lifted her chin and met his gaze, refusing to cower.

"She's got spine, son," he called across the room to Hunter. "I approve."

Finally, a stiff smile crossed the man's face, as if he knew she'd been holding her breath, then he guided her into a cozy den dominated by a chocolate brown sectional and a huge flat screen. Kata relaxed, but wondered . . . what had the Colonel expected?

Hunter settled her mother on the sofa and wrapped a blanket around her. The TV flickered mutely in the background. Kata sat beside her mother, holding her frail hand. Carlotta drifted off almost instantly. Between the illness and the medication, she was exhausted.

"Clearly your mother needs rest." The Colonel stared at her mother. "I'll make certain she gets it."

Mamá didn't like being idle, but in this case, it was good for her. "Thank you."

He turned to Hunter with a scowl. "You say her husband wanted her to make dinner?"

"Yep. Was cranky that she hadn't."

"Fucker," the Colonel said under his breath, then glanced her way. "Excuse my language, but my opinion of him stands."

Kata shrugged. "You'll get no arguments from me. He is a fucker. I hate him."

The Colonel threw his head back and laughed. "She's definitely not like those twits you used to spend time with. Logan still hasn't learned his lesson. He'd been here all of five minutes when he started sexting with some local hussy begging for a dose of pain."

"Give it a rest, Dad."

Kata whirled at the new voice from the edge of the room. He had the same piercing blue eyes that his father and older brother possessed, the same large frame and intimidating stance. The similarities ended there. His hair was like midnight, his skin naturally bronzed. The cleft in his chin a throwback to another side of the family. This had to be Logan.

As if on cue, his phone beeped. He took it out, slid the keyboard open, and muttered as he typed. "I said midnight. Natalie definitely needs a spanking." Then he pocketed his phone. "Hey, bro!"

With a laugh, Hunter crossed the room. "How the hell are you?"

The two brothers embraced and gave each other hearty slaps on the back. "Damn fine."

"I thought you'd be in Dallas."

Logan shook his head, peering around his brother to stare at Kata. "Wouldn't miss meeting the woman who snared your heart."

"Kimber called with news of your surprise wedding," the Colonel said wryly.

Hunter rolled his eyes. "Our little sister needs to keep her mouth shut. God, why doesn't she just send an announcement to the paper? Or plaster it all over Facebook?"

"I'm sure she'll do both as soon as she's recovered from childbirth," the Colonel assured. "I saw her and Baby Caleb this afternoon. He's got a fine, healthy set of lungs. And seems to have the Edgington eyes."

"Agreed," Logan threw in. "Precious baby. Deke is in love all over again."

Wincing, Hunter admitted, "I meant to see Kimber and the baby this morning when I reached the hospital, but I got . . . sidetracked."

By the sight of her sitting on Ben's lap. Kata cringed. Being with Ben hadn't been emotional or sexual for her, but the incident had caused an argument, forced painful revelations—and Hunter to miss seeing his newborn nephew.

Logan's phone beeped again. He glanced at the screen, raised a displeased brow, then pocketed his phone.

"Who wants Chinese food?" Hunter's brother asked, as if everyone in the room didn't know that some impatient woman was dying for his discipline.

"Good idea," Hunter agreed.

Twenty minutes and a straight-up whiskey later, Kata sat with the men at the round, utilitarian table, trying to stay awake. The eventful morning and hours in the car piled on top of the days' worth of vigil in the hospital were catching up with her. Resting her head on her hand, she closed her eyes. What she wouldn't give for a bed and eight uninterrupted hours of sleep.

Then Hunter mentioned the one subject guaranteed to rile all the other alpha males in the room.

"What do you mean, someone is trying to kill Kata?" Logan glared at his brother.

Their father followed suit, eyeing her protectively. "Suspects?"

Oh, she didn't need more drama—or testosterone—right now. "No one has made a move against me since Sunday. Maybe . . . he's given up. Or the hired killer who died in jail took his secret to the grave. Or someone realized they had the wrong girl."

"Or maybe they're hiring someone new as we speak. Between the fact that I've tried to protect you and you haven't stayed in one place for too long, we've been lucky," Hunter stated.

Kata wasn't feeling acquiescent. "Really, who would be trying to do *me* in? So I pissed off a gang thug by issuing a warrant for his arrest. I'm a probation officer," she supplied for Logan and the Colonel when they looked confused.

Hunter shook his head. "I don't think a punk from some street gang has the kind of connections to hire an assassin with that kind of equipment."

"Professional?" The idea looked like it pissed Logan off.

"All the way." Hunter nodded.

"What do we know about this guy, except that he's dead?" her father-in-law asked.

"Not much. He had no ink or affiliations that we could find. Guy was iced ten minutes after hitting lockup. They still haven't ID'd the body."

Logan whistled. "Quick work. Someone wanted their loose ends covered."

"Yeah, and fast." Hunter grabbed her hand, squeezed. "Jack knows all the local cops. As soon as they figure out who this John Doe is, he'll call me. Maybe that will be a clue. For now, Kata can't think of anyone trying to kill her, other than this Cortez Villarreal."

"Something's not adding up." Arms crossed, the Colonel stared her way.

He looked like he wanted to interrogate her, and frankly, Kata wasn't in the mood. "Damn it, no one else has cause to be angry with me. I don't know who else would want me dead or why. If I did, I certainly wouldn't be keeping it to myself."

The Colonel raised a thick, tawny brow at her.

Hunter looked like he was repressing a smile. "Kata hasn't had a good night's sleep or a real meal in two days. This morning was particularly . . . demanding."

Oh, he didn't just say that, grinning with that cat-that-ate-the-canary expression. The second she got him alone, she was going to kick his ass. Still, she felt a flush crawl up her face.

As Logan's phone beeped with a new text message, he grinned broadly at them. Even the Colonel had a knowing look in his eye. Kata glared at Hunter, the rat bastard, then excused herself. No one laughed—but they wanted to, she was sure.

She walked into the next room and sat on the sofa, taking Mamá's hand in hers. A second later, the doorbell rang, startling her mother awake.

Logan grabbed the food and dispensed with the delivery boy in less than sixty seconds. Hunter set out paper plates, grabbed beers and bottles of water. The Colonel headed her way.

"Carlotta, time to eat. I'll make you some eggs and toast."

Mamá turned and saw all the little white cartons and the pile of fortune cookies on the table. "No need to trouble yourself, Caleb. Chinese is fine."

"You're taking heavy antibiotics. Spicy foods may upset your stomach."

"Really, do not trouble yourself for me." She reached out to Kata for a hand up.

The Colonel edged Kata aside. "I'm going to take care of you properly. No arguments."

Before her mother could speak, the big man bent and lifted her mother into his arms.

Mamá looked Kata's way, shock spreading across her face. "Caleb, I assure you, I can walk. I do not wish to be a bur—"

"Barely twenty-four hours ago, your fever was one hundred three. That's a serious illness. You're family now. You'll find the Edgingtons take care of their own."

Her mother gaped at the tight-lipped soldier. "My husband would not approve of you holding me this way."

The Colonel's expression turned even more grim. "With all due respect, Carlotta, any able-bodied man who expects a woman to cook for him hours after being released from the hospital doesn't deserve the privilege of having a wife."

True, but the Colonel was matter-of-factly making sure her mother didn't exert herself . . . and not really hearing her discomfort. Kata winced.

Mamá's mouth pursed. "I—I would prefer to walk."

"When you're stronger."

"Colonel, I can help her. We'll be fine," Kata assured.

"Hunter says you're only staying until tomorrow afternoon. It's best that your mother and I get used to each other. I mean to take care of her until she's well."

End of conversation, at least as far as the Colonel was concerned. Mamá surely heard that tone, too; neither she nor Kata argued again.

If the man was going to insist that her mother eat something bland, like eggs and toast, then Kata could fix it and put her mother at ease.

As the Colonel set her mother at the kitchen table, then tucked the throw blanket around her, Kata headed for the kitchen. "Eat your dinner while it's warm. I'll make Mamá's meal."

Hunter frowned as he followed her into the kitchen. "Honey, you're about to fall down. Sit, Kata. Eat."

"Mamá needs my help, and I'm fine," she lied as fatigue crept in. "The snack earlier helped."

He grabbed her arm. "I'm willing to bet that you don't last ten minutes. Stop being so stubborn and let me do this."

Yanking away, she anchored her hand on her hip. "Do I need to get a string? You remember I told you that if you tried to control me outside the bedroom I would string you up by the balls?"

"Fine," he said, his hands up, wearing a hint of a smile. "Let me help you at least."

It went against his grain not to demand, and Kata appreciated his offer, but she wasn't helpless. "Bacon and eggs aren't hard. Really, I'm good."

Hunter didn't say a word. He merely watched as she rummaged through cabinets until she found a pan and set it on the stove with shaking hands. Exhaustion pulled at her.

"Do you think your mom will want juice?" Hunter asked, opening the fridge. "I can get you some, too."

Hell, why hadn't she thought that Mama might want juice? Worse, her hands wouldn't stay still.

Right now, she didn't have the strength to string Hunter up by the balls even if she wanted to.

"Sure. Thanks."

Hunter poured the juice, setting a glass aside for her and giving the other to his dad, who stood waiting with a frown.

Ignoring them, Kata trudged to the refrigerator. Her legs felt weak as she withdrew the staples she needed. Gripping the door handle to keep her upright, she dug for the energy to lift the bacon and set it on the counter behind her, then grab the carton of eggs. She drew in a bracing breath.

As she made her way across the kitchen again, eggs in hand, her weary legs gave out for a split second, and she stumbled. Tears filled her eyes as she realized Hunter was right; she didn't have the energy to do this.

Hunter was there to catch her with an arm around her waist and a hand under the eggs. His voice was a soft warmth on her cheek. "Honey, are you okay?"

Damn it, she didn't want to admit weakness. "I'm just tired. Give me a minute." She reached for the juice glass and gulped some. "I'll be fine."

The "family" face he'd been wearing all evening dissolved. The "Dom" face took over. "Don't lie. Time for you to rest. Dad, will you take care of Carlotta? Kata and I are going to have a chat."

With that, he dipped down and picked her up, bringing her against his chest.

"What are you doing?" she screeched.

Logan did his best to smother a laugh.

Hunter didn't answer. Marching down the hall, he shouted, "Save us some dinner."

Kata wriggled . . . but he wasn't letting go. "Damn it, put me down! Don't you dare embarrass me like this."

No response. A dozen steps later, he kicked the door shut behind him, then dropped her. Kata felt the bed at her back. Her fury seethed. Was he fucking serious, dragging her away in front of everyone like a child in need of discipline?

But she couldn't deny that the bed felt heavenly soft. Kata was sorely tempted to close her eyes and sink into sleep.

"This is totally ridiculous." She struggled to find her feet and get them under her.

"I agree." His big body came over hers. His face, even in the shadowed room, said he was very serious. "I love your spirit, but if you don't take care of yourself properly, I'll intercede."

Every word out of his mouth sounded too much like the Colonel talking to her mother, commanding and making decisions, without regard to her feelings. Without really listening.

Kata sagged back to the mattress, closing her weary eyes, though thoughts ricocheted through her brain. Were they both destined to be like their parents? The awful question crashed over her. Hunter behaved like a younger replica of his father—determined, protective, bossy, unbending. Just this morning, she had realized that she was more like her mother than she'd ever imagined.

A part of her had been hoping that Hunter was right, that the budding love between them would prevail. But how, when every day brought more proof that this relationship would probably destroy her—and she, slave to the increasing submissive weakness inside her, would let it happen?

Hunter leaned over and placed a brief kiss on her forehead. Even while furious, the connection between them sparked across her skin. Everything inside her yearned for more.

The truth hit her—a slap across raw cheeks. She'd fallen in love with a man who would steal her independence, even as she became addicted to his touch and was ruined for every other man.

The Colonel had cowed her mother into silence in less than five minutes. Granted, she was beat down with sickness and years with Gordon. But Kata wondered how long would it take Hunter to twist her into the same submission. Five years? One? Less? How long before she lost herself to him and her self-respect?

That was a question she had to make certain she couldn't ever answer.

Chapter Seventeen

HUNTER and Kata emerged from the bedroom to find that the Colonel had fixed Carlotta's dinner, as he should have, in Hunter's estimation. He'd spent the last twenty minutes with his lips against hers, his hands soothing her aching muscles. He wished she'd sleep, but she was too worried about her mother to do that now. Once Carlotta got settled, he'd be sure that Kata did the same.

Rolling his stiff, still-healing shoulder, Hunter reheated the Chinese food, then sat down to a plate of steaming vegetables, kung pao chicken, and steamed rice. Carlotta watched Kata pick at her beef and broccoli—and sneak a puzzled glance every now and again at his father.

After the meal, the men cleaned the kitchen with efficient silence, admonishing the women to stay put. Then the Colonel lifted Carlotta in his arms. Despite the woman's tired protests, he carried Kata's mother to her bedroom upstairs, down the hall from his own.

Kata followed the pair, then gave her mother some medicine, tucking her in. After Kata planted a kiss on her mom's cheek, and

Carlotta gave her daughter a weak smile, the woman drifted off. Hunter watched from the doorway as concern fell across Kata's face.

"She's going to be just fine." He caressed her shoulder. "She'll get plenty of rest."

"If she takes a turn for the worse, I'll get her back to the doctor ASAP," his father vowed.

"Thank you," she addressed the Colonel. "Remember that she's hurting more than physically. She needs not only your care, but for you to listen to her."

With that, Kata shouldered her way past them, out of the room. Hunter saw his father wince.

"I guess that's your wife's way of saying I've been a bulldozer. She's right."

"She thinks the same of me." Hunter shoved his hands in his pockets. "You and I, we're cut from the same cloth. I don't know a different way to take care of Kata. I love her."

The Colonel shot him an unreadable stare. "Tread carefully, son. If you hold on too tightly, she'll force you to let her go."

Hunter heard the voice of reason, experience.

"Is that what happened with you and Mom?"

He shouldn't ask. Hunter knew it . . . but damn it, to this day he didn't understand why his father had simply let Amanda go. The Colonel had never explained, and after she'd left, Hunter had never seen his mother again. Maybe understanding would help him with his own disintegrating union.

"In retrospect, yeah. I controlled so much of her life to avoid losing her that it became a self-fulfilling prophecy." The Colonel rubbed the back of his neck. "Amanda wanted more affection, wanted to know I valued her feelings and opinions. The only things I was good at were protecting her and, when I wasn't deployed, showing her how much I desired her. It wasn't enough."

Hunter damn near choked. It sounded too fucking parallel. "She wanted to leave. I get it. But you gave up and let her go so easily."

"You think that was *easy*?" the Colonel growled. "Letting her go was the fucking hardest thing I've ever done. I loved her, but didn't know how to be what she wanted. I gave her some space, agreed to the separation. I'd hoped the strategy would show her that I'd changed. But then I found out she'd been seeing someone else. I was so furious, but up until the day she was killed, I kept hoping that she would come back to me. Eventually, I realized that I'd loved her enough to set her free. She just didn't love me enough to come back. And I couldn't force her."

Hunter felt every word down to his bones. His mother had been so miserable being controlled that she'd walked out on a husband and three children and never looked back. Kata had been fighting him since before they said "I do."

Dread rolled through his belly as the years peeled away. He remembered his parents' ugly fights, the rage his mother had spewed. Her pleas for freedom. She'd finally grabbed it the only way she'd known how. Even in middle school, Hunter had become aware of the depression and anger that plagued his mother. Still, he'd been shocked when she left. He'd always assumed his father would keep the family together.

That should have been love's role. When the Colonel had finally realized it, he'd let her go.

"I've known for years that you disapproved of me not fighting to keep your mother."

His gaze snapped up, and he met his dad's head-on. "I lost respect for you that day, sir."

"You weren't good at hiding it. I could hardly keep Amanda against her will. I did what I thought had the best potential for long-term success." He shrugged as if he'd finally accepted years of pain and loneliness. "But after years of not hearing her unhappiness and not doing enough to change my ways, I was going to lose her, regardless."

In that moment, everything crystallized inside Hunter. "You're right. It takes a wise man to know when he can't win. And a brave one to let his woman go."

Hunter didn't know if he was that brave.

The Colonel sent him a sad smile. "Apparently not too wise. Carlotta isn't even mine, and I'm smothering her already. I know how I should behave, but I'm not good at implementing it. I suggest you learn, too."

Or Kata will be gone.

Under the tangle of anxiety, denial, and anger, Hunter knew his father was right. And it made him sick to think that, in all the time he'd been trying to show her how much he loved her, he'd also been hurting her.

"You know that biblical verse, 'Love isn't selfish. It's patient and kind . . .'"

Hunter closed his eyes. Yeah, he knew, just as he knew he'd been selfish, impatient, and pushy. "Fuck."

"Things between you and Kata aren't as smooth as you'd like, are they, son? It's hard when you're newlyweds."

"She already wants a divorce." He forced the words out, pinching the bridge of his nose. It hurt to admit just how much he'd screwed up, but his dad was being so damn honest.

The Colonel sucked in a breath. "What do you want?"

"I love her. I can't stand the thought of her not being mine."

His father clapped him on the shoulder in understanding. "But if her heart isn't with you, then she's not yours anyway. Sometimes . . . you have to let go. Better to do it now, before she comes to hate you." His voice cracked as painful memories twisted his strong face.

Hunter watched his father leave the cozy room. He turned to Carlotta, seeing a lot of Kata in her slightly lined face. It hadn't escaped his notice how disturbed Kata had been by her mother's interaction with his father. Hunter just hadn't been able to curb his own need to care for her in much the same way. But he saw now that if he didn't change fast, he was going to lose her for good.

With a heavy sigh, he turned out the lights in the little bedroom, then wandered downstairs. Kata had gone off to bed, according to Logan, whose phone continued to beep.

"Insistent girl," Hunter commented.

Logan shrugged. "Three of them now. All pain sluts." He ran his hands across the top of his buzz cut. "It's a game with them. They each want to be the one I finally sleep with."

Hunter shook his head. Granted, with his own love life a wreck, he was the last one who should be offering advice, but he had to try to help his younger brother. "How long has it been?"

The question made Logan look away. "I don't know. Maybe five years."

A small eternity. Logan was too young and vital to be voluntarily going without. "Your palm chafed raw yet?"

Logan scowled and punched him in the shoulder. "Fuck off. I make sure they get what they need. Xander delivers the sex and aftercare."

"Is sending in your clean-up man good enough for them? For you?" With a shake of his head, Hunter admonished, "Bro, you're going to have to move past T—"

"*Don't* say her name," he snarled. "Don't."

Hunter held up his hands in a defensive gesture. "Fine. You try talking to her again?"

Longing and misery crossed his face. "She slammed the door in my face."

His shrug told Hunter just how futile the whole mess felt. It was a feeling that Hunter feared he was going to know all too well if he lost Kata.

The Colonel sauntered into the room with a grimace. "Couldn't help overhearing. Her prick of a stepfather still lives in the same house. Adam Sterling smiles at me when I jog the neighborhood, as if he enjoys reminding me that his little princess broke my son's heart."

Hunter wouldn't be surprised. Logan growled something ugly and anatomically impossible.

Before Hunter could point that out, his phone rang. He glanced at the clock as he pried the phone off his belt. Who would be calling at eleven thirty?

Hunter looked at his display, his belly tightening as he pressed the button to talk. "Jack, talk to me."

"I've finally got some information, and you're not going to like it."

He hadn't liked anything about Kata's would-be assassin since he'd popped up. The whole thing stank.

"Kata's hired hit man was ID'd through fingerprint records earlier this evening. I just found out. His name is Manuel Silva. The name mean anything to you?"

"Nothing. You find something out?"

"Yeah, this is where it gets ugly. He's a well-known hit man, originally from Bogotá."

The words sucked the air from his lungs. "Colombia? You're sure?"

"One hundred percent. I made some of my local friends let me see the records before the CIA stepped in. Apparently, he was a person of serious interest to them. I'm still trying to learn why. The INS deported him a few years ago. He's done a lot of jobs for lowlifes in the drug trade. He was last seen slinking around New Orleans a few weeks ago. His services were *very* expensive, probably close to one hundred grand a whack." Jack sounded grim, and Hunter's blood ran cold. "Whoever wanted Kata iced went to a lot of trouble and expense. The question is, why?"

For the first time in his life, he felt almost numb with fear. "I don't know."

"Kata doesn't know anyone from New Orleans who might want her dead?"

"She's never mentioned it. I'll ask."

"Good. I'll keep seeing what else I can find and call you with any new information."

"Thanks, Jack." Though the news was really shitty. "Keep me posted."

"What is it, son?" the Colonel asked as soon as he ended the call.

Hunter drew in a deep breath. "The assassin, Silva, is from Colombia. Probably came from New Orleans. I can't figure out the connection. Cortez Villarreal deals in dope, but how would a small-town street thug from Lafayette even know the kind of badass killer who's a person of interest to the CIA?"

"If Villarreal didn't put that contract out on Kata, any ideas who did?"

"None." It wasn't adding up, but he honestly had no other suspects.

"Just because the connection isn't obvious does not mean it doesn't exist," Logan surmised. "For all we know, Silva and Villarreal are friends, family, or one owed the other a favor. Or maybe he was hired because he was out of left field."

"How could Villarreal afford Silva? But you may be right; I shouldn't judge a book by its cover. Maybe there *is* a simple connection; I'm just not seeing it."

Maybe. Whatever the case, Cortez Villarreal was the only suspect he had. Hunter would have preferred to hit the ground, shake people up, ask questions, dig up answers. But he was running out of time. Logan rose from the table, searching for his shoes, reminding him that it was nearly midnight, the dawn of a new day. He had just under three days to put this danger to bed once and for all. Thoughts raced as he made plans, discarded them, fine-tuned others. He wasn't sure which would suit best without more information, but he hated all of them.

Hunter rang Jack again. As soon as the bodyguard answered, he fired off questions. "Do you know where to find Cortez Villarreal?"

"Exactly? No, but rumor is that he's in the area and been laying real low over the past few days. I've been keeping tabs in case we need to have a meaningful conversation with him."

"I think it may be time. When you find him, let me know."

"I'll get on it and call you back."

The Colonel leaned in his face. "What are you thinking, son?"

Hunter gripped the phone, tamping down rising panic for Kata's safety. "It's time for something drastic."

* * *

SUNLIGHT streamed through the windows Friday morning when Hunter heard someone grip the doorknob. He came to, sat straight up, and reached for his SIG on the bedside table. When the door opened, his wife, hair tousled across heavy breasts barely covered by a thin white tank top and wearing black lacy pajama pants that clung to her hips, entered. Damn. Hunter was always ready for sex with her, but the sight of her made far more than his cock ache.

"Sorry if I woke you."

He glanced at the clock. Nine a.m.? He never slept that late. Then again, he'd spent all night holding Kata close, fearing their days together were numbered. He hadn't fallen asleep until after five. "I'm glad you did. I need to get up. Honey, does the name Manuel Silva mean anything to you?"

Her blank stare told him everything he needed to know. "Should it?"

"Do you know anyone from Colombia? Where is Villarreal from?"

"I don't know. I didn't exactly read his family tree when I was assigned to him."

"Does anyone in New Orleans have a beef with you?"

She blinked, shrugged. "Not that I know of. I haven't been there in a few years."

At this point, Hunter had to assume there was some connection between Silva and Villarreal that he simply couldn't see. He had nothing else.

"What's this about?" She crossed her arms and stared expectantly.

"Maybe nothing. How's your mom?"

Kata's face closed up as she sat on the edge of the bed. Hunter tried not to be distracted by the fact that he could see her rosy areolas through the little white tank.

"That's why I came to talk to you. I appreciate all the trouble you and your father have gone through for her, but she's not comfortable here. This morning, your father insisted on cooking for her again, carrying her out to the porch for fresh air, assisting her from room to room. He's been glued to her side, jumping up with a box of tissues or her cough medicine every time she sniffles."

In other words, his father knew what to do, and even after having his heart ripped out, he still couldn't manage to change. Then again, Hunter hadn't done much better last night at giving his wife space.

He cleared his throat. "Kata, having someone take care of her is good for her recovery."

"Not if she can't *relax*. The Colonel is being . . . a general. She isn't comfortable with him hovering. She wants to go to Mari's house, so I talked to my sister—"

"No. No way in hell am I taking either of you back to Lafayette now." This wasn't a good time to be inflexible, but damn it, she had to see the problems with her plan. "What if whoever wants you dead tracks you or your mother down? What if Gordon coerces her back home? Carlotta needs to give it more time here. She's uncomfortable because she's not used to others caring for her. She'll adjust."

Kata shook her head. "I don't think so. Believe me, someone trying to kill me scares me, too, but I can't leave Mamá here to get worse."

"Carlotta won't get much rest with two rambunctious grandsons underfoot. I'll bet that she ends up waiting on them."

Kata bit her lip and paused. "I was very clear with Mari that she can't be out of bed."

"Mari will have her hands full with her job, her kids, and a husband who lacks discipline. Your mother will naturally want to help. She can't afford to."

"Your father is totally overwhelming her."

"The Colonel is too . . . attentive. He knows that and will work on it. I'll talk to him."

"You?" she sputtered incredulously. "*You're* going to talk to him about backing off? Um, Pot, meet Kettle."

He bridged the space and grabbed her wrist, pulling her against him. "You're not using your head, Kata. You want to make your mother happy, but think about what's best for her. Do you want her returning to Gordon? Because if she's at Mari's, he'll browbeat her into it. If she stays here, the Colonel won't let that happen."

"Because he'll smother her even more. Mamá doesn't want to be here." Kata tried to pull away. "I saw your point, now you need to see mine."

He couldn't afford to. "I can't risk taking you or your mother to Lafayette now, with a potential assassin on the loose. I'm sorry. We're staying."

Kata rose and grabbed her suitcase. "You always have to be in charge, don't you? It's not just a bedroom thing, so stop pretending it is. And while you're at it, sign those damn divorce papers. Mari is tied up at work today, so I'm calling Ben. He'll give us a ride home."

With that, she slammed out the door. Hunter scrambled out of bed to find his pants. As he shoved his way into them, he heard the slam of the nearby bathroom door, heard the shower start. She was batshit crazy if she thought he was going to let her put a door between them so that she could fucking call Ben and leave.

But he also couldn't mow down her free will, or he'd lose her.

Hunter cursed, wishing for a convenient terrorist to put his fists into. Fuck, he didn't want to sign those papers. But while he was on active duty, Kata could proceed with the divorce without him—and he'd be powerless to stop her. Regardless of his dad's words of wisdom, he wasn't ready to stop fighting for Kata.

As Hunter reached for the bathroom door, the phone in his pocket rang. A glance at the display made him groan. "This better be fucking good, Andy."

"Remember who you're talking to, Raptor."

Shit. Andy Barnes was now his commanding officer, not just a buddy. He'd better suck it up. "Sorry, sir. What's up?"

"Your leave has been cut short."

"*What?* Twice in the same leave?" This was fucking unheard of unless it was a goddamn national emergency. "Is something happening?"

"The Sotillo organization is definitely gathering. The big arms-for-drugs sale that we anticipated earlier this week will go down Saturday night. We need you there."

Hunter struggled to wrap his head around Andy's words when he could still hear Kata threatening to call Ben in his head. "How? Víctor is dead. If you read my report, I received intel on my last trip that his brother, Adan, was killed, too. Who the hell would be organizing this?"

"Sotillo had underlings. I guess it's one of them. Víctor's death created a vacuum of power. Of course someone will want to step into it. We're going to send a small four-man team in there—"

"Four men? If they're going to conduct major business, both parties will come with a frigging army. Four men aren't going to get the job done."

"Four men will be able to slip in under the radar undetected and clean house. Too many men and too much equipment means that the potential for detection and fuckups is greater."

So was the potential for ineffectuality. This mission sounded like pure suicide. "I want it on record that I disagree."

"Duly noted." And boy, did Andy sound pissed off. "We'll need you back at base by fifteen hundred tomorrow."

With that, Andy hung up. Numbly, Hunter pressed the off button on his phone. Three o'clock tomorrow afternoon, in barely thirty hours. How the fuck was he supposed to save his marriage and ensure that his wife was completely safe before he had to leave?

Hunter didn't see a way to do both, and any good soldier learned how to prioritize mission objectives when things started going to hell. Between those two, he had no doubt which came first. Mentally, he sifted through his possible tactics. He had only one left.

And it hurt like hell.

Gritting his teeth, he reached for his phone and called Jack, who answered on the first ring.

Hunter didn't even let the man greet him before diving in. "We've got to move tonight. I'll be out of the country indefinitely tomorrow."

Jack cursed, sighed bleakly. "Okay, we'll make it work. Word on the street is that Villarreal is tired of dodging cops and is ready to wring your wife's pretty neck. I know the connection between him and Silva isn't obvious . . ."

"But what you're saying definitely lends credibility to Villarreal's motive and seems to validate him as the prime suspect." Goddamn it, Hunter felt the walls closing in around him—the danger to Kata, her distance, his job. He had to get his house in order quickly, and keeping her safe was top priority.

"You know anything about him?" Hunter hated feeling impotent. Usually, he'd be in there digging for answers and making heads roll accordingly. Staying near Kata and protecting her must take precedence.

"I've done a little research," Jack said. "Villarreal likes throwing his cash at flashy strippers. Sexy Sirens' grand reopening is tonight. I'll have Deke ask Alyssa to put out the word that he'll be a VIP if he shows up. Deke and I can grab him and have a 'friendly' chat with him until he agrees to leave Kata alone."

"Good. I'm going to keep Kata busy tonight while you bag this fucker. I'll be around in the morning to talk to him so we can settle this."

After agreeing to coordinate later that evening, Hunter made two more phone calls—both necessary evils. Then he threw on the rest of his clothes, brushed his teeth, found Kata's phone, and gave it to his dad for safekeeping. No way was she calling Ben to come take her away when she was in danger. Preferably not ever.

Rubbing damp palms on his denim-clad thighs, Hunter stood in front of the bathroom door Kata had retreated to and let out a deep breath. It didn't help; every muscle remained clenched. If there was another fucking way . . . But there wasn't, and he knew it. This was it.

His heart pounded as he pushed into the room. The fragrant, humid air wrapped around him. Everything smelled like her: spicy amber, sweet lilies. Beyond arousing. Like always, he turned hard and aching in an instant.

God, he loved this woman.

Seeing him, she gasped and scrambled for her towel on the basin. He grabbed the damp terry cloth first, loving the hell out of her in nothing but a lacy, baby blue thong. Her smooth olive skin and lush breasts with those tight, rosy brown nipples tempted him like nothing ever had. The dark ropes of her wet hair dripped down her back, framing her freshly scrubbed face. He couldn't wait to get back inside her, hold her again. Yesterday, she'd been dealing with too much, so he'd backed off, hadn't pressed his way into the snug, silken clasp of her pussy.

Tonight, all bets were off.

Realizing that he wasn't going to give her the towel and that he blocked the path to her clothes, Kata faced him squarely, chin raised. "What now? I've told you how I feel and what needs to happen. If you're here to stop me from leaving, you can't."

Ah, that stubborn streak of hers that intrigued him so much. Normally, he'd argue until he wore Kata down or seduce her until she gave in with a well-sated cry. This situation was far from normal. Until dawn, his most important role was to keep her safe. Nothing mattered more. Hunter had only one way left to do that . . . and give her what she wanted.

It was going to tear his fucking heart out.

He had no illusions; he'd never be the same. He'd be every inch the miserable bastard his father had been for the last fifteen lonely years, that Logan was now. Hunter had always sworn he'd do whatever it took to hang on to the one woman meant for him.

Goddamn it, in a handful of hours he'd have no choice but to let her go.

Hunter crossed his arms over his chest, restraining the urge to embrace Kata, stroke her tempting flesh—and never stop. "First, if you go home, you're not only putting yourself in danger, but your family, too. You might not know everything about this asshole threatening you, but he knows you. Why wouldn't he come after those you love?"

Kata's stubborn chin rose, but she nodded. Though she didn't want to, she saw his point. Now he had to put all his cards on the table, even though he had the losing hand.

"I have a proposition, honey: Today, I'll do whatever it takes to neutralize the threat against you. Tomorrow, you'll be free in every way." He clenched his fists. "I'll sign the fucking divorce papers."

As soon as he choked out the words, Hunter wished he could take them back. For him, she was it—had been since the moment he laid eyes on her. He wished he could make her understand, but unless she came to love him in return, accept his needs and her own, they were doomed.

Surprise flashed across her face, along with something else—regret, maybe . . . or was that his own wishful thinking?

She smoothed out her expression. "T-thank you for finally being reasonable."

Reasonable? In five seconds, she wouldn't think so. "I'll do that, *if* you spend tonight with me."

Chapter Eighteen

HE *was going to sign the papers?* Kata swallowed as conflicting emotions rushed her. She expected relief. After all, the emotional rollercoaster ride she'd been on the past few days was ending. Instead, dismay crashed through her. After tonight, she'd probably never see Hunter again. She blinked back blindsiding tears that burned like acid. Her heart felt as though it were bleeding out of her chest.

Was she crazy? She'd demanded this divorce. The minute Hunter relented, some twisted part of her wanted to stay with him?

God, she'd fallen in love with him.

Kata closed her eyes. Fine freaking time to realize it.

"Did you hear me?" He leaned against the doorframe, his gaze hot on her body.

He was cocky, challenging. Damn it, it didn't seem like his heart was breaking. He loved her so much that he was throwing in the towel after a mere four days? After he got another piece of ass and stole another bit of her soul, of course. Then he'd let her go.

Or maybe he'd finally realized they were a losing bet.

"Yes." She cleared her suddenly tight throat. "Spend tonight with you, and you'll sign the papers."

Even saying those words felt like a hot knife carving a jagged hole in her chest. But Hunter wasn't going to change. His dominance disturbed her. That his parents had split up over his father's controlling nature didn't bode well. Spending the day with Caleb had proven that leopard wasn't going to change his spots. And Logan seemed made from the same mold, if the demanding, growled phone calls she'd overheard with his BDSM bunnies were any indication. Perhaps she was too sensitive, but she'd rather roll over and die than let any man have the kind of dominion over her that Gordon held over Mamá.

She and Hunter had shared the best sex of her life. Kata always knew that she'd fall for someone who had a core of honor, straight-up honesty, a decisive bent. Dominance aside, Hunter was everything she could want in a man. It made sense that she had feelings for him. But she'd never be the kind of woman he needed. And she'd ultimately make him miserable.

She had to find the strength to let go before they hurt one another any more.

Hunter speared her with a haunting blue stare. "And?"

"I'll do it." Her voice was scratchy, thin. "What about the killer?"

"I have a plan. Jack and Deke are helping. By morning, everything should be over."

In that, she trusted him completely. Leaping into a marriage with Hunter might be as scary as jumping off a cliff, but she knew that he'd *never* let anything or anyone hurt her. And whatever else had happened between them, she probably owed him her life. "Thank you. I don't know how you accomplished it, but I'm very grateful."

"I'll explain once it's all settled."

That rankled a bit, but Kata nodded. That was Hunter's way. She couldn't change him, but she wanted to touch him, cup his cheek, plant a soft kiss on his mouth. It was too much like something a woman in love would do, so she did nothing. "Thanks."

"You're welcome. Be ready at five, suitcase packed. The Colonel and Logan have agreed to stay with your mother. I'll get Dad to back off. But you can be assured that she's in good hands. Tomorrow, you're both free." He paused, glanced down at her lacy blue underwear. "But tonight . . . no panties."

With that, he turned and left, closing the door behind him with a quiet click.

Kata stared at the solid oak portal between them. That was it? No kiss, no embrace? She'd certainly wanted it—even though tonight was good-bye.

A fresh wave of desolation overcame her, leaving her bereft in its wake. Hunter seemed all but done with her.

Kata frowned at her reflection in the lightly steamed mirror, then closed her eyes against the crush of emotion weighing on her. Everything inside her resisted ending this. How had Hunter ingrained himself in her heart so quickly that she suddenly wasn't sure how she'd live without him?

Kata shook her head. She'd lived without the man for twenty-five years. She'd find a way to manage for the rest of her life. First, she had to focus on making it through tonight. Because Hunter would strip her bare, all the way down to her soul, expose everything she was inside, then take it all. She feared she'd never be the same again.

* * *

HUNTER drove across town in silence. Kata wanted to ask where they were going, but his tight-lipped silence didn't encourage conversation. Wherever they were headed, she knew he would keep her safe.

Kata had no such assurance where her heart was concerned.

Finally, they pulled up in front of a big house as dusk began to fall. Just outside of town, on an isolated lane, the sprawling brick house with its black shutters and large windows beckoned from a long stone walkway bracketed by pairs of towering oak trees, their lofty branches reaching up and over the quaint walk. Flowers abounded in pots here and there. An air of old money and wealthy decadence lingered.

As she exited the truck, Hunter came around and held her door. She noticed another truck, a black one, already against the curb in front of them.

"Is someone else here?"

He closed and locked the truck behind her. "Come with me."

"Who lives here?"

"The owner won't be here tonight. No more questions."

He definitely had his Dom face on. The hard edge to his voice and the distance he put between them now tore at her. Fighting it would only hurt more in the long run, but she ached to throw her arms around him, press her lips to his, and ask him to share himself with her.

The way he'd been trying to coax her from the beginning. She winced at the thought.

He took her by the elbow, led her up the stone walkway, reached for the doorknob. And she couldn't stand the thought that their last night together would be impersonal. As much as he'd pushed and shoved his way into her life, her psyche, and even her heart, the Hunter who stood at her side now was so remote she wanted to scream.

"Wait!" She swallowed down her nerves. "I—I don't want it like this. You . . ." She tried to gather her racing thoughts, find the right words. "It's like you don't like me, even want me, anymore. If that's the case—"

Kata didn't even finish the sentence before Hunter dragged her closer and captured her mouth with his own, fists in her hair, lips tangling with hers, heart racing against her own. He urged her open and dove in. The kiss turned instantly deep. Intimate. He swirled his tongue around her own as if he planned to stay all night. With a devouring pace, he engulfed her senses, silencing her worries. Kata pressed to him, curled her arms around his neck, losing herself in Hunter's familiar flavor. God, she never wanted the kiss to end.

As she moaned, he pulled away, his mouth pressed into a grim line. "I want you. Never doubt that. Come inside."

He opened the front door, and Kata had the impression of warm-toned walls, tall ceilings, lots of Tuscan details before he hustled her down a long hall. She bit back questions. He'd reveal to her his intentions when he was ready. As much as she hated to admit it, he knew her body well. Whatever demanding, restraining, subjugating things he had planned, she'd likely love it.

He led her to the very last door and pushed his way into a large bedroom, steeped in shadows. Just inside the door, he flipped a switch. Low, golden light flooded the bedroom. Beige and white striped the walls. A traditional white headboard framed by heavy brocade drapes dropped from a white cornice box affixed to the ceiling, a wood-burning fireplace tiled in traditional marble and a gleaming white mantel all lent the room an air of elegance. Not a piece of BDSM equipment lay anywhere in sight.

Kata turned to Hunter with a question in her gaze.

He swallowed. "Do you like it?"

The cozy, romantic feel appealed, for sure, but . . . "I do. I guess I was expecting something that looked more like your brother's living room."

An expression she couldn't discern crossed his face. "Tonight is about you, honey. Whatever you want, it's yours."

It was on the tip of her tongue to ask him why he could just be with her this way tonight and not every other night, but she knew. He simply wasn't wired that way for the long term. Tonight, Hunter was willing to put aside his desires for her.

It made her love him even more.

She pushed back tears. "That's . . ." *Incredible.* "Thank you."

Hunter looked like he wanted to say more but shook it off. He shoved his hands in his pockets. "Tell me how you want this to go."

With him, it had never been anything but a whirlwind of desire so intense, it was like standing in the middle of a raging storm. For days, she'd wished he would ease off, not try to overtake her mind and soul. Now that he was giving her what she wanted, Kata wasn't sure what to say.

"Can you just . . . be with me? Soft, maybe a little sweet?"

For a second, the hard angles of his male face tightened with uncertainty. Finally, he caressed her shoulder, cupped his palm around her neck. "For you, yeah."

Her heart was about to break. Kata knew that as soon as he leaned in and kissed her softly, his lips lingering over her own, a velvety brush of tongue. She clung to his wide shoulders and pressed her mouth to his. He didn't hesitate to open to her, deepen the kiss until she felt herself drowning in the sweet stirrings of pleasure.

"Do you want to lie down?"

Of course. This good-bye was going to be long and poignant. She didn't want to be rushed or try to join with him standing up. Tonight called for soft sheets, rumpled covers, breathy sighs—a cocoon for lovers.

"Please."

Hunter reached up to the switch and killed the lights.

From their argument their first night together in Vegas, she knew that he preferred full light, wanting to see the effect he had on her. He'd given her darkness now as another concession.

Funny thing, she no longer felt self-conscious around him. In fact, she'd rather have the lights on to see every expression on his gorgeous, familiar face.

Before she could say so, he took her hand in his. "Lead the way."

Kata frowned. She knew he was letting her set the pace, trying to give her what she wanted, but this behavior was so unlike him, she wondered if making love tonight was going to be like being with him at all.

Biting her lip, she led him over to the plush queen-sized bed. He followed without word, waiting until she sank down to the mattress, her whole back enveloped in something cloudlike, heavenly.

He stretched out beside her, taking her hand in his, turning his face in her direction. Their stares met in the shadows, his questioning . . . and so damn resigned, she felt a sob rise up. Kata turned to him, threw her arms around him, pressed their bodies tight.

Hunter slid his arms around her. "Tell me what I can give you tonight, honey. Whatever you need, it's yours."

That would be his parting gift. She heard it in his voice.

A mix of sadness and panic gripped her. She trapped a sob in her chest and covered his mouth with her own, desperately trying to sink down into the male flavor of him, his gentle embrace. He returned the kiss, every breath, every brush of lips, every slide of tongue. She tried to drown in the heavy, honey-sweet sea of desire he usually created inside her. It wasn't there.

"What's wrong?" She stared at him in the dark, trying to understand.

"Nothing." He caressed her face. "I'm doing my best to give you what you want."

Yeah, he'd said that, but something didn't feel right. "Tell me what *you* want."

He sent her a regretful smile. "Everything you don't. So let's not dwell on what isn't meant to be. Let me give to you tonight."

Hunter was trying to be something he wasn't—for her. Hunter was letting her go—for her. Suddenly, she knew what she wanted.

"Be yourself with me," she blurted into the silence.

He sighed. "Kata . . ."

"I know I've been afraid before." Of him seeing too deeply inside her, of falling for this man who enthralled her so much. No matter how she'd tried to stop him, he'd worked into her soul and stolen her heart. She couldn't protect what he'd already taken. "Tonight is our last time together. I want to be with *you* completely."

This once, that would be her gift to him—for both of them.

His grip at her neck tightened. "Are you sure?"

Yes and no. Hunter was going to strip away her every defense and artifice, but for once in her life, she didn't want to be too afraid to give her trust, her love. Tomorrow, she could return to her sarcastic, defensive, barbed-wire self. Tonight, she wanted to connect to Hunter in a way she never had . . . and never would with any other man again.

She smiled. "Yes, Sir."

He hesitated, then pulled her to her feet. "All right, honey. Come with me."

Kata squeezed his hand as he led her out of the cozy bedroom, then across the hall. In front of another door, he stopped. She waited as he pulled a black, silky cloth from his back pocket. He held it up in front of her, as if waiting for her to object. She flattened her lips together and kept the hovering question to herself.

"Very good," he praised her restraint. "Thank you. I'm proud of you."

Then he turned her away. Kata fully expected him to tie her wrists together. Instead, he lifted the cloth over her eyes and tied it around the back of her head.

"Can you see, Kata? Be honest."

"Nothing." That was the frightening truth.

She heard a soft click, then a long creak. A rush of cooler air greeted her as Hunter urged her forward, guiding her with an arm around her waist and his hand on her hip. Then she heard the door close behind her.

Kata swallowed nervously. What didn't Hunter want her to see? Her mind flashed back to Logan's living room. She shivered. Hunter had admitted that he was no stranger to all that equipment, and he'd known it freaked her out. Was that why he blindfolded her now?

"Your safe word tonight is "red." Are you clear?"

"Red. Yes." Kata knew without asking that if anything Hunter did frightened or hurt her that she could say one word and stop everything, no hesitation.

She frowned. When had she come to trust him so unequivocally? The man had seduced her, married her when she was too drunk to know better, dominated, spanked, and punished her. He'd also given her more pleasure and devotion than she'd ever had in her life, and he'd never gone back on his word. He wouldn't hurt her now.

He also wouldn't be in her life after tonight.

The reality of that swamped her again. Panic flared, along with a need to feel him close. What was the matter with her? Was it the vulnerability that being blindfolded gave her? Or those useless feelings for Hunter creeping in?

Afraid to answer the question, she turned to where she sensed he stood and wrapped her arms around him.

"Whoa." He steadied her, brought her closer. "You all right, Kata?"

"A little afraid." She wanted to say more but forced herself to keep silent, trust him. Please him.

"You'll be fine. Tonight, you didn't choose what you've been telling yourself you want. And I'm glad." She could hear the sincerity in his voice. "Let me give you what you need. Surrender to me."

Kata reached out to touch him. "Yes, Sir." Then Hunter set his mouth over hers again with hungry demand, and she was lost.

She might regret it later, but she opened to him completely. If this was their last night, she wanted that connection deeper than ever, wanted to know that she'd been with him without artifice, barriers, or fear.

Kata knew that might hurt tomorrow, but he would do whatever necessary to give her absolute pleasure. She put herself in his hands and let go.

"Strip, Kata. Shoes first, then shirt, pants, bra—in that order. Fold the garments, putting them on the table beside you as you go. Once you're finished, hand them to me."

Her stomach lurched, as if she'd jumped off a cliff. A week ago, she would have hated his tone, even as it melted her. Now, she focused on the sound of his voice, on giving herself over, pleasing him, experiencing all they could be. Tonight only.

"Yes, Sir." She slipped off her shoes and groped for the table, finding it directly beside her. She followed by unfastening her shirt, one reckless loosening of each button after another until she peeled it off her shoulders. Folding it as best as she could, Kata set it aside. Then she took a deep breath. Now for the most frightening command. But she tore at the fastening on her low-rise jeans and pushed them down. Per Hunter's earlier instructions, she'd worn no panties.

Kata shoved the denim down, folded it up, then set the pants on top of the rest. With a deep breath, she shoved them in his direction. Hunter was right there, taking the clothes from her hands, settling a soft kiss on her mouth.

Naked, she stood before him, heart pounding, blood racing. Proud, scared—ready.

Hunter took her by the hand, led her across the room, then guided her to stand before him, easing her back against something padded. Everything inside her stuttered, and she wanted to ask what he planned. But she didn't. "Spread your legs."

Drawing in a bracing breath, she complied. Something cool and leathery-soft slid around one ankle. It fastened with a quiet click. He repeated the motion with the other leg. Caressing his way up her thigh, her belly, her breast, Hunter reached for her wrist and dragged one over her head. Soon, she felt the supple straps and the cool metal of a buckle. Finally, he reached for her other hand, linked her fingers in his, then raised her arm.

Kata seized up. God, by binding her so completely, how powerless would he make her? And yet, with his groan of approval in her ear and his body pressing against hers, urgent and hard, she felt the power she had over him.

The buckle fitted around her wrist, then he trailed his fingertip down the inside of her arm, over her breast, stealing across her nipple until he pinched with just enough pressure to be just shy of pain.

Hunter leaned in and feathered his lips across her shoulder, her neck, her ear. "We're being watched, honey."

She froze, her breath catching. There was someone in the room with them? Who?

Hot eyes roamed her skin, assessing, caressing. She shivered, an icy thrill racing over her. Vulnerability hit her, and she became aware of every taut inch of her skin, the tight beads of her nipples, the wet folds of her pussy sliding against each other with lip-biting friction whenever she moved. And a complete stranger could see it all.

As if he could hear her racing thoughts, he murmured, "Shoulders back. Hair behind you. Show him how fucking sexy you are. Make him know that I'm the luckiest bastard on the planet to be fucking you tonight."

Him? The thought, Hunter's words aroused her . . . even as insecurities tried to take over. "A stranger is looking at my hips and thighs."

"They're gorgeous and lush. *I'm* looking, too. If you can't commit to submitting tonight, use your safe word. Or let me touch you while he watches."

Kata should be horrified by the thought of a stranger's eyes on her. Anxiety about her appearance niggled at her, but Hunter demanded her compliance. And she wanted to please him.

This was so much like her fantasy. She held her breath. Oh God, did he mean to give her the *entire* fantasy? As possessive as he was, would he really share her with another man?

Hunter brushed his thumb across her nipples, scattering her thoughts. He pressed his body against hers, kissed his way down her neck—and made her feel sexier than any man ever had. She sighed, willed herself to relax. For him.

"Yes, Sir."

"So fucking sexy," he groaned against her skin as he kissed his way down the swells of her breasts, laving all around the tight peaks of her nipples.

Electricity flashed through her as if someone had jolted her. Pleasure flowed between the peaks and in a straight arrow between her legs. Her first instinct was to press her thighs together, but her bindings made that impossible. She whimpered.

She could almost feel Hunter smile as he sidled closer and fastened his mouth on her breast, sucking hard at the peak.

His first strong pull was a jolt. She mewled, her entire body alive, racing. The familiar sensations blossomed, yet somehow as fresh as new spring. Pleasure, dormant since he'd last touched her, now burst wide, nerve endings unfurling.

Then he slid his hand down her abdomen and into her wet folds, settling unerringly on the aching bundle of her clit. And someone she may or may not know could see her pleasure.

She put herself entirely in Hunter's hands. No control, no responsibility, no telling what would happen next. A week ago, she would have been hard-pressed to think of anything that she'd tolerate less. Now, she could hardly think of anything she wanted more.

"So wet," he murmured against her skin. "You smell incredible. I'm dying to taste you."

The thought of Hunter's mouth on her, driving her beyond her control while someone watched, ratcheted up her desire another notch. Kata clenched her fists, struggled to draw in her next breath as the ache between her legs tightened again.

His large, deft fingers skimmed her clit again, circling the little bud in an unpredictable rhythm that had her gasping. Every time he touched her, he shoved her to the edge of pleasure. When she could barely catch her breath, he pulled away. Her body tightened, and she bucked against her restraints.

"Please . . ." she murmured.

But Hunter never veered from course.

"He's watching us. Be a good girl and take what I give you."

God, that voice. She was willing to endure torment to please him. "Yes, Sir."

Before she could take another breath, Hunter knelt at her feet and gripped her hips. Her heart stuttered with anticipation when she felt his hot breath on her pussy. Kata tensed, waiting.

The first touch of his mouth wasn't tentative or gentle. He dove in hungrily, devouring her slick flesh, his tongue slipping between her soaked folds and nestling right against her clit for a strong lap that made her rise on her toes and nearly come out of her skin. He chuckled softly, then did it again. And again. Every press of his mouth went deeper, felt more intimate, as if he meant to sate himself somehow. As if he was leaving his mark on her forever.

The pleasure soared, and Kata wanted so badly to touch Hunter in return, feel the soft stubble of his military cut under her fingers, the bulge of hard shoulders against her palms. Restrained and bound, she could only endure the delicious torture.

Suddenly, a man's heavy breaths in her ear joined the rhythm. *Oh God, the stranger,* she thought—just as Hunter's lips seized her clit. Watching Hunter consume her was arousing the stranger. The ache between her legs coiled tighter.

Her pounding heart roared in her ears. The precipice of orgasm loomed; just one more sweet caress of Hunter's tongue would put her over the edge. Instead, he eased back. The cuffs came off her ankles, then her wrists. He rubbed them both with firm, gentle hands until she felt the warm rush of blood in her fingers.

"What are you . . . ?" She reached for him, her body boneless against his, the chafe of his slightly starched shirt and jeans against her hypersensitive skin nearly throwing her into sensory overload.

"Not a word," Hunter warned with a bite in his voice and a slap of his hand on her ass.

Kata whimpered, her entire body aching. She was like a grenade with the pin pulled, going to explode at any second. His hot hand across her backside only magnified the explosion building between her legs.

"Turn." He gripped her hips and faced her away from him, right at a wall of male heat that smelled like musk and pine—something vaguely familiar that she couldn't place. Suddenly, she felt Hunter's harsh breath ruffling her hair, in her ear. "Kiss him."

The stranger? Anticipation and fear gripped her stomach at equal turns. Kata wanted to ask so badly who he was . . . but that hadn't been her fantasy. And it wasn't Hunter's will.

Firm lips brushed over hers, soft and slightly minty. Pleasant. She relaxed, opened into the kiss. The stranger pressed their lips together, brushing her tongue with his. Excitement swirled in her belly, grabbing her between the legs and pulling unmercifully.

Then Hunter reached around her, settling over her clit with a ruthless, rhythmic touch. "No coming."

"But—"

The stranger cut her off with another hard kiss, and she grabbed his solid biceps and hung on as Hunter drove her body higher. She gasped, and the stranger swallowed the sound with his mouth. This kiss was short on patience, long on hunger as he dove deep.

"Pull back," Hunter growled.

Immediately, the stranger tore his mouth away. Kata was still processing Hunter's command, trying to understand it. Then his fingers left her clit and rose. He painted her juice across the soft surface of her lips, top and bottom. Her stomach flipped.

"Kiss him again."

No hesitation. If the stranger had been determined before, he was downright demanding now, plundering her lips, licking them, soaking up her taste with a growl.

"I'm too selfish to give him your orgasms," Hunter whispered in her ear. "They belong to me, but I can see he likes the taste of your pussy, honey. I want him to tease you until you scream."

Kata whimpered.

"Sound good, man?" he asked the other man.

The stranger whispered against her lips, "Fuck, yeah."

Again, a slightly familiar voice, but her senses were too scattered, her body rioting.

He grabbed her face and planted another urgent kiss on her lips, short and hungry and passionate. Then he was gone, drifting down her body, his mouth trailing over her neck, the swell of her breast. He lingered to take one nipple in his mouth, nipping, sucking. She gasped and filtered her hands through his severely short hair. He chuckled against her skin.

The stranger eased down her abdomen, then dropped to his knees. She barely had a moment to feel his unwavering stare and hot pants before he opened her pussy wide with his thumbs. Kata's breath caught, as he latched on to her clit, sucking gently but deep.

She cried out, reaching behind her, wrapping desperate arms around Hunter's neck, holding on to him like a lifeline.

"You like that, honey?" he whispered in her ear, his thick cock digging hard and urgent through the denim of his jeans into the curve of her ass.

She'd liked it better when Hunter had gone down on her, but knowing that he was watching, that this aroused him, was a turn-on all its own. She mewled her reply.

He chuckled in her ear, moving her hair aside. Then he pressed sweeping kisses across her shoulder and thumbed her nipples until they stood stiff. The stranger's head bobbed between her legs, his tongue swiping against her hard bundle of nerves again and again. The friction nearly unraveled her. Kata focused on pushing down the orgasm, but the stranger . . . he was good. She clung to Hunter even tighter.

Him murmuring, "You're so fucking sexy, honey," only drove her higher.

God, she was so close, lava flowing hot through her veins.

"Ease off, man," Hunter said. "She's about to come."

Instantly, the stranger backed off, the devouring pulls of his mouth reduced to gentle licks. Kata whimpered in protest.

"I told you, your orgasms are mine. But I love knowing you're on edge. Spread your legs wider for him."

Kata bit her lip. Hunter controlled her utterly, even through another man's touch. She squirmed, perspiring, feeling overheated and needy. Hunter caressed her arms, his teeth nipping into her shoulder. She wanted more.

He turned her face toward him, and Kata pulled his head down, bringing his lips close to hers. He resisted.

"You're not complying. Do you need a spanking, Kata?"

He was going to make sure the stranger kept her on the edge for as long as he liked, and there wasn't a damn thing she could do to stop it. Even as it turned her on, she wished it was his mouth touching her so intimately, his tongue driving her so close—yet so far away—from bliss.

Finally, she eased her thighs farther apart.

"More," he murmured against her lips.

With a moan, she did.

"Pretty. Press your hips forward," he said over her shoulder, looking down as she complied. "Yeah. A bit more. Perfect."

The stranger's lips were there, and he licked his way through her slit, prying her apart again so he could swirl his tongue around the base of her clit, flick over the tip. Sensation slashed through her reserve, and she jerked forward—right into his waiting mouth.

He accepted the invitation immediately, opening his mouth over her pussy, sinking his tongue in deep, cradling her clit right on the flat and rubbing until the friction made her claw at Hunter desperately.

The torture went on forever, suspending her with a pleasure sharper than a bed of nails. Every sharp point dug under her skin. And Kata knew it wasn't because a stranger touched her; it was because Hunter instigated it so he could grant her fantasy.

And at some point, he was going to wrest control of her body from this man and give her everything she was dying for. The very thought drove her to the edge.

"Back off," Hunter instructed. "She's close again."

The stranger unleashed a frustrated groan but backed away. Hunter rounded her until he stood beside the stranger. Cool air rushed over her overheated skin as she heard the rustle of cloth. Were they getting naked? Goose pimples broke out all over her body.

Then the powerful press of hands on her shoulders urged her down before Hunter spoke. "On your knees."

Those words pinged shock through her system. Did he want her to suck off a stranger while he watched? A foreign thrill mingled with discomfort. Could she do it? Did he really want her to, or was this just him granting her the fantasy that he'd ended the night they met?

"Kata." A warning, stern, harsh.

To please him, she could do this. Succumbing to the pressure of his hands, his voice, she fell to her knees onto the plush carpet.

A gentle hand stroked her hair from peak to crown before urging her forward. The velvet head of a stiff cock met her lips. Gingerly, she opened, not certain who it belonged to. As soon as she licked the crown, Kata knew this wasn't Hunter. This man tasted salty, woodsy, earthy—foreign. The stranger groaned.

"Deeper," Hunter demanded. "To the back of your throat."

The command ricocheted around inside her, an erotic blend of shock, forbidden thrill, and a desire to please. She opened her mouth, stroking her tongue along the underside of the thick erection, then swallowing it as deep as she could.

The stranger's smothered groan told her that she'd gotten to him. So she did it again.

As she opened her mouth to take a third pass at the stranger, Hunter gathered up her hair in his fist and tugged her away from the other cock to his own. His familiar weight and taste hit her tongue, and her arousal soared. This was what she wanted. *He* was who she wanted.

If this was their last night together, she didn't want a fantasy inspired by an old book fulfilled; she wanted every bit of Hunter. Their relationship might be futile, and she might be too scared to hope that they belonged together forever, but she couldn't deny that she loved him.

Kata eagerly devoured Hunter's cock, taking him all the way to her throat. Lovingly, she wrapped her tongue around him, laved the head, plumped her lips at the crown, then repeated the process.

"Holy fuck," the expletive slipped past Hunter's lips. His hands tightened in her hair. "God, I love your mouth."

And she loved pleasing him. Knowing that her lovers were satisfied in the past had been good enough for her, but Kata wanted to be Hunter's best, the one he couldn't forget. Selfish? Probably. But she knew damn well she'd never forget him.

Tonight, she wanted to soak in every memory she could.

"I want you," she admitted, breathing against the ridges of his abdomen. "Is it okay if I only want you?"

In a heartbeat, Hunter lifted her to her feet, gripped her shoulders. "You're sure? This is supposed to be your fantasy, the one I took from you."

"Do you really want to share me?" She reached for the blindfold to tear it off.

The stranger's hands stopped her. "If I'm not staying, I'd rather just slip out anonymously," he whispered.

Kata lowered her hands, then sidled closer to Hunter.

He cupped her face in his hands. "Honey, I never want to share you. If I had my way . . . Well, I think you know." He pressed a hard kiss to her mouth, then turned to the other guy. "Beat feet, man."

The stranger groaned, but after a rustle of cloth and the creak of the door, he was gone.

Hunter ripped off her blindfold. "We're alone. Whatever happens next is your call, honey."

"Take me," she whispered. "In every way you want."

"You're sure? I won't go easy on you."

"I know. Please, Sir."

He hesitated, looking as if he had something to say. Then, with a nod, he directed her across the room to a sawhorse-looking item and bent her over it. She went without a word.

After flipping on every light in the room, Hunter clipped her wrists into cuffs on the sides, then repeated the process with her ankles at the front of the equipment. Then he grabbed her hips, lined his cock up with the empty ache between her legs, and plunged so deep in one stroke, she knew she'd never be the same.

Covering her back with his powerful body, he thrust into her with a frightening, lightning pace, then growled in her ear, "No one feels like you. No one will ever replace you."

Kata clawed the side of the wooden apparatus, shoving back against him. The pleasure she'd been holding off when the stranger's mouth had been on her soared again, this time undeniable. Her heart beat, swelled.

Deep, then deeper Hunter forged and thrust, claiming her utterly. She clenched on him, and he brushed over her wet curls, strumming over her clit. "I've had the most fucking vivid fantasies of you as mine always, bare pussy, a little ring piercing the hood of your clit so my tongue would always have a toy to drive you mad . . . matching rings in your nipples with little weights a constant tug. If I got to keep you, honey, I'd want my stamp of possession on every inch of you. I'd want to see it, touch you every damn day, possess every part of you. I'd be the most attentive lover and husband ever." He closed his eyes, groaned loudly.

His words were driving her up. The vision exploded through Kata's brain. Her pussy clamped down on him again, her muscles gripping him. He wanted her bare? Pierced? She'd never considered doing that for a lover, refused to alter herself to please any man. But the thought of doing it for Hunter made her beyond hot.

His slick fingers glided over her clit again. She gasped, teetering right on the edge again.

"Not yet, honey."

"Hunter . . . please."

He gripped her waist possessively and pounded into her again, again. "I know. I fucking know." His growl was like a curse. It dripped need, bled desperation. "If you come, I'll follow you, and I'm not ready to let you go yet."

Kata wasn't sure she was ready to let him go, either. Parting was smart and would save them heartache in the long run, but . . . she clenched her fists, desperately wishing that she could touch him.

"Deep," she begged. "Slow. Love me."

"Yeah." He set up a grinding, excruciating pace, an unhurried pounding that had her babbling in incoherent pleas for relief.

"I love you." He slammed into her again. "So fucking much. I can't hold back. Come with me."

With those words she detonated with a throaty wail. He stole her breath, her mind—and every bit of her heart. Behind her, he stiffened and roared, pulsing inside her as she gripped him fist-tight, taking everything from him that he could give. Tears burned her eyes, ran down her cheeks. Hunter did this to her every time, ripped her open, stripped her to her core, connected them stronger, deeper.

He gripped his fist in her hair and tugged until her mouth was under his, then covered her lips with his own. He moaned into her, and Kata felt him all the way through her body, deep down to her heart.

With a groan, he withdrew and unclipped her quickly, then turned her into his arms, pressing her damp body against his sweat-drenched skin. Their heartbeats fused together as he took her mouth again and carried her across the hall, to the cozy bedroom.

He set her on the bed, then crawled in after her. "Let me hold you."

Jumbled and exhausted, Kata nodded mutely. She didn't want to let him go—ever. He aroused her, inflamed her, challenged her. Tonight, he'd pushed her farther than ever, and she'd given all she could. What if . . . she asked him not to sign the papers?

What had changed? He'd still be so much like his father, and she was apparently too much like her mother. Eventually, they'd make each other miserable. She had to let the inevitable happen.

With her heart breaking, she turned into his arms and sobbed.

Chapter Nineteen

Hunter never closed his eyes. Kata snuggled up beside him now, though he'd rolled her over twice in the past few hours and taken her again, a deep, soft fusing of mouths and bodies until she cried out in ecstasy beneath him. She'd slipped into an exhausted sleep afterward, and as much as he wanted to slip inside the tight clasp of her pussy and make love to her again, he couldn't.

Desperation tightened every muscle in his body. He was leaving her for all the right reasons. She'd submitted beautifully tonight . . . but she insisted that she wasn't built for this in the long run. After meeting Gordon, Hunter knew why she thought so; he just didn't agree. And he couldn't force her to conquer all her fears for him. As much as he hated the way his parents had split up, the Colonel was right. Hunter couldn't hold Kata against her will. She had to want to stay. She had to want to conquer her own fears.

They were fucking doomed.

He glanced at the clock. Almost three a.m. He could measure

the time they had left together in seconds, and it was ripping him apart. What the hell was he going to do with the enormous void she'd leave in his heart? No one was ever going to fill it. The best Hunter could hope for was that, someday, she'd be happy.

On the bedside table, his cell phone vibrated. Quickly, he snatched it up. Jack's name popped up on his display. His time with Kata was up.

He went into high alert. "Talk to me."

Jack heaved a long sigh. "We found Cortez Villarreal. He never appeared at Sexy Sirens, so we had to hunt him down at a rundown meth lab here in town."

"And?" Hunter sat up, easing Kata's head onto a pillow, then anchoring his feet on the floor.

"He's dead. According to the homicide detective, he's been dead for somewhere between forty-eight and seventy-two hours."

Shit. That probably explained why no one else had come after Kata since Silva had taken potshots at her. Villarreal probably hadn't had time to hire anyone else before his untimely demise.

"Cause of death?"

"Bullet to the brain. This was gang style, all the way. In fact, one of Villarreal's rivals is taking credit. He's got details of the murder that no one but the killer would know. It's legit. I swiped Villarreal's cell phone and laptop before the cops arrived. If they have anything, I'll let you know."

Relief eased through Hunter. "Thanks."

They hung up, and he opened the blinds so the silvery moonlight rushed in, glowing over Kata's skin. He stared at her with a sigh. This was it. The end. He had no reason to linger here . . . except that he loved her. Since it looked as if the danger to Kata had passed, he'd ask Jack and Deke to watch over her for a while, just in case. But he'd promised to sign her divorce papers and get out of her life. Even if it fucking killed him, he'd live up to his word.

Swallowing, he grabbed his phone and flipped it to camera mode. Just one image. He needed it, his own personal heaven and hell. Hunter wanted to remember Kata like this, his wife, in his bed, her soft expression sated, peaceful.

As soon as he clicked the button, he glanced at the picture, knowing this would be the first of a million times he'd look at it. The image was perfect. She looked absolutely beautiful and lush, her lips swollen, her hair in a wild tangle, almost covering the swells of her breasts . . . but not quite.

Squelching all his urges to wake her, take her, try to reason with her again, Hunter rose and shoved into his jeans. He dug into his pocket and fished out the rumpled papers inside and flattened them out. The word "Divorce" screamed out from the top of the first page. Cursing, he flipped to the back and saw Kata's signature. Beside it sat a blank line, ready for him to add his name and legally declare this union over. He grabbed a pen, hesitated, damn near choking on rage and grief.

If the divorce would make her happy, he loved her enough to let her go.

Hunter pressed the pen to the page and forced himself to scrawl his name at the bottom. Resisting the urge to slam the pen down, he set it down gently, leaving both on the nightstand.

Before he could think any harder, he tossed on the rest of his clothes and headed for the door. One last time he glanced back at Kata sleeping in a lush tangle of silky hair, soft arms, and cotton sheets. His heart twisted in his chest. But there was nothing left to say or do, except leave.

He shut the door behind him with a quiet click. The finality of it swept desolation through him. Hunter leaned against the door, scrubbed a hand down his face.

Never had he done anything this fucking hard. He felt like he was breaking into a million pieces.

Suddenly, Tyler appeared in the hall. "You gone?"

"Yeah." He glanced back at the closed door. "Take her back to my dad when she wakes up. Thanks for the offer to drive Kata and her mom to Lafayette."

"Have to go back anyway." Tyler shrugged, sandy hair falling over his green eyes. "You sure you want to do this? Kata is a hell of a woman."

Fresh anguish swept through Hunter. In his head, he knew it wasn't Tyler's fault, but that didn't stop him from grabbing the guy's shirt and slamming him against the wall. "I know how you feel about other men's wives. Even though I signed those divorce papers, she is *never* available to you. I will dismantle you limb from limb if you ever touch her. And last night never happened."

With a pointed glance at Hunter's fist in his shirt, Tyler went very still. "You done making an ass of yourself?"

Yeah, he probably had, Hunter conceded—and released Tyler.

The guy smoothed out his shirt. "Like you said when you invited me, I'm in love with someone else. But I gotta tell you, I think you're bailing prematurely. Kata's definitely got feelings for you."

Feelings, yes. But those feelings didn't trump her fear, and he wasn't sure they ever would. Hunter loved her. He wished like hell that was enough.

* * *

KATA woke as the first rays of sun crept into the bedroom. *Hunter!* She opened her eyes, only to find the rest of the bed empty. She touched a trembling hand to the sheets where he'd lain. It was cold.

Just beyond, on the nightstand, familiar, rumpled pieces of once-crisp paper lay faceup, all pages folded back at the staple to reveal the last one. A black pen lay ominously on top.

Dread banged through her, like mute cymbals crashing, their silence deafening.

As if they might bite her, Kata eased her hand toward the papers, picking them up slowly. A glance told her that Hunter had signed. In a few short months, they would no longer be husband and wife.

No, no, no!

Kata closed her eyes, and tears welled up. Everything between them last night had been perfect. If she could survive one night under his domination, she could do it again. And again. Couldn't she? Hunter would never hurt her, never mean to run roughshod over her. Had she let the best man to ever come into her life go because she was too damn afraid to trust her heart?

Sobbing, Kata reached out for his pillow, dragging it to her chest. God, it smelled like him, wood, summer rain, and pure male. She clutched the pillow tighter against her body.

"He left a few hours ago."

Gasping, Kata turned toward the voice. Tyler emerged from a chair in the dark corner across the room. He stood, approached. His musky-pine scent drifted across the room. Memories slammed her. He had been her stranger last night.

Instantly, her face flamed, her body twinged . . . but she clutched the pillow even tighter to her bare breasts. The thought of touching Tyler now left her cold. They might have been intimate the night before, but this was morning. All her intimacy belonged to Hunter, the man who had given Kata her wish . . . and her nightmare.

He winced. "Wow, didn't take you long to figure last night out. While it might be interesting to proposition you, Hunter would kill me. And you're not interested."

Sadness settled into the shadows around his strong face, and Kata's heart went out to him. She wasn't sure she'd ever seen such loneliness on a man. "You're in love with Luc's wife."

"There is that. I'll give you a minute to . . ." He looked at the neatly folded pile of clothes on the nearby table. "Dress."

"Thanks," she choked out. "Did he say anything when he left?"

Kata was almost afraid of the answer, but she had to know.

"Villarreal is dead. As planned, last night Jack and Deke hunted him down, found his body. We think someone in his own gang killed him. The threat is over."

Wow. So that was everything.

As planned? Kata paused, frowned . . . then something dawned on her. Last night hadn't only been about saying good-bye. He'd hidden her until he knew she was safe, and he'd bribed her with the divorce she'd been fighting him for since their marriage began just so she wouldn't run home and put herself in danger. He'd done that, at his own expense, for her.

Kata's heart plummeted to her knees. Pain battered her . . . even as love welled up. She bit her lip, shoving down an urge to bury her face in her hands and cry. No matter how he felt, he'd promised to live up to his end of the deal. He might take control from her in the bedroom, but when it counted, he'd given her the ultimate power.

"If it's any consolation, he was one miserable bastard. That man loves you."

No, hearing that wasn't any consolation at all. She felt fucking wretched.

"Where is he?" Maybe they could talk, slow things down while she got her head together, work it out. His leave wasn't over for another thirty hours.

Pity crossed Tyler's face. "Gone. His CO cut his leave short again. I'll bet he's out of the country by this afternoon."

For at least six months. *Oh, God.* She wrapped her arms around her middle and fought new tears. God, this couldn't be the end, not this way.

He closed the distance between them and put an awkward arm around her. "I'll um . . . there's juice and toast ready in the kitchen once you're dressed."

As soon as he stepped out, Kata swiped away the tears on her cheeks and tossed on her clothes. She stalked down the hall to the cheerful kitchen and the smell of burned wheat with peanut butter.

"Where's your phone?" she demanded.

Tyler shook his head. "Unless you're really sure you want Hunter for good, let it go. Don't jerk his heart around anymore."

"I love him."

"But can you live with him? The way he is?" Torment whipped across Tyler's face, and he blew out a tense breath. "Don't start this if you're not sure. Alyssa did that to me before she married Luc. She cared, but . . . she didn't want what I wanted. Once, she tried." He shook his head with a curse. "We didn't make it far before she called it off. It fucking crushed me. I'm not it for her; I get it, but I wish she hadn't tried me on for size. It would have been easier if she'd just walked away."

Kata's heart stuttered. Was she ready to be with Hunter in every way he needed? Last night, he hadn't enslaved her. She'd felt strong, connected. So empowered that she'd let go. But was she ready to be with him that way for a lifetime?

"If you have to think about it that long, then you're not sure."

She tried to swallow down a rush of denial, but it bubbled back up. "He won't be home for months, and by then he may have moved on."

"If he isn't for you, then you'll have moved on, too. Problem solved."

At the moment, with her lips still swollen from Hunter's kisses and his scent still clinging to her, Kata didn't believe that, for her, Hunter would ever be solved.

* * *

AFTER forcing down some of the extra-crispy toast and too-tart juice, Kata rode in silence with Tyler back to the Colonel's house. Logan greeted her in jeans and a white tank clinging to a body slabbed with muscle that obviously got a lot of exercise. He sent her a cold glare but let her in, locking up tight behind her.

"Your mother is upstairs. She wants to talk to you." He turned away.

Kata grabbed his arm. "Did Hunter come by here before he left?"

"Yes." Logan stood almost frozen—except for the living fury on his face. "He signed your papers, despite the fact it killed him. If you ever fuck him over again, I swear I won't be responsible for what I do to you."

With that growled warning, he turned and marched to the back of the house, slamming cabinets in the kitchen as he went. Kata flinched, then pressed a trembling hand to her mouth. She'd really, truly hurt Hunter. She'd been so wrapped up in her own fears that she hadn't really seen the depth of his pain. God, that realization hammered guilt through her. What the hell had she done?

"Kata?" her mother called down the stairs.

With a sigh, she rubbed her hands down her jeans, then ascended two steps at a time. If Mamá wanted to talk to her this early in the morning, something was up. Maybe hearing her mother's problems would take her mind off her own. "Yeah, coming."

At the top of the landing, she glanced into the airy bedroom the Colonel had settled her mother into, right beside his own. She rocked in an antique wooden chair, a thoughtful smile on her face. That peaceful look wasn't her mother at all.

"Morning," Kata greeted, testing the waters.

"*Mija!*" Then she frowned. "You need a shower. And some way to cover the love bite on your neck."

Instinctively, Kata raised her hands to cover herself. Hell, Hunter had a propensity to leave behind his mark when he made love to her.

And she'd never have another mark of his possession. More misery pressed down on her, and she choked back fresh tears. This was about her mother now. Her own heartbreak could wait. God knew, she'd have a lifetime of it to deal with it.

She pasted on a plastic smile. "How are you feeling today? You look better."

"I feel better. I am at peace for the first time in years. You can thank Hunter for that."

Kata sent her mother a puzzled stare. "Because he took you away from Gordon?"

"And he urged me to talk to his father. Caleb and I are fine now. We will be good friends, I think. He is a good man. They both are."

Good friends? "Yesterday, you couldn't stand the overbearing man."

"Hunter pointed that out to him. They had something of an argument . . . which I overheard. Do not worry about me, *Mija.*" Her mother grabbed her hand and squeezed. "I will recover here with Caleb. I am going to divorce Gordon and go back into nursing."

"Really?" She'd decided all of that in one night?

At Mamá's broad smile and nod, joy infused Kata, sugary . . . but bittersweet. She had tried for years to help her mother see another future but had encountered one barrier after another. Enter Hunter. He'd gently taken charge of Mamá. In doing so, he'd given Kata another precious gift. She'd be eternally grateful to him. Even if her life was falling apart, Mamá was getting hers together. That meant so, so much to Kata.

"That's great!" She hugged her mother. "This will be good for you. Mari will be completely over the moon."

"She seemed so when I called her this morning, yes." Then something sad flitted across her face. "My sweet girl, why did you not talk to me? I cannot tell you how sorry I am that I set a poor example for you. I made you doubt yourself and cost you a marriage."

"No," She wanted to reassure her mother. "I . . ." What? She couldn't reassure her mother that she'd played no role in it. "The decision not to stay in the marriage was mine."

Mamá's expression chided her. "Sí, because of me. I heard Hunter and Caleb arguing. It never occurred to me that you would be afraid to become like me. You?" She shook her head. "It is impossible. You are so strong."

"Maybe today, but look what the years with Gordon have done to you."

"Because I let them. It was not that I lacked strength to stand up to him; I lacked will." Her mom squeezed her hand. "When your father died, I was barely thirty-three. With three growing children, no money, and a broken heart, what was I to do? When I met Gordon, he seemed like the answer to my problems. Believe me, I knew not long after the wedding that the solution was not perfect. Joaquin hated him after he overheard Gordon talk down to me. But you kids had a roof, food, good schools. Me, I did not matter so much."

"Mamá, you married him for money? For us kids?" Until now, she'd never hinted that the union had been anything but a love match.

"It is not the first time a woman has put her children before herself. Gordon knew I did not love him, and this made him feel small, I think. So he made me feel small in return. After Joaquin moved out, and the doctors and I lost that little boy during surgery . . ." she shrugged. "Well, every day I felt my love of life dimming. I no longer cared that Gordon treated me badly. The routine of seeing to him and the house was numbing, especially after the car accident. For that, I was grateful."

Kata shook her head slowly, shock racing through her brain. "All this time you acted as if Gordon was the man for you, but you knew . . ."

She nodded. "I did not want you kids to feel any guilt for my choices. After I turned forty and shattered my foot . . . I resigned myself to life with Gordon. I was no longer young or had most of my life ahead of me."

"You're wrong!" Kata insisted. "You're wonderful and deserve every happiness. Sometimes you have to fight for it and go after what you want, but—"

"Is that right, Kata?" Mamá sent her one of those cat-that-ate-the-canary smiles. "Have you fought for Hunter? He may be demanding and, at times, difficult. He is, after all, a man. But it's unlike you not to chase what you want. Your zest for life reminds me of your father. He never let anything stand in his way." She frowned. "All this time, I never imagined that you were keeping men at a distance for fear of becoming like me."

When Mamá put it like that, her behavior sounded cowardly. "I'd watched Gordon browbeat you. I knew that you had to be unhappy, but you didn't say so, didn't change the situation."

Her dark eyes softened with love. "Kata, you have always had far more courage and strength than I, at least until Hunter. I let your father's death and Gordon's behavior take mine from me, but you . . . I am proud of you, *Mija*. Do not make the wrong choices simply because I did. If Hunter is the other half of your heart, you should not let him get away."

That's exactly what she'd done, let fears and dark possibilities ruin her chance to be happy.

"Hunter overwhelms me sometimes, and I thought . . ."

"That if you stayed long enough you would become me? He knows that. Today he returns to active duty and will not be home until Christmas. You have time to sort this out. He will need the time to think, to heal. Never fear, *Mija*. I believe he will come back still as in love with you as ever."

For the first time since Hunter had promised to sign their divorce papers, she genuinely smiled.

* * *

ACROSS the street from Kata's apartment, Hunter sat in the Colonel's Jeep. He'd driven to Lafayette this morning to talk to Jack and Deke, see Villarreal's body for himself. That grim task behind him, he had a few hours to kill until he had to jump on a plane and head back to Venezuela.

Barnes was smoking crack if he thought all the men he sent on this mission were going to make it back alive. So he'd spent a little time this morning making sure the navy was informed of his change in marital status. If he died before the divorce was final, no reason Kata shouldn't have everything she was entitled to as a SEAL's widow.

He also visited Kata's sister. As an attorney, he figured she didn't see many clients on Saturday. As he'd predicted though, she'd made an exception for him, and agreed to meet with him, in fact was beyond eager to see him. And unload on him. After a little heart-to-heart, Mari still didn't love him . . . but she knew the score, knew that he would always love her sister. He had the skeleton of a nice, new will, leaving everything to Kata, as a result of the meeting.

Shifting in the leather seat as the early June afternoon heated up, Hunter stared out the tinted windshield. The only thing that was missing now was for Tyler to drop Kata off safely on his way home.

He'd fight down the urge to go to her and persuade her that last night wasn't a fluke, that she could be both a strong woman and his sweet submissive and still respect herself tomorrow.

If she hadn't figured it out yet . . . chances were that she wasn't going to. For her sake, he had to let it go.

On the seat beside him, his cell phone vibrated. Jack's name popped up. Hadn't they already hashed most of the crap about Villarreal?

"What's wrong?" he barked into the phone.

"Plenty. You've got good instincts. Sure you don't want a job with Deke and me?"

Maybe if he and Kata had a future and— He cut the thought off. Pointless. "Tell me."

Jack sighed. "I scanned Villarreal's phone. Deke scrubbed his computer. It's all the normal criminal shit, calls to local thugs and drug dealers. There's just one thing missing . . . No sign of communication between your boy and the assassin. He hasn't talked to anyone out of the 337 area code in the last month. Unless someone was hiring a hit man on his behalf, Villarreal didn't hire Manuel Silva."

Hunter's blood ran cold. His first instinct had been that Villarreal was too small-time for a hit like that. In the absence of any other evidence or suspect, he'd let himself be swayed by circumstantial shit.

He pounded his fist on the steering wheel. "Goddamn it to hell! I've got to get on a plane in two fucking hours, and I have no idea who's trying to kill my wife. Or why."

"There's no one else in her life who would want her dead?"

"No. Her mother thinks she's a saint. Her sister adores her. Brother is all but MIA with work undercover somewhere."

"The buddy who set you two up in the first place? Could he be the jealous type?"

"Ben? Hell no. If he wanted to kill anyone, it would be me. But he won't fuck with me. I'll wipe the floor with him. I've done it before and have no problem doing it again. "

"I'm not even sure I'd want to cross you."

Hunter snorted. "That would be an ugly fucking fight. Man, I've got to solve this."

"So no one in her life who would want her dead," Jack mulled. "How about someone in yours?"

Hunter paused. That didn't seem possible . . . but he couldn't afford to rule anything out now without examining the possibility thoroughly.

"Jealous ex-girlfriend?"

"No." He hadn't done much more than one-night stands in years. Once he'd joined a team, his love life had been one of the first casualties.

"Anyone who would want to hurt you by hitting where it counted?"

The list of assholes who wanted to hurt him was probably long and would take too long to cull. Better to just take the logical approach.

Pushing down the panic threatening to eat away at his composure, he walked through the sequence of events. "If someone I knew wanted to hurt me by killing Kata . . . who even knew last Sunday when Silva attacked her that we'd married the night before? The people we partied with that night, whom we've never seen again. Ben, who wouldn't do this." Hunter kept moving forward chronologically. He'd only told one other person before that attack on Kata.

He froze.

"Andy Barnes." He gripped the steering wheel, suspicion and fury poisoning his veins. "My CO."

If he was truly guilty, Hunter vowed to rip the fucker apart limb from limb.

"Why would he want your wife dead?"

Motive was the big question mark. "We used to be buddies. His last promotion was one I turned down first. We've come up the ranks together. I always thought it was a friendly rivalry, but since this last promotion, he's turned into a prick."

Jack started tapping on a keyboard, the clacking sounds audible through the phone. "Give me all the info you've got on him. Full name, DOB, anything."

Hunter had always had a head for numbers, and he thanked God now that it hadn't deserted him. In minutes he spit out Barnes' DOB, phone number, address, and a few other miscellaneous facts.

Less than a minute later, Jack whistled long and low. "I just tapped into your CO's phone records. He makes a lot of calls to South America."

"That's not a surprise." They had contacts down in Venezuela, informants and former government officials who didn't like the way their country was headed now. "But he did ask quite a few questions about Kata."

"On Saturday, he made a flurry of phone calls to a mobile phone in New Orleans. They stopped abruptly on Sunday. And based on his financials, he wasn't in particularly good shape until he received a small wire transfer Sunday morning. It's the kind of amount that makes me think it's a down payment on a bigger job, you know. But the payoff hasn't come."

Because Kata was still alive.

"I don't know who Barnes would be taking from . . ." Hunter skimmed his interactions with his CO. It had to be work related, and in the last two years, he'd devoted most of his missions to stopping Sotillo and his thugs. "Shit, Barnes cut my leave short to send me back to Venezuela tonight, to intercept a meeting between a drug lord and an arms dealer. The last mission with that objective was a waste. This one is suicide."

"Maybe he wants you out of the way. Oh, your CO just received a text from someone with a Venezuelan mobile phone. It says, 'Reaching target's apartment in three minutes.'"

Venezuelan? Someone from Sotillo's gang?

Hunter's heart nearly fucking stopped in his chest. Maybe Andy had hired a new assassin to kill Kata. "Can you trace the number?"

A long pause and a few clicks later, Jack sighed. "Disposable phone."

Shit, no tracking the possible assassin that way.

Someone in Sotillo's organization wanted Kata dead. But why? To crush Hunter by killing his wife? If so, why not wait until he was out of the country, where he couldn't protect Kata? Whatever the motivation, Hunter knew that if Barnes was on the take and the Sotillo organization planned to make a move on her now, this was going to get ugly.

Chapter Twenty

As soon as Hunter asked Jack and Deke to come for backup, they ended the call; then he sent a text to Tyler not to let Kata out of his sight. Tyler didn't answer, but he'd called earlier to say they were en route to Kata's apartment. That probably meant they were still driving.

Briefly, he considered calling someone above Barnes' head, but the chances of reaching anyone willing to set aside politics and make a quick decision was about nil. Besides, this was going to go down too fast. He'd ask for forgiveness later. Fuck permission.

Formulating a plan, Hunter took stock of his surroundings. Nothing suspicious, just kids playing in the park ahead, people starting their weekend errands, and joggers atoning for the week's laziness. Rush to Kata's place and secure it or wait here and see if he could head the assassin off at the pass?

Hunter no sooner thought the question when Tyler pulled up and parked his black truck at the curb across the street, in front of her apartment complex. Hunter watched through the tinted windshield of the Colonel's Jeep as Tyler climbed out, his gaze crawling all over their surroundings, then came around to help Kata with her suitcase. She'd showered, dressed, and looked so lush. His heart twisted in his chest.

Hunter wanted to rush out of the vehicle and warn them, but in case the assassin had them in his sights, he stayed put. He didn't want to give up the element of surprise unless forced. Instead, he watched.

Tyler set his hand at the small of her back and helped her into the atrium-style complex. Hunter wished the guy would get his paw off Kata, but if Tyler protected her, Hunter would let it go.

Soon, they disappeared down a shaded path between a cluster of buildings. Still, he didn't see anyone following them.

It was now or never. From the seat beside him, Hunter grabbed his SIG and tucked it into his waistband, then shoved an extra round of cartridges in his pocket. He slammed out of the vehicle, dodging traffic as he crossed the busy public street, and followed the others at a discreet distance, ducking behind trees and bushes for cover.

Still, Hunter didn't see anyone or anything that looked out of place, and that made the hair at the back of his neck prickle. He had a bad feeling that this was all going to go down—quickly.

Tyler followed Kata down the path paved in river rock as she fished the keys from her purse and headed for the stairs. They rounded a corner, then disappeared from sight. Hunter cursed and grabbed the gun from his waistband, ready for anything. He hated to potentially involve any civilian who might trek this path, but if they saw him and got out of the way or, even better—called the police—Hunter was all for it.

Watching for danger and innocent bystanders, he followed the signs affixed to the sides of the buildings that denoted the apartments in any given building. From reading Kata's driver's license last weekend, he remembered that she lived in unit 251D. He wished he could get ahead of her and secure the perimeter, but they'd reach the apartment way before him. Fuck.

Creeping behind a tree nearly choked by Spanish moss, he caught sight of the two again, this time climbing a set of stairs to her unit, Tyler carrying the suitcase in one meaty hand as Kata reached the door and unlocked it.

Hunter held his breath as he began creeping up the stairs until he could just see above the next rise. Kata opened the door, pushed her way in. Tyler followed.

Suddenly, gunfire erupted. Tyler shouted. Glass shattered. Then Kata let loose a bloodcurdling scream.

Adrenaline spiking, Hunter ran for the door as quietly as he could. He didn't want to spook her or tip off the assassin to his presence. But he had to get up there and fight to keep her safe.

During a mission, he could block out his anxiety and simply focus on the tasks at hand. This wasn't a mission, though. This was his wife. His heart drummed so loudly in his chest that he couldn't hear whether his feet slapping the pavement were too loud . . . or whether Kata was begging for her life.

He'd likely have seconds to kill this motherfucker before he killed Kata—if he hadn't already. Shoving the thought aside, Hunter forced himself to focus. If he started thinking she was already dead, he'd fall apart.

The door hung wide-open. As he reached the top, he saw blood. The sun streaming through the jagged shards of a broken picture window along the back wall blinded him for a moment. As he hit the door in a crouch, shielded his eyes, and stepped inside, Tyler was nowhere in sight. What Hunter could see made his heart stop.

Víctor Sotillo stood in the open doorway, his back to the enormous shattered window, using Kata as a shield. He held a gun to her temple. She shivered, her body shuddering with wide-eyed terror. Hunter wished like hell that he could comfort her. But he had to get her away from Sotillo, save her, first.

Hunter wondered how this was possible. Was he seeing a fucking ghost?

"Drop your gun," the drug lord demanded.

If he did, everything would be over. The man had no mercy and wouldn't hesitate to kill Kata—or incapacitate him and make him watch. Hunter had to come up with plan B.

Hunter could only imagine that Sotillo had shot Tyler and the blast had propelled him out the window, to his death. He shoved down the regret and dread.

"How are you still alive?" Hunter didn't really give a shit, but if it bought him time until Jack and Deke showed up, maybe he and Kata would make it out alive. "I shot you in the chest."

Sotillo's mustache curved up, along with his thin lips. "Modern medicine, it is a miracle, yes? I . . . how do you say, flatlined on the way to the hospital. But the very talented doctors revived me, so here I am." Then his face darkened. "They were unable to save my brother after your bullet lodged right in his chest."

Damn, he'd shot the wrong brother. That mistake might cost him everything. "I'm sorry, Víctor. From what I hear, Adan was a much better human being."

Rage gripped Sotillo, and he jammed the gun harder against Kata's head. "Adan was a good man. It is your fault he's gone. You and your team attacked us as we were leaving my *abuelita*'s house. You killed him."

His grandmother's house? Bullshit. If he'd gone to visit an old lady, why were there so many armed thugs and little baggies stuffed with white powder strewn all around the place?

And Andy had lied about Adan being alive and running the cartel, likely to hide the fact that Víctor was still alive.

Hunter caught her gaze and tried to send a calming vibe. He needed her to understand that she wasn't alone. She still shivered, but anger had overtaken some of her fear. She was getting pissed.

Excellent. There was the Kata he knew and loved. She was going to have to fight to make it out of here alive. The chances of them both making it out . . . well, the odds of a cataclysmic asteroid hitting the earth were probably better.

"So what? You want to kill me, Víctor?"

Kata's eyes went wide, silently asking if he'd gone crazy. He ignored her encroaching panic.

Sotillo shook his head. "Suffering the anguish of loss is much harder to bear than simply closing your eyes forever. I want you to *feel* that void like a bleeding wound. Originally, I asked Barnes to return you to duty today. I arranged to sneak into the country this morning. My transportation was scheduled to leave tomorrow, but I must return sooner. Big deal going down. Barnes told you about it, yes? I believe you called it a suicide mission, but you'll be long dead before then." Sotillo smiled.

The puzzle pieces fell into place for Hunter. Thank God Sotillo's schedule had changed because of the big deal. Otherwise, Hunter would have been out of the country while Kata was being stalked . . . and killed. Hopefully, he could save her now.

"This plan works much better," Sotillo murmured. "Now, I will *see* your anguish when I kill your wife before your eyes. This is much better than merely hearing of your pain."

Hunter choked down his fear. He couldn't lose Kata, especially to revenge for something he'd done in the line of duty. "And my commanding officer helped you determine just the right person in my life for you to off, didn't he? For the right price, of course."

Behind him, Hunter heard the cocking of a gun.

"That's right, asshole." Andy Barnes crept behind him, through the open door. "Put down your gun."

Hunter didn't comply. Dropping the gun meant giving up and dying. Instead, he tried to keep Barnes talking. "You had to know I was going to figure this out, Andy. "

"It took you longer than I thought. If you hadn't been busy fucking this Latina whore, I'll bet you would have guessed right away."

Anger poured through him like scalding acid. Hunter forced himself not to do something rash. He restricted himself to grinding his teeth. "You're a disgrace to your country and your team. How much did you sell me out for?"

"Enough to pay off a few bills, along with my house, and buy my wife that vacation she's wanted for years. My fucking country doesn't pay as well as Sotillo. I'll leave the patriotism to idiots like you."

"You hired Manuel Silva?"

"As soon as you called to say you were married. It was the lucky break I'd been looking for. It didn't take me long to find Silva, who was only two hours away from your wife's apartment. If she hadn't gone to her office building, which took time to break into, giving your friends time to arrive, she would already be dead. I had to make a few more phone calls to find a cop willing to ice him in jail.

"I cut your leave short on Monday, thinking that would make her easy to pick off. But I couldn't figure out where you'd stashed her quickly enough. By the time I tracked her down at the hospital with her poor, sick mother, too many of your personal security buddies were crawling around the place."

Shit, Hunter had always known that Barnes had a clever streak. He'd underestimated how devious the bastard could be.

"I called you away early today for the same reason." He shot Sotillo a rancorous stare. "Víctor changed the plan."

"So did you do all this for the money, Andy?"

He laughed coldly. "The money was icing. I did it for all the times you thought you were better than me, were offered promotions before me, were given medals that should have been mine, and swaggered your way through gorgeous women I'd have given my right nut to fuck. It will be sweet to stand here and watch you die inside after we kill her."

Then Barnes planned to off him. After all, now that Hunter had seen his face and heard his admission of guilt, his CO couldn't let him live.

Sotillo sneered. "You will indeed suffer. The day I buried Adan, I held my sobbing mother, then began looking for a way to find the person you love most so I could rip them away from you. Barnes was very helpful in telling me about your life. Your father and brother are hard men to track down and ever-vigilant. Your very pregnant sister was a tempting target, but her husband made things too difficult.

Then Barnes told me of your lovely new wife and your deep attachment to her."

He trailed a finger down Kata's cheek, into the hollow of her throat, over the curve of her breast, and Hunter buried the urge to kill the fucker on the spot. He had to convince Víctor that Kata wasn't important, or she would be dead quickly. And just like the bastard wanted, he would know anguish beyond measure. Kata might not be his for much longer, but he would always protect her, always love her.

"I hate to tell you this, but you came after Kata for nothing. We're getting divorced," Hunter said. "The guy she was with—I assume you already iced him before he fell out the window? I saw them naked together last night." Technically, that was true, and Hunter tried to be as accurate as possible. Andy was an ace with body language. "If you'll let her into her purse, you'll find the divorce petition. We've both signed already."

"You're lying," Barnes snapped. "You love her."

He did. No way he could lie about that. "Check her purse. You'll see the papers."

"Katalina?" Sotillo asked her.

Hunter tried to catch her gaze, hoping she'd understand the ploy.

"He's right," she told Barnes. "We married on a whim. I was drunk, and he was horny. It was Vegas. But Tyler dropped in last night . . ." She shrugged. "Then Hunter saw us. By this morning, he'd signed the papers and left. End of story."

"Fuck!" Barnes shouted. "Let me see those papers. Get them— carefully. Nothing funny, or Víctor will put a bullet in your brain."

Once more, Hunter willed Kata to look at him. She met his gaze for a second, then took a deep breath and dug into the depths of her purse. *Hold on, honey.*

Moments later, she withdrew a stack of papers and, with shaking hands, flipped them to the last page, all but shoving them in Sotillo's face.

Víctor frowned, then dropped them back into Kata's hands, glaring at Barnes. "He does not lie. For this, I will kill you."

"I swear, he loves her. I can tell. He's putting on an act so you think he doesn't."

"Complete with legal documents?" Kata's tone told him to get real as she shoved the papers back in her purse. "It just wasn't going to work out."

Before Hunter could lament the fact, she sent him a weighty stare.

Shit, Kata was going to do something. What? Fear kicked Hunter in the balls. He tried to give an imperceptible shake of his head. She had no business playing the hero. But she ignored him, raised her hand from her purse just a fraction. The gleam of her handgun she kept there for self-protection shimmered for just a second, then she cast a meaningful glance over her shoulder toward Sotillo. Shit, he'd forgotten about it. She'd used it and almost gotten a jump on Silva. He couldn't let her try on Sotillo, not with Víctor holding a gun to her temple. Hunter frowned, silently begging her to use caution.

"What's going on?" Andy demanded. "You, get your hand out of your purse!"

Hunter stepped between them, turning his back on Sotillo. It was a calculated risk. The Venezuelan prick didn't want him dead, at least not yet. And he wanted Hunter to watch Kata die. He wouldn't kill her behind his back. Andy had already proven he was unpredictable. Hunter had to take Barnes out first, before he had the opportunity to pull that trigger and harm Kata.

"What the hell are you doing?" Barnes jumped, snapping his gun inches from Hunter's face.

He stared down the barrel. If his sacrifice saved Kata, he'd count it as a win. If not . . . he'd make sure that somehow, some way, he took Sotillo down with him as he took Barnes.

Waiting for Kata to be ready with the gun in her hand, Hunter wrapped his finger around the trigger of his own gun.

Andy didn't miss it. "Drop your gun. Now!"

Behind him there was a scuffle. Sotillo growled. Gunfire resounded, deafening in the small space. Kata screamed. Sirens began to wail, closing in. Andy's attention veered for just an instant . . .

Hunter took the opportunity, knowing it would probably be the only one.

"No." Adrenaline spiking his bloodstream, he whipped his gun up, firing almost point-blank in Andy's chest. Barnes was dead before he started falling to the ground. "Sir."

Hunter didn't wait for him to collapse. He turned to see Kata elbow Víctor in the gut. Sotillo released her with a grunt. She whirled and fired. In an instant, he was bleeding from an open wound in his side, staining his pseudo-military uniform dark. His face was mottled, rage blaring from his eyes as he grabbed Kata again and pressed his gun into her temple so hard that she began to bleed. His finger hugged the trigger. "Die, *puta*."

Desperate to do anything, Hunter raced through possibilities, but Kata's body blocked a clear shot at Sotillo. He couldn't risk shooting her himself.

Frenzied and furious, Kata stomped down on Víctor's instep. His body jerked, arm flailing up as he jerked his injured foot from the floor. His weapon fired, deafening in the small space. Chunks of the ceiling rained down as Kata whipped her gun over her shoulder and pulled the trigger, hitting Sotillo in the jugular. Blood spurted everywhere. Víctor screamed, trying to stem the flow of blood with one hand. Kata kicked the gun from his hand, and he stumbled back, grabbing her hair as if it was a lifeline.

Hunter dove into the fray, trying to pry Sotillo's fingers from Kata's thick tresses. But the dying bastard gripped tighter, staggering back again—right for the open picture window, broken and ominous right behind him.

"She dies with me," Sotillo gurgled.

Hunter lunged for them, but the bastard glared with hate and pulled Kata closer as he fell out the window to his death. With an evil smile, he took her with him.

Chapter Twenty-one

Christmas Eve

HUNTER stalked out of the terminal at DFW airport and reached for his coat. Shit, coming from Venezuela, where December was damn near eighty degrees, to Dallas, where he'd be lucky if the temperature reached fifty, was always a bit of a weather shock.

Slinging his duffel bag over his shoulder, he walked through the automatic doors, out to the chill. Right on schedule, Logan waited for him at the curb in the Colonel's Jeep.

His brother hopped out of the car, opened the hatch in back, then stuck out his hand. "How's it going?"

Shitty. Fucking miserable. Hunter shook his hand. "Okay. You?"

Logan shrugged. "It's Christmas, so let's play happy, huh? Deke, Kimber, and the baby are driving down tonight. They'll stay a few days."

"How are they? I'll bet the baby has really grown."

"Absolutely! Little Caleb is going to be a bruiser. He's got the temper to match."

Hunter dumped his duffel in the back of the vehicle and smiled faintly, glad everything had worked out well for his sister and her husband after such a rocky start. "Of course. Neither Deke nor Kimber has ever had a problem expressing when they're pissed off."

Logan laughed and jogged for the driver's seat. "C'mon, before the overzealous traffic cops around here write me a ticket."

With a nod, Hunter made his way to the passenger door

"Let's see . . . what else?" his brother mused. "Carlotta is already at Dad's."

Hearing that was a punch to Hunter's solar plexus. Carlotta would just remind him of all he'd lost. Kata had survived the fall out her window because Sotillo had landed under her, breaking it. She'd suffered a concussion and a broken arm, lost some blood, and gone into shock, but they'd whisked her away to the hospital and stabilized her quickly. Hunter had gone insane worrying about her, but the police had insisted on asking inane questions, tying him up. Then military brass had demanded his presence soon thereafter, subjected him to a shitload of red tape. He'd told them to shove it until he knew that Kata was going to be fine. But after the doctor's assurance that her injuries were minor and an admiral called, threatening court-martial if he didn't appear and explain why he'd shot his commanding officer, he'd been forced to leave. The Colonel had given him frequent updates on Kata's health until she'd healed completely.

Back on active duty, he'd tried to write Kata, but he couldn't wrangle his feelings onto a page. Besides, she'd wanted a divorce and never contacted him to say anything contrary. So he'd stayed silent. Since then, he'd buried himself in one mission after another, turned down another promotion . . . and spent time deciding what to do with the rest of his life.

He still had no fucking clue.

Hunter pushed the pain of Kata's loss and all his uncertainty aside. He didn't feel like celebrating the holidays, but he'd put on a good face for his family. "Carlotta doing good?"

"Yeah, her divorce to Gordon is almost final. She's got her own place now in Tyler and a job at Mother Frances Hospital as a surgical nurse. She's been rehabbing her foot." Logan nodded. "She's making great strides and seems really happy. I think Dad may be sweet on her, but if there's anything there, they're taking it slow."

Maybe someone would come out of this mess happy, and if anyone deserved it after over a decade and a half of misery, it was the Colonel. He'd sacrificed his heart to make his wife happy and hadn't been the same since. Hunter knew that wretched feeling. But if Kata was happier apart from him, he'd bear it.

"Carlotta isn't going to spend the holiday in Lafayette with Mari or her other family?"

Logan shrugged. "Guess not."

"You doing any better, little brother?"

"No better, no worse." He navigated through the airport's twisting roads to the main thoroughfare and the toll gates. "Don't worry. I'm fine."

"Not if you still haven't had sex in the last five years."

Logan slanted him a livid glare. "How much sex have you had in the last six months?"

None. He hadn't had many opportunities . . . but he also hadn't had any interest. Hunter looked out the passenger window, knowing he'd walked right into his brother's trap. "It hasn't been that long since we split up. You've had a dozen years to get over T—"

"*Don't* say her name," he growled. "Or I swear I'll stop this car and take you apart."

Hunter understood his brother's anger. He could barely think Kata's name without getting choked up and pissed that he'd somehow let her slip through his fingers. He hated to think he'd still feel the same way years down the road . . . but it was damn likely.

"Sorry. I'm having a hard time. She's in town for the holidays." Logan stared bleakly at the busy road.

"I understand." No doubt, the situation was rough. So close . . . yet so far away. To this day, he didn't really know what had happened between them, but whatever it was had left Logan broken.

"Hey," his brother broke into his thoughts. "With so much

company and all the beds in the house taken, we drew short straws to see who'd have to find other bunks. You lost."

"I wasn't there to draw for myself." Hunter frowned. "You cheated."

Logan winked. "Sucks to be you."

They hit the highway, and the long drive to Tyler passed with loud alternative rock and a smattering of conversation. Once they left the bustle of Dallas behind, the barren spindles of tree branches flared across gray skies as one mile rolled into the next. Pastures that had been green in June were now brown, dead. Like he felt inside.

He whipped out his phone and stared—yet again—at his contraband picture of Kata. As always, it never failed to both soothe and destroy him.

God, he'd give anything to go back and change . . . what? If he'd been any different with Kata, he would have been lying to them both. She feared the sort of relationship he needed and had only felt free to really submit when she'd known it was good-bye. Everything about that night had been bittersweet. He'd had hope when she'd wanted to make love to only him, but . . .

"How's Tyler doing?" he asked. Anything to avoid treading the same mental ground he'd stomped on a thousand times.

"Still rehabbing his back, but he's nearly a hundred percent. I still think it's incredible that the fall didn't paralyze him."

"No shit." The blood loss from the shot to his arm had actually been worse than his fall out the window. Hunter had been very relieved when a couple of minor surgeries had fixed the majority of Tyler's damage. He didn't need anything else to feel guilty about.

The outskirts of town appeared, hovering on either side of Highway 69. The holiday decorations up on the shops and restaurants should have helped Hunter get in the spirit. Nah, he was more depressed than ever.

He drew in a deep breath and broached the one subject he dreaded most. "Did the final divorce papers come to Dad's house?"

Logan hesitated. "No. Why would they?"

"Just asking, since they didn't come to my barracks. The only thing I received was a letter telling me that my request for married housing on base had been approved. I guess when I told the navy I'd married, they thought I'd want a real house."

He wished so fucking badly that he could share it with Kata.

"You'll figure it out," Logan drawled.

"After Christmas, yeah." No way was he dealing with it now. It would only depress him more. "I'm home for two weeks this time. I told my new CO that he'd better not call me once unless the world was coming to an end."

"I hope he lives up to that."

Hunter snorted, despite his misery. "He didn't seem eager to give me a reason to shoot him."

"Makes sense. You've gained a hell of a reputation for being hard on a CO." Logan drove for a minute, then exited the freeway, stopping at the first red light. "You've asked me about everyone except Kata."

God, even hearing her name hurt. He knew now why Logan couldn't stand to be reminded of his ex-girlfriend.

Sucking in a sharp breath, Hunter tried to pass off the question with a shrug. "I assume that someone would tell me if something's not right with her."

"True." Logan turned right, away from the Colonel's.

Hunter frowned. "Where am I staying?"

"I cooked a little something up for you. This place belongs to a friend who's away for the holidays."

That grin worried the crap out of Hunter. Since when did Logan let anyone close enough to actually call friend? The only people who remotely qualified were all the hard-core folks at that BDSM club he frequented. "What the hell are you up to?"

Logan stopped the car beside the curb of a nondescript little house about six blocks from his family. "Got a surprise for you inside. Merry Christmas, bro."

When he got out of the car and grabbed the duffel in the back,

Hunter followed reluctantly. "If you're trying to set me up with one of your pain groupies, please don't. Just let me see Dad and everyone else—"

"Sorry." Logan darted for the door and fished the keys from his pocket. He slung the duffel in Hunter's direction, then tossed him the keys. Hunter caught them reflexively. "I'll be back for you by dinner. If you'd rather stay in, just text me."

What the hell . . . ? Hunter turned on his brother and stormed down the concrete walkway, toward the Jeep. "Damn it, I don't want this."

"Yes, you do." Logan got in the car and locked the door, rolling down the passenger window. "Trust me."

With that, he drove off.

Hunter sighed. He'd be furious if it didn't take too much energy—something he hadn't been able to muster much of in the past six months. Shaking his head, he stalked into the house.

A female lived here, he knew the instant he hit the threshold. The décor didn't give that fact away as much as the smell. Vanilla-scented air fresheners were the top note. Musky amber and lilies hit him next—a scent that made him freeze in his tracks.

Kata? It was her scent, but she couldn't be here. Maybe he'd finally lost his mind. It would be a welcome change.

Heart pounding ridiculously fast, he closed the door behind him and stalked through the house. He was going to find out what was happening here and get some fucking peace.

The cozy living area was filled with buttery tan leather and wrought-iron tables, which led into a kitchen with earth-toned paisley patterns and cherry cabinets. The scent he sought had weakened, so Hunter turned, wending back the way he'd come, until he found a hallway.

He inhaled more of the gorgeous smell. God, it was stronger here, perfect. For the first time in what felt like forever, he had a raging hard-on. He tried to will it away.

Two bedrooms down either side of the hallway proved empty

and lacking the scent he craved. The corridor dead-ended with a closed door. The master bedroom? Likely, he'd find it empty, and this strong scent the work of a candle or something, but . . . that didn't keep his heart from beating like mad, his hope from soaring.

Hunter gripped the knob and shoved the door open.

Inside, he found a Dom's paradise. It was a shadowed room filled with toys, tables, and restraints galore. In the middle, a woman knelt naked on her knees, head down, palms up, thighs spread, glossy dark curls swirling around her body.

Shock spread over him. Everything inside him froze, stuttered, then began racing a hundred miles an hour. "Kata?"

"Welcome back, Sir."

What the hell was going on? Why was she here, waiting for him like his perfect fantasy? "Look at me."

Slowly, she raised her head, her familiar hazel eyes rimmed in black liner. She met his gaze with a languid, sure sexuality that made his entire body tighten—and love. Then he looked down.

Since he'd last seen her, she'd embellished her body into his most potent wet dream. A delicate weighted hoop dangled from each nipple. Down lower, her pussy was completely smooth and bare. A little silver ring winked from between her slick folds. Dear God . . . He staggered back a step.

Hunter was about two seconds from pouncing on her like a starved man. It damn sure looked like she was offering herself but . . . "Explain."

She swallowed. "I'm signaling my willingness and availability to you."

The submissive pose was generally meant to convey that, but . . . coming from Kata? "We've been down this road. You didn't want what I wanted. Not to say I don't love the way you look." Hell, he loved everything about her—except the fears that kept them apart. "But we're divorced for a reason. I haven't changed."

"I have," she assured softly. "I want to submit in whatever way you need. I want to please you, husband."

Everything about that statement filled him with questions, but he focused on the most important. "Ex-husband, right?"

She reached onto the bed right beside her and pulled down papers that had escaped his attention. Not surprising since her gorgeous, naked form had captured it. With a trembling hand, she handed the papers to him.

Mind racing, erection nagging him like an infected tooth, he unfolded them, knowing full well what they were.

He frowned. "The petition for divorce. We both signed. What happened?"

Finally, she looked nervous. "I never gave them back to Mari so she could proceed. I wanted to see you again, apologize for everything, submit to whatever punishment you deem appropriate, then let you decide what happens next."

The words sank in. Shock pinged through him. Hope crept back in. "We're not divorced?"

"No, and we won't be unless you want to. I love you."

Her hazel eyes filled up with tears, sincerity pouring from their depths. Hunter's breath caught. His heart seized up. He wanted to cover her body with his and take all she offered. What little logic he still possessed made him pause.

"You were terrified of me and the sort of relationship I wanted. You sought this divorce. Now you love me?" He shrugged, struggling to balance his hope and fear. "Yes, I see you're pierced in exactly the way that turns me inside out, and I won't deny that the sight of your bare pussy is arousing as hell, but it's going to take more than that for me to understand what's different."

She bowed her head, her silky hair sliding over her soft shoulders. The gesture, the intimation—hell, everything about the woman—was about to undo him.

"Our last night together was a revelation to me. When I wasn't afraid about the future and put my trust in you, I simply let go and discovered how connected I felt to you. How strong. You're not Gordon. I'm also not my mother, settling for a man who takes pleasure in bending me low to cause me pain. The last few months, I've worked a lot of issues out. I'm at peace. I've learned to submit with grace and calm. Unless you no longer love me and have moved on, I want nothing more than to be your wife in every way."

Hope crept over Hunter, damn near blocking out rational thought. In Kata's head, she'd worked through their issues. Maybe. God, he hoped so. But what if she went running again the first time he overwhelmed her? He didn't think he could stand the torment of losing her again.

"My love for you was never the question. I'm always going to love you, but if we can't be together in the most basic way . . ." He narrowed his eyes as he stared at her, trying not to focus on the little piece of jewelry dangling between her luscious thighs that made his tongue twitch. "Why should I believe that anything has truly changed?"

"I talked at length to your brother, along with Jack Cole and his wife. They introduced me to Cheyenne, a Domme. We're . . . friends."

Hunter stared hard at her, a bolt of jealousy piercing him. "You submitted to her?"

"Often, yes. For the practice. It wasn't sexual."

For most submissives, the act of opening themselves up to another's will opened them up sexually. "You never came for her?"

She couldn't have missed his skeptical tone, because she flushed. "When she wielded a paddle in one hand and a vibrator in another, it was impossible to resist. You are welcome to punish me as you see fit." Kata lifted her gaze to him, so open and welcoming. "Please touch me, Hunter. Try me."

The strength of her conviction, along with his enduring feelings for her, made him stand and hold out his hand. As she placed her fingers in his palm, his heart slammed against his ribs. He couldn't help but notice that they both shook.

"Afraid?" He helped her to her feet.

"No. Just nervous."

Yeah, he was, too. She might be placing her body in his grasp, but he was placing his heart completely in her hands. If this didn't work out, Hunter knew it would crush him—and he didn't know if he could ever find his way back.

"I won't go easy on you."

Kata nodded. "I haven't earned anything else."

She definitely knew the score. There was only one thing left to say. "Your safe word is "divorce." You say it, and we're done. I'll disappear forever."

"You'll never hear that word from me again."

The possibility of a thousand bright tomorrows stretched out in front of him. Having this woman by his side for each and every one was his biggest fantasy of all.

Unfamiliar with the setup in the room, he prowled to the closet. *Bingo!* He found exactly what he needed in seconds. Grabbing a few items, he shoved them in his pockets, then turned back to Kata.

"Turn on every light in the room."

"As you wish." She flipped on the switch near the door. Light flooded the room from a fixture overhead. It shined on her bare skin, glowing golden across her shoulders, down her back, on the bare skin of her buttocks.

His mouth watered. His chest clenched. God, how badly he wanted her to be his forever . . .

Kata turned on the lamps at both the nightstands flanking the bed. Intense light flooded the bed, white, bright, unforgiving.

"Good." But he hadn't asked anything particularly taxing of her. Yet. "Now get on the bed, flat on your back, legs spread wide."

She jumped to do his bidding without hesitation.

With this light, she had to know he would see any flaws she'd tried to hide in the past. But she didn't flinch once, just arranged herself on the double bed, head on a pillow, heels hugging the edges.

Jesus, she looked gorgeous. He wanted to pounce on her, affix his mouth to her pussy, feel her explode on his tongue, then fill her with every aching inch of his cock. Hunter fought the need, forcing himself to think this through. He had to know if she could really be free to submit, not just for him, but for herself, too.

"Arms above your head."

Again, she complied, no hesitation. He climbed on the bed and grabbed her wrists, then withdrew handcuffs from his pocket. Quickly, he clapped one around each wrist and attached the dangling chain between to a fastening screwed into the headboard.

Squelching the urge to kiss Kata until she was putty, Hunter focused his attention lower. Could she submit without being seduced into it? Could she give her will over to his because they both needed it, nothing more, nothing less?

"I'm going to inspect you." He stared at her with a raised brow, waiting for her to flinch or protest or close her legs.

She did nothing.

Making his way slowly to the end of the bed, he knelt between her thighs and looked at her bare flesh and the pretty piercing in the hood of her clit. Fuck, nothing got to him faster than knowing she'd done that to please him, and on Kata the sight ramped him up like he'd never known before.

Reaching out with one finger, he trailed it up the smooth, damp skin in the crease between her pussy and her leg. At his first soft touch, she gasped.

"Quiet, unless I say otherwise."

No rancor or annoyance crossed her face. "Yes, Sir."

"Is your pussy shaved or waxed?"

"Lasered. It's permanent. Cheyenne recommended someone really great to me."

She'd committed to keeping herself bare for him? The thought made desire coil inside him even tighter. Damn, it was going to be tough to focus on putting her through her paces and not fucking her like a rabid animal on the spot.

Breathing deeply, he forced himself to hold back and ran that same finger over her clit. "And the piercings?"

Her muscles tensed. Her breathing hitched. But she answered his question. "Cheyenne recommended me to Bruce. He did them all. He's very gentle."

Which meant that Bruce had seen his wife naked, and Hunter didn't like it one bit. He swallowed the urge to hunt the asshole down and focused on the fact that Kata had seemingly gone to great lengths to please him.

Flicking the little ring with his finger, she tensed, then forced herself to relax. Hope sprang a little higher inside him.

"How long ago was this done?"

"Middle of July."

So plenty of time to heal. Plenty of time for her to take them out if she'd reconsidered the kind of commitment he sought. Then her words hit him all over again. She'd done this shortly after getting out of the hospital. She'd been thinking of him while he was thousands of miles away, miserable with the distance between them. Had she, even then, been looking for a way to bridge the chasm so they could be together?

Hunter released a shuddering breath, but nothing was going to stop the freight train of desire slamming through him. Kata got to him, now more than ever.

"I don't like another man seeing you naked."

Her lips curved up, but she said nothing.

"What's that smile about?"

"I like that you're possessive. I feel . . . loved. Safe."

"Not controlled or run over?"

"Try to tell me how to do my job or how to manage my out-side responsibilities, and we'll have fights. I'll invest in a whole lot of string for your balls. Keep me all to yourself in the bedroom, and we'll be great."

Exactly how he wanted her. "No more fantasies about me sharing you?"

She shook her head. "Thank you for the offer. I know having Tyler with us wasn't easy for you."

He froze. "Is that why you refused?"

"No. I did it because I only wanted to be with you. Being shared was just a fantasy, but the reality of you and me together is so much better."

Damn, could she be any more perfect for him? They'd had a tough road, both learned hard lessons. They'd both had to compromise. Was it possible that would pay off for the rest of their lives?

Unable to resist, he swiped his tongue through her wet slit, teasing the little ring piercing the hood of her clit. *Hmm, sweet.* Her body tensed. Her breath caught. The taste of her sank onto his tongue, and he reveled in having her this way again. As he sucked her clit gently into his mouth, he slid the base of the ring against her bundle of nerves so it created a friction she couldn't resist.

Up he drove her, higher, higher. Her breaths became moans. Her hips arched up.

Hunter held her down and gave her the sternest expression he could muster. "Be still. You can't force your orgasm with this wriggling and silent begging. You'll get it when I think you're ready. *If* you get it. Are we clear?"

"Yes, Sir." Her voice emerged as a high-pitched squeak.

He repressed a smile. "I'm enjoying my treat. Do you know how fucking hungry I've been for the last six months? You don't want to spoil it for me."

Kata shook her head and tensed every muscle in her body as he set his mouth back on her cunt and lapped slowly, hungrily, losing himself in her taste. He wanted her so far on the edge that she could see the chasm of destructive pleasure below but still want it so badly that she was willing to risk anything for it, for him.

Her fists clenched, unclenched, along with her jaw. She tossed her head as he tongued that little ring again and plunged two fingers into her soaking pussy, feeling around for that one spot . . . *Yeah.*

Perspiration broke out across her skin and she flushed a dusky rose everywhere. Her labia swelled. Her clit turned hard. She rippled around his fingers, but clamped down, trying to control her response.

She'd done well, so far. Now it was time to challenge her.

Forcing himself to pull back from her sweet taste, he eased to the edge of the bed and slapped his fingers down on the pad of her pussy. Kata cried out, bucked. Then brought herself under control.

"I'm sorry," she panted.

She knew she hadn't followed his instructions to be still and silent. He didn't have to remind her at all.

"Turn over. Present your ass for a spanking."

She hesitated, and Hunter tensed. Yes, she'd enjoyed the last thorough spanking he'd given her . . . eventually, but not without a lot of persuasion and coercion. She'd fought him all the way to orgasm.

Finally, she turned over, arms crossed over her head, knees beneath her.

"You hesitated." He rubbed her backside. He hoped like hell the touch was at least a tad threatening, and she was thinking about the paddling she'd soon get. Mostly, he couldn't keep his hands off her ass.

"Permission to speak?"

"If you're going to enlighten me, sure."

"I'm very close to the edge, Sir. A spanking will put me over quickly. I took a moment to compose myself. I'm sorry."

Candor, an admission that his discipline excited her, *and* an apology? That set him back on his heels. She'd come so far and obviously done a great deal to work through her issues. He was so damn proud of her, he was about to burst. And so encouraged, so happy, it was all he could do not to tear off his jeans and sink tightly into her body, stake his claim for good.

But he had to remain steady. "That will cost you five extra swats. You understand?"

"Yes, Sir."

"Count them." He smacked her right cheek dead center. Her flesh made a satisfying smack against his hand, and she breathed through the sting.

"One."

Nice. Nodding, he brought his palm down on her left cheek, first at the top, then the bottom, hitting a bit harder each time.

She tensed, forced herself to relax. "Two. Three."

As soon as the words were out, she sank deeper into the sensation, body going lax, her head dropping to the bed. Hunter could see the outline of his hand on her ass, and he nearly clawed his way out of his clothes to get to her.

He forced patience. He'd tested her a great deal . . . but hadn't crossed all her boundaries. Conversations with Logan, Jack, and Morgan seemed to have emotionally prepared her for submitting. This Cheyenne woman he hadn't met had certainly given her practice. But there was one boundary that another woman couldn't cross with her.

Suddenly, he was eager to take her there, find out if she could really be his in all ways.

Palming her ass once more, he rained down a series of blows on it, high on her right cheek, on the fleshy part of her left, straddling the luscious parting of those globes. He spared her no mercy.

"Four, five, six." Her voice grew calmer with each word. Her skin actually glowed with a healthy sheen of perspiration and blood pooling just under the surface.

Hunter slipped a hand under her, to swim through the moisture wetting her sweet pussy. Her clit was still a tight knot, and her body begged to be fucked. As he pressed his fingers inside her again, she rippled around him. But she breathed through the pleasure-pain, finally relaxing everything but her pelvic muscles. With those, she held on to her need to orgasm tightly.

He smiled wide and hefted four more hearty smacks on her ass, one right after the other. No yelping, crying, begging, arguing. Kata merely took them in stride.

"Seven, eight, nine, and ten," she breathed out.

"Excellent." Hunter tried to sound in control, but the truth was, he'd lost it. Knowing he was with Kata and that she was submitting so perfectly . . . That had been the stuff of his fantasies for the past six months. The need to hold her, the yearning to have her under his hand as she still wore his ring and he saw love in her eyes, had nearly strangled him. Now it seemed that everything he wanted was within his reach. Nothing on earth was going to keep him from her. Elation swelled inside him.

With jerky motions, he shoved his jeans down his thighs and guided his cock to her wet entrance. With one shove, he pushed his way in on a tortured groan. Her body parted for him, like warm water flowing around a rock, she caressed and clung until Hunter wondered if he was going to lose his ever-loving mind with the sublime joy.

In long, deep strokes, he began to fill her, pushing his way over her most sensitive spots, all the way up to her cervix. He leaned his body over her back and put a hand on her chest. "Breathe with me, honey."

He waited a moment until their breathing synched up, until he felt a measure of calm overtake them both. Fucking perfect. She felt like home, and he never wanted to leave her again.

Clutching Kata tightly, Hunter fucked her, each stroke ending with a mutual indrawn breath, every withdrawal punctuated with a moan. God, he could feel her, her rising excitement, her peace in the knowledge that she was pleasing him.

It was as if the last six months of separation hadn't existed. They fell away, and he wasn't the same bastard who'd been looking for a reason to get out of bed each day, snapping guys' heads off at every opportunity, wishing every night that he drank, because drowning in alcohol sounded like a damn relief. Now he was purely in the moment, more connected to Kata than ever.

Gripping her hips, he thrust in faster, faster, reaching under her to circle her engorged clit with his fingers. She was damn close.

"You want to come?"

"If you think I've earned it, Sir."

Damn, even an obedient answer, and it went straight to his cock. "Yes. Come!"

Almost immediately, her body began convulsing. Her sex sucked him in deeper, gripping him so tightly, Hunter had to breathe hard through the urge to climax and flood her. Six months without sex was damn unpleasant. Six months without Kata had been excruciating.

Knowing he either had to pull out of her tight clasp or come now, he withdrew, still having one question mark in his head about her submission. This didn't have to go perfectly, and if she was still coming to terms with it . . . he'd deal. She'd already come so far.

Fishing into his pockets, he extracted the plastic tube he'd shoved in there and dabbed a large dollop on the small pink rosette between her cheeks, then slid even more inside her.

Every time he'd touched Kata's ass before, she'd resisted in some way. Now? She relaxed and pushed down on his fingers.

"I'm going to fuck you here." He pressed deeper. "You'll tell me if I hurt you."

"Yes, but you won't. Cheyenne helped me with a variety of plugs, each bigger than the last. I made sure I was prepared for you."

If he'd been shocked before, her answer completely blew him away now. She'd willingly had her body prepared for the ultimate act of his submission?

"Why?"

"Because I want you to have me this way if you desire it." Her eyes sparkled, filled with life and joy as she looked at him over her shoulder. "And because I think it will be hot as hell."

His heart clenched. There she was. His hell on wheels Kata was right below the surface, waiting to tease and drive him mad. She would submit in the bedroom, but the partner he loved more than his own life had merged with the submissive he needed.

He wrapped his arms around her middle and trailed kisses along her shoulders. All the reserve he'd been using to hold himself back until he'd been sure . . . it was gone now, dissolved in the blush of her pure acceptance.

"Sweet Kata, goddamn it, I missed you so much."

Her breath caught. "I missed you, too, Hunter. Every day, I

thought about nothing more than you coming home and us having another chance. I was so afraid. I'm not anymore."

"I know, honey. I see you, so obedient and so brave. So strong. I'm proud."

"Take me."

Her husky, pleading tones charged through his veins. No way to deny that request.

Fitting the head of his cock to her tight hole, he pushed gently to the ring. She pushed down and back. The resistance gave way quickly—and he found himself sliding into heaven. He gripped her hips, hissing in a breath as fire breathed through his body.

She groaned. "This is so different than a plug. So much better."

"I want to help you enjoy it. Tell me what feels good."

He drew back, then stroked in again. And again. Around him, her insides tensed, and her body flowed with him, hips catching his rhythm for one deep thrust after another. God, he was so deep into her, Hunter knew he'd never find his way out. His body craved hers. His heart . . . well, she might be his wife and submissive, but no doubt, he was the one enslaved.

Diving back into his pocket one last time, he pulled out a little vibrating bullet and switched it on. He wasn't going to last much longer, but damn it, if he went over the edge into pleasure, she was going with him.

He flipped it on and shoved it right against her clit. Kata jolted, cried out. Her body tightened around him almost unbearably. Gnashing his teeth, Hunter tried to keep it together.

But he was fighting a useless battle.

"Come for me." He barely got the words out before his own climax slammed across his senses, taking out his ability to breathe, to see, to do anything but feel Kata shudder around him as she found her own pleasure. He shouted, his cries mixing with hers.

They collapsed to the bed in a heap, and as soon as he could feel his legs again, Hunter withdrew carefully, shucked his pants, then found an attached bathroom. After gathering a warm, wet wash-cloth, he entered the bedroom again and went to Kata's side.

He cleaned her gently, then uncuffed her. As soon as they were face-to-face, her hazel eyes sought his, the apprehensive questions lurking there a silent shout in the room. She wanted reassurance that she'd pleased him—the most basic instinct for a submissive.

Warmth spread all through Hunter, and he wondered that he didn't goddamn glow. With a smile, he pushed the dark curls from her face and caressed her cheek. "You pleased me very much. Never in my wildest dreams did I imagine that you'd be waiting for me today, much less so prepared to accept everything I've wanted to share with you. You can't know how proud I am of you or how much I appreciate all you've done for me. No more fears?"

Joy suffused her golden face. "None. Hunter, I know now that I can be me and still love you. You should know that I will still kick your ass when you need it. But I'm not going to run again. I would conquer my fears twenty times again just to be with you."

His heart fucking exploded with joy as he clutched her close and pressed a sweet kiss to her lips. "Thank you for that."

Somehow, some way, his gut had led him to this woman from the moment he'd laid eyes on her. She'd come to feel the same way, and had been willing to fight for their happily-ever-after. He felt like the luckiest bastard in the world.

"You know, Kata, 'Sir' is someone you're testing out, to see if you can share a relationship. 'Master' is the man you intend to stay with." He held her hand, relieved to still see that band of gold he'd put on her finger all those months ago. "Surrender to me forever?"

She reached up and cupped his jaw, bringing her mouth to his for a slow kiss that was a sharing of breaths and souls. "Yeah, Master. Forever is how long I intend to love you."

Shayla Black

The author of more than twenty-five sizzling contemporary, erotic, paranormal, and historical romances, national bestselling author Shayla Black (who also writes as Shelley Bradley) lives with her husband, her munchkin, and one very spoiled cat. In her "free" time, she enjoys reality TV, reading, and listening to an eclectic blend of music.

She has won or placed in more than a dozen writing contests, including Passionate Ink's Passionate Plume, the Colorado Romance Writers Award of Excellence, and the National Readers' Choice Awards. Romantic Times has awarded her Top Picks, a Historical K.I.S.S. Hero Award, and a nomination for Best Erotic Romance of the Year.

A writing risk-taker, she enjoys tackling writing challenges with every book.

Visit her website at www.shaylablack.com.

Belong to Me

She's undercover and in over her head . . .

When FBI analyst Tara Jacobs's fellow agent and best friend goes missing while investigating a sex ring, Tara goes undercover as a submissive in a Dallas BDSM club called Dominion. But no man can top a woman with Tara's moxie convincingly enough—until an edgy, dangerous Dom takes control of the scene and sets her heart racing with a single, commanding glance. Too bad he's also the man who stole her innocence years ago—and one to whom she will never submit.

He's got everything under control . . . until he falls for her again.

Navy SEAL Logan Edgington once left the woman he loved to save her life. He knows Tara will never forgive him, but he has no doubt that he possesses the knowledge to help her master her fears and the strength to guide her through an unfamiliar world of pleasure and pain. He alone can protect her on a dangerous mission that reveals both wicked depravities and terrible secrets. Logan relishes the exquisite torture of holding her again and feeling her uninhibited response. No matter how much Tara insists their fling will end after this mission, he's determined that she will be his once more—and this time, he'll never let her go.